USA TODAY bestselling author **Debbie Herbert** writes paranormal romance novels reflecting her belief that love, like magic, casts its own spell of enchantment. She's always been fascinated by magic, romance and gothic stories. Married and living in Alabama, she roots for the Crimson Tide football team. Her eldest son, like many of her characters, has autism. Her youngest son is in the US Army. A past Maggie Award finalist in both young adult and paranormal romance, she's a member of the Georgia Romance Writers of America.

Beth Cornelison began working in public relations before pursuing her love of writing romance. She has won numerous honours for her work, including a nomination for the RWA RITA® Award for *The Christmas Stranger*. She enjoys featuring her cats (or friends' pets) in her stories and always has another book in the pipeline! She currently lives in Louisiana with her husband, one son and three spoiled cats. Contact her via her website, bethcornelison.com

D1350815

Also by Debbie Herbert

Appalachian Prey
Appalachian Abduction
Bayou Shadow Hunter
Bayou Shadow Protector
Bayou Wolf
Siren's Secret
Siren's Treasure
Siren's Call

Also by Beth Cornelison

Rancher's Deadly Reunion
Rancher's High-Stakes Rescue
Rancher's Covert Christmas
Rancher's Hostage Rescue
Cowboy Christmas Rescue
Rescuing the Witness
Rock-a-Bye Rescue
Guarding Eve
The Return of Connor Mansfield
Protecting Her Royal Baby

Discover more at millsandboon.co.uk

UNMASKING THE SHADOW MAN

DEBBIE HERBERT

COLTON 911: DEADLY TEXAS REUNION

BETH CORNELISON

MILLS & BOON

First Published in Great Britain 2019
by Mills & Boon, an imprint of HarperCollins*Publishers*
1 London Bridge Street, London, SE1 9GF

Unmasking the Shadow Man © 2019 Debbie Herbert
Colton 911: Deadly Texas Reunion © 2019 Harlequin Books S.A.

Special thanks and acknowledgement are given to Beth Cornelison for her contribution to the *Colton 911* series.

ISBN: 978-0-263-27443-1

1019

MIX
Paper from
responsible sources
FSC **C007454**
www.fsc.org

This book is produced from independently certified FSC™ paper to ensure responsible forest management.

For more information visit: www.harpercollins.co.uk/green

Printed and bound in Spain
by CPI, Barcelona

UNMASKING THE SHADOW MAN

DEBBIE HERBERT

This book is dedicated to Karen Groce; thanks for being such a great beta reader!

And, as always, to my husband, Tim; my dad, J. W. Gainey; and my sons, Byron and Jacob.

Chapter One

The scratching began again. *Skreek.* A heartbeat of silence. *Skreek. Skreek.*

She could sleep through the blare of traffic in Atlanta, but this teeny noise in her mom's old house in rural Virginia had roused her from deep sleep in a mere nanosecond.

It was the sound of her nightmares. The ominous scratching that had preceded the worst moment of her life and hounded Harper to this day. It was inexorably tied to the image of her sister Presley's body lying on the kitchen floor as smoke swirled and fire licked the darkness. Harper sat up in bed and waited for the scratching to resume. But this time, the only noise was a faint swish of something soft brushing against a wall.

Probably just a mouse scampering behind the old Sheetrock, or so she hoped. Disgusting as that was, she'd welcome the prospect of mice infiltration over creepier alternatives. As a child, she'd wondered if the house was haunted by a ghost—or an even scarier type of supernatural horror.

Harper pictured the wraithlike, filthy creature she'd glimpsed the night Presley died. The thing—she wasn't sure if it was a person or some remnant from a dream—had loomed over her sister's lifeless body. She'd screamed, and the pale figure had vanished into the shadows. Never to be seen again.

Nobody had believed her. There'd been no signs of forced entry, and a search of the old Victorian had revealed nothing unusual. Presley's death had been ruled accidental.

But even now, the skin at the nape of her neck prickled at the memory.

This wouldn't do. After all, she'd returned to Baysville in order to settle her mom's estate and make peace with her own disturbing past. Time to discover what was real and what was imaginary. Over the years, she'd pushed that night's events to the back of her mind.

Of course, she wasn't always successful. At unexpected moments, a vivid image of pale skin draped on a frail, gaunt figure would crystallize from the hazy memories of the night Presley died.

Sleep was no longer possible, so Harper climbed out of bed and turned on the bedside lamp. The light reassuringly spotlighted the familiar and mercifully vacant room. All was in order. The peach-colored walls cast a comforting warm glow. Her white French provincial bed and dresser were old but classic and had served her since childhood. She could have taken the larger master bedroom across the hall, but it still felt like Mom's room. Probably always would, no matter how many years passed after her death.

Harper donned her comfy, though tattered, pink robe and opened the bedroom door, flipping on the hall lights. The recently polished oak floors gleamed golden and reflected the bright sheen of her red hair. She gripped the iron railing of the staircase, surveyed the stairs, and then her eyes darted involuntarily to the kitchen. After all these years, she still checked to make sure no flames or smoke billowed from the room. Grimly, Harper made her way down the steps. Would she ever descend them without remembering that night?

At the bottom of the stairs, she stopped abruptly. Heat spread from her bare feet and then up her spine, tingling like an electrical shock. Someone was here. Watching. Swiftly, she turned and surveyed the empty staircase behind her. Nothing was there except for the same old portraits that lined the stairwell wall. Generations of grim Catletts stared back at her, as if in silent rebuke of her foolishness.

Skreek.

The scratching started up again. And had she heard an echo of a footfall? Harper's ears strained, but she detected nothing else. The old house had gone eerily quiet.

Stop creeping yourself out. Nothing's here but you and the rodents.

Harper strode to the den, flipping on every light switch along the way. She turned on the TV, and the reassuring voice of a morning news show filled the house's quiet void. Then she marched to the kitchen and started coffee. Familiar sounds and smells eased the niggling worry in her gut.

See? You did it. Spent another entire night by yourself here. A couple more weeks, and you won't think anything of it. Easy peasy. Onward and upward until she'd satisfied every speck of uncertainty about what had happened that night.

In the meantime… "Exterminators," she said aloud, with a determined nod. Coffee mug in hand, Harper sat at the kitchen table and fired up her laptop. This wouldn't be just any old routine extermination. No, she was booking the full Monty—the entire house wrapped in a toxic bubble by men dressed in hazmat suits. She pulled up a list of local companies and dutifully scribbled down a couple of numbers to call when their businesses opened this morning.

Taking that action, however small, made her feel more in control. One step at a time, as her mom would say. And if anyone had reason to believe in that mantra, it was Ruth Catlett. She'd buried a husband and a child, yet every day she'd risen before dawn to work at a local diner one block down the road. And if her spirits had never quite recovered from Presley's death, she managed to put on her game face in public.

And now there was one. Harper was the last of her family. Oh, sure, there were a couple of aunts and uncles and cousins scattered about Baysville, but it wasn't the same.

Harper sighed and sipped her coffee as she stepped onto the front porch. Streaks of purple and orange illuminated the sky and were reflected in the Pagan River's rippling water. Many of the quaint shops lining the riverfront had already turned on their lights. Baysville was awakening to a new day. She'd forgotten how beautiful her hometown was. The Tidewater region of Virginia was steeped in history and picturesque in a way that a big city like Atlanta could never match. She sat in the glider for several minutes, enjoying the slower pace. No clients to meet, no ringing phones or assistants to send on errands. She'd been much too busy this past year with her interior decorating business. In some ways, it'd been therapeutic after her breakup with Doug, but she was over that disappointment. Any man that fickle and gun-shy over commitment wasn't worth the heartbreak.

The streets gradually began to fill. Slow pace or not, it was time to go in and get dressed before someone she knew spotted her in the grungy but comfy robe that was the epitome of ugly.

Inside, Harper strolled to the kitchen table and picked up the exterminators' phone numbers. There were four new emails in her inbox. She supposed she'd better check them in case of pressing business in Atlanta. Sitting down, Harper opened her email, and her eyes were immediately drawn to one subject line that blared at her in all caps:

GET OUT OF THE HOUSE

With trembling fingers, she opened the email. No message in the body of the email, only the ominous warning from a sender: loser@life.

HARPER WALKED BY the front door of the Baysville Police Department three times before resolutely squaring her shoulders and marching in. Behind the charming brick facade of the station, the interior was utilitarian and stark. The designer in her was aghast at the yellowed linoleum floors, cheap metal chairs and institutional-green walls of the lobby, but taxpayers were paying for a service, not a pleasing office aesthetic.

At the counter, a bored woman handed her a clipboard. "Write down your name and reason for coming."

Dutifully, Harper printed her name, then paused. Reason for coming? They were going to laugh her out of the station if she wrote "disturbing email." This had been a terrible idea. Growing up, other kids had merely looked at her strangely if she mentioned the thing she'd seen that night. Worse, she hated that look of pity as they scooted away from her. As though she was a sort of magnet for disaster. It had been high school before her friendships had returned to normal, and that was due in large part to making the cheerleading squad and becoming friends with the popular Kimber Collins. Harper had learned to fit in with her peer group, keep her mouth shut and act as if all was well in her world.

"Never mind," she told the city employee, handing back the clipboard.

She blinked at her behind thick glasses. Before the woman could ask questions, Harper flashed a fake smile and turned away.

"Excuse me, miss, are you sure about this?" the woman called out.

The few others slouched in the lobby waiting area looked up from their cell phones. Harper ignored them, too, as she waved a hand, the phony smile still in place. She looked and felt like an utter fool. All she wanted was a quick exit and...

Oomph. She crashed into a solid object and began tumbling backward. Hands gripped her forearm.

"Whoa, there. You okay?"

Dark, amused eyes flashed before her face. Bryce Fairfax.

Harper's face and neck heated. "Fine," she mumbled. Maybe if she hurried, he wouldn't recognize her. She tried to pull away, but he held fast.

"Harper Catlett, Presley's little sister," he said, flashing his infamous grin that had had all the girls swooning in high school, including Presley. Truth be told, Harper had secretly crushed on him, too, although he was a good nine years older than her.

His smile faded. "Sorry to hear about your mom. I imagine you've been busy with her estate and settling loose ends."

"Yes, thanks."

His grip loosened but still remained. "What brings you to my station? Is there anything I can help you with?"

"Well, no. It's not important."

Bryce tugged at her arm and guided her back into the station. She fell into step beside him, wishing like hell that she'd never come.

"I'd do any favor for Presley's little sister. Did you know that in high school, she used to tutor me in algebra? If it wasn't for her, I might have failed that class. As it was, I managed to slip by with a D-minus."

His self-deprecating laugh eased some of her tension. Bryce was as charming as ever. He had a knack for drawing people to him, especially women. He'd kept his athletic physique, and the crinkles at the corners of his eyes and forehead only made him look more interesting.

"Yes, I knew about the tutoring. Presley was so smart. Wish she'd been around when I struggled with math classes."

Bryce shot her a sympathetic nod. "Such a tragic accident."

"If it was an accident..." Harper clamped her mouth shut. No sense reminding anyone about her so-called mystery monster.

His brows rose, but he didn't respond as they passed through the lobby and into the bowels of the station. From here, the slamming of iron doors and loud voices emanated from the county jail connected to the back of the building. It was disquieting. Any moment, she expected an escaped convict to pop out of nowhere, looking for a hostage.

At the end of a narrow hallway, she followed Bryce into his private office. She'd expected more from the police chief's office, although she shouldn't have been surprised, given the rest of the station's decor.

Bryce slid behind a massive desk constructed of dark-stained plywood. A simple nameplate on his desk displayed his name and title. "About what you said back there—" he clasped his hands on the desk and leaned forward slightly, all business "—are you saying that you believe Presley's death wasn't accidental?"

"Not at all. I mean, I was only a child when it happened. What do I know?"

His dark eyes pierced her, as if trying to read her mind. "I remember the rumors. You claimed to have seen something—or someone—by Presley's body right after she fell."

She swallowed hard. "Like I said, I was a kid. One with a vivid imagination and who had awakened from a bad dream. A bad combination."

"Describe what you saw, again."

Harper shifted in her seat, uncomfortable with the request. "It sounds so silly now. I thought I saw a stick-thin person wearing filthy rags and staring at me with huge eyes."

They were like the alien eyes that people drew after supposed encounters with UFO creatures, unnaturally large and black. But she didn't elaborate on the details. Even now, the memory unnerved her. Harper rubbed the goose bumps on her arms.

Another cop entered the room and shoved a piece of paper across the desk to Bryce. The man was tall and exuded authority in the firm set of his shoulders. He shot her a curious glance, his gray eyes quickly assessing her. She had the feeling he'd overheard some of the conversation. Probably pegged her as a wacko. A nuisance taking up the boss's time.

Bryce nodded at the cop. "I'll call him back in a few minutes. Stay a moment while I finish up here. I have some questions for you on this matter. Harper, this is Officer Andrews."

"Hello," she said politely.

"Harper Catlett was born and raised here in Baysville," Bryce told Andrews.

The chief turned his gaze back to her. "I can assure you the case was thoroughly investigated by this office and the fire department. No signs of forced entry, no evidence of foul play."

Great. Now she'd insulted him. "I'm certain everyone here did an excellent job," Harper hastened to agree. "I'll never forget your father was the first firefighter to respond at the scene."

"Must have been tough on you and your mom. And now she's passed away, too. Lots of bad memories here for you in Baysville. I imagine you're itching to sell the old house and get back to Atlanta."

"You know I live in Atlanta now?"

Bryce gave an easy chuckle. "You forget how news travels in a small town. Kimber mentioned it after your mom's funeral."

"Oh. Of course." She and Kimber had kept in close touch over the years.

"Sorry I missed the funeral—I had to testify in a case south of here. I did make it late to visitation one night, though. Fifty-two years old. That's way too young to die."

Just like with her father, death had crept up sudden and silent—in the form of a heart attack. Harper would always wonder if mourning over Presley's death had been a contributing factor in her mom's early demise.

"So what brings you here today?" Bryce asked, cutting through her reverie.

"Right." She removed her cell phone from her purse and punched in the password, conscious of two sets of eyes on her. "It may seem like nothing now, but I was a little concerned this morning when this email popped up on my laptop."

"Some kind of cyberthreat?" Bryce asked. "I assure you, we take everything seriously."

Harper's brows knotted with worry. The threatening email was gone. Had she accidentally deleted it? Quickly, she scrolled through her email trash folder. Not there, either. "I, um, it seems to have disappeared," she explained reluctantly.

"That's too bad," Bryce said smoothly. "What did it say?"

"To get out of the house."

Silence greeted her words.

"Anything else?" Bryce asked.

"No. That's it, except for some strange noises in the house. Probably mice," she admitted sheepishly. "In the light of day, in front of two cops, all this doesn't sound so bad." Harper rose. "I've wasted enough of your time. Good to see you again, Bryce. Nice to meet you, Officer Andrews."

Bryce also rose. "Come back anytime. Let us know if it happens again."

His words were kind, but she felt as though he was impatient to return to work. With a quick nod and smile, she hurried to the door, glad to make an escape.

Halfway down the hallway, she turned at the sound of approaching footsteps. Officer Andrews bore down on her. "Would you like to file an official report?" he asked.

"No. Forget it. I'm sure it's nothing."

"I wouldn't say that."

She blinked at his earnest kindness.

"Especially since you believe a family member may have been murdered in that house."

He had overheard her conversation with Bryce. "I didn't exactly say that," she protested.

"Not in so many words. I don't know if Chief Fairfax mentioned it, but there's been a long string of unsolved murders in Baysville. Would it make you feel safer if an officer searched your house sometime this afternoon or evening?"

Harper hesitated. *Yes*, she wanted to scream. On the other hand, what would people say if they observed an officer in her home? The hell with appearances, she decided. She was only going to be here a short while. Might as well be able to get a sound sleep in the evenings.

"Yes, that would be great, actually. Thank you." She withdrew a pen and paper from her purse and wrote down her address and phone number. "Whoever you send, just tell them it's the last house on the left at the end of King Street."

"Got it," he said, tucking the paper in his uniform shirt pocket. "I'll have no trouble finding your place."

Was his kindness merely a scam to put a move on her? She rejected the suspicion immediately. Doug had really done a number on her mind for her to be so suspicious of a local cop doing a favor.

Harper made a quick exit, pausing at the lobby entrance. She turned around and caught both Bryce and Officer Andrews standing in the hallway, regarding her soberly.

A string of unsolved murders, Officer Andrews had said. They weren't dismissive of this threat at all. Harper didn't know whether to be relieved or worried about their concern for her safety.

Chapter Two

Harper leaned against the pillows on her mom's head-board and wearily brushed a hand through her tousled hair. Six cardboard boxes lay scattered on the floor, filled to brimming with her mother's old clothes. On the bed, she'd kept out a few things she couldn't bear to part with—a couple of Mom's old silk scarves, the flannel night robe she'd worn for decades and several sweaters that were still stylish. The rest would be donated to charity. The sooner everything was packed up, the sooner she could hold an estate sale for the furniture. Whatever didn't sell would also be given away.

Coffee was in order. Tonight, she wanted to finish the master bedroom and then move on to either the basement or attic in the morning. Harper kicked aside boxes and headed to the kitchen.

Twilight cast its dusky hue along the riverfront. Today had gone by much too quickly. There was so much to do before she returned to Atlanta and her normal routine. Without Doug. It wasn't so much that she missed him, it was being alone yet again. And now, with Mom's passing, the thought of Thanksgiving and Christmas on her own was depressing. Maybe she should book a tropical cruise and pretend the holidays weren't even taking place.

The idea lifted her spirits. Her business was successful, so why not have a little fun after this sad year?

Humming, Harper measured water into the coffee-pot. Might as well fill it to the brim—Officer Andrews had called earlier, saying he'd stop by after work. Didn't all cops love coffee and doughnuts? Tonight, cheese-cake would have to do. Speaking of which, a tiny slice now would be a reward after all her hard work cleaning and packing. She got the dessert out of the fridge, then frowned at the dwindling size of the cheesecake. Had she really eaten that much of it in the past two days? Ev-idently, she had.

She limited herself to only a couple bites, eaten over the kitchen sink. A neighbor across the street, Mrs. Hen-ley, walked down the driveway to collect her mail, which reminded Harper to check hers as well. Outside, the air was a bit chilly for October. Harper hugged her arms as she sprinted for the mailbox. She waved at Mrs. Henley, an old friend of her mom's, and then withdrew a hand-ful of envelopes.

An icy finger of fear trickled down the nape of her neck. Someone was watching her. She lifted her head and caught a faint swish of the lace curtain hanging in her attic window. Harper drew a deep breath. Inhale, hold for four counts, and then a long exhale—just as her yoga teacher advised for easing stress. *Nobody's there.* The house had been locked up tight ever since Mom died. A couple more therapeutic breaths and she dismissed the silly feeling of being watched. The prank email this morning had her jumpy, that was all.

Quickly, she flipped through the envelopes. Mostly junk, but a couple of utility bills were due. *Call and can-cel utilities for next month*—Harper added the chore to her mental checklist. By then, the house would be on the market, and…

A flash of something large came toward her at break-neck speed. A whisper of tires on asphalt, the faint scent of car exhaust—Harper's head snapped up in alarm. A black pickup truck barreled down on the wrong side of the road and aimed straight at her, its headlights blinding. Paralyzing fear kept her rooted to the spot for a couple seconds.

Get back. Her body caught up to her brain's screaming message. Harper lunged off the curb and rolled onto the sidewalk. The truck crashed into her mailbox, and then its engine revved, increasing speed. Gaping at the truck's fading taillights, she lay on one elbow and watched as it sped around King Street's sharp curve, disappearing into the night as quickly as it had arrived.

"Harper! Harper, are you all right?"

Mrs. Henley's voice seemed to come from a great distance. Harper tried to catch her breath, to let her neighbor know that she was okay, but damned if the words wouldn't form past her numbed lips.

Pain radiated from the palms of both her hands and her right hip. Blood formed beneath the ripped knees of her jeans. She raised her hands to eye level and stared blankly at the deep abrasions marking the tender skin.

"Oh my God, Harper. Tell me you're okay." Mrs. Henley knelt beside her and wrapped an arm around her shoulders. "The nerve of some drivers! He could have killed you with his recklessness."

The reality that she'd been seconds away from possible death or disfigurement finally sank in, and Harper trembled uncontrollably. Reckless? It had seemed deliberate.

She sucked in deep breaths of the crisp air and managed a wan smile. "I'm okay, thanks."

"Let me help you up."

"No. Wait a minute." She needed to collect her wits.

"Of course." Mrs. Henley nervously scanned her prone body. "Where all are you hurt?"

Good question. "I—I think just my knees and hands and hip." She drew a deep breath and sat up. "Okay, I think I'm ready to stand now."

Mrs. Henley placed her hands under Harper's right forearm. "I'll help."

She surveyed her neighbor's somewhat frail body. "That's okay. I've got this."

The sound of a racing motor set her heart skittering. Had the truck returned to finish her off? Harper twisted around. A Baysville Police Department sedan screeched to an abrupt halt by her fallen mailbox. Officer Andrews was halfway out of the vehicle before the motor turned off.

"What happened? Are you injured?" he called, running toward them.

He was beside her, his brow furrowed with concern, assessing the situation. Harper had the oddest sensation of falling into the warmth of those gray eyes. She wanted nothing more than to lean into the broad expanse of his chest and shoulders—to draw momentary comfort from his strength and kindness.

"Some fool driver nearly ran her over," Mrs. Henley jumped in to explain. "He nearly gave me a heart attack! And he didn't even stop, just kept right on going."

"Did you get a plate number?"

"No. Sorry, Officer. It happened so fast."

Andrews turned back to Harper. "What about you?"

"All I can tell you is that it was a large black pickup truck."

"Catch the make and model?" he asked hopefully.

"No." Even if it hadn't been for the darkness and her shattered nerves, Harper couldn't have relayed that information. Vehicles were just vehicles, and she'd never bothered learning different manufacturers' specifications. Not that Officer Andrews needed to know all that.

"How bad are you hurt? Should I call an ambulance?"

"No, don't. I'm fine. Was just going to stand when you drove up."

Andrews held out his hand, and she took it without hesitation. He wouldn't let her fall. His grasp was strong, an anchor to momentarily lean on. She winced, though, as the raw patches on her palm pressed into the hard strength of his hand. Luckily, her legs and ankles were uninjured, and she stood on her own two feet again. She gave him a nod, and he released his hold.

"Thank God, you're okay." Mrs. Henley held up the stack of envelopes Harper had dropped as the truck came at her. "I believe I've gathered all your mail."

Harper took the envelopes and shook her head. How unimportant the mail seemed now.

"Let's go inside, and I'll fix you something to drink while I take your statement."

Andrews's deep voice washed over her scattered senses like a balm. "I wouldn't mind a cup of coffee."

"I can do that for you," Mrs. Henley chimed in.

"That's okay, ma'am. Thanks for your help."

Harper shot him a grateful look. Mrs. Henley meant well, but once she came in the house and settled down, she was likely to stay for hours, wanting to chitchat. While her neighbor was a perfectly lovely person, Harper didn't feel up to that.

Andrews guided her in the house and helped her get seated at the kitchen table.

"Let's get you cleaned up. Where are your first aid supplies?"

She pointed to the hallway on their left. "Second door

on the right. Should be alcohol and bandages below the sink. At least, there used to be, years ago."

He left momentarily, returning with an old, dusty bottle of rubbing alcohol, a washcloth and several square packages of gauze. Kneeling by her feet, he gently cleaned the abrasions on her knees and palms. At her slight, involuntary hiss as alcohol touched the wound, he bent low and blew on her skin to ease the pain.

Holy hell. The tender intimacy of the gesture bulldozed her senses with as much impact as when she'd crashed to the ground dodging the wayward truck. After he wrapped her palms with the gauze, he moved on to her knees and she gulped hard, fighting back unexpected tears. What was wrong with her? Was she so broken that a kindly ministration reduced her to a puddled mess?

He finished, cocking his head to the side as he regarded his handiwork. "Might want to pick up some antibiotic cream tomorrow. Just to be safe."

She cleared her throat, determined to keep her voice steady. "Thank you. I've made coffee, and there's some cheesecake in the fridge," she told him. "Help yourself."

She instructed him where to find cups and dishes. He set to work, and she watched. Andrews's presence filled the kitchen, and she was again struck by his aura of confidence. He wasn't handsome in the conventional sense like Bryce—his features were a little too sharp, his body more lean than overly muscled—but Harper was drawn to him nonetheless.

Bet the man was sorry now he'd offered to stop by and check her house. Seemed she was one problem after another lately.

Andrews sat across from her. "About that truck— I'll need to file a report on the incident."

"Okay. Sorry Mrs. Henley and I are no help in providing anything more specific, Officer."

"Liam."

She blinked. "Huh?"

"My name's Liam."

Liam. The lovely syllables washed over her.

"Why don't I get started on the house search while you finish your coffee?"

"Okay. Be warned, it's a bit of a mess with boxes everywhere. I'm getting ready to sell the place."

"Understood." He rose and regarded her with something that seemed like…interest. "So, you'll be here, what, a couple more weeks?"

"More or less."

He nodded. "I'll start in the basement and work my way up."

"Sure. I'll tag along with you. I'm fine now."

Her legs were still shaky, and she hoped Liam didn't notice. He followed her to the basement, and she was conscious of his large form so close to her own. A stirring of excitement whispered through her body. How pathetic was she? The man was merely paying a kindness. Harper flipped on light switches and flushed a bit as he examined the junky, damp room.

"Lots of Dad's old tools are still down here. Plus, Mom always kept a large pantry of canned goods and stored holiday decorations in the basement, too. Got loads of work to do clearing it all out."

Liam shone a flashlight on the narrow overhead windows. "No sign of forced entry here."

And didn't she feel foolish. Going to the cops over a few scratching noises and a silly email?

"Onward and upward," she joked. He followed her upstairs, and they made their way through each room.

Liam opened all the closets and checked the windows. With each passing room, her embarrassment grew. In the attic, he walked through and inspected the cramped space filled floor to ceiling with plastic bins. "More holiday decorations," she explained. "Mom went all out for every holiday—Valentine's, St. Patrick's Day, you name it, she had knickknacks to commemorate its occurrence." An unexpected pang of nostalgia for the old days hit her in the solar plexus. *Old* meaning the years before Presley died. There hadn't been much need to celebrate anything after that.

"This house is huge," he commented as they made their way back to the kitchen. "Come from a large family?"

"Nope. There were only two of us kids and Mom and Dad. My dad used to talk about quitting work at the factory and turning this place into a B&B. But once he died, Mom lost all interest in the project. Truthfully, I don't think she was ever gung-ho about the idea. She enjoyed waitressing at the diner. And Presley and I didn't like the idea of sharing our home with a bunch of strangers, either."

"Sorry about your sister's accident."

Speaking of which… "How did you know of it? Were you outside the office when I spoke with Bryce?"

"Couldn't help but overhear," he said easily. "I don't like to barge in when he's in the middle of a conversation."

"Ah, I get you. Well, it's been seventeen years since she died, so you don't need to walk on eggshells when it comes to discussing what happened." Harper cast an involuntary look back over her shoulder. "She fell down in the kitchen and passed out. The soup she had on the stove caught fire. She died from a combination of a head wound and smoke inhalation."

"I see." His kind gaze sent waves of comfort through her body. Lots of people acted weird when you brought up tragedies and tried to immediately change the subject. To his credit, Liam did not. "That must have been awful for your family."

"Yeah. She was only sixteen."

"Were you two close?"

"As close as you can be when you're seven years apart. I looked up to her as a kid. Presley was smart. *Genius* kind of smart. Used to earn extra money tutoring students, including your boss."

She motioned to the table, and they sat down, this time side by side. She was hyperaware of his arms and shoulders so close to her own. Harper gripped her coffee mug with both hands to resist an impulse to reach out and touch Liam. "What about your family?" she ventured. "How long have you lived in Baysville?"

A contented smile washed over his face. "I have a huge family. Three brothers and two sisters. Most of them live in Arlington."

"Parents still living?"

"Yep. Both still kicking."

"You're lucky."

A heartbeat of silence fell between them, a locked gaze that lasted a second too long to be casual. Liam scooted his chair. "Time for me to get moving. You going to be okay here by yourself?"

"Yes, of course." They both rose at the same time, and Harper almost sighed. It would be ridiculous to start anything with her moving so soon, and she wasn't into one-night stands. Damn it.

"What the hell?" Liam frowned and strode toward the back window of the kitchen.

"What is it?"

"Look outside."

Dutifully, she walked over and stood beside him. An elliptical flashlight beam pierced the marshlands abutting the far side of her property. Liam hurried out onto the back porch, and Harper grabbed the flashlight she always kept on the chifforobe for emergencies. By the time she joined up with Liam, they were halfway across her yard.

"Get back," he ordered. "I'll check it out."

"Alone?"

"I'm a cop."

"Shouldn't you at least call a dispatcher before you take off to investigate potential danger?"

"It's one person with a flashlight. And I have my cell phone on me. Not to mention a sidearm. Stay inside," he added. "Until I'm sure the area's safe."

But instead she fell into step behind him. "I'd feel safer with you."

They walked away from the lights of town and into the dark silence of the marshes. Cordgrass leaves brushed against her thighs, and her sneakers sank slightly into the muck covered by black needlerush. In the distance, flowing river water lapped against the shore, and the occasional hoot of an owl punctuated the night. Moonbeams glowed silver on the tips of cypress trees and wax myrtles.

Again, the inky blackness was pierced by a flashlight beam, but it was farther away now.

"Whoever it was, they're leaving," she whispered.

Liam turned her flashlight on full beam and directed it toward whoever had been lurking. "Damn. If I thought I could trust you not to run after me, I'd give chase."

"Good thing I'm here, then."

He shot her a severe frown. "I'm going in a little closer anyway to see what he might have been up to."

"We're getting near the railroad tracks. Probably a vagrant wandering the area."

"Awful brave of him, considering the several recent murders."

"Several?" she asked in alarm.

"Over the past ten years, six have been reported. All were vagrants. You weren't aware of this?"

"I'd heard of a couple over the years, but I didn't realize there were so many. That's awful. Have they been fighting among themselves, like some sort of gang war?"

"That's one theory," he said drily.

"I take it that's not your favorite theory."

The rev of an engine sounded from far away, but no headlights appeared.

"Think that's our flashlight man—or woman?" she asked.

"If it is, he's definitely up to no good."

"Or she," Harper remarked. "I'm an equal-opportunity crime theorist."

"Fine. You go home and theorize up a storm. Can you see well enough to make it back?"

"Sure. I left the porch light on."

"Great. I'm going to investigate."

She'd said she could see the way home, but not that she'd obey. "Be careful," she answered, turning around and taking a few steps. Once Liam was out of sight, she stopped and waited. Better to be here and learn what he'd found firsthand than to sit at home waiting and wondering. And no doubt every tiny rustle in the house would set her imagination down a fearful path she was sick of traveling.

Headlights beamed from far off, appearing for an instant and then vanishing along the winding county road out of town.

Harper shivered and wished she'd thought to grab a jacket from the porch. Liam moved quickly through the marsh, the flashlight beam set on high and shining in an arc over the wetland field. Whatever was out there, she hoped it wasn't dangerous. She wished they would return to her house and call for backup—in case of trouble.

A hoot owl screeched, and chills bristled her skin. According to legend, the night's predatory raptor had cried a message of death.

Chapter Three

There. He'd almost stepped on the prone body lying facedown in the boggy soil. Liam shone his light on the victim, automatically categorizing details—Caucasian male, approximately six feet tall, long brown hair, wearing jeans, army boots and a flannel jacket shredded in the back upper torso area. Beneath the jagged slits, blood oozed from multiple lacerations.

It fit the pattern.

As he'd told Harper, this had been going on for years. Whoever the murderer was, he was smart enough to space the crimes out. The choice of victims was calculated, too. Usually, the homeless had cut ties with their families, and no one would report them missing for years—if ever. It was entirely possible that his missing uncle Teddy had met a similarly violent end in the backwoods of some small town. Perhaps even this one. Liam shook off the speculation to focus on his duty. Before he called out a team, he wanted to take a good look at the scene for himself. He knelt and searched the ground near the body for small clues—a button, a gum wrapper, anything the killer might have left behind unnoticed.

But there was nothing incriminating to be found.

Not only was the killer smart, but he was as cowardly as he was vicious. Each victim had been attacked from behind and stabbed multiple times. Liam pulled out his cell phone, hit the dispatcher contact button and quickly explained the situation.

A limb snapped nearby. "Officer?" a deep voice called out from the darkness. "That you, Officer Andrews?"

A group of about half a dozen men approached, in various states of dishevelment and sporting long hair and beards. Liam recognized a few of their faces.

One of the men stepped forward while the others lingered in the dark. "It's Gunner, sir. We out here lookin' for our buddy—Larry."

"When did you last see him?"

"It were morning time. He gathered up our spare change and offered to go into town to buy us a few veggies for our stew tonight. Nobody seen him since."

"Does your friend have long brown hair? Dressed in a flannel jacket?"

"Yes, sir. You seen him?"

"Unfortunately, I believe I have." Liam waved him over. "Brace yourself. It's not a pretty sight."

Liam turned the flashlight on the body for a brief second. "That look like him?"

Gunner sank to his knees, gagging.

Liam gave him a moment, then asked, "Did you see anyone roaming around here minutes ago?"

"We saw a light and headed right over in the general direction."

"Larry have a beef with anyone in town that you know of?"

"No, sir. He ain't been in Baysville but a week or two."

That was often their way. Ride the rails, then jump track to stay in a town for a bit until the urge hit to travel again. It made tracking someone damn difficult. Easy to get lost in this counterculture. Years ago they were referred to as hobos, a word probably derived from poor migrant workers who traveled from town to town toting knapsacks and a hoe for working the fields.

Baysville had once been a boomtown for them. Plenty of work in the old tobacco and corn fields. During the off-season, they could sometimes find jobs in the pork-processing factories. But these days, Baysville's largest industry was tourism, and those farm and factory jobs for transients had almost dried up.

"If you don't mind, I'd like you and your friends to stick around a bit longer. Might have a few more questions for y'all after forensics arrive and we search the area."

"Yes, sir."

Gunner clearly would rather slink away than face a group of cops, but Liam figured he knew better than to take off.

Looked like he'd be here awhile as well. Might be best to call Harper and explain the situation. After they were through here, it'd be too late to stop by her house. There was no reason to return, anyway, except to leave her flashlight on the porch and retrieve his car from the driveway. He'd checked her home and found no cause for alarm.

He ran a hand through his hair. Damn if the night didn't feel a little colder and lonelier. He called Harper's number but got no answer. Maybe she was getting ready for bed. Liam left a voice message that he'd found a body and would be tied up the rest of the evening.

Blue lights strobed on King Street at the same moment his phone rang. Liam held the flashlight straight up in the air as a beacon and verbally guided the officers to his precise location.

"What's happening? What did you find?"

He whirled around at the familiar voice. "Thought you'd gone back to the house."

"Fat chance," Harper said, looking around the scene.

He knew the exact moment she spotted the body. She inhaled sharply. "Is he…is he—"

"Dead," he confirmed. "We have the situation covered." He briefly pressed her small, trembling hand. "Go on back," he urged.

The police car bumped along the field and parked close by. A detective and the forensics examiner exited the vehicle and immediately set to work taking pictures and putting the body in a bag while Liam filled them in on what he knew. A siren sounded in the distance, and another cop car pulled up by the small crowd. Liam frowned when he recognized the driver.

Bryce Fairfax strode over, hands on hips as he surveyed the scene. His eyes widened at the sight of Harper. "What are you doing out here?"

"We saw a light in the marsh, and Liam… Officer Andrews…wanted to check it out."

Bryce shot him a stern look. "Civilians don't need to be at a crime scene—unless they've witnessed a crime, of course."

Liam clamped his jaw tight to prevent an angry defense. His boss never failed to find something to criticize in his work. It had been like that almost since he'd transferred to the Baysville PD five months ago.

"It's not his fault," Harper said quickly. "He told me not to come out here, but I did anyway."

"So I see."

Bryce shot him another look that promised he'd speak with him later about this matter. What a jerk.

"I'll go on home," Harper said, giving Liam an apologetic smile before handing him her flashlight. "I won't need this now."

"I'll have you escorted," Chief Fairfax said, motioning to one of the responding officers.

For the next hour, they took statements and searched for forensic evidence. Bryce questioned the homeless men. His condescension was evident in his smirk and sharp, pointed questions. Bryce released them with a warning not to leave town. Liam predicted they'd be hopping the next train that passed through. Bryce had to realize that as well, which meant another unsolved vagrant murder.

"That should wrap it up for tonight, men," Bryce said, hitching up his belt and puffing out his chest. "Appears this is nothing more than another case of vagrants killing one of their own. Probably arguing over alcohol or drugs, I bet."

"You're forgetting the car," Liam pointed out. "There was someone roaming the field, and then we heard a vehicle driving off."

Bryce chuckled. "Probably just some teenagers making out. You know how kids are." He nodded at the other two men. "Sam, stay here and keep the crime scene secure until another officer arrives from the midnight shift. George, go on home now. I need to speak to Andrews."

George left with a wave, Sam resumed searching the ground and Liam was alone with his boss.

"What were you doing over at Harper Catlett's place?"

"I offered to search her house. She seemed upset this morning about the noises and that email. And someone tried to run her down with a truck. I'll be writing up a report."

Bryce popped a stick of clove chewing gum in his mouth. "Let me fill you in on Harper. Her sister, Presley, died in that house seventeen years ago. Harper was only nine at the time. She was the first one on the scene. Claimed she saw a sickly looking man—or creature— hovering over her sister and that he just disappeared into thin air. The police thoroughly searched the place. Nobody had been in that house. Nobody, you understand?"

"So she told me. What are you saying? That she lied?"

"*Lie* is a strong word. Maybe a better word is *imaginative*. After all, she was a kid. Probably woke up from a nightmare and then suffered a trauma when she saw Presley dead. Or it could have been she was thinking of the Shadow Dweller."

"The Shadow Dweller? What are you talking about?"

"A local legend. Some people—mostly kids—claim to see a filthy, emaciated creature that vanishes the instant he's spotted. They say he peeks out of house windows or deserted buildings, especially whenever the mailman passes by." Bryce chuckled. "When items go missing— a jacket, a pecan pie, a blanket—folks blame it on the Shadow Dweller."

Liam mulled over the new information. "And you think Harper's mind leaped to the legend when she found her sister?"

"Could be. Took a long time before kids stopped giving her grief about what she claimed to have seen."

"Kids can be cruel. What did her parents say about it?"

"Her dad had died a year earlier. Ruth, her mom, made Harper go to grief counseling."

A stab of sympathy shot through him. Must have been pretty tough for Harper. "And you bring all this up because…?"

"Isn't it obvious? Again, she's claiming to hear noises in the house and that she received a threatening email. Weird how the proof happened to disappear."

Anger thrummed along his temples at the insinuation. "Harper's not crazy." He'd seen her abrasions from the near run-in with the truck. Those were real, and there had been a witness to the incident.

"Now, now. I didn't say that."

"You implied it."

"I'm merely laying out the facts for you. Might want to take what she says with a grain of salt. You found nothing in her house, correct?"

"Correct," he reluctantly admitted. "But someone did try to run her over—"

"Just watch your step, that's all I'm saying. You entered her house, still in uniform, and spent time alone with her. Use caution. Who knows what goes on in that head of hers? I don't want my department getting a hare-brained sexual harassment complaint because Harper's made up some fantasy in her head about *you*."

"Your fears are unwarranted," he said stiffly. "Doubt I'll even see her again before she leaves."

"Might be for the best."

Although it was offered as a suggestion, Liam understood his boss meant it as an order. Bryce hitched up his pants again and strolled to his car.

Alone in the marsh, Liam ran a hand through his hair and sighed. Porch lights shone from Harper's house, and he could make out her silhouette where she stood, waiting. He'd return her flashlight and then be on his solitary way. Although he disagreed with his boss as to Harper's state of mind.

Reluctantly, he returned. Harper opened the screen door and beckoned him inside, but Liam only climbed the porch steps and held out the flashlight. "Thanks for the loan. It came in handy."

"No problem." She met him halfway on the steps and took the flashlight. "Can I offer you coffee?"

"Sorry. I need to go back to the station and write up a report. I'll be on my way."

She reached out to him, and the heat of her hand bled through his uniform sleeve. "I appreciate you coming over." An uncertain smile lit her pale face. "Thanks for taking this matter seriously. Not everyone does that for me. But you did."

"So I heard."

Harper winced. "Bryce must have filled you in on my past. That didn't take long."

"It doesn't matter what other people think."

"Easy for you to say." Harper shrugged. "It took a long time for all that stuff to blow over. Should have realized no one's forgotten it, though. Hell, I'm not sure I even believe what I saw anymore."

"I see why you want to sell this place and get back to Atlanta. Lots of bad memories here."

"And good ones from when all four of us were alive. It wasn't all bad. Guess all families are complicated that way."

"Right." He dug his car keys out of his pocket.

"Maybe I'll see you around?" she asked.

The wistful note in her voice tugged at him. "Maybe."

He turned away and started down the steps, conscious of her watching. His legs felt as though they weighed a ton. He didn't want to leave Harper. That murder had been way too close to her house, right after someone had nearly run her over, and the night grew darker by the minute. What if the murderer had seen them leave her home and head into the marsh where he'd just killed? Unlike Bryce, he didn't believe it was an instance of the homeless killing one of their own. His boss was lazy, too quick to dismiss the murders as unimportant casualties of the transients turning on one another.

Liam would never forgive himself if he left Harper alone and something happened to her. He had to do more to keep her safe.

Liam turned back to Harper. "Want to go to the store with me? I need to pick up a few things before it closes at nine."

Her face lit up. "Actually, I'm wound up too tight to relax, and I could use a few things. I'll grab my purse and meet you out front."

What Bryce didn't know wouldn't hurt him. He liked Harper, and he'd been in law enforcement for years. Not as though he were a rookie about to be taken in by a deranged woman. No, he was capable of making his own decisions about a person's character. Bryce might have distant knowledge of Harper through her sister and mutual acquaintances, but that didn't mean he knew the woman she'd become.

Soon, she stood by the vehicle, waiting with purse in hand.

"That was quick." He opened the door for her, and she slid in.

"No time to waste if we want to make it by closing."

Liam entered the driver's side and started the engine.

"Is your fridge totally empty?" Harper asked. "That happens to me all the time in Atlanta. I'll work long hours and forget to shop. I end up eating way too much fast food."

"The groceries aren't for me."

She shot him a questioning glance as he backed out of the driveway.

"It's for the men we met tonight," he admitted reluctantly. "Gunner, I guess you could call him their leader, mentioned they'd been searching for the victim. They'd scraped together money for him to buy provisions for a stew tonight."

"You're buying the food for them? You're a kind man."

Liam shifted uncomfortably in his seat at her look of admiration. He shrugged. "It's no big deal. I have a soft spot for the homeless. My uncle used to be one. For all I know, maybe he still is. We haven't heard from him in years."

"That's terrible. Were you close?"

"Not me, but my mother was close to Uncle Teddy. She still harbors an irrational hope of reuniting with him one day." Liam crossed an intersection, bemused at his admission. He didn't normally open up to people so quickly.

"Anything's possible. He might turn up one day out of the blue."

"I've asked around about him, of course. Over a decade ago, he was arrested several times in Baysville for public vagrancy and for living in abandoned buildings. After the last arrest, he spent a few nights in the county jail. Probably a welcome change from cold and hunger. Never was seen or heard from again. I've showed old photos of my uncle to Gunner and some of the older guys, but they didn't recognize him."

"At least you tried. I'm sure your mom appreciates that."

They fell into a comfortable silence as he drove through town. A few couples strolled the river walk, and others exited from the main street restaurants that were closing. The scent of crab cakes and lobster was strong enough to detect even in the car. One of the many advantages of living in a tourist town were the great restaurants and bars.

He'd be sad to leave when the time came. His stint

in Baysville was temporary, although his boss and co-workers didn't know that. Only one person knew his real reason for coming, and Liam trusted him to keep that knowledge secret.

"This seems like a great place to grow up," he noted.

"Mostly. If only…well, if only Presley hadn't had that accident and I hadn't seen what I did." She hesitated. "Or what I thought I saw."

"Can you describe it again? In more detail?"

"A man hovered over Presley. Extremely pale. When he looked up at me, I couldn't really read his expression. His eyes were large and full of contradiction—anger, surprise, but mostly fear. Although he couldn't have been more afraid of me than I was of him."

"How tall was he?"

"Hard to say since he was bent over, but I don't think he was a tall man. He wore dirty clothes that were ragged, and his face and arms looked as though they were crusted in dirt. If not for that, he might have been glow-in-the-dark pale. Very sickly looking."

"The legendary Shadow Dweller, perhaps?"

The corners of her mouth turned down. "Bryce was awfully chatty tonight, wasn't he? And here I thought he was my friend—that we shared a connection through Presley's memory."

A false belief like that could be dangerous. He shouldn't say anything, and yet… "A word of warning," he said reluctantly. "Don't trust Bryce Fairfax one hundred percent. He might not be all that he appears to be on the surface."

Chapter Four

She should be tired. Bone weary after the night's events. Instead, Harper tossed underneath the covers. Even when she wasn't consciously listening for an out-of-place sound, her brain remained on high alert. So far, coming home hadn't eradicated her fear of old ghosts and things that went bump in the night. Yet, she owed it to herself to stay and confront the memories head-on. With each bit of clothing donated or trash discarded, with the stripping away of each material possession tied to the house, Harper hoped to sweep away the remaining cobwebs of mystery and sadness.

Sighing, she admitted defeat. No matter how much she needed eight hours of shut-eye, sleep eluded her. Experience taught her that when all else failed—a hot bath, yoga, warm milk and a misting diffuser of lavender essential oil—the best remedy was to read the most boring material available. Harper climbed out of bed, strolled to her mom's bedroom and emptied out a drawerful of old papers from her desk. Might as well kill two birds with one stone, get rid of outdated paperwork and read until her eyes became so blurry she'd be forced to close them and drift off to never-never land.

She carried a stack of papers to the bed, fluffed a pillow behind her back and dug in. Outdated checks, old warranties and instruction manuals—Mom was clearly old-school and didn't trust keeping records on a computer. But two-thirds of the way through the stack, an official government record caught her attention.

Her breath caught at the heading: Autopsy Report of Presley Lee Catlett. The yellowed sheet of paper shook beneath her trembling fingers as she read on. "Cause of death: Asphyxiation from severe spinal cord injury at the fourth cervical vertebra." Paragraphs of further medical description continued, describing the damaged tissue on the base of Presley's skull and trauma to internal organs, all consistent with smoke asphyxiation. "Other findings: Deceased was nine weeks pregnant. Signed, Dr. Thomas J. Lumpkin, Pathologist."

Pregnant? In stunned disbelief, Harper slapped the report against her thighs. "Presley was pregnant?" she squeaked in the silent room, as if someone was nearby and could respond. Why hadn't her mother ever mentioned it? Harper stood and paced, running a hand through her tousled hair. She'd imagined herself all cried out years ago, but a fresh well of grief burst inside. Nine weeks, so her sister had to have known about her condition before her unexpected death.

And so had Mom. Yet she'd never mentioned a word of it to Harper. Why not? Did she imagine shielding her from the news would make her sister's death any less painful?

Who else knew about this? Did the biological father know? Harper abruptly stopped pacing, recalling Presley's old boyfriend, Allen Spencer. They'd broken up days before Presley's accident. She hadn't thought much of it at the time, but now she couldn't help wondering. Did Allen break up with Presley when, or if, she told him about the pregnancy?

A sliver of muted light shone through the lace curtain. Another day dawning. And yes, learning about the pregnancy made Presley's early death even more tragic.

Would Presley have kept the baby? Harper rather thought her sister was the kind of girl who would do just that. And maybe, just maybe, that had enraged her ex-boyfriend. Maybe even enough to kill her.

Harper crawled back in bed and rubbed her temples. Allen was no killer. The man was a well-respected preacher now, had been for many years. Last she'd heard, he was married with three kids. Besides, whatever she'd seen or not seen that night, it certainly wasn't Allen.

She had to get out of the suddenly stifling house. The only place open this early in the morning would be the Dixie Diner, Mom's old place of employment. A chocolate crème–filled doughnut and a vanilla latte would provide a welcome sugary distraction. On a whim, Harper whipped out her cell phone and texted Kimber to see if her old friend had time to join her calorie fest.

She was in luck. Kimber agreed to meet her there in thirty minutes.

"I CAN'T BELIEVE that murder last night was so close to you," Kimber said with a shudder. "Practically in your own backyard."

Rhoda, a waitress, hovered nearby, smoothing her hands over her apron. "Heard about it on the radio this morning. Not what you needed after all you've been through." She patted Harper's shoulder in sympathy before returning to wait tables.

"Did you see or hear anything?" Kimber asked.

"I'd rather not talk about it."

Kimber nodded. "Okay. I get it. If you change your mind later, give me a buzz."

Harper soaked in the sweet, heady scent of chocolate, coffee and fresh-baked doughnuts that permeated every square inch of the rustic diner, which sported turquoise Formica tabletops, waitresses in white aprons and local folks sipping white mugs of steaming coffee. It was like stepping into a 1950s soda shop. Even the windows were clouded with condensation, and Harper imagined herself embraced in a cozy cocoon of warm deliciousness. Just what she needed after last night.

"Here ya go, honey," Rhoda said, returning with Harper's food and drink. She patted Harper's shoulder. "I think of your mom every day." The two had worked the morning shift together for nearly three decades. She shook her head, her gray curls straining against a black hairnet. "Keep expecting her to breeze through the door any minute and put on her apron." Rhoda turned to Kimber. "What'll it be this morning, sweetheart?"

"Toast and black coffee." Kimber smiled at Harper's wince as Rhoda sauntered to the kitchen. "What can I say? I've been on a perpetual diet since having kids."

"You look great," Harper assured her. And she did. Kimber was a tall, cool blonde with terrific bone structure and a homecoming queen aura, even if she'd finished high school eons ago. Smart, too. Owned a successful real estate company and ruled her roost of husband and three kids with an easy aplomb that Harper couldn't help but admire.

"How's the house prep coming along?" Kimber asked. "Don't forget, I have a cleaning crew that can make short work of it for you. Reasonable rates."

Harper waved a dismissive hand. "I remember. I need to go through a lot myself, but after that, I'll give them a call. Text me their info."

Kimber nodded. "I understand. Lots of old memories

tied up in the place. How much longer you reckon it'll take? Aren't you worried about your business in Atlanta?"

"I'm going to call my assistant today and have her take over a couple of outstanding jobs. She can contact future customers and explain there'll be a short delay due to a family emergency."

"I'm sure they'll understand. Just give me the word when you're ready to place your house on the market. It might be difficult—it's an older home—but I'm the best."

"Even after what happened to Presley in the house?" she asked doubtfully.

"It won't be the first home I've sold where tragic accidents have occurred, so even though it's an obstacle, I know how to overcome it. Not all agents do." Kimber laughed. "Not that I'm trying to rush you for a commission. Hell, I wish you'd move back to Baysville." Her classically sculpted face grew pensive. "I could use a friend."

"You?" She scoffed, surprised at Kimber's words. "You've got plenty of friends. You've lived here all your life."

"Mmm-hmm," she murmured, not revealing anything. "But small towns can be lonely places."

Harper frowned at Kimber's uncharacteristic vulnerability. "Is something wrong?"

Kimber folded her hands on the table and gave a tight smile. "Not at all. Just an off kind of morning."

She studied her friend's blue eyes—the exact shade of Pagan River's navy hue. Harper had always viewed it as a sign that Kimber perfectly fit in with Baysville. But what did one ever really know of another person's secret trials? Presley had carried a huge secret on her teenage shoulders, without a word to anyone, as far as Harper could tell. Weren't small towns supposed to be an open book where everybody knew everybody's history and where gossip ran rampant?

But not a word of Presley's pregnancy had been whispered about in the grapevine. Not that had gotten back to her, at any rate. Harper leaned forward, keeping her voice low. "Have you ever heard any rumors about Presley?"

Kimber blinked. "What kind of rumors? I mean, she's been dead for years."

"Before she died, did you ever hear talk of anything about her, um, sex life?"

"She dated Allen Spencer. Whether they slept together, I haven't a clue. Why do you ask?"

Harper silently debated. What did it really matter after all these years? But Presley had kept her secret, and it didn't seem right to spill the beans now. "Never mind. It's not important. I've been going through old family stuff and it's made me maudlin, I suppose."

"Understandable. Your sister always kind of kept to herself. But I remember Presley as smart and very likable. Just don't put her on a pedestal, though…after all, she was very young. Whatever it is you've found, if Presley was less than perfect, so what?" Kimber lightened the mood with a wink. "The two of us did plenty of questionable things as teenagers."

"True enough. Guess I'm in an off mood as well. My house is still…unsettling."

"The memories?" she asked sympathetically.

"Yeah. And other things… Sounds, senses…something. I know there has to be a logical explanation, but it gets to me." Kimber was the only one she could talk to about it. Everyone else either shut her out or stared at her with eyes full of pity. She hated that look.

"Here y'all go." Rhoda set down their food and drink. "Enjoy."

"Breakfast of champions," Harper grinned, biting into the doughnut.

Kimber stoically bit into her dry toast and downed it with a sip of black coffee. "I'm glad you texted about meeting this morning. There's something I've been meaning to ask you."

Harper raised her brows and kept eating.

"I have a proposition for you." Kimber straightened, assuming her professional Realtor mantle. "As I said, your house presents certain challenges to a sale. Even though I know I could meet them, there's a simpler solution to its marketability issues—I'd like to buy it."

"Why?" She was taken aback at the offer. Kimber and Joe lived in a rambling old farmhouse outside town that they'd renovated into a showcase. It was her pride and joy. "Thought you loved your farmhouse."

"Oh, we do. We have no plans to move. Your house would be an investment. I've studied the market carefully, and I believe I could turn it into a profitable bed-and-breakfast."

An unexpected twinge of sadness swept through her. "You know, that's what Dad always wanted to do with the place. Mom had started to warm to the idea before Presley died. She gave up on dreams after that."

"I remember. That's what gave me the idea. Besides making a nice profit, I figured it would be a blessing for you as well. A win-win. I'd buy it immediately, and you could return to Atlanta without worrying about selling it." Kimber's face brightened with enthusiasm. "Not only would the house be in good hands, but also it'd bring your dad's dream to light."

All true, so why didn't the arrangement make her happy?

Kimber's smile dimmed. "What's wrong? You don't like the idea?"

"It's just unexpected."

Kimber patted her hand. "If you don't want to, no hard feelings. But think about it, okay? And, of course, I'd hire you to do all the decorating. That way, you'll always have a presence there. Might even entice you to visit Baysville more often if you could spend the night in your old home."

"You're the best, Kimber. Let me consider it for a few days, and I'll let you know."

"Of course."

She still wasn't sold, which made no sense. Her friend's offer would hasten cutting all ties to her hometown. Wasn't that what she wanted? More people bustled in the diner, grabbing breakfast or coffee before heading to work. Several uniformed officers entered, and she recognized Liam and Bryce heading to the counter. At the sight of Liam's tall figure, her heart kicked up its heels.

Kimber's cell phone buzzed, and she picked it up, a slight frown tugging her face. "Business calls," she said crisply. "I've got an unexpected client meeting. Sorry, I've got to run."

"No problem. Quick question, though. This cleaning crew of yours, can they handle large jobs?"

"They've done everything from hauling off old furniture in vacated houses to fire damage renovation. Nothing's too big or too small."

Harper dug the spare house key out of her purse and slid it across the table to Kimber. "Consider them hired. I need a good set of muscles to haul off all of Dad's old tools and benches in the basement. They can donate anything in good condition to charity and dump the rest. Stop by anytime and go down there to assess the fee. I don't need to be home."

"I'll do it today," Kimber promised. After they made a dinner date for later in the week, she bustled off. Harper watched through the window as she quickly walked to her car and climbed inside. Sell the house to Kimber? She tried to convince herself to accept the offer. It was the rational move to make, and yet…

"Harper?" Liam approached her booth. "May I join you?"

"Please do." He slid in opposite her, and his gray eyes bored into hers, as if he could read all her secrets.

Bryce stopped by the booth. "Morning, Harper. Any more threatening emails or unexplained noises?"

Several customers shifted their gazes to them, and her face warmed. Did he have to boom out the question within earshot of so many people? "Not in the past twenty-four hours."

"Good, good. We're always here if you need us. You coming, Andrews?"

"In a few minutes."

A look passed between them, a tiny beat of tension. "Don't stay too long—we've got a full load today." Bryce turned from Liam to her and rapped his hand on the table. "See you around, then. Hopefully not in my official capacity."

She sipped her drink, relieved to find the other patrons resuming their own conversations. Liam leaned in, keeping his voice low. "You sure you're going to be okay? You look…weary."

"I didn't get much sleep last night," she admitted. "I kept thinking about that poor guy killed nearby. I tried to tackle a project, to get my mind off the murder, but I read something in Mom's old papers that disturbed me."

"Want to talk about it?"

The loud rev of an engine distracted her. Outside, Bryce backed a police cruiser out of his parking place.

"Don't you need to get to the station? What with the full load Bryce mentioned."

"No hurry." Liam kept his eyes pinned on her.

Somehow, she found herself telling him about the autopsy report. Strange how she felt so free to confide in him instead of her longtime best friend. Maybe because he never knew her sister, it felt like less of a betrayal to confide about the pregnancy.

"Damn, what a horrible way to find out."

"I can't believe Mom never told me."

"She might have been trying to protect you from more pain."

"Probably. But I wish she had talked to me. Mom shut down after Presley's death. Her life became a matter of merely going through the motions of living."

"Do you think this report has any bearing on your sister's death—on what you saw that night?"

"No. Her boyfriend, Allen Spencer, looks nothing like whatever I saw on the staircase. Although—I do wonder if Allen knew." She set down her drink. The sugary sweetness that had tasted so good going down now roiled in her belly.

"I can ask him for you."

"Seriously? You don't think that would be presumptuous? I barely know the guy, and you don't know him at all. Won't you get into trouble for asking about his teenage behavior—wouldn't he think you were harassing him?"

"It's all in the approach. I'll tell him I'm searching for answers about what happened to Presley since some new information has come up. It's the truth."

"He's a minister now. He's sure to be taken aback by you questioning him and his reputation. Let me do it. At least I won't be a stranger."

"I don't know..."

"He's a minister. He knew my sister. Knew of her tragic death. Surely he'll respond with compassion."

"All right. But I'll go with you. Not in an official capacity. I'll change into my civilian clothes but let you do all the talking."

His kindness tugged at her heart, yet an ugly suspicion arose inside. Why was he being so helpful? He barely knew her. "Why?" she asked abruptly.

"Why what?"

"Why are you being so nice?"

"Maybe I'm just a decent guy."

Of course, that was one explanation. Why must she always be so suspicious of people's motives? If alive, Mom would advise her not to look a gift horse in the mouth. "Okay, let's do this. When's a good time for you?"

"When I get off work this evening. Find out the minister's schedule, and we'll work something out." Liam finished the last of his coffee and set it down. "One last word of advice—don't warn him we're coming."

She hadn't expected that. "Why not?"

"He might not have been the man you saw that night, but say he and your sister argued about the pregnancy. Maybe she wanted to keep the baby, and that infuriated him. Enough so that he hired someone to hurt her."

"A teenager hiring a hit man? Bit of a stretch, I think."

"I've seen it all in my line of work. Never underestimate what people will do when they're in a rage or feel cornered. By the way, I filed the report on that truck that came at you. Nothing's come up yet, but I'll let you know if something does." Liam slid out of the booth. "I'll buzz you later."

She continued to sit for a few more minutes, pondering Liam's parting salvo. The Allen she remembered had been a quiet, slightly nerdy kind of guy. But what was that old line about how you always have to watch the quiet ones?

"You doing okay, sweetie? More coffee?" Rhoda appeared at her side, a fresh pot in her hands.

"No, thanks. I'd better get going." Harper slapped a generous tip on the table and eased out of the booth, only now noticing several people standing at the entrance, waiting on a clean table. No wonder Mom used to come home with aching feet and a sore back from serving a steady stream of customers.

She waved goodbye to the staff and headed outside, gazing forlornly at her car. Everyone else seemed so busy and content, full of things to do and people to meet. The way she had been not so long ago. And now? Nothing waiting on her but a creepy house that still needed more cleaning and decluttering. She didn't even want to return to her childhood home—how sad was that? If she had any sense, she'd call Kimber immediately and accept her offer to buy it. In two days, she could be back at her old job in Atlanta, slipping into a comfortable routine.

Funny how that hardly appealed to her, either.

Harper pushed her shoulders back and strode forward. The thing was to keep busy. She'd sleep on Kimber's offer tonight and call her in the morning with a decision.

"Harper? Harper Catlett?"

The deep, booming voice sounded familiar. She swung around, spotting Captain Carlton Fairfax bearing down on her. Make that ex-captain. Bryce's father was a negative image of his son. Where Bryce was muscular, Carlton was stocky. Bryce's dark good looks and affable smile managed to look downright smarmy on his dad, although the family resemblance was there in the strong jaw and in the confident aura both exuded.

He held out a beefy hand, and she shook it, almost wincing at his tight squeeze. Was that a male dominance tactic—show her who was stronger? There she went with the suspicions again.

"Knew it had to be you with the wild red hair." He grinned.

She forced a smile, reminding herself that he had been kind to her and Mom after the accident. Not to mention he'd been the first responder at the scene that night and had whisked them away to safety.

"Sorry about your mother. She was a good woman, that Ruth. A hard worker."

"Yes, sir."

"Reckon you'll be heading out of Baysville in the next few days?"

She felt a perverse desire to contradict his assumption. "I might just stay." The admission surprised even her.

His smile slipped a notch. "I'd have thought Baysville wouldn't hold much attraction to a young lady with a fancy decorating career in Atlanta."

It almost sounded as though he wanted her to leave. "Isn't the mayor your buddy? Don't imagine he'd find your portrayal of Baysville very flattering."

He barked out a laugh but hardly appeared amused. Harper opened her car door. "Good to see you again." She shut herself inside, ending the conversation. From the rearview mirror, she saw him watch her as she backed out of the parking space and then onto Main Street. His stare was oddly unsettling. Probably a guilt by association thing. Since Liam had warned her that Bryce might not be a particularly reliable person, she assumed his dad was cut from the same cloth. It felt odd to be wary of them when she'd looked up to Bryce as a girl. But she was starting to view him in a different light now, especially since he'd refused to take her fears seriously.

She turned on the radio, determined to shake off her uneasy mood. Obviously, last night's discovery still played on her emotions, too, making her mistrustful of everyone and their motives. For now, she'd concentrate on her upcoming interview with the preacher.

Chapter Five

The nearly deserted church had an eerie vibe. On either side of the main sanctuary, the rippled surface of stained-glass windows sparkled like deep-hued jewels in the waning sunlight. A weighty silence blanketed the room, as though thousands of prayers were compressed between the walls.

From a distance came the sound of a girl's high-pitched voice—out of place and jarring. Liam couldn't make out the words, but he guessed from her tone that she was agitated.

"The youth group always met in the basement on Thursday nights," Harper said in a near whisper. "If memory serves, it should begin in about fifteen minutes. When I called earlier, the church secretary told me that Allen personally conducts their meetings and would be available."

"Hmm…so he knows we're coming?"

"If the secretary told him. I know you didn't want to alert him to our visit, but she asked if I wanted to see him."

"No problem. The basement it is, then." Liam nodded, amused that he'd also lowered his voice, as though conversing in a normal tone would violate the reverent atmosphere. "I meant to ask, did Allen conduct the funeral service for your mother?"

"No, we went to a different church across town."

They stepped from the sanctuary into a dimly lit hallway lined with rows of closed doors with placards designating various Bible study groups. A sliver of light shone from the last door on the right, casting a patchwork of shadows on the linoleum floor.

"Allen? Where are you?"

That same querulous voice he'd heard in the sanctuary drew closer, emerging from the staircase to his left. A young girl rounded the second level of the stairs, blinking at them in surprise. Skinny and with a short pixie cut feathering her face, her eyes looked impossibly large.

"We're looking for him, too." Harper veered from his side and walked toward the stairs. "Are you part of the youth group?"

"Yes, ma'am. Sort of."

A muffled rustling sounded from down the hallway, much more interesting than this conversation with the girl. Liam quietly padded toward the occupied room, tuning in to whispering voices and the unmistakable metallic clicking of a zipper. He reckoned he'd either found the missing preacher or two brazen teenagers who'd arrived early for the youth meeting and decided to engage in a little fun first.

The doorknob turned, and a fortysomething man appeared, running a hand through his short hair, his reading glasses slightly askew on his delicate features. He pasted on a nervous smile. "Did I hear someone calling for me?"

"Allen Spencer?" Liam asked.

Allen quickly shut the door behind him and walked away as if in a hurry to get somewhere. "Yes? Do I know you?"

"Where ya been?" The teenager pushed in front of Liam to confront Allen, eyes narrowed.

Now wasn't this all very interesting. The man was hiding a secret. If he had a consensual thing going on with an adult employee, Liam couldn't pursue that in any official way. But the inappropriate flash of suspicion and jealousy in the teenager's eyes gave him pause. Did Allen flirt with these young girls and lead them on? Perhaps something even worse was happening here.

"Patience, Kristen." Allen frowned a warning at the girl before catching sight of Harper. He squinted and tentatively offered his hand, ignoring Liam. "Aren't you—"

"Harper Catlett. Presley's sister."

They shook hands. "Yes, yes. There's a resemblance. I heard about your mother. So sorry. What brings you here tonight?"

Liam's suspicion increased as the preacher drew them toward his office—and away from the closed door of the Adult Disciples room. Harper glanced at him with raised brows, a silent acknowledgment that she was also aware of the man's odd behavior. Allen flipped on the lights and bade them enter, motioning them to sit on the couch across from his desk. "Come in, come in. I only have a few minutes, though, before the youth group starts. Kristen, will you please go downstairs and set up the chairs for me?"

Kristen pouted, and Liam thought she was about to refuse, but the girl huffed out of the room, producing a surprising amount of noise as she stomped down the stairs. Liam remained standing at the door while Harper seated herself.

Allen perched behind the desk, folding his slender fingers together atop its mahogany surface. "This must be a difficult time for you after losing your mother," he began in what sounded to Liam like practiced, professional rote. "But death is not really the end, it's—"

"Thank you, but that's not why I'm here," Harper interrupted.

"Oh?" Surprise lit behind the thick lens of his glasses.

The landline phone on his desk rang, and he winced. "Excuse me a moment. I never know when it might be someone in the congregation who needs my assistance."

Perfect timing. Liam raised a finger toward Harper. "Be right back," he murmured.

She nodded in understanding. Allen appeared wrapped up in his phone call. Liam closed the door behind him and made his way back down the hall. If he found a grown woman trying to discreetly slip away, then there wasn't much he could do if she was part of a consensual affair. It would make Allen a hypocrite and adulterer, but not necessarily a lawbreaker. If, however, the man was fooling around with underage girls, that was a different story entirely. Allen was in serious trouble in that case. At the last room on the right, from which Allen had originally emerged, he quickly opened the door and stepped inside.

All was quiet. A corner lamp softly lit the unoccupied room where a circle of metal folding chairs was arranged. On the walls were shelves of books and angel statues. Had he missed whoever had been there a minute earlier? "It's okay, you can come out now."

From the corner of his eye, he caught a slight movement to his far left. There. A young girl's head peeked out from behind the back of a large, wing-backed chair positioned near the back window. They silently, warily eyed one another.

"Who are you?" she whispered.

Automatically, his right hand reached for the back pocket that held his wallet and police identification. He thought better of it. The girl was nervous enough without throwing that bit of information into the mix right off the bat.

"Liam Andrews," he answered simply. "Come on out."

She emerged from behind the chair, nervously running her hands through her shoulder-length tangle of curls. "I, um, I'd lost an earring and was looking for it."

"In that case, it might have been helpful to turn on the overhead light."

"Yeah." She gave a self-deprecating giggle and stuffed her hands in the front pockets of her jeans. "You're right. My bad."

He commanded her gaze. "How'd you lose the earring?"

She lifted her shoulders and raised her palms in a whatcha-gonna-do gesture. "Oh, you know..." The girl shuffled past him, her head bent low.

"Hold on there," he said.

She spun around. "Yes, sir?"

"How old are you?"

"Fifteen. Why?"

A minor then. This was bad. "What was going on in here?"

"Wh-what do you mean?" A blush scoured her cheeks even as guilt flashed in her wide green eyes. Her hands left her pockets, and she again played with the loose curls framing her girlish face.

"You can tell me. I'm a cop. I'll help you."

Her eyes darted to the door.

"Would you rather discuss this with a female officer?" he asked gently. "I can call someone in."

White teeth scraped at her bottom lip. Slowly, she started walking backward toward the exit door. "I'm, um, late. I gotta go."

"What's your name?"

"Mary Smith."

If he wasn't so concerned for her, he'd have been angry at the blatant lie. "What's going on here is wrong," he said gently. "Like I said, I can help you. But I need your real name. And your parents' phone number."

Mary—or whatever her name was—visibly paled, and her mouth dropped open in fear. She bolted.

Liam rushed into the hallway after her as she streaked through the sanctuary, swift as a scared bunny.

Allen's study door opened, and he poked his head out, furtively scanning the hallway. "Everything okay out here? Emily, what's going on?" he called after the girl.

Harper pushed past Allen and joined him in the pursuit.

"Emily, wait!" she pleaded. She looked back at Liam, and said softly, "She might talk to a woman."

The girl halted and peered over her shoulder.

"Can we talk a minute?" Harper asked, approaching her slowly, holding out a hand. "Just you and me."

Allen caught up to them, huffing from the short run. "Why are you running, Emily? What's going on?"

Liam's jaw clenched at the man's faked air of innocence and the deliberate, warning frown he gave the young girl. He stepped in front of Allen, blocking his view of Emily. "Harper, do you mind taking Emily inside while I deal with Mr. Spencer?"

"What do you say, Emily?" Harper smiled softly, draped an arm over the girl's shoulder and guided her to the sanctuary. "Everything's going to be fine, honey. You'll see."

Thank heavens for Harper's assistance. The arrest would be so much easier without the victim witnessing it and possibly trying to protect her abuser, denying that anything wrong had occurred.

"Get in my car," he ordered Spencer. "I'm taking you into the station for questioning."

"Questioning? Wh-what are you talking about?"

"I'm a cop. It's my job to investigate this." Liam took a grim satisfaction at Allen's widened eyes and the sudden slump of his shoulders. He stepped forward, his face within inches of Allen's—close enough to smell his sweat, even through the mentholated scent of the man's aftershave.

"But I haven't done anything wrong," he protested, clear blue eyes awash with barely contained panic. "You can't make me go."

"Get in the car."

Allen's shoulders slumped as he complied with the order. Liam caught up to Harper and pulled her aside from Emily. "Just wait with Emily in an empty room and don't discuss anything with her about what just happened. I'm calling in an officer who specializes in this kind of possible crime, and she'll talk to Emily about the matter."

Harper nodded. "I understand. Don't worry."

Liam called in to the station and arranged for an officer to come over and speak with Emily at once. He returned to his car and confronted Allen. "Here's what's going to happen," he said shortly. "An expert officer in the field is going to interview Emily. Whatever was going on in there, it's all going to come out. I suggest you tell the truth. Now. It might go easier on you that way."

"I was counseling that girl. How dare you! What will my parishioners think? You'll ruin my reputation."

Liam continued. "Didn't you hear me? Admit to everything now."

Allen shook his head, as though dazed. "This can't

be happening. Please. I was counseling Emily. Nothing inappropriate happened."

"Really? And that's why you were in a dimly lit room with her behind closed doors?"

"I can assure you that—"

"We practically caught you in the act."

"You have no proof," he insisted. Allen's skin looked ashen, and he licked his thin lips. "Okay, I'll admit that my behavior has been somewhat inappropriate, but I've never crossed a certain line—"

Disgust filled Liam. "She's a minor. You admit to having physical contact with her of a sexual nature?"

"Yeah, but like I said, we never actually—"

"You're under arrest," Liam interrupted. "I'm taking you to the station."

Allen started to tremble. "My reputation will be in ruins. I'll lose my job."

"Should have thought about that before you crossed the line with a minor. Now stay in here a minute until I return."

Liam made his way into the church and followed the sound of low murmurs coming from Allen's office. Harper and Emily glanced up at him as he entered. Emily's face was tearstained, and her hands shook as she swiped a tissue at her eyes. Harper stood, patting the girl's shoulder as she exited the room and slipped beside him in the hallway.

"What's going on?" she asked. "Did you arrest Allen?"

"I did. How's Emily?"

"She's seems scared to death and called her parents, who, by the way, are on their way over."

"Good. You didn't speak to her about anything that happened?"

"I didn't."

"Excellent. I'm taking Spencer to the station. An officer should be arriving here momentarily. We'll make arrangements to get you a ride home."

"Don't worry about me." Harper crossed her arms and glanced at Emily. "What happens next? I find it hard to believe Emily is his only victim. Maybe Kristen needs to be interviewed as well."

"We'll thoroughly investigate."

"Thank heavens. That man needs to be stopped."

"I agree. Did you get to question him about your sister?"

"Yes, but I didn't learn anything. You just do what you have to do tonight, and I'll see you later."

He nodded and returned to his vehicle, his mind teeming with questions. Could there really be a connection between Presley's pregnancy and her death? He wished he could talk it over with a colleague, but that was way too risky. Word could get back to Bryce and his boss would have yet another reason to dislike him. Already, he probably skated on thin ice with tonight's arrest of a prominent citizen. Bryce would worry about how his department looked if the charges against Spencer didn't stick. The Baysville police chief was hung up on public image, his officers following a strict chain of command, and he exerted control over every facet of the department. So far, Liam hadn't been able to uncover whether this was due to the man's insecure personality or whether it was an attempt to cover up wrongdoing.

As always, the reminder of why he was really in Baysville set him on edge. Did he really want to get involved in Harper's need to poke around in her past? After all, how serious could she be about finding the truth when she was only going to be in town such a short time?

Yet every time he saw Harper, the more he liked her,

the more he wanted to be close to her—and not just for official business. She was kind and intelligent and cared about people in the community. He'd just have to keep a tight rein on his emotions until the questions surrounding her sister's death and the truck that had tried to run her down were either resolved or dismissed. Spending more time with her was probably not a good idea—personally or professionally.

But he'd never been one to shy away from trouble. It was obvious Bryce had no interest in looking into Presley Catlett's death or the truck incident, and he felt like both deserved an investigation. Wherever his attraction to Harper might lead, it would have to be put on hold for now. Which might be easier said than done.

Chapter Six

Harper smiled with pleasure at the sight of Liam on her doorstep the next morning. "I was hoping you'd come by today," she said, gesturing him inside.

He held up a hand. "Sorry, I can't stay. I was in the area and just wanted to ask what, in particular, Spencer said to you about your sister when you questioned him last night."

"I didn't get much of anything out of him." She strode to the porch swing and patted the seat beside her. After a moment of hesitation, Liam sat beside her.

"I can't stop thinking about poor Emily. Hope she's the only victim."

"That would surprise me if she was. Sexual predators rarely fixate on one person."

Harper still couldn't get her head around Allen as a criminal. Maybe sexual misconduct wasn't the only violent secret in his closet. She shook her head. "At any rate, while you were out of the room, I told Allen about the autopsy report revealing Presley was pregnant. He claimed they were never intimate, even saying they had broken up a good two or three weeks before Presley died and that they'd never been serious."

"Do you believe him?" Liam asked.

"I don't know what to believe anymore. Mom always

insisted on meeting Presley's dates, not that she dated that much. Matter of fact, Allen was one of only three guys I can recall Presley introducing to us."

"If you ask me, it sounds like his complete denial was too quick."

"Guess we'll never know for sure." She drummed her fingers on her lap a moment and then admitted in a rush of breath, "I've never mentioned it to anyone before, but I used to hear Presley sneaking out of the house after Mom went to bed at night."

"Think she was meeting Allen?"

"It's what I always assumed. I asked her about it, but she claimed she was just hanging out with a couple girl-friends. I never believed her story."

"How often did this happen?"

Harper cocked her head to the side, thinking. "As far as I know, only a few times. All occurring in the weeks right before her death."

"What—"

The two-way radio crackled and spit out a message.

"Duty calls," Liam said. "Let's put our heads together later and figure out our next step."

"Sure. Was that an emergency call?"

"No."

He didn't volunteer any more information, and she re-garded him quizzically. She imagined having a serious re-lationship with a cop would be filled with moments such as this—worry every time they were called out to a scene.

"Hope everything's routine on the call."

He nodded, and she watched as he returned to his vehicle and sped off. Mrs. Henley waved her over, and Harper walked to her neighbor's house, chatting with her for over an hour before finally returning home.

That smell.

The stench wafted through the foyer—putrid and acrid, a mixture of something rotten mixed with sweat and urine. But the worst part? She'd smelled it before. That horrible night. Even over the acrid tinge of smoke, when whoever or whatever had been there brushed against her to escape into the shadows, an odor had momentarily pervaded. A very distinctive miasma of stink that triggered a gag instinct.

Harper lifted the hem of her T-shirt and covered her mouth and nose, blinking against the insistent tang. She tentatively entered the kitchen, scanning the room to determine the cause of the smell. Had something crawled in the house and died? She could think of no other explanation. The floor and counter were as she'd left them earlier—clean and wiped down. No left-out food, spilled milk or dirty dishes in the sink. The day's garbage had already been taken out. Pinching her nose, she thrust open the kitchen window. The chilly October air she could handle, not so much the smell.

Her search continued room by room. Along the way, she flung open windows and kept breathing through her mouth. And still no explanation to account for it. Upstairs, the smell dwindled to a tolerable level. In her bedroom, Harper wrapped herself in a fleece robe and opened every window before turning to the bed for the throw blanket she always kept neatly folded at the end of the mattress. Next step would be to light candles and spray every inch downstairs with air freshener. Huddling under the warm fleece blanket, she opened her night table drawer in search of a candle and matches. It was then that she noticed it—a yellowed sheet of paper scribbled with her mother's handwriting. How did it get here? Forgetting everything else, Harper sank on the bed and began reading. The letter was addressed to her mother's sister and dated three months after Presley's death.

Dear Ana,

Every day, just as I begin to believe things couldn't possibly get worse, they do. The autopsy record arrived in the mail today. It held one whopper of a surprise. Presley was pregnant. I hardly know what to think. It makes it all the more sad. Lately, it feels like I'm holding on by a thread. I'm unraveling inside. Maybe…maybe it's even affecting my mind? I'm hearing things, sis. Strange noises in the night that keep me awake. I tell myself it's because of what Harper claimed she saw that night, but I don't have the strength to figure it out.

I wish I could just pick up and move out of this place. Go somewhere like Florida where the sun always shines and the beaches glisten with white sand. My hope is that someday Harper will have a better life, far from this town with all its bittersweet memories. But I can't afford to leave. Instead, I work my butt off at the diner and dread coming home in the evenings to my mostly empty house, where the only other person there cries nearly as much as I do. I know what you'll say—to be strong for the only daughter I have left. I'm trying. I really am. But I'm a shell with nothing more to give, and I suspect Harper picks up on that.

The letter ended there. Unfinished, unsigned and undelivered. Her mom hadn't written anything Harper didn't already know, but still. Anger and hurt warred within her heart. Twin emotions both caused by the pain of realizing that her mom had no love left to give once her husband and oldest child had died. It was as though she'd grown up in a foster home with no parents to provide love or security.

She crumpled the aging paper in her fist and flung it on the floor. Anger won out over sorrow and she marched downstairs, sprayed air freshener and then gathered candles and lit them in every room.

There had to be a rational explanation. Yes, the odor had been particularly strong the night Presley died, but every now and then the same mysterious stench of something rotten had appeared over the years, although very faint. Thank heavens the exterminators were arriving in the morning. She'd made the appointment after settling on a local business with great online reviews. Between that and getting rid of all the old possessions in the house, the problem would be removed—or at least, it wouldn't be her problem to deal with anymore. If she had any sense, she'd call Kimber right now and accept her offer.

I have nothing left to give.

Her mom's words echoed round and round in Harper's mind until a tight knot of anger balled in her gut. Presley's death had been tragic, and heartbreaking for Mom, but damn it, she was a victim in all this, too. Her childhood had sputtered to an end. If for no other reason than to satisfy her own questions, she was staying on in Baysville until she either figured out if foul play was involved in her sister's death or accepted it as truly accidental.

Decision made, Harper called her assistant in Atlanta and talked over taking an extended leave of absence. Muriel was understanding and more than capable of filling in for now. There was money in the budget to hire other designers on an as-needed, temporary basis if the workload became too heavy with existing staff. A twinge of guilt hit her as she hung up the phone, but she'd make it up to her assistant when everything returned to normal. Once all this was over, she'd offer Muriel a partnership in the firm.

The house smelled habitable again, if not peachy keen. Harper closed all the windows, sat at the kitchen table and went to work making a game plan on how to proceed with her quest. So far, the only motive she had for foul play was a boyfriend murderously unhappy about the pregnancy.

She drummed her pencil on the notebook but could think of no other lead to pursue. At least not for now. The unexplained noises and smell at home didn't concern her as much as the message to "get out of the house" and the truck that had barreled down on her by the mailbox. Sure, it was possible that both were random, unconnected incidents—but it was also possible that someone did not want her in Baysville. If that were the case, it had to be related to Presley. She had no conflict with anyone in this town.

Unease hammered her temples. From here on out, she'd have to be extra vigilant to ensure that all windows and doors stayed closed and tamperproof.

The lockdown began now.

"You've reached your destination. On right," the disembodied voice of the GPS announced.

Here? Liam frowned at the sight of an ugly cinderblock house that appeared to have been randomly dropped in the middle of a no-man's-land of marsh. Weeds grew up the sides of the moldy structure. A rusted Chevy truck was parked haphazardly on the side of the windowless building. At the back of the property stood an old barn, its rotten roof half collapsing in on the building. The place looked forlorn and neglected, as though no one lived within miles.

Unease lifted the tiny hairs on Liam's arms and the nape of his neck. It was way too quiet out here. Someone had anonymously reported a break-in at the house and left an address, but no name or phone number. Liam got on the two-way radio and reported his location and findings to the dispatcher.

"Want to wait on backup before approaching the house?" the dispatcher asked.

He hesitated. They were chronically short staffed, and it was close to quitting time for the first-shift crew. Already, the October sky had darkened. Only a few dying rays of sunlight cut through the gray clouds.

"No. The place appears deserted."

"Stay in radio contact," the dispatcher advised.

"Ten-four." Liam pulled the cruiser near the front door and shut off the engine before easing out. The quiet was deafening, a heavy pressure that rang in his ears. A flock of starlings abruptly flew out of a sweetgum tree, their collective wings flapping as noisily and erratically as his heartbeat. The birds made their way skyward, still in search of the perfect night's roosting spot.

Cautiously, Liam approached the house and knocked at the door. Complete silence greeted his overture; not even the whisper of movement could be detected from within. He knocked again. "Anyone home?" he called out. "It's the police."

Nothing. Liam backed away and peered into the first front window. Through a thick layer of dust, he made out a single cot surrounded by trash. Did anyone even live in this place? At the second front window, he observed a small room that held an old couch that had stuffing bursting out of threadbare upholstery and more trash scattered on old carpeting. He made his way to the back of the house, which only had one door and window. Again, he looked through the window into a tiny kitchen, where dirty pots and pans overflowed from a sink, and more trash, mostly empty fast food containers, littered the counter and floor.

There wasn't anything even worth stealing from this place. If anyone had wanted in, it would be merely to seek temporary shelter from the coming night. Liam glanced over his shoulder at the decrepit old barn. Might as well search it to be thorough. He headed there then stopped, surprised to find a pattern of flattened weeds and grass. Someone had driven by recently. His gaze followed the tire tracks where they wound to the back of the barn.

This didn't feel right.

Might be best to return to his vehicle and drive around back to check out the area. Liam switched on the two-way. "Nobody found at the residence," he reported. "But I'm—"

A loud pop cracked, and a whizzing torpedoed the air, invisible and swift. A crushing swath of fire radiated from the side of his left leg.

"Officer Andrews? Are you all right?"

On instinct, he dropped to the ground on his belly and withdrew his sidearm, flicking off the safety. The cold ground rumbled beneath him at the same moment he heard rustling from the barn. A large figure, clad all in black and wearing a knitted black ski cap, burst from the barn and ran, headed to a copse of pines not twenty feet away.

"Halt," he ordered. "Police!"

"Officer Andrews?" The dispatcher's voice came again. "An officer possibly down!" she cried out, quickly calling out the address.

The man kept running. Liam shot into the air—but the fleeing felon never even slowed. Damn it. The man had a getaway vehicle or another driver waiting that was parked nearby and out of sight. Warm dampness spread down his left leg, and he noted the scent of blood. Liam pushed down the injury aftereffects; he'd deal with that later. For now, he needed to seek cover in case his pursuer took another shot. He struggled to his feet, wincing as his left leg crumpled at the slightest weight. The twenty feet to the barn felt like a mile as he limped to shelter. From a distance, an engine came to life. Through the barn slats, he witnessed low, narrow beams of light heading in the opposite direction of the main road. His shooter was escaping in a four-wheeler.

"Officer Andrews?"

He raised the walkie-talkie to his mouth. "Here," he responded breathily, surprised at the effort required to speak. Now the danger had passed, his adrenaline bottomed out and pain registered through his former numbing shock. He stretched his leg, wincing at the stabbing agony. The vortex of pain was localized about three inches above his left knee on the outer side. Luckily for him, the bullet hadn't landed a smidge farther right and shattered his kneecap. But that didn't mean he was by any means grateful for the burning bullet now lodged under his skin.

A siren sounded. It felt odd to realize it was his own signal that help would shortly arrive. Usually, he was the man responding to other people's emergencies. Grimacing, he again stood and painstakingly made his way out of the barn, fighting back a sudden wave of nausea and dizziness.

He recognized Sam as his fellow officer exited the cruiser and ran toward him. *His fellow officer.* Running to help him despite any threats of danger. What would Sam and the others think if they knew the real reason he was in Baysville? Would they view him as a traitor?

And what if that bullet had been meant as more than a mere warning—if the shooter had aimed at his heart?

Chapter Seven

Harper threw her car keys on the counter and picked up a note from Kimber. The cleaning crew she had recommended would arrive tomorrow morning. At least that was something. Today's library research had been a bust. Surprisingly little had been written on Presley's death.

She headed upstairs, sipping a glass of wine. On her bed, she hit the remote button to turn on the TV and rubbed her eyes, still bleary from viewing internet articles and microfiche documents. Lethargy set in and the dark abyss of sleep beckoned. And yet, her mind resisted the vulnerability of sleep.

Something about this house was all wrong. She could deny it all she liked during the day with her rational brain, but here, alone at night, fear insinuated itself like a chilling fog rolling over her in waves. Here, her childhood home held no charm or happiness. No comforting memories of love. No cheery reminiscences to indulge in. Instead, it contained pain and loss and sorrow. Even more, the house oozed a sentient, living vibe, as though the very walls were listening to her every breath. Watching her every move. Possessing an unknown menace that could pounce upon her at any moment.

Just as it had done to Presley.

All wrong, all wrong... The warning refrain echoed

through her. But her weary body accepted the peace and promise of rest. Just a few minutes to recharge. What could it hurt?

Skreek.

Worry clawed at the back of her sleeping mind, a frantic warning that all was not right.

Skreek. Skreek.

An explosion of noise erupted close by, and she awoke in a flash of panic. There was no disorientation or gradual floating back to consciousness. One second she'd been dead to the world, lost in a cocoon of oblivion, and then the next second she sat straight up, clutching a pillow. The small TV set on the dresser gave off an artificial glow that cast deep shadows in the bedroom. A reporter's monotone voice sounded over video footage of a riot somewhere in a country far away. Maybe the noise had merely been gunfire from the TV news broadcast.

She willed her mind to accept the rational explanation. What else could it have possibly been? Yet her heart rate barely slowed its frantic pace.

The sound came again. *Bam bam bam bam bam...* A dozen mini bombs detonating in rapid succession, followed closely by loud rolling swishes—as though a bag of marbles had been upended onto the hardwood floor.

What the hell? Her heart pounded as though trying to break free of her rib cage.

Heavy breathing pervaded the air. A menacing pant— slow, deep, deliberate.

She couldn't move. Arms and legs stiffened into paralysis. There was only the rapid rise and fall of her chest.

A cackle broke out, witchy and guttural.

Her tongue lay thick and heavy in her dry mouth; she couldn't have answered even if she'd wanted to.

This couldn't be happening. She glanced at the nearly

empty glass of wine on the nightstand. The alcohol, perhaps? But no, it had never affected her this way before.

The breathy voice chuckled with a tinny echo. It held no familiarity to her ears. A whimper escaped past her numb lips, and she scooted backward, her spine pressed into the wooden headboard.

The eternal scratching started up, like a mischief of mice. "Go away," she cried, flinging a book against the wall.

Don't you love me, Harper? You're my sister. My baby sister.

She should run, get the hell out of the house and never come back. Unexpected silence descended, and she tensed, waiting for the next round. Because it always came back. Every. Damn. Time.

The tinkling of shattered glass erupted, followed by a sniveling, as though a person was crying.

There was a knock—a sharp rap that sounded loud enough to splinter wood. Harper clamped her hands over her ears.

"Get out of here! You aren't real. You can't be." She was officially losing her mind now, talking to a make-believe person in her head.

All sound ceased, but the threat lingered in the darkness. A promise. A harbinger of doom. It would come back again one night. Harper was sure of it.

She'd come home to get answers. And if the answer was that she was crazy, then she'd have to accept that and get counseling. Harper waited, hardly daring to breathe, in case the noises returned.

They didn't. Not this time. Maybe it had been her imagination, after all. Maybe she was oversensitive to normal sounds old houses made.

She turned up the volume on the TV and downed what

was left in her wineglass. There'd be no more sleep to-night. For a distraction, she changed the channel to watch the late-night news. It held little interest—until the an-nouncement that a local police officer had been shot.

Harper gasped and leaned forward at the video of EMTs pushing a stretcher into an ambulance. The injured officer was strapped down, but she caught a glimpse of sandy-colored hair.

Liam.

Her heart pinched at the brief glimpse of his pale face. How badly was he hurt? What if... She couldn't bear to think of it. Liam would recover. He'd been conscious as the camera had panned over his body. A good sign.

Liam hadn't been in Baysville too long, and she knew for a fact that his relationship with Bryce was strained. The other times she'd observed him with his fellow cops, it seemed as though there was a reserve in their inter-actions.

Her instinct was to rush down to the hospital, to be a friend.

The least she could do was pay him a visit and offer to sit with him until family or a friend arrived. She'd rather be in a bleak hospital room all night than tossing and turning in bed.

Decision made, Harper strode to the mirror and ran a hand through her tousled hair. With only a moment's hesitation, she left her bedroom and went to the bath-room, splashing her face with cold water. She reached for the towel, but her hand grasped air. What the hell? Had it dropped on the floor? Mystified, she glanced around and then shrugged. Must have thrown it in the wash and forgotten to replace it with a clean one. Ablutions com-pleted, Harper flipped on all the lights as she made her way downstairs.

STARK LIGHTS, UNFAMILIAR voices and an antiseptic chill in the air sent goose bumps down his arms. Liam narrowed his eyes and caught sight of a man in white, a stethoscope dangling from his neck. That's right—he was in the hospital. Evidently, he'd lost consciousness for a bit. A blessing considering the pain radiating like a heat wave from his left leg.

"We've removed the bullet," a doctor assured him, leaning over the hospital bed. "You're going to be fine. Might be a bit sore for a few days, though. Best if you stay off your feet. We're going to give you a numbing shot and send you home with a prescription for pain pills."

The sharp jab of a needle punctured the wound's tender flesh, immediately followed by a blessed cooling. A nurse wheeled him out of recovery and to a temporary room for a couple more hours of observation. No sooner had he transferred from the wheelchair to a cot than Bryce entered the room, deep worry lines etched in his broad forehead.

"Damn, Andrews," he said, running a hand through his dark hair. "Looks like you had a close call tonight."

"Not really."

"Looks that way to me. I talked to my men who arrived at the scene and got your statement."

The nurse interrupted, pointing to the metal drawer beside the cot. "Your clothes are in there. Let me know if you need help getting into them. Once you're dressed, we'll see about sending you home. Although, like the doctor told you, it would be best if you remained overnight."

"Thanks, but I insist on being discharged. I can manage on my own," he assured her before turning to Bryce. "If the shooter had meant to kill me, he had ample opportunity. This shot was a warning."

Skepticism flashed across his features. "A warning? About what?"

"Don't know yet." Liam scooted off the bed, placing all his weight on his right leg and testing the left. Even with the numbing shot, it tingled. He sat back down and withdrew a plastic bag of bloody clothing from the nightstand. No way he was putting those on.

Bryce lifted the bag he held in his hands. "Take this. A new uniform. Figured the old one would be shredded."

"Thanks, man. I'll take my badge off my old shirt and throw the old uniform in the trash."

"Let's get back to what you said about the shooting being a warning," Bryce said. "You probably just caught a robber unawares. Plain bad luck."

"Doubt that old house had anything worth stealing. Couple that with the anonymous phone tip, and I'd say that shooter was waiting on me."

"The dispatcher traced the call, but—"

"Let me guess. It was to a throwaway phone." Liam untied his hospital gown and donned the new uniform shirt.

His boss nodded as he buttoned his shirt. "Even more reason to suspect it was a warning." Bryce scraped his face with a broad palm. "Not a very good warning if you don't know what it is you're supposed to be warned away from. You got any ideas?"

Did he ever. But Bryce was the last person he'd confide in. Liam observed him closely as he cautiously pulled up the new uniform pants, careful to avoid touching the bandaged wound, taking his time as he adjusted to the twinges of pain. His boss looked like hell, as though he'd been too long without sleep and stressed to the max. Had Bryce discovered what his newest employee was up to?

Had his cover been blown? "Not a clue," Liam dead-panned. "What about you? You got any theories?"

"Can't help wondering if it somehow relates to Harper Catlett. Trouble seems to follow that family."

"Why? Because her sister died in an accidental fire?"

Bryce winced but doggedly continued with his theory. "The minute she returns to town and starts asking questions, look what happens. She drew you in with her claims about a possible stalker and now this. We've never had an officer shot in Baysville before."

"Coincidence," Liam insisted. If he played it smart, he'd let Bryce continue with his delusion. Keeping his boss focused on the wrong path could only help Liam preserve his cover. But he hated Harper being wrongfully suspected of anything to do with tonight's incident.

"I don't believe in coincidences."

"Why are you suddenly turning on Harper, linking her to this? You made it clear from the start that you believed her fear was all in her head. That her sister's death was an accident and anything strange happening in the house was only her imagination."

"Call it intuition."

"You don't believe in coincidences? Well, I don't believe in intuition." With that, Liam zipped his pants and then sat on the bed as he slipped into his old, muddied uniform shoes, hiding his pain as he bent to pull them on.

Bryce quirked a brow. "You've never had a gut feeling on the job?"

"Sure. But what people often call a gut feeling is actually based on fact. Like last night, I had a feeling something was wrong when I was merely picking up on environmental clues that I too quickly discounted—the isolated location, the anonymous call, the subconscious awareness that somebody was watching me."

"Semantics. You're quibbling, Andrews. Harper's bad news. I tried to warn you."

Liam shrugged. Either Bryce was too dense to understand his illogical distrust, or—worst-case scenario—Bryce had found out about the undercover investigation and was taking aggressive measures to scare him off track. Either way, Liam had never quit an assignment, and he wasn't about to start now. Whatever it took, he'd get to the bottom of the vagrant murders and discover if the Baysville PD were involved in some sort of cover-up.

"Can I give you a lift home?" Bryce asked.

"If it's not too much trouble, then—"

They both turned at the sound of a light knock on the semiclosed door. "May I come in?"

A bolt of warmth shot through his gut at the familiar voice. Before he could answer, Harper's head peeked around the door.

Bryce sighed and strode across the room. "I suspect you'd rather ride home with Harper than me. Take as much time off as you need to recover, Andrews," he called over his shoulder. He nodded at Harper and quickly exited the room.

Harper strolled over, her red hair practically ablaze under the merciless fluorescent lights. He wanted nothing more than to brush his face against its sweet warmth and run his hands through the silken fire. After his abrupt rejection the previous night, Liam couldn't have been more startled at her appearance. Or more grateful.

"I heard what happened on the news. Hope you don't mind me dropping in." Her eyes slowly scanned his body from head to toe. "Are you okay?"

"I'm fine. Just a flesh wound. They've already dug out the bullet and stitched me up."

Her lips trembled. She reached out a hand as though to

touch him, then thought better of it and dropped it down by her side. "Bryce said you could use a ride home?"

Damn, he hated not being able to drive himself. Being dependent on anyone made him nuts. "Looks that way. But if you'd rather not, I'll call a cab or an Uber."

"At this time of night? Not happening in this town."

"Right."

They regarded one another awkwardly. As for himself, Liam recalled lying in the marsh, bleeding, in pain and waiting for backup—and all he could think about was Harper.

"When this is over," he began slowly, "if you're still in town, then maybe…" His voice trailed off.

"Maybe," she breathed. Harper ran her fingers lightly down his face, and he closed his eyes, marveling at the soft caress that made his entire body heat. His whole adult life he'd been an outsider, always on the outskirts of intimacy and true friendship. Because of his undercover work, everyone was either a suspect or not to be trusted in keeping his secret.

But Harper felt like home after a long trip. When this case was over…

"Excuse me. Looks like you're ready to check out," a nurse said, entering the room.

Harper dropped her hand and stepped away. The nurse practically winked. "Let's get your paperwork in order and you can go home."

Home with Harper. Suddenly, the night didn't seem all bad.

Chapter Eight

She hurried into the hallway, eager to pull her car around front to the hospital's main entrance. Liam should be signed out and waiting by then. The two nurses on night duty didn't even glance up from their charts as she walked by. On each side of her, most of the patient room doors were ajar. Machines beeped and hummed, emitting an industrial green glow punctuated by the flashing of red buttons. People lay quiet, attached to IVs and tubes. Thank goodness Liam hadn't been severely injured and facing a prolonged stay.

Her sneakers scrunched on the polished linoleum and echoed through the labyrinth of hallways, a stick-slip squeak of rubber.

Another set of rubber-soled shoes chirped from behind. She stopped and swiftly turned, hoping it wasn't a nurse unexpectedly canceling Liam's discharge orders.

The hall stood empty, save for an open patient door that swayed slightly, as though recently entered. Her throat tightened. *Probably just a nurse dispensing medication.* Harper continued to the elevators and punched the ground-floor button, quickly getting on when it arrived almost immediately. As it lowered, she exhaled a sigh, glad to be on her way. She exited and made her way through the now-empty lobby.

Squeak, squeak.

The mystery person was back. He must have taken the stairs when she'd opted for the elevator. Discreetly, Harper slightly turned her head, but she only caught a glimpse of a tall person in a white coat as he whisked by a coffee kiosk. Absolutely no reason for the sensation of spiders skittering down her spine. She frowned, noting the absence of blue-uniformed cops hanging around the entrance door. They'd probably all migrated to the ER section, where any action would be taking place.

To top it off, a storm had arrived. Trees swayed in the wet gusts and the clatter of rain on the roof and pavement intensified several decibels. Of course, she'd left home in a hurry with no umbrella. Nothing for it but to brave the elements. Harper rushed into the night. By the time she'd crossed the street, her clothes were drenched and her hair plastered to her cheeks and neck.

Only a few vehicles remained in the concrete parking deck. She spotted hers right away and dug out the keys from her purse.

There was no inexplicable warning sound, only the mechanical hum of the overhead lights, but Harper knew the instant she was no longer alone. Probably another visitor like herself, but she quickened her pace and clicked the remote to open her car door. The responding beep of her vehicle in the parking deck echoed, loud and jarring, accompanied by the explosive flash of her headlights.

Harper got in the car and locked it before starting the engine. *See, you're fine.* Nearby, another car engine sounded, but no headlights flashed on. She hit the gas and exited, relieved to leave the gloomy concrete lot.

Liam waited at the door with a nurse when she pulled up to the entrance.

"Take good care of him," the nurse said, waving good-bye.

Liam eased into the seat, a wince creasing his face.

"I hope they gave you some pain pills in case you need them before the pharmacy opens."

He held up a plastic bag. "They're in here, though I don't plan to take one."

She drove away and followed his directions, on past the outskirts of town, leaving behind the quiet, deserted streets for a country road without streetlamps. Inky darkness pervaded while sheets of rain slashed at the windows.

"Another mile before we get to my place," Liam said. "Sorry you have to drive in such bad weather."

Headlights suddenly flashed from behind, drawing closer and closer. As though rushing forward to consume them. She pressed her foot on the gas pedal. Liam turned in the seat, frowning.

"They're going way too fast and getting way too close. Especially on these wet roads."

"Too bad we aren't in your cruiser. Bet if we turned on the blue lights they'd back off in a hurry."

Harper lifted her chin to peer at the rearview mirror. Through the pounding rain, she was able to make out the vehicle's outline.

"Oh, great, not again," she muttered. "A black pickup truck." Not her favorite after nearly being run down by one on her own front lawn.

An explosive sound rang out. "That wasn't thunder, was it?" she asked.

"Hell, no. They took a shot at us." Liam reached for

his right pocket, then swore. "Bryce took my sidearm at the hospital for safekeeping."

Harper's heart beat painfully as she floored the accelerator. The tires squealed, and the vehicle swayed from side to side as she hydroplaned. *Stay calm.* She eased her foot off the gas and steered it back to the right side of the road.

Liam called for emergency assistance. But by the time help arrived, it would be too late. She had to do something, anything. *Think.* The truck started to pull up around her on the left. Its headlights were on bright and the beams blinding. Time for drastic measures. Less than an eighth of a mile ahead was a cutoff road. Again, she sped up and at the last possible second, turned the steering wheel sharply to the right.

"What the hell?" Liam braced his hands on the dashboard as her car skidded dangerously. But their pursuer was in an even worse predicament. The driver slammed on his brakes and the truck spun in circles.

Harper took a deep breath. Up ahead was another turn she could take and then reverse direction to head back in town. With any luck, the truck driver would either lose sight of them or he'd be reluctant to pursue them once they'd hit city limits.

"I think you've managed to lose him," Liam said, staring back at the truck. "Way to go. There's already an officer responding."

"Who are they after—you or me?"

"Maybe both of us."

From a distance, sirens wailed. Harper turned on a side street.

"Damn. He's getting away." Liam returned to the dispatcher on the phone and reported that the truck was speeding north on County Road 78.

"Think they'll catch up to him?" she asked.

"Doubtful." Liam eyed her appreciatively. "Smart thinking back there. Probably saved our lives."

"Now what? Shall I drive to the police station?" They were back in Baysville, and her tight grip on the steering wheel relaxed.

"Pull over a minute." He held up a finger, listening to the dispatcher. Harper stopped the car by the side of the road and watched his face for long minutes.

"Thanks. Not a bad idea. See you in the morning." Liam punched a button and laid the phone down.

"Well?"

"The truck was long gone by the time they arrived. Bryce is sending an officer to periodically drive by my house all evening, just to be safe. I think you'd be safer staying with me tonight than driving home and being alone."

"Can't say I relish the idea of being alone, either."

Harper pulled back onto the road and drove to Liam's, keeping a wary eye out for another round with their mysterious truck driver. By the time they arrived at his home and got out of the car, her knees were unsteady, and exhaustion had set in. They made a dash through the rain and then Liam unlocked the door.

She entered his neat, well-kept ranch house. Leather furniture, a large-screen TV, wooden coffee and end tables—it all screamed Standard Bachelor Decor. No knickknacks, artwork, pillows or froufrou of any kind graced the masculine abode. Which was fine—minimalism was a statement of its own, and as an interior designer she could appreciate the style. Yet it lacked a personal touch.

"You're renting this place, I take it?" she asked.

He hobbled over to the couch, eschewing her out-stretched arm offering support. "How'd you guess?"

"Nothing on the walls. No photos anywhere." Or books or anything else to indicate his tastes or family life. "Can I fix you something to drink?"

"I'd say a beer, but I imagine that's off-limits with the meds they plied into me at the hospital. Water, please."

She found a water bottle in the fridge and returned to the den. His face was pale, and fine lines pinched the corners of his eyes and lips. He was obviously still in some pain, whether or not he wanted to admit it. Pinpricks of guilt assaulted her. She couldn't shake wondering if her poking into Presley's death had anything to do with everything that had happened tonight. "Need anything else?" she asked, handing him the bottled water.

"I'm good. Thank you…for everything."

He took a long swig while she fidgeted with the cuffs of her sweater. "Do you think the shooting and tonight's chase had anything to do with you helping me look into Presley's death?"

Liam slowly lowered the bottle and shook his head. "Don't see how."

"Maybe Allen…" She let the suggestion slip unsaid into the gulf between them.

"Spencer might be a creep and scumbag, but a rogue shooter? He's too much of a coward. I don't see it."

"He could have hired someone to do the dirty work," she insisted.

"I don't believe he's that creative or has those connections, but I can have another talk with him."

She nodded and took a look around. "So do you have a spare bedroom? If not, I can sleep on the sofa. It's only a few hours until dawn, anyway. If you need me for any reason, I'll be here."

"Your idea has one serious flaw."

"What's that?"

"We should stay in the same bed." He quickly held up a hand. "I'm not saying we should have sex." Liam's voice dropped to a deep, gruff tone. "Although if you want to…"

A smile crooked one side of his mouth.

It shot through her like lightning, then relief—and a tad of disappointment—whooshed out of her lungs, and she gave a shaky laugh.

"Seriously, though, after all these potshots at us, I'd sleep better where I can keep an eye on you." Liam rose to his feet, still careful to keep most of his weight on his right leg.

Heavy static suddenly crackled through the den, and she spun, searching for the source.

"It's okay, I've got a police scanner and a two-way radio," he explained, pointing to the maze of boxes and wires on top of a table on the far side of the room. "Even an old-fashioned landline phone and an answering machine."

Disembodied voices talked in some kind of cop code about an incident three streets over. She gathered that a citizen had called in complaining of a strange person creeping through their backyard.

"Must be the Shadow Dweller," she said with a tired smile.

He groaned. "Not you, too. Any time property goes missing or someone's roaming where they shouldn't, y'all are quick to blame it on this mysterious Shadow Dweller."

"He's a local legend." She walked to the scanner, her hand hovering over the power button. "Don't you want me to turn this thing off? Listening to it is above and beyond the call of duty. Especially when you're supposed to be resting."

"Leave it. I like to keep a pulse on what's happening, in case I might be needed. That's why I even keep the landline as a backup to my cell. Never know when something big might break."

"What kind of things go on in our small town?" she asked curiously.

"You'd be surprised. Besides the homeless men killings, there's plenty of talk about a gambling and prostitution ring, not that I've been able to verify it."

"Here in Baysville? I've never caught wind of that kind of activity."

Liam hobbled across the den and into the hallway. "It's kept on the down low." He glanced into the kitchen. "Hungry?"

"I'm good. Want me to fix you anything?"

"Nah."

She followed him into a clean, though stark, bedroom with dark wood furniture and utilitarian blinds over the lone window. The bed loomed before her, and again her face flushed with heat. Liam sat on the edge of the mattress, kicked off his shoes and patted the empty space beside him. "Come here."

Self-consciously, Harper kicked off her shoes as well and eased onto the bed beside him.

"I want you to feel safe, and I want to know you're safe. You can sleep here on the bed. I'll lay a few blankets down and sleep on the floor."

The thought of him, with his injuries, sleeping on the hard floor, appalled her. "No, you won't!" she said forcefully, and then wondered if she was sending the wrong message. "I'll take the floor if you'd rather not share the bed."

"It's not that I don't want to share. I want you to be comfortable."

"I am comfortable. I trust you."

His fingers interlaced with hers, and they lay together staring into the darkness, a falling rain pattering on the roof like a lullaby. The warmth of his body beside her was both comforting and intimate. So much nicer than tossing and turning in her own bed at home, waiting to hear unexplained scratchings and whispers that defied rational explanation. His fingers lightly traced a pattern, circling up from her palms and then the inside of her forearms up to her elbows. She'd never considered that an erogenous zone, but everywhere Liam touched her leaped to an awakening of her senses.

"You must be exhausted," she finally commented.

"A little, but also a bit wound up. Talk to me awhile if you're not too tired. Tell me more about your family."

"It's too sad. They're all gone. I'd rather hear about yours. What are your parents and siblings like?"

A tired grin ghosted across his wan face. "Noisy. Full of energy. Growing up with three brothers and two sisters, plus all of their friends that hung out at our place, there was always something going on."

It sounded wonderful to her. The Catlett home had been much too quiet after Dad and Presley's deaths. The kind of heavy silence that weighed on a person's mind and soul, a dreadful emptiness that hammered at the heart from the absence of loved ones. "What about that Uncle Teddy of yours you mentioned? Is he the reason you're so kind to the homeless men that hang out by the railroad tracks?"

"I don't do that much for the men," he protested. "Just take them out some food and clothing from time to time.

I'd like to think that someone did the same for my uncle when he passed through here."

She rolled on her side and regarded him in surprise. "How do you know he was ever in Baysville?"

"He'd been arrested a couple times for holing up in vacant buildings. Even spent a few days in the local jail."

"That's so sad."

"Let's not talk about sad stuff tonight," Liam said softly, gently squeezing her fingers. "Thank you for being here."

For a few moments, they rested in silence, but she could tell he couldn't sleep, and neither could she. There was a connection between them, something beyond the case of her sister's death, the homeless man's murder and Liam's shooting. She genuinely cared for him. She wanted to be closer to him, and after the events of the past few days, she wasn't in a mood to wait.

She kissed him full on the lips, conscious of the heat of his body, the woodsy scent of him. Her core tightened with hunger, and she moaned in protest when he broke the kiss.

"I promised to keep my hands to myself," he explained gruffly.

Maybe I don't want you to. But she bit back the words and squeezed his hand. The poor guy had just taken a bullet to his leg tonight and was pumped up with pain meds. He needed rest.

Harper settled into a peaceful lull as Liam slowly drifted to sleep, listening to his slowed breath, her hand resting on the rise and swell of his chest. The *rightness* of this moment couldn't be denied. Liam had come into her life for a reason, she was certain of it, even if the timing was all wrong.

Liam made her feel as though no obstacles were too

difficult to face. A resurgence of optimism made her lips tug into a smile. Quietly, she eased off the bed and tiptoed into the hallway. A small glass of water, a trip to the bathroom, and then she'd lie back down beside Liam and—hopefully—fall into untroubled sleep.

"Andrews, you there?" The deep, male voice cut through the quiet house—abrupt and demanding. "It's Eason. Pick up the phone. We need to discuss the next gambling game and arrange a meeting with the women."

Harper pulled up short. Gambling? Women—as in *hookers*? What did Liam have to do with any of this?

Mattress springs squeaked, followed by heavy footsteps pounding the floor. Liam raced past her, surprisingly fast considering his injury, and grabbed the phone in the den. "Eason? Why are you calling me on this line?" A short pause and then, "No. Not yet. I need more time. Obviously, I've made progress. If you come now, it'll ruin everything." Another pause. "Yeah, yeah. I'm fine, no problem."

Liam hung up the phone and slowly turned to face her. The blue glow from all the equipment on the table cast an unnatural pallor on his harsh features. She didn't know this man like she thought she did. *He's not who he says he is.* What else didn't she know about him? And to think she'd been so content moments ago. Harper swallowed past the knot in her throat.

"Who are you?" she whispered.

BLOODY HELL. JUST WHEN they'd reestablished trust. But it was his own damn fault. He'd forgotten to take his cell phone to the bedroom. Naturally, Eason was worried once he'd gotten wind of the shooting and there'd been no response to his text messages. He'd been much too distracted from his usual routine by a combination of sedatives and a certain beautiful redhead—who now stared at him with a wide-eyed skepticism.

He approached slowly, palms held open at his sides. "I don't suppose there's any chance you could just forget what you overheard?"

"Not a chance."

He sighed. "Didn't think so."

Her eyes darted past him, to her purse lying on top of the coffee table. Was she actually afraid of him and wanting to make a quick getaway? There was no hope for it. He had to come clean. *Even if it means blowing your cover? Sacrificing all these months of work?* He could practically hear Eason's outraged words at what he was about to disclose.

"What's going on?" She took a step back, eyes narrowed.

The easiest way out of this mess was to show her. Liam walked forward, and she backed against the wall, avoiding his touch. "I'm going to get my wallet out of my pants pocket," he explained.

He strode past her and flipped on the bedroom lights, picked his pants up off the floor and retrieved his wallet. He turned, relieved to find that Harper stood in the doorway—he'd half expected her to grab her purse and run. Liam pulled a badge from his wallet and handed it to her. "I'm working undercover for the Virginia ATF field division.

"ATF?" she asked, squinting at the badge.

"Bureau of Alcohol, Tobacco and Firearms."

She handed him back the badge. "What's that got to do with gambling and prostitution?"

"The name doesn't fully encompass our range of authority. We also investigate any threat to public safety from organized crime."

"Really?" Her lips twisted, and she placed her hands on her hips. "Seems like your bureau could have chosen more likely towns than ours to infiltrate. We must be small potatoes compared to larger cities."

"But not all towns have a string of unsolved murders like Baysville."

"The homeless killings?"

"We have reason to believe the killer, or killers, are involved in an organized crime ring related to gambling and prostitution."

"The mafia? Here?" Her voice rose in disbelief.

"Not on that kind of scale." Her blue-gray eyes regarded him with a mixture of hope and wariness. How far was he willing to explain his undercover discoveries without knowing if she'd even believe his story?

"The crimes in Baysville are localized, without ties to a larger crime ring," he hedged.

She tapped an index finger against her lips, considering his words. "Tonight's shooting was no random robbery gone bad. And someone was after you on the drive home as well. You're getting too close to the truth. Which is making someone very nervous."

Relief melted the twisted knots in his shoulders. Harper understood. "Exactly. It was a warning."

"But who…" She paused, studying his set face. "You can't tell me. Probably not a good idea for me to know anyway."

"Knowledge can be dangerous."

The numbing injection at the wound site was wearing off, replaced by an itchy burning. Standing around arguing all night wasn't what the doctor ordered. He ran a hand through his hair, silently giving in to the weariness.

"You need to rest," she said, taking him by the elbow and guiding him back to bed.

HE SETTLED INTO the warm cotton covers. Again, he sought her hand, and their fingers interlaced. Heaven help him, he could get used to this. To Harper's sweet body beside him, making love to her every night and waking with her in his arms every morning. Dangerous, forbidden longings. Lethargy overcame his whirling thoughts, and yet one more thing needed saying aloud.

"Thank you again," he murmured.

"It's the least I could do after you believed in me when I reported that email threat. And for not believing Bryce when he hinted I was mentally unstable. Even if…well, never mind about that."

He was wide-awake now. Liam switched on the bedside lamp and leaned on an elbow, staring down into her troubled eyes. "Never mind about what?"

"Shouldn't have opened my big mouth. You're not the type to let something go."

"So tell me then."

She sighed and ran a hand through her red tresses that pooled on the white pillowcase. "There've been more strange noises at the house. It seems to be getting worse."

Liam sucked in his breath. "There has to be a logical explanation. There's no such thing as ghosts."

"That's what I used to think." She laughed without mirth. "Either my house is haunted, or everyone is right about me. I'm a basket case."

He smoothed a lock of hair from her cheek and tucked it behind her ear. "I reject both those posits."

"Then how do you account for the weird noises?"

"I don't know," he admitted. "But we'll figure it out. Together."

Chapter Nine

Daytime is safe.

Liam had insisted on going in to work today, hoping to get a lead on the possible owner of the truck that had chased them last night, and she had her own agenda of things to do. Harper sprinted up the steps to her house.

She felt herself grin, remembering her awakening next to Liam. If she'd thought their first kiss had been spectacular, it was child's play compared to this morning's toe-curling kiss. She bounded inside, 100 percent more lighthearted than when she'd left.

First things first. Harper entered the basement and gasped at the change. Kimber's crew had done amazing work. Every shelf, tool and box was gone, just as she'd requested. They'd even swept the floors and washed the high windows. Worth every damn penny. She promptly called her friend and invited her over for coffee. Just mailing a check seemed too impersonal.

Harper proceeded upstairs and into Mom's room. Today, she'd take all those packed-up boxes to Goodwill and check off another section of the house as completed. After more than a dozen trips up and down the stairs, Harper loaded up her car and then headed to the kitchen to start the coffee. The aroma of fresh-ground beans revived her flagging energy, and she happily pulled cups and saucers from the cupboards. There was a pack of chocolate chip cookies, not homemade but they would have to do. Kimber wouldn't take but a couple of nibbles anyway.

Tires crunched gravel, and she glanced out the window to spot Kimber emerging from her Town Car. She wore an expensive-looking navy pantsuit and the same tight, worried expression Harper had witnessed at their last meeting. What had happened to the bright-eyed, happy cheerleader from high school? Now she thought about it, Kimber's temperamental descent had been gradual over the last few years. At first, Harper had attributed it to stress from building her real estate career and managing a large family. Now, she wasn't so sure. Marital problems, perhaps? She and Richard always seemed so perfect for one another, so in love. But no one could ever know what went on with a couple behind closed doors.

Harper threw open the front door with a welcoming smile, determined to cheer up Kimber. "Hey there, come on in." She gave her a hug, holding it for an extra second before ushering her to the kitchen table. "You sit down and relax while I fix you a cup."

"I can't stay long, I have an open house in less than an hour." Instead of sitting, Kimber walked down the hallway, peering in rooms. "Looks like you've made progress clearing out the place."

"A room a day. That's the game plan."

"So, by that rate, I take it you'll be finished here within the week." She returned to the kitchen and perched on the edge of a chair. A ball of nervous energy always ready to take flight.

"More or less." Harper set their drinks on the table.

"Have you thought any more about my offer?"

"I'm staying put for the time being. If I decide to sell later, I'll let you know."

Kimber's eyes flashed. "What do you mean? Don't you need to get back to your job in Atlanta?"

The sharp edge in Kimber's voice caught her unawares, and she sipped her drink to consider her next words.

"I've made arrangements, so everything's covered in my absence." Harper slid a check across the table. "Thanks for your help. I included a little extra money so you can tip all the workers."

Kimber stuffed the check in her designer purse, then sipped her coffee, her face pensive.

"Is everything all right, Kimber? I mean, you don't have to tell me the specifics if you don't want to, but you seem a bit wound up. I'm concerned about you."

"Me?" She set down her cup with a decided thud, her brows drawn together. "I'm perfectly fine. Why would anything be wrong?"

And yet, Kimber's smile was brittle, and that sharp edge remained in her tone.

Harper regarded her somberly. Kimber had never been one to confide if she were having problems. She liked everyone to think her life was perfect, that she could handle anything on her own.

"I'm not trying to pry into your business," she said gently. "It just appears to me like—oh, I don't know—like you don't have any joy in your life lately. You're always busy or stressed."

Kimber sat up straighter, bristling with indignation. "I own my own business. Of course I'm busy. And you of all people should know how stressful that can be. Plus, I have a family and you…"

"Don't," she supplied drily.

To Harper's surprise, Kimber's eyes filled with tears.

Harper grabbed a tissue and handed it to Kimber. "We've been friends a long time. You've seen me at my worst and took me under your wing from middle school on up. I'll never forget that. So if there's a problem and you want to talk, I'm always here."

Kimber blew her nose and sniffled. "It's nothing. Just stress from trying to keep up with everything. Teenagers. A business."

Harper nodded sympathetically and waited for her friend to elaborate if she wanted.

But Kimber stood, clutching her purse like a lifeline. "Can't sit around all morning blubbering about my problems. Maybe one day next week you can come over to my place for a home-cooked meal. Richard will be glad to see you."

Harper doubted that. Richard was wrapped up in sports and motorcycles—two things she had no interest in. Not that she had anything against him or his hobbies—they just had nothing in common. And maybe she and Kimber didn't, either. Not anymore.

With a heavy heart, she walked her friend out to her car, where they exchanged perfunctory goodbyes before she returned to the house. Absentmindedly, she gazed out the window. A dreary pall fell over her spirits—until she thought of Liam and waking up in his arms. Harper straightened her shoulders. If he could go back to work this morning, she could do the same. From her research at the library, she'd garnered a list and phone numbers of Presley's old friends to call. Not that she planned on spreading the news of her sister's pregnancy, but she was curious if Presley might have confided in someone about her condition or problems she had with anyone.

Filled with renewed determination, she sat at the

kitchen table and began making the calls. Over an hour later, Harper surveyed her dwindled list and notes. A couple of names had been scratched through as out of service, but most of Presley's old friends had been glad to reminisce about memories and old times. It cheered her that so many people remembered Presley with such fondness.

She tapped her pen on the table, trying to determine what action to take next. The old grandfather clock loudly ticked away the minutes, and she couldn't shake the feeling of impending doom. Maybe she and Liam could brainstorm later about the next course of action. With any luck, he'd have a few names of black-truck owners to investigate.

Decision made, Harper grabbed a container of shrimp scampi from the freezer and dumped it in a pan to heat up for lunch. This dish had been her sister's favorite. If Presley was still alive, the two of them could enjoy it together. Unexpected sadness pinched her heart.

A booming static infiltrated the quiet bustle of the kitchen. As if someone were in the next room and had switched on the TV or radio to an unclear channel. The fine hairs on her arm rose as she turned down the stove burner and nervously wiped her hands on her apron. She should go investigate. Yet her feet remained unmoving.

It stopped as suddenly as it had begun. She started to draw a relieved breath—*see? All is well*—when a stomp of slow, deliberate footsteps sounded from the basement.

She wasn't alone. Someone was in the house.

Harper stilled, struck by a frightening paralysis. The kind she experienced in dreams when danger approached and she couldn't run from an oncoming threat.

The basement door rattled. "Go away," she screamed, as though trying to reason with a ghost.

At last, her feet unglued from the tiled floor and she crossed over to the cabinet drawer that held the cutlery. She picked up the largest, sharpest knife available and gripped it tightly.

The stomping resumed, louder than before.

Harper crept across the dining room floor. A quick glance out the back window of the property revealed nothing out of the ordinary. She inched forward until she faced the closed basement door. Again, the stomping ceased as suddenly as it had begun.

What lay on the other side of the door?

Her need to know overcame her fear of the unknown. One quick, deep breath and Harper grabbed the doorknob with her left hand and jerked it open.

Cool, damp darkness awaited.

"Anybody down there?" she called out. *As if they would answer.* But the sound of her own voice was reassuring in itself.

Utter silence greeted her words.

Harper licked her dry lips and slowly stepped down the first three steps. Leaning forward, she surveyed the dark, still shadows. Thanks to the work of the cleaning crew, little remained in the basement. No place for anyone to hide. No explanation for the clomping footsteps.

She retraced her steps, careful not to turn her back on the darkness. Just in case. At the head of the stairwell, she shut the basement door, the sound of her own breathing loud and thick in the hushed house.

There had to be a rational explanation. Though not a one came to mind. In the meantime, she'd go to the hardware store and buy a lock. It might be useless and irrational, but it would help her sleep at night.

Harper returned to the kitchen and tossed the knife on the counter. The smell of burned butter had created a stench, so she turned off the stove and set the pan in the sink. Any desire to cook flew out the window. She wanted a break from being inside.

Air. She needed fresh air.

Harper went out the front door and into the yard, rubbing her arms. What the hell had just happened back there? It made no sense.

Mrs. Henley emerged from her cottage across the street, bundled in a sweater.

"Harper?" she called out. "What are you doing standing in the yard without a coat? It's cold out here."

The nip in the air had nothing to do with her body's involuntary shaking. Could she confide in Mrs. Henley?

"I, um, thought I heard something inside the house, and it freaked me out a little," she ventured.

Mrs. Henley shook her head in sympathy. "Your mom used to say she heard noises, too. But like I always used to tell Ruth, it's just the old house settling. Happens at my place all the time."

The news brought her up short. Mom heard weird stuff, too?

"Did Mom say what kind of noises?" she asked. "Or mention if she thought the place might be haunted?"

Faded blue eyes danced with mirth. "We used to joke about it. I'd mention that Fred—my late husband—had been rattling around my house the previous night, making a general pest of himself. Then Ruth would tell me if she'd heard anything at her place. It was quite the joke between us."

Harper grabbed a fistful of the hair whipping about her face. Too bad she could find no humor in the joke.

Mrs. Henley laid a hand on her forearm. "Are you okay now?"

"I have an idea," she said, forcing joviality into her

voice. "Would you like to come inside and keep me company while I make lunch? It would be a kindness."

As Harper suspected, her neighbor was delighted with the notion. She clasped her hands together at her chest. "Why, I'd love to. It'll be like old times with Ruth. We spent many an afternoon chatting over coffee. Why we'd talk up a storm about the latest books and TV shows and…"

Harper half tuned out the constant barrage of chatter. Had her mother humored the elderly widow by keeping her company, or had she really been lonely? Of course, she had been living all by herself. A guilty pang hammered her heart. She should have made an effort to visit more, to understand her mother better. Now it was too late.

They made their way to the front door, and even with Mrs. Henley by her side, Harper felt the familiar foreboding as she reentered the kitchen and turned on the stove. As her neighbor chattered away, Harper heated the shrimp scampi with unsteady hands, ears straining for any unexplained noises or whispers.

Of course, with a witness on hand, there wasn't a peep out of the resident ghost.

Chapter Ten

The sight always depressed him.

A cluster of dingy, sagging canvas tents and a few shelters that were nothing more than large strips of blue tarp hung between two trees. A huge campfire burned in the center of the vagrant gathering, and several men huddled over the warmth, the more fortunate holding sticks with hot dogs or other food scraps. The aroma was distinctive—burning oak mixed with roasted food and an unfortunate underlying note of rot. Empty tin cans, plastic jugs and other trash littered the outside edges of the tents. His mother would be dismayed to know that her brother had willingly chosen such a lifestyle, so Liam never filled her in on the finer details of the modern homeless living conditions.

He'd read reports estimating that over twenty thousand people chose this kind of fringe existence, but their numbers were dwindling and their culture drifting from the strict moral codes of the past. No one bemoaned this more than Gunner, who proudly claimed he'd jumped freight trains for decades traveling the country, although it was much harder now and at his age much too dangerous to continue.

As usual, Gunner was the first person to greet him. Liam limped over and waved.

"What happened to your leg?" Gunner shot a mostly toothless grin. "Did ya hurt yourself jumping the rails?"

"Not hardly. I don't have your physical agility," he joked, holding out the bag of groceries he'd brought with him.

The half a dozen other men scrambled to their feet and strode over, their faces pinched with cold and hunger. He knew all the regulars' names now, Sam, Grady, Biff, Tick and Buster. It'd taken Liam weeks to gain their trust so they'd accept his offerings of free food. Pride could be found in even the most humble of men.

Gunner doled out the provisions, equitably distributing the canned goods and other staples. The sandwich meat and bread he kept in the bag. "For supper tonight," he declared to the men before facing Liam again. "You need to speak with me?" he asked, lowering his voice.

"Yeah. Let's sit in my car a bit and warm up."

Once they were out of earshot of the others, Gunner cast him a worried frown. "So what happened to your leg?"

"Bullet wound. It's not as bad as it sounds. Just won't be suiting up for work a few days."

Gunner gave a low whistle but said nothing else until they were safely ensconced in Liam's car. "Any of this related to what happened to Larry?"

"I feel sure of it. Proving that there's a correlation is another matter."

"We're starting to get scared. Baysville used to be a good resting spot, but now there's talk among the guys of moving on. Maybe heading farther south, at least for the winter."

"That's probably not a bad idea."

Gunner scrubbed at his lined, weathered face. "Don't feel like no place is safe no more," he admitted. "'Specially not at my age. The younger crowd that passes through here are rough. Drugs got 'em bad. No moral code. Ain't like the old days."

"Tell me about Larry. He one of the younger guys into drugs?"

"Nah, he seemed like a good dude. Always seemed to have a little cash on hand, although none of us knowed how he come by it. He'd disappear for hours and sometimes days, then show up with food and folding money."

"Dealing drugs, perhaps?"

"Not Larry. He had a son OD from drugs and was dead set against it."

"What about Ash, the guy killed last year? Did he spend time away from camp and return with cash?"

Gunner's eyes drifted upward and to the right as he cocked his head to one side. "I'll be damn. He sure did. Is there a connection, ya think?"

"I need to find out who they were working for. Could be the key to unlocking the killer's identity. You have folks drop by here looking for work?"

"Sometimes. But work's more plentiful in the warmer seasons, when farmers are tending their fields or people need some painting done or some other odd job."

Liam thought it over carefully. He'd pieced together an illegal gambling operation that had recently begun expanding into prostitution. The homeless murders had to be tied in somehow—he just needed to figure out how. And for that, he needed Gunner.

"I suspect that with Larry's recent demise, someone else will approach one of you, offering cash in a shady business arrangement. Will you let me know if they do?"

"Sure thing, boss."

"I'll pay you for information."

"Ain't no need. We appreciate the groceries you bring out every week."

"I insist." He felt guilty enough involving Gunner in the mess. But whether or not Gunner turned informant, his life—and the other men's lives—were already in danger.

"Tell you what you can do," Gunner began, rubbing his scruffy chin.

"Name it."

"When this is over, help me find a job. A real job. Steady. Enough so's I can afford a proper shelter."

Liam regarded him with surprise. "You're giving up the life?"

"Case ya haven't noticed, I'm getting old." Gunner cackled and straightened his tattered pants. "The wanderlust has faded. I regret nothing. I seen the entire country and lived like a free man. But the truth is, I'm not sure I can make it another winter out in the cold."

"Say the word, and I'll take you to the local YMCA now and help you find a job."

"But you need me here."

"I can use Buddy or one of the other guys, Gunner. Just tell me which one you think's the most trustworthy."

Gunner shook his head. "Nah, sir. I'm going to earn my keep and fulfill my end of the bargain."

"Promise me you'll be careful. Trust no one," Liam warned. "Not even the cops."

Especially the cops. For the crimes to go on for so long, they were either turning a blind eye or, worse, they were ringleaders.

"If there's any danger, call me and I'll swoop in. Still got your phone?"

Gunner fished it out of his jacket pocket and held it up proudly. Thank heavens for the government policy that made it possible for the homeless to be given free cell phones. It was a lifeline for them, a connection to the world.

"Can't tell ya how grateful we are for these," Gunner said, returning the phone to his pocket.

"No problem." Not long after arriving in Baysville, he'd made sure each of the men obtained one, using the address of the nearest shelter as their place of residence.

Gunner held out a hand. "I get you info you can use on your case, and you can set me up at the Y. Deal?"

"Deal." No matter what happened, he'd find a way to convince Gunner to leave camp. He could only hope that some kind stranger had done the same for his uncle.

He reached his destination, and Gunner got out of the car. After a quick goodbye, Liam slowly eased out of the field and back onto the main road. Harper's home was just ahead and to the right. She'd probably fuss at him working in the field when he was supposed to be laid up in bed taking it easy, but Liam couldn't resist stopping in to see her.

A KNOCK SOUNDED at the front door, and midstir on the soup, her hands stilled. A quick glance at Mrs. Henley and Harper breathed a sigh of relief. Her neighbor had heard it, too. This was no phantom noise.

"You stay put. I'll get the door," Mrs. Henley said, pushing herself up from the table. "Were you expecting someone?"

Harper spotted Liam's red pickup truck in the driveway. She'd been so wrapped up talking with her neighbor she hadn't heard his arrival.

"It's Liam."

Mrs. Henley's brows rose. "Who?"

"Officer Andrews. You met him the night that truck almost ran me over."

"Ah." She grinned. "I thought I noticed a spark between y'all. Maybe he can talk you into staying in Baysville where you belong. I'll let myself out so you two can be alone."

"You don't have to do that," she protested.

Mrs. Henley winked. "Sure I do."

"If you won't stay for supper, at least take some soup home with you. I'll fix it up while you get the door."

Her heart tripped at the sound of Liam's deep voice as he crossed the threshold. And when he entered the kitchen, the sight of his tall body and gray eyes that smoldered like gunmetal set off butterflies in her tummy. Harper tried to rein in her smile. Liam had no business driving all around town with his injury.

"You shouldn't have—"

"I'm fine."

She wasn't so sure. "You have no business driving with that injury."

"What injury?" Mrs. Henley cut in.

"Have a seat," she ordered Liam, pulling out a chair.

"It was nothing. A minor—" he began.

"He was shot in the leg yesterday."

Mrs. Henley gasped. "What's the world coming to? People actually shooting at our police officers." She shook her head as she accepted the plastic container of soup from Harper. "Thanks, dear. And you be careful, young man."

"Yes, ma'am."

"Smells amazing in here," he said after she'd left. "What have you been cooking?"

"Sautéed shrimp and she-crab soup. Hope you don't have a shellfish allergy."

"You could have picked up fast food burgers for to-night and I'd be happy—as long as we're together."

The warm glow flowing through her body had nothing to do with the kitchen heat. Damn, even his voice sent her heart rate into overdrive. "I better stir the sauce."

She returned to the stove, checking the burner. It was a bit of an obsession with her to closely watch the stove. One kitchen fire was enough for a lifetime.

"To answer your earlier question, I was speaking with Gunner and the other homeless men at their camp down by the railroad track."

"Did you talk to him as part of your undercover work, or were you taking them more food?"

"Both."

Satisfaction flooded Harper at his admission. Liam must trust her at least a little bit to divulge his business. She continued stirring, waiting to see if he offered more of an explanation.

"I'm beginning to think there's a connection between the vagrant murders and the illegal gambling and pros-titution rings."

"Why?" she asked, removing the pan from the burner. Everything was ready.

"It makes sense that whoever runs them would hire transients for muscle work."

"Like roughing up people who don't pay their gam-bling debts?"

"Right. And making sure the prostitutes fork over a large percentage of the money they take in."

She returned to the table, shaking her head. "Hard to believe this kind of thing has been going on under our noses."

"Enough of work. What have you been up to all day?"

Liam had opened up about his undercover work;

couldn't she trust him with the latest bit of weirdness at the house? Would he think she was crazy? Honestly, though, she'd love an objective opinion. If Liam believed her nuts, then there was no relationship to be built. Best to find out now.

"Actually, something did happen today," she admitted, smoothing the denim on her thighs. "It's hard to talk about. I don't want you to think I'm nuts. It only happens when I'm alone and—"

"Just tell me." He tipped her chin with a crook of his index finger, forcing her to meet his eyes. "I've heard lots of strange tales as a cop. I won't judge you. Are you hearing strange sounds again? Receive any more threatening emails?"

"More noises," she said past the burn in her throat.

No shock or flicker of skepticism crossed his face.

"If you think my train has boarded for crazy town, just tell me," she prodded.

He stood and scanned the room, as though searching out things unseen. "When was the last time you heard them?"

"Last night, before I went to the hospital to see you. I'd had a glass of wine and drifted off to sleep only to wake up to all the weird sounds. I heard more this morning, too."

Liam circled the room, eyeing everything top to bottom.

"One of the strange noises I'm hearing sounds like a pebble hitting a window. It made me flash back to the past."

"How's that?" he asked, continuing his search.

"I know I told you that I'd caught Presley sneaking out a few times at night. Once, I heard pebbles bouncing off her bedroom window. I guess a signal someone was outside waiting on her. I was only nine at the time and didn't want to rat on my big sister. Maybe if I had…" Harper swallowed hard. "Maybe Mom would have read her the riot act and Presley would still be alive."

Liam was back at her side, kneeling at her feet. "No," he said firmly. "Stop it right there. You aren't responsible. It was a horrible accident."

"Or was it?" she whispered hoarsely. "There was that *thing* standing by her body."

Liam stood. "One mystery at a time. Were you in the bedroom when you heard the noises?"

"Yes. The first time."

"And the second time?"

"I was in here, in the kitchen. Only this time it wasn't at night. No way it was a dream or the effect of a glass of wine. There's no rational explanation for it at all."

"Creepy. You must have been scared. Which no doubt was the intent behind it."

"The noises are awful—the basement doorknob rattling, hard breathing, scratching and even the sound of a child crying." An involuntary shiver racked her body. "If Mrs. Henley hadn't come inside with me, I might have driven straight to your place."

"Let's go take a look."

"At what?" she asked in confusion.

"Your bedroom, for starters. I'm going to sort this out immediately."

He headed up the stairs, and she reluctantly trailed behind him. "I don't know what you're expecting to find. I can assure you that as long as someone else is in the house, you won't hear anything unusual."

"All the more reason to be suspicious."

He breathed hard, rubbing the wound on his leg, but

she knew better than to mention it. Liam was undeterred once his mind was set.

Harper gripped the polished mahogany rails as she climbed. Each step felt like hiking a mountain. Once inside the bedroom, Liam methodically scanned every corner and searched behind every piece of furniture. He seemed so out of place in the feminine room, and she was eminently conscious of her bed—the place where she'd indulged in more than one fantasy of the two of them together.

She cleared her throat. "What exactly are you searching for?"

"I'll let you know when I—" He pulled something from the top of an old watercolor painting on the wall opposite of her bed. "And here we go."

"What is it?"

"A camera," he said grimly. "Bet there's hidden microphones or speakers, too."

What did it mean? Where had they come from? Harper shook her head. "It's not mine. I don't understand."

"It's planted. Someone is trying to scare you." He skimmed his hand along the top of her dresser. "Aha! Found them."

She hurried to his side, where he extended a hand. Tiny black speakers and wiring rested in his upturned palm. Harper backed away as though he held a nest of baby vipers.

"This explains the noises."

"But—how?"

"Everything must be operated remotely by computer." His gray eyes were as cold and stormy as the autumn sky. "Who's been in your bedroom?"

"I—I don't know. Nobody!"

Liam stormed out the door and down the stairs.

"Where are you going?"

"To find the rest of them."

She scrambled after him, only to trip halfway down the stairs. One moment she was stepping on solid ground, and the next her feet flailed into emptiness. Before she could scream, strong arms grasped her beneath her legs and back.

"I've got you," Liam said.

She buried her head against his broad chest; the crisp linen of his dress shirt smelled detergent-clean, and Harper relaxed against him until the wild beating of her heart mellowed.

Liam picked up several tiny metal objects from the steps. "What's this?"

It couldn't be—yet, she couldn't deny the solid proof in front of her. "Jacks."

"Like—in the kid's game?"

She retrieved the jack from his hand and closed her fist around the six-pointed metallic piece with enough pressure that the sharp nubs indented her flesh. This child's game piece was real—nothing ghostly about its solid substance.

"Yes," she whispered. "Presley and I used to play jacks together all the time."

"That doesn't explain how they got here."

The world went fuzzy as she bent down to pick up the toys. Surreptitiously, she swiped at the wet pools that formed in her eyes. Jacks was the one game she could beat her older sister at. They'd have mammoth games of onesies, twosies and on up to fivesies, which was the edge of Presley's maximum pickup skill. As for herself, she'd practiced until she'd mastered ascending to the tenth level. She pictured the two of them, cross-legged on the bedroom floor, shrieking with glee as they picked up the pieces before the tossed rubber ball bounced down.

Harper picked up the scattered pieces, counting eight in all. "Two are still missing. The game comes in sets of ten," she informed Liam. Her eyes swept the stairs, but she couldn't locate any more.

"That's hardly the point," Liam said. "How did they get here to begin with? Did you drop them earlier?"

"I haven't even thought of jacks in years." These had materialized from thin air.

Liam shook his head. "Gaslighting. Someone is seriously messing with your head."

"But why? What would be the point? I don't have any enemies."

Harper followed him into the kitchen, where Liam began the same methodical search he'd conducted upstairs. From behind the toaster oven, he pulled out yet another camera and speaker. "And here we go," he announced in grim satisfaction.

Harper plopped down at the kitchen table, squeezing the eight jacks. The pain kept her grounded to the surreal discoveries in her home. The place where she ate, slept and bathed—all the time under the assumption she was safely sheltered from the world. Bathing… "Check the bathrooms," she croaked. Had someone seen her naked—at her most vulnerable? And if so…were they recording the images to blackmail her?

"What if there's a place on the dark web with nude photos of me?"

Liam's face darkened. "Normally, I'd say that's highly unlikely. That's not the reason why your tormentor snuck hidden cameras through your place."

She wasn't sure if Liam's reasoning was reassuring or

not. No matter what, her privacy had been invaded, and she'd never feel the same here again.

"I'll check it out." His footsteps echoed through the house as she laid her head on the table and shut her eyes. If only burying her head in the sand was a real possibility.

Liam's steps grew louder, and she lifted her head.

"Good news. Nothing in either of the bathrooms."

"Suppose I should be grateful for that."

"I want the names of everyone who's been in here the past couple days." Liam pulled out his cell phone and swiped the screen.

"It can't be anyone I've let in," she protested.

His lips pursed into a straight line. "Don't count it out. Consider everyone a suspect."

"Okay. Let's see. Kimber's been over. And her crew cleaned out the basement while I wasn't home." She latched onto that idea. "Must have been someone on that crew, right? Some sicko playing a joke on me—the old crazy girl living alone in the house where her teenaged sister died. He and his friends are probably having a good laugh right about now." Anger replaced apprehension. "We'll get all their names from Kimber. Think you can pick out the culprit in the interviews? Could be the whole crew is in on the joke."

"Anything's possible," he conceded, his fingers flying over the keypad as he made notes. "Who else has been here that you know of?"

"Nobody."

"That's not true. Mrs. Henley just left."

"Lurlene Henley?" She gave a disbelieving laugh. "You can't be serious."

"Oh, but I am. Deadly serious."

"She's a sweet old lady who's lived across the street

from me all my life. A friend of my mom's. What possible reason could she have for gaslighting me?"

"If she has a motive, we can find out. Anyone else?"

"A delivery man was here yesterday afternoon, but he was never out of my sight when he set a heavy package in the foyer for me."

"That's it?"

"Yes."

Liam clicked away and then returned the cell phone to his back pocket. "I'll report this to Bryce and have a couple men do a thorough sweep to make sure no more cameras or speakers remain."

"Thank you."

He regarded her silently.

"What?" she demanded.

"Didn't you tell me your friend wanted to buy this house?"

"Yeah. So what?"

"How bad does she want the place? Enough to scare you into selling?"

"That's ridiculous," she snapped. "We've been best friends for years. Kimber's a highly successful Realtor. Buying my house will hardly make or break her business."

Liam dug out his phone once more. "What's her last name again?"

"Collins," she said tightly. "As in Collins Realty."

"Got it."

"It's not her. Don't blame Kimber."

"We'll see."

"I don't want you antagonizing my friend."

"If she's got nothing to hide, then she won't mind a few questions to help us get to the truth. As your friend, she'll have your interests at heart."

Harper sighed. Damn his logic. "You make an excellent point. Can't argue that."

Liam nodded with satisfaction. "Great. Because I don't want to argue with you. What do you say we enjoy our dinner and table this discussion for afterward? Frankly, I'm starving."

"Doubt I'll enjoy a bite. Must be nice to compartmentalize your emotions," she grumbled. Although, to be fair, the ability to do so must make his job a heck of a lot easier.

Liam's hand rested on top of hers. "Whatever we discover, remember that the truth is never as painful as living a life in fear."

She nodded. "You're right. It's hard to even sleep here at night anymore."

"Stay with me, then." His gray eyes smoldered as his thumb stroked her hand.

"But I can't—"

"Just stay with me—at least until all this is over."

"No. It doesn't feel right. Running away never solves a problem."

"You'd be doing the Baysville Police Department a favor. They'll still be patrolling my house at night until we discover who shot at us. If they also have to do drive-by patrols of your house, it will be stretching them thin."

She hesitated.

"Do it for me?" He shot her the sexy smile she found hard to resist. "I have enough to juggle without lying awake at night worrying if you're safe. Plus, together, we'll be stronger."

"In that case, I accept."

Chapter Eleven

K-i-m-b-e-r C-o-l-l-i-n-s.

Liam hit enter on the keyboard and waited while the Baysville PD's computer network packaged bits of data in cyberspace, searching for a recognizable hit. Not that he expected anything. Harper was confident that her friend was aboveboard and a well-respected member of the community who'd been born and raised here.

He had enough years of law enforcement experience to recognize that a prestigious pedigree had no bearing on a person's morality. Ethically challenged or desperate people came from all walks of life.

While he waited, Liam read the updated file on his desk regarding the Allen Spencer investigation. Two more underage girls had come forward as victims. The judge had set a very high bond for Spencer, but despite any support from the community, Spencer had rounded up the money and was now out awaiting trial. He was forbidden any contact with minors and had been dismissed from his church.

Ding. The tiny beep signaled the computer had found some sort of match. Liam clicked on the rap sheet PDF document and quickly scanned its contents. Four counts of check fraud, all within the last month. So, Harper's friend wasn't the entrepreneurial success she imagined.

Or maybe Kimber just lived way above her means and it had finally caught up with her. It wasn't like Kimber Collins had committed a violent crime, but she was no angel, either. These weren't merely bounced checks—she'd written them fully aware there were insufficient funds in her bank account to cover the amounts. The bounced checks totaled over five thousand dollars, and she'd written more than three in a five-day period—which made the charge a felony instead of a misdemeanor, punishable by a two-year sentence. Currently, she was on bail for the offense.

He tapped a pencil on his desk, pondering the implications. From his office window, he watched as a couple of trustee inmates raked leaves. A loud rap on his open office door shifted his attention to Bryce, who leaned against the door frame, a scowl etching his face.

"You shouldn't be here," Bryce ground out. "You're no good to any officer if we're called out for a disturbance. Matter of fact, you'd be a hindrance."

"That's why I'm sticking to paperwork. Limited-duty stuff for a couple more days." He met Bryce's scowl. "You're welcome," he added sarcastically.

Bryce pushed away from the door and sat in a chair opposite him. "What kind of paperwork are you doing?"

"Filing incident reports, taking complaint calls. That kind of thing. Figured I'd help out doing what I could."

His boss had the grace to look contrite as he opened a stick of clove-flavored gum. "Appreciate that," he mumbled, stuffing the gum in his mouth.

"Any specific reason you wanted to see me?"

"Heard you'd arrived for work, so I wanted to warn you not to go out on calls."

"Hadn't planned on it."

"Good. Because as it stands now, you're a liability."

At least I'm an honest cop—unlike you. But Liam bit back the words. "I'll consider myself warned to stay put."

"Good." Bryce nodded, apparently mollified that his authority had been validated. "Dad and I are going out for a bite to eat. Want me to bring you back a burger? It's the least I can do for an injured officer."

The conciliatory offer caught Liam by surprise. "No, thanks, I'm meeting Harper in a bit."

His boss didn't make the usual eye roll at the mention of her name. "Surprised she hasn't left town yet."

"Why should she be in any hurry?" Liam stared his boss down. "Seems to me that someone wants her to leave pretty badly."

"What are you talking about? That phantom email warning her to get out of her house?"

How much could he probe his boss for information? "That and a couple other incidents, like the truck nearly running her down," he said, keeping any other information vague. "How well do you know Kimber Collins?"

"I've known her all my life. She's married to Richard, a good friend of mine. Why do you ask?"

He gave a nonchalant shrug. "I was reviewing the arrest log, and her name jumped out at me since she's friends with Harper."

"Right. They appear to be in some financial straits lately."

"What kind of work does her husband do?"

"Sells insurance. I thought he'd been doing well with it. Guess the bad economy's getting to all of us."

"Maybe. Or maybe Richard, or the both of them, have expensive vices."

"They live in a beautiful house and drive nice cars. Their kids go to the best private school in the area—so

I bet the bills all add up while their income's taken a hit. No need to suspect anything more dire than that."

"Or it could be your friend has a problem." Liam decided to test the waters. "Like drugs or gambling or even taking up with hookers."

Bryce flushed crimson and jumped to his feet. "Richard wouldn't cheat on his wife. He's crazy about her. He might drink a bit—but drugs? No way."

He noticed his boss skipped one of the vices he'd mentioned.

"What about gambling, then?" Liam pressed. "I've heard rumors there's some big-time action taking place right under our noses."

"First I've heard of it."

Bryce was lying. His face had gone from crimson to pale. Either he was incredibly naive, stupid—or part of the problem. Liam's money—if he were a betting man—was that his boss was well aware of everything that happened in Baysville. But he said nothing while Bryce gained his composure.

"I'll put my ear to the ground. Even ask Dad if he's heard the same rumors. If you get any concrete leads, fill me in."

Like hell he would. "Of course, boss."

With a satisfied nod, Bryce sauntered away.

About time he headed out as well. A quick burger and then he and Harper had a date to meet Kimber Collins at her office, ostensibly to get the names of her crew. But he wanted more than that, although he'd have to exercise caution. Harper was already angry he thought of her friend as a suspect, and now he'd learned that Richard was buddies with Bryce.

Small towns often made for sticky social situations.

THE INTERIOR OF Collins Realty vibrated with an understated elegance. From the expensive crystal chandelier to the plush carpeting and mahogany furniture, it telegraphed glamour and wealth. Not the unattainable kind of wealth—but a step above the run-of-the-mill kind of American dream. Harper cast an appreciative glance at the cream-colored walls and the splashes of turquoise and coral accent pieces that offset the heavy masculinity of the dark furniture. A place both men and women would be comfortable as they discussed the finer points of house bids and mortgage rates.

"I wasn't expecting you to bring company," Kimber said, her eyes flitting from Harper to Liam.

Harper gave her a reassuring smile. "This is my friend Liam. We had lunch, and I invited him to come along and meet you. Hope that's okay?"

"Of course." Kimber nodded and gestured at the white sofa. "Have a seat and I'll get you the crew list on my desk. I've printed it out."

This already felt awkward, and Liam hadn't even said a word yet. Must be the police uniform making Kimber uncomfortable. Harper should have asked that he wear street clothes instead. This might have been easier if she hadn't called ahead of time and told Kimber about the gaslighting attempt.

"Here you go." Kimber held out the list to her as she sat in the wingback chair across from them. "But I'm confident none of my employees had anything to do with whoever's trying to scare you."

Harper looked it over.

"Do you know the people on the list?" Liam asked.

"A couple are familiar, but not all. But if Kimber vouches for them, that's good enough for me."

"I'll run them through the police department's computer, see if any of them have a record."

"They don't," Kimber asserted. "I do thorough background searches on everyone I hire."

Liam folded the paper and tucked it in his jacket pocket. "Not all criminals have records."

"What possible reason would one of them have to harass Harper?"

"That's what we need to discover. Seems like someone's afraid of her asking so many questions about Presley and the past."

Kimber crossed her legs and casually began swinging the top one as she leaned back into the chair. Harper was glad to see her visibly relax. Of course, Kimber was assured there was nothing to fear. She'd done nothing wrong.

"'Fraid I can't help you there, Officer. But if you're ever in the market for a new home, give me a call."

"She's the best Realtor in town. She's even offered to buy my house and turn it into a B&B if I decide to sell later."

"A B&B?" Liam turned to Kimber. "Have to admit that offer surprises me. How would you have time to run your own business and think about taking on another full-time job at the same time?"

"I'd hire a manager for the B&B, naturally."

"Still would be a formidable task managing both enterprises at once. Especially initially, what with finding staff, marketing and everything else that goes into such a venture."

Kimber lifted her chin. "I can assure you, I'm extremely capable and up to the challenge."

"I'm guessing you hope the B&B would help with your current cash-flow problem."

Cash-flow problem? What was he talking about? Harper glanced from one to the other, trying to figure out what caused the sudden tension in the room. Kimber gripped the sides of the chair, and her lips pressed into a thin white line while Liam sat unnaturally still—a lion ready to pounce on unsuspecting prey.

"What's all this about?" she asked, breaking the awkward silence. She tried to get Liam to face her, but he was intent on staring down Kimber. Resentment slashed against her ribs. He'd promised not to antagonize her friend, but he was doing just that.

Kimber wiped her hands on her navy pencil skirt and then smiled bitterly at Liam. "I see you've been checking up on me."

"It's all part of my job to be thorough. And I'm especially serious when it comes to Harper's safety. She's reported several recent incidents of hearing noises in the house."

"I would never hurt Harper." Kimber flashed her a panicked help-me-out-here look.

Harper stood. "Enough. We've got the list. Let's go."

"Maybe I've looked at this from the wrong angle," Liam said slowly, leaning back and throwing an arm across the back of the couch. His intent to pursue this matter couldn't be clearer. "Maybe everything going on at the house was an attempt to motivate Harper to sell to you."

"You've got a lot of nerve." Kimber's composure crumbled, and she leaped to her feet, shaking in outrage. "I've known Harper all her life. Who are you to come in here and fling such wild accusations?" She switched her gaze to Harper. "You believe me, don't you?"

Harper opened her mouth to say yes, but the word stuck in her throat. She glanced at Liam, and something in his sturdy, calm demeanor gave her pause. Gray eyes pleaded with her to have a little faith in him. How could she deny Liam the benefit of the doubt? After all, he'd trusted in her from the very beginning, even when his boss insinuated she was mentally unstable. She drew a deep breath. "I think we should listen to what Liam has to say."

Liam's eyes glowed with silent appreciation, but Kimber gasped as if she'd been slapped across the face. She pointed at the door. "You can both get out of my office. I won't be insulted and accused of something I didn't do."

"We found hidden cameras and speakers, Kimber. If I ran tests, would your fingerprints be on that equipment?"

"How dare you! I should sue you for harassment!" Despite her forced anger, her red lips trembled, and she abruptly sat back down.

Harper noticed that Kimber hadn't answered Liam's question outright, though, and her heart sank at the betrayal by her friend.

Liam leaned forward, as though moving in for the kill. "If I got a search warrant to have all your home and office computers and cell phones and other technical devices examined for evidence—"

"You have no grounds to invade my privacy on such flimsy evidence," she scoffed.

"If you have nothing to hide, then why not let our computer and audio forensics guy take a look?"

"I have a lot of confidential information on my computers, about clients. I could never let you go through them without a warrant." Kimber turned her gaze from Liam and faced Harper, and her normally cool blue eyes were as frightened as a cornered kitten. "You believe me, don't you, Harper?"

She cast a glance at Liam. "You believe she's guilty?"

"Yes."

Who to trust? She didn't want to believe Kimber would play such a nasty trick on her, but desperate people did desperate things. "I don't want to believe it's true," she admitted at last. "But if it *was* you, please tell me. I need to know the truth."

"Come clean and this will go easier on you," Liam urged.

"I wouldn't press charges. Just be honest."

Kimber regarded them silently and then keened forward, dropping her head onto her knees. Beneath the cotton fabric of her shirt, her shoulders shook. Harper stood stiffly, watching the woman she thought she knew get herself together.

Kimber lifted her head. "I'm so sorry." Her voice was strangled, and her cheeks were smudged with black mascara. Nothing like the poised, in-control Kimber she was used to seeing. But then, perhaps she'd never seen the real woman until now. Before, she'd always regarded Kimber as her savior wrapped with a mantle of kindness.

"Why?" she whispered past the lump in her throat.

"We need the money. So bad. Richard gambles. It started small—a few bets on sports games between friends—but then it escalated over the years. It got so bad I took him off our credit cards and hid the checkbook from him. Somehow, he always finds a way to get the money, though."

Harper picked up the box of tissues on Kimber's desk and pressed one of them into Kimber's hand.

"We're about to lose everything, even our house," Kimber confessed. She blew her nose and swiped her face, which only served to make the black smudges worse. "I—I thought I could make a success of the B&B. Even with all of us living there, we'd have a couple of spare rooms to rent out. Plus, I was hoping to eventually add on more rooms through reconstruction."

The Collinses' beautifully restored farmhouse. A showcase home that she'd painstakingly decorated for a decade. And now Kimber was about to lose it all. Pity tamped down her initial anger at Kimber's deceit.

"Why didn't you tell me all this earlier? I would have listened. I wouldn't have held out for a better deal."

Kimber shrugged her shoulders. "I was trying to fix our problems without Richard's business being affected. And...pride? I know how you always looked up to me. I didn't want you—or anyone—to know just how bad it's gotten."

"Bound to come out when your check-fraud cases go to trial," Liam said drily.

"I keep hoping for a miracle," she admitted. "I know. It's stupid. But I can't bear everyone knowing I've failed."

"You'd rather torment me out of my own home than have everyone know you aren't perfect. That's pretty sick."

"I don't blame you for being angry. I would be, too."

She had to get out of here. Harper grabbed her purse and strode to the door.

"You aren't pressing charges—right?" Kimber's voice rose. "Isn't that right, Harper?"

She should reassure Kimber, but her heart wasn't in it. Not yet, anyway. Let her sweat it out a bit. After all, how many nights had she lost sleep—too afraid to sleep in her own bedroom? All because of Kimber.

On the porch she closed her eyes and inhaled the crisp clean air.

"You okay?" Liam draped an arm across her shoulders.

The heavy warmth spread comfort through her body—

a balm for her troubled spirit. "I should go back in and reassure Kimber I'm not pressing charges. Right?"

"It's okay to think about yourself now. She betrayed your trust. I wouldn't be in any hurry to offer comfort if I were in your shoes."

Chapter Twelve

Home.

It felt great to be back, to know that she was safe inside her childhood home. The danger had been eliminated. Police officers had come by earlier today and done a clean sweep of the house. No other cameras and speakers were found. So no more hunkering down at Liam's place.

How could Kimber have done such a thing?

Resolutely, she tamped down the anger and upset. Kimber had caused enough trouble—she didn't need to waste any more of her time dwelling on that confrontation. She ran her hands along the smooth oak table that had been there ever since she'd been a little girl. Happier times when the whole family had been together. Her gaze drifted to the fireplace mantel in the den and the large photograph of the entire family smiling the kind of bright, carefree grins one sported before life kicked you in the butt.

And then she noticed something else. *That* smell had returned. Only a trace, but enough that her nostrils flared in distaste. She'd deal with that again another day. For now, she'd fix iced tea and then head to the master bathroom for a long, scented bubble bath. Only two years earlier, Mom had installed a whirlpool tub to help ease the pain of her arthritis, and it made for a lovely retreat.

She poured a glass of tea and reached into the cookie jar to grab a snack, but only crumbs remained. Her brow furrowed. She'd just filled the jar a couple of days ago. The officers who'd searched her home must have helped themselves. Which was fine—the least she could do to show her appreciation. Tomorrow she'd send a written thank-you letter to the police department. In the bathroom, her mom's old radio, now dusty, sat on a shelf, and her eyes were magnetically drawn to the old-school device. How many times had she and Presley heard Mom playing classical music from this very room? Some people retreated from life's demands by taking a nap or settling in front of the TV with a cup of coffee, but their mom had opted for long bubble baths and classical music. Really loud music. Mom had been deaf in one ear, the result of a childhood infection.

On impulse, she retrieved the radio and pressed play. The invigorating chords of Johann Strauss's "Blue Danube Waltz" blared in the small space. A memory, long forgotten, surged forth—she and Presley impromptu waltzing through the house to this very piece. What they lacked in elegance they made up for with youthful enthusiasm as, hands on each other's shoulders, they leaped and skipped about the kitchen and hallways.

Nostalgia, bittersweet as baking chocolate, smacked Harper's senses as she filled the tub with hot water. What was that old saying—in for a penny, in for a pound? Might as well go all the way for the full effect. She located Mom's old bottle of gardenia-scented bath salts before stripping down and stepping into the tub.

Heavenly. The stress of the day began to ease as she enjoyed the water's warm, liquid caress. Mom's method of escape was a winner. She closed her eyes, imagining herself dancing at a Viennese ball, the Danube River flowing magically in the background.

Everything would get better now. No more strange voices and unsettling emails. No more treacherous friends manipulating her mind. To top it off, Liam was quickly healing from his wound, and their relationship grew deeper every day. Languidly, Harper traced her lips with an index finger, recalling his kisses. In many ways she was a lucky, lucky girl.

A loud rustling erupted from outside the bathroom window. Shrubbery scraped against the frosted glass pane. A small animal, perhaps? But no, a cat or dog couldn't cause that much ruckus.

But a human could.

Fear prickled along her neck and shoulders, and—despite the bathwater's heat—her arms broke out in goose bumps.

A silhouette appeared—a broad outline of head and shoulders. She wasn't alone. Frantic, she glanced at her robe hanging on a hook on the wall and out of arm's reach. Much as she loathed stepping naked out of the tub, lying there like a sitting duck for the Peeping Tom was an even worse option. With a giant splash, she climbed out, snatching the robe from the hook and wrapping the tie around her waist.

"Get out of here! I'm calling the police right now."

Rounded eyes and a gaping mouth regarded her from the other side of the glass. Even through the distortion of the frosted window, something in the shape and angle of his face seemed familiar. Anger melted her fear. Did everyone in this town have a hidden sinister nature underneath their masks of smiles?

The man vanished.

This probably wasn't the smartest thing to do, but if

she wanted to know the creep's identity, this was her only chance. The guy was fleeing after all, not trying to break in and harm her. Harper flung open the window.

She recognized that slight-built frame. "Hey!" she shouted. "What are you doing here, Allen?"

His head whipped around, his eyes wide pools of panic. He froze, head twisting from side to side, as though debating whether to flee or face the music.

"Get back here," she ordered. "Talk to me before the police arrive. Might go better for you this way."

Allen's shoulders slumped, and he shuffled back to the window. "Damn it."

"Is that anyway for a preacher to talk? Oh, that's right," she continued, voice dripping in sarcasm. "When he's caught peeping in a woman's window, that's the least of his worries."

"It's not what you think," he protested, holding up his hands like a shield. "Please don't call the cops. Please. I'm already in enough trouble."

"Why should I care?"

"If not for me, then will you do it for my family? My wife and kids will be devastated. Give me a chance to explain."

This ought to be good. Harper crossed her arms. "You've got one minute to explain yourself."

He glanced around the yard. "Meet me on your porch? In case anyone walks by and wonders what I'm doing. This doesn't look right."

She laughed. He'd been creeping around in the shrubs by her window and *now* he was worried what people would think?

"Don't you dare run off," she warned.

"I won't. I can explain this misunderstanding. Meet

you around front. And make sure you put some clothes on first. I have a reputation to maintain."

The nerve of that sanctimonious hypocrite.

Quickly, she threw on a pair of jeans and a T-shirt and ran to the front porch. To her surprise, Allen hadn't left. He sat in the glider, awaiting her appearance. Anyone passing by would think he'd come to pay a call, exercising his pastoral duties.

The creep.

"I thought teenage girls were more your forte. Why were you peeking in my bathroom window? Only one answer comes to mind."

Allen winced. "It's not what you think. I didn't know that was a window on a bathroom. Really. Sit down and let's talk."

"I'll stand right here, thank you very much."

"All right then." He drew a deep breath and exhaled loudly, running a hand through his thinning hair. "I was just trying to find you to talk. Your car's in the driveway, so I knew you had to be home. I knocked at the front and back doors for over a minute, and you didn't answer."

"Which would lead anyone normal to figure that the person was indisposed for company."

"I wanted to take advantage of this moment. You're either not home lately, or that *cop*"—he practically spat the word—"is with you."

"Anything you have to say to me, you can say in front of Officer Andrews."

"Not really. You see, he's the problem."

She quirked a brow, waiting on his explanation.

"He's ruined my life. I was fired from my church, and my marriage is in shambles. I'm facing financial ruin, too. No one would help me in posting bond. You have no idea what it's been like for me."

"Spare me your sob story. Wouldn't hurt my feelings if you hadn't been released on bond. I'm worried about Emily and any other victims that might turn up during the investigation."

"I'm begging you, Harper. Talk to him and see if he can help me out in some way."

Allen was delusional if he thought there was anything Liam could or would do to help him.

What had Presley ever seen in this creepy wimp? "Preying on minors is breaking the law. You should be put in jail."

"I never admitted crossing a certain line. What I did was wrong, but I can seek treatment. Start over."

"She's a child. Don't try to justify anything to me. And I'm really supposed to believe you weren't trying to enjoy the show in my bathroom?"

"I couldn't see anything through the frosted glass. You're not going to tell him about that, are you? I was only trying to find you."

A shudder of revulsion passed through her. "Stay away from me, Allen. Don't ever come back here."

"For Presley's sake—can't you at least grant me a little kindness?"

"You're pathetic. Even you admitted she'd broken up with you weeks before she died. You have no claim on my pity."

"What if I told you I might have information?"

A pulse of nervous energy sparked in her chest. "Like what?"

"You came to me wanting to know if I got her pregnant. I didn't. But I know who Presley was secretly seeing after she broke up with me."

"Who?"

Allen wagged a finger. "First, you agree not to tell

Liam I was at your bathroom window. Second, I want special consideration when my case comes to trial."

"I'm not agreeing to anything. Give me the information or give it to Liam. You know you can't keep it secret."

He gave a long-suffering sigh. "All right, all right. What do I have to lose? I've lost almost everything anyway. But if you could see it in your heart to help me, put a word in for me..."

"Who was it?" she demanded.

"Bryce Fairfax."

THE PHONE RANG, and he recognized the caller number. Liam pressed the Answer button on his vehicle's Bluetooth device. "What's up, Gunner?"

"I've been contacted."

Finally. A break in this case. "By who? What did they ask you to do?"

"He didn't give me his name. Guy come down to camp, and I seen him chatting up with Buddy. But Buddy shrugged him off and walked away. He don't cotton to strangers, you see. Then the guy goes over to Buddy and I stroll over real quiet like to see what he's up to."

Liam grit his teeth in exasperation. All he needed was the man's description and what he wanted with Gunner. But he'd learned not to interrupt Gunner once he'd started a story; it would only take him twice as long to gather his thoughts and start the whole story all over again.

"When he mentioned a job enforcing dudes to pay their gambling debts, why, I motioned Buddy to walk away, too. Then I eased up next to the fella and told him I'd be interested in making a little cash."

At Gunner's brief pause for breath, Liam jumped in. "Did he give you an assignment already?"

"I'm getting to that, boss. So, when I told him..."

Liam pulled over to the side of the road and grabbed pen and paper to write down information. Absently, he rubbed a hand over his gun wound that was more uncomfortable than truly painful. He'd find the bastard responsible for this.

"Then *he* says that I didn't look fit for the kind of job he had in mind. He needed muscle to manhandle a welsher. Ticked me off big-time. I told him I was scrappy and had won many a fight at camps over the years. That I could hold my own with anybody. Guy didn't look convinced but said he'd give me a test job. Pay me one hundred dollars, cash, to go rough up this dude who needed to be taught a lesson. And I says…"

Liam couldn't stay silent. "What's the target's name?"

"The target? Oh, you mean who I'm supposed to rough up? Well, I'm getting to that. So, I told him I wouldn't take any less than one hundred and fifty bucks. You know, just to make it seem like I weren't too interested in taking the job. Didn't want him to be suspicious of me. So the guy agreed to that. Gave me fifty bucks and said I'd get the rest tomorrow when I completed the job."

Liam's heart hammered with anticipation. "Who are you supposed to beat up?"

"Well, at first he didn't want to give me a name. Just an address. But I told him I needed at least the target's name, and a photograph would be even better. Told him I wanted to make sure I didn't hurt the wrong man, see? I could tell he didn't like that, but he got out his phone and showed me the guy's picture. Looked like a real preppy kind of dude. Know what I mean? Fancy clothes and a trendy kinda hairdo you don't get at a real barbershop. Must have gone to a girly beauty parlor to get it done, know what I mean?"

"Go on." Liam refrained from banging his head against the dashboard. But just barely.

"Did I tell you the guy also said there might be an occasional need to force a call girl to pay up all the money she'd collected? Now, I draw the line there. Told him so, too, but that I'd find someone willing to do it. And he said, what are you? King of the hobos? And I said…"

He glanced at the dashboard clock. He was already late meeting Harper for dinner, but work came first. If they continued seeing each other, she'd come to realize that grim reality. Could be a deal breaker for her, but it wouldn't be the first time a woman had decided that he wasn't worth the aggravation. Although he quietly admitted to himself that if Harper felt that way, it would shake him.

"Anyway, we exchanged cell phone numbers. I'm supposed to call him after I finish the job."

"Excellent. Give me his number. Probably a throwaway phone, but I'll check it out." He scribbled down the number Gunner provided.

"How's this going to work now, boss? What's gonna happen when I don't show up for the job? Makes me a little antsy to have this guy ticked off. Worried he might come hunt me down."

"I'll contact the target and squeeze him for information on the players in this racket. Hopefully, we'll get this shut down quick. In the meantime, I'll pick you up now and take you to a safe location."

"I appreciate that, boss, but wait until tomorrow. If I suddenly leave it'll look funny to my guys. And what if this man shows up at camp again in the meantime and I'm not here? It'll blow up everything."

Gunner was right, but Liam didn't want to place him in a vulnerable position. "I'll take that chance."

Gunner chuckled. "Truth be told, I kinda want to spend tonight with my friends. One last time, ya know?"

"Are you sure?" This didn't sit well with him. The old man played a dangerous game.

"Positive." In a sudden show of brevity, Gunner added, "Gotta go. Meet me about four o'clock tomorrow at the clearing. Oh, and the target's name? Richard Collins."

Collins…a jolt of recognition coursed through him. Had to be Kimber's husband. Time to pay the man a visit earlier than he'd planned.

He was so close. Liam could almost feel the answer to his questions settle into the palm of his hand. Squeezing the steering wheel, he eased his truck back onto the road.

Chapter Thirteen

"Where are you headed?" Liam's voice called to her from the cab of his vehicle as Harper descended her porch steps to her car. She was on her way back to Kimber's to re-assure the woman she wouldn't press charges. As angry as Harper was, she knew Kimber was hurting, and she didn't want to inflict pain on her when she herself had suffered enough.

After sharing this news with Liam, his eyebrows shot up. "Not a good time," he said stonily.

"Why? Are you headed there? I could go with you."

"It's police business, Harper. I just happened to be heading past your place."

She sighed. "Tell me. You know I'll find out soon enough. And you won't stop me from heading there, too."

When he explained his mission, she got in his car without asking permission. "I can help," she announced. "Richard and Kimber know me, and they're in my debt for not pressing charges. Besides, I need to get out of the house."

"Why? Did anything happen?"

On a sigh, she told him. "Allen Spencer paid me a visit earlier."

Liam scowled as he drove. "What did he want?"

"The usual. For us to back off."

"No way."

"That's what I told him."

Liam grasped her hand and raised it to his lips, kissing the inside of her wrist. "This meeting with the Collinses won't take long," he promised. "And if anything else is bothering you, we'll work it out."

She gazed out the passenger window until she spotted the 1830s farmhouse with its redbrick, federal-style architecture rising with a quaint charm in the wide meadow where several horses grazed. "Isn't it beautiful?" she said wistfully. "And wait until you see the inside. Interior brick walls in the kitchen, fireplaces in every room, vintage appliances—"

"Sounds like they sank a fortune in this place," he commented wryly. "No wonder they're up to their eyeballs in debt."

"Richard's gambling is at the root of their problem, not the restoration." Her knee-jerk defense of Kimber surprised her—considering how Kimber had tried to scare her out of her own home.

"They can pay off house loans, but gambling ones just get bigger and come with strings attached," she added.

"Whatever the reason, they're in serious trouble," he said.

Liam pulled into the semicircular cobbled driveway and stopped the car. "Why don't you wait here while I conduct my police business? What if Richard doesn't react well?"

"All the more reason to go in with you. He'll react better if I'm there as a reminder of what he and Kimber owe me for not pressing charges," she countered, exiting the car. They walked up the pathway to the front door.

"You should see this place in spring. Kimber planted

roses and herbs along the border, and it looks and smells like heaven."

But Liam didn't respond. His jaw was set in determination—a look she'd come to think of as *full cop mode*. He pressed the doorbell, and they silently listened to the deep chime echo inside. Moments later, a pigtailed girl in Hello Kitty pajamas opened the door and stared up at them with welcoming curiosity alight in her eyes—the same shade of blue as her mother's.

"Miss Harper!" she threw herself on Harper, wrapping her small arms around her thigh.

"Hey there, Courtney." Harper smiled at the child's enthusiastic welcome. "Good to see you, hon."

"Who's at the door? I told you not to answer it unless..." Kimber emerged from the den and then stopped in the hallway, surprise and uncertainty clouding her eyes.

Liam had felt that an unscheduled visit would be more strategic. That way, he could speak without an attorney or anyone else from the Baysville PD involved.

"May I have a word with you and your husband?" Liam asked.

Kimber's hand flew to her throat. "Go back in the den, Courtney."

They all watched as the little girl raced down the hall. Once she was safely out of sight, Kimber faced them. Her eyes darted back and forth between Liam and Harper. "You aren't..." She wet her lips. "You aren't here to arrest me on more charges, are you?"

"No, ma'am. But I have serious business to discuss with you and your husband. Is he home?"

"Yes." Reluctantly, she gestured them inside. "Let's go to the sunroom, where the kids won't be able to hear us."

"Richard?" she called out. "We have company."

Harper strolled down the familiar hallway, feeling oddly…disloyal. Which was crazy. Kimber was the one who had betrayed their friendship, not her. And yet, how many times had she been in this same house, feeling like part of the family?

Not anymore.

They followed Kimber into a sunroom furnished with white wicker furniture. Baskets of lush ferns hung from the high beams. Glass panels afforded a view of the surrounding woods. At a rustic pine table, Kimber stiffly gestured for them to have a seat. A moment later, Richard appeared in the doorway, dressed casually and sporting his usual easygoing grin.

That smile faltered at their somber expressions. "What's up?"

"Shut the door. I don't want the kids to hear."

"Sounds dire." He tried to joke, but it fell flat in the strained silence. Richard took a seat, folding his hands on the table.

Liam extended a hand. "Liam Andrews."

The men shook hands, and Richard gazed at all of them expectantly.

"I did something really stupid you don't know about." Kimber's lips twisted, and she dropped her gaze to the floor.

"That's not why we're here," Liam cut in.

Richard kept his eyes focused on his wife. "What did you do?"

"I was desperate to get my hands on Harper's house. You know I've always thought it could be converted to a profitable B&B. And we need the money so bad."

Richard scowled, clearly unhappy with their financial situation being discussed openly.

"You can explain that to your husband later. Like I said,

that's not why I'm here, and Harper's already told you she's not pressing charges." He faced Richard. "Actually, you're the reason we're here today. You're in deep trouble."

"Me? You've got to be joking." He snorted with disbelief. "And I don't even know who the hell you are. What's your business with us?"

Kimber tapped his folded palms in a quick warning. "He's a cop, Richard."

Chagrin washed his face. "Guess I better listen up, then."

"It's come to my attention that you've been gambling heavily—to the point where you're overdue on your losses."

"Not again!" Kimber pushed away from the table, eyes blazing. "You promised me you'd stop."

Richard looked down at his hands, and a flush crept from his neck to his face. Harper's heart went out to him. She'd never seen him look anything but carefree and confident. And she knew he was crazy about Kimber. Gambling must be a sickness with Richard, a compulsion that drove him despite his best intentions.

"Have you even been attending the counseling classes?" Kimber continued. "Or have you been lying about that, too?"

"I have. It's just… I thought a couple of wins and I could ease the strain. Pay a few overdue bills."

"Same old story." Kimber shook with indignation. "It does me no good to work so hard when all you do is gamble everything away."

Richard raised his head and faced Liam, ignoring his red-faced, accusing wife. "How did you find out about my uncovered losses?"

"I have my sources," he answered evasively. "It's reached the point where they're through with the verbal threats. Tonight, they plan to physically coerce the money from you."

Stunned silence greeted that news.

Kimber recovered first. "What do you mean?" she whispered.

"Oh, my God. What have I done?" Richard groaned and scrubbed at his face. "I'll go to the bank now and pay them off."

"What good will going to the bank do? There's nothing there. You've ruined us!"

"*I've* ruined us? What about you? You just had to buy this place and go crazy fixing it up."

The sunroom door squeaked open, and Courtney stuck her head out. "What's wrong?" she asked, her little face puckered in dismay. "Why are you screaming?"

"See what you've done?" Kimber said in a whispered hiss at Richard. She pasted on a fake smile. "Everything's all right, sweetie. Go back in the den and watch TV with your sisters."

Courtney teetered on her feet, her gaze flickering back and forth between her parents.

"Go on," Richard said gruffly. "We'll be there in a few minutes."

Their daughter didn't appear convinced that all was well, but she obediently left, her shoulders drooping as she shut the door behind her.

"Thanks for the warning," Richard said, using the table to push himself up. To Harper, it appeared his spirit had been sucked away. "I'll take precautions."

"But what about us?" Kimber faced Liam. "Are those men coming after me and the children, too? Are we in danger?"

"I won't let them touch you or the kids," Richard vowed. "I promise."

"Yeah, right. Like you promised you'd quit gambling?"

"Y'all can stay with me a couple of nights. Or until the danger's passed." Harper surprised even herself with the offer. Despite what Kimber had done, the thought of Courtney and her sisters being in danger pulled at her conscience. She had plenty of room at home, and it was only for a short time.

"You'd do that for me after…after everything I've done?" Kimber swiped at the tears streaming down her face.

"I want Courtney, Anise and Layla to be safe," she hedged. Harper turned to the scowling Liam. "Won't this make it easier for you to set up a sting tonight?"

"Maybe," he conceded.

"I can handle this on my own. I don't need your help. Or any…sting operation."

They all stared at Richard in disbelief. Liam was the first to recover. "Suppose you do manage to dodge an enforcer tonight. What about tomorrow night and then the next night? You can't be with your wife and children 24-7."

"Don't be stupid, Richard. Accept his help. Hear him out." Kimber lifted her chin in determination. "If you don't, I'm leaving you. I won't subject my children to danger. We'll go, and no judge will ever award you custody. Care to gamble on that?"

Richard sat down abruptly, shoulders rounded in defeat. "You don't understand."

"Enlighten me," Liam urged.

"You can't beat city hall."

"Meaning?"

"Why do you think this gambling operation has lasted so long?" Richard said with a sigh. "I can give you the name of the guy that manages the poker games and who collects our cash. But it won't do you much good to lean on him. He's bragged before that his job is risk-free... The cops are in on it."

LIAM HAD SUSPECTED as much all along, but his first reaction was a knee-jerk denial that the men in blue were so corrupt.

"And I don't just mean they turn a blind eye," Richard continued. "They're over the whole thing. You see my predicament. There's no escape for me but to pay them off."

"How do you know that for sure?"

"Rumor," he admitted. "But it makes sense, doesn't it?"

It did. Liam drummed his fingers on the table, debating his options and quickly discounting telling Richard that he worked undercover. Should he call in the big guns now? His gut screamed no. Until he apprehended the enforcer paying Gunner, he had no proof of anything. He needed to bring in the enforcer and wrangle a confession in exchange for fingering the masterminds. Folding now would severely jeopardize his chances of bringing down the criminals.

"Can't you put a hidden mike on Richard at a gambling game?" Kimber suggested. "Get the guilty to incriminate themselves?"

"Are you trying to get me killed?" Richard asked with a snort. "Divorce isn't enough for you?"

"There's a better way," Liam suggested. "The best chance of arresting the head of it all is to put the screws on the middleman. Which in this case means catching the enforcer in the act of getting paid off."

"You mean be willing to let some dude beat the crap out of me and then arrest him for assault? No, thanks."

"Hear me out a minute—"

"No way." Richard stood again, grimly shaking his head. "Y'all can leave my house now. I've heard enough."

"Cooperate with Liam," Harper urged quietly. "We don't have the money to buy your way out of this mess. And even if we did, what about the next time you lose? Liam's offering you a way out."

Richard sank back in his seat, and Liam shot Harper a grateful look. She knew this couple well, and they trusted her to have their best interest at heart.

"Do it, Richard." Kimber briefly laid a hand on her husband's shoulder and then faced Liam. "You promise to keep him safe. Right?"

"I will."

Harper rose. "Why don't we pack overnight bags for the girls and head over to my place?"

Liam gave her a grateful nod. She'd instinctively realized he'd have a better chance of talking Richard out of acting alone if he was out of earshot of his wife.

"Thank you. That sounds like a good idea." Kimber nodded, seemingly eager to get away.

"Call me in a bit," Harper said to him. "We'll go over the plan."

He nodded.

Kimber cleared her throat. "Goodbye, Richard. Stay safe."

"Do you really care?" he asked gruffly.

They stood and faced each other; their hands, like magnets, seemingly drew out to one another and their fingers entwined. Despite the hurt and pain, it was obvious the couple was still in love. The two men watched as Kimber and Harper left the sunroom.

"What's the game plan?" Richard asked, running a

hand through his short shock of hair. "I'll do anything to keep my family from being hurt by my stupidity."

Could he trust this man not to call Bryce the moment he left? Harper had warned him that Bryce and Richard were friends, that they'd played on the same high school football team for years. But those high school days were long gone, and he'd witnessed the way Richard looked at Kimber and his daughters. The man cared about them.

"If you don't one hundred percent cooperate with me and keep your mouth closed, I'll arrest Kimber for criminal mischief."

"Kimber? What the hell did she do?"

"Long story short, she planted cameras and speakers at Harper's house, trying to scare her into leaving Baysville and selling her the property. Your wife is obsessed with the idea of turning the place into a B&B. She seems to think it's the answer to your financial problems. Sell this place, move into Harper's house and then rent out the extra bedrooms."

"She'd be willing to sell our farmhouse?" Wonder flickered in his eyes. "She loves this place. More than she loves me, I suspect."

"Doesn't sound that way to me. She was desperate to fix this problem."

For the first time in their visit, Richard's eyes lit with hope. "Whatever you have in mind, I'm game."

"First thing I need is for you to tell me who collects the gambling money," he said.

"Fair enough." Richard gave a long sigh. "The man's name is Mitchell Sullivan. He's the pharmacist that owns the Baysville drugstore."

Liam's brows rose at the name, although nothing should surprise him in this line of work. Greedy people came in every socioeconomic level. "And Sullivan takes these payments at his place of business?"

"Yep." Richard ran a hand through his hair. "We text him when we arrive, and he goes around to the back door to collect our money that's discreetly folded inside plain-covered envelopes. He treats it as though it were a business transaction. Which, I suppose one could argue, it is."

Chapter Fourteen

Liam kept his sight on Harper as she led Gunner through the dark woods. He didn't like her being here, but she'd insisted, and he was afraid if he left her out, she'd turn up on her own, increasing the danger to herself.

Water squished around his feet, threatening to suction him down into the swampy morass. His socks slightly dampened inside the supposedly waterproof boots. Good thing he'd brought along a spare set for Gunner, although the guy was probably used to wet socks and much worse. Luckily, the moon was close to full, providing plenty of light as they made their way along the back edge of the properties. The flip side? The full moon made detection easier.

He stayed well behind them, trying to keep his footsteps quiet and his back bent in a crouch when they hit clearings between the woods. Gunner claimed not to need a backup as he hiked to the Collinses' farmhouse, that it was bad enough he had to follow Harper, but Liam insisted on providing protection. He had an uneasy feeling about this.

Something swooped nearby, and a small limb broke off a tree less than ten feet away. Must have been an owl. Liam drew to a complete standstill, ears straining, but there was only the rustling of trees and shrubs and an occasional, far-off dog barking. Even Harper and Gunner barely made any noise as they quickly walked along. Harper was familiar with this area and had mapped out the direction earlier for them but insisted that they still needed her eyes as they hiked unfamiliar territory.

At long last, a light shone from the clearing ahead. This was it. Liam observed the tall, thin lines of Gunner and Harper as they quickly strode to the designated area of the Collinses' farmhouse and lifted a window that had been left unlocked and slightly ajar.

There was no reason for the tingling at the back of his neck. Nor any explanation for the foreboding that filled his gut with dread. Yet, Liam couldn't shake the feeling of being watched.

A scream erupted from the farmhouse. "No, don't! I'll pay. Stop!"

Even though the entire scenario had been prearranged down to the smallest detail, including the fake begging for mercy, his unease continued to mount. Could be that the enforcer had a policy of watching the first assignment of a new recruit and they were all being observed from somewhere in the darkness.

Shadows shifted and moved. To his right, a tall, muscular person, dressed entirely in black, slipped from behind the trunk of a large oak and sprinted across the field. As the man was a good fifty yards away, Liam couldn't make out any identifying details. The figure again disappeared into the night. Seconds later, the sound of a motor roared to life. An elliptical beam of headlights strobed the field and woods—and then the vehicle sped down the county road.

Once the engine noise faded away, Liam walked directly to the farmhouse and knocked on the back door. No need to hide any longer. As he suspected, the enforcer spied on his newest henchman. What was he to make of Gunner having a companion? Hopefully, the guy wasn't *too* concerned as long as he'd witnessed Gunner fulfilling his end of the bargain. The enforcer probably assumed Gunner had brought along one of his homeless friends.

"Who's there?" Gunner called out behind the door.

"Liam. All's clear."

The door immediately swung open, and he entered. Both men stood in the kitchen, anxiety palpable in their agitated stances. Harper leaned against the counter, looking calm and confident. As though she had done this a dozen times before. The woman had unplumbed depths.

Richard hurried to lock the door. "Anyone see you out there?"

"Probably not." Liam wished he could offer more assurance. "But, Gunner and Harper, y'all were being watched. Not long after you entered, a man slipped out of the woods and took off in his vehicle. Once I was sure he was gone, I came."

"We heard the engine, too." Gunner shook his head. "These guys mean business, don't they?"

"Once you get the payment, I'll arrest the enforcer," he promised. "Agents will wire money into your bank account first thing in the morning to cover the debt. After the arrest, I can call in for backup."

"The state guys, right?" Richard asked. "The local police will do more harm than good."

"They're standing by for my call. After tomorrow, we'll have at least two arrests. The enforcer paying off Gunner and the man accepting your gambling payment. Between the two of them, I'm confident at least one will give a full confession."

Richard nodded, but it was clear he didn't share Liam's

full confidence. But if he were in Richard's shoes, he'd also be uneasy until the matter was resolved.

Harper took off the knitted black cap she wore, and her red hair gleamed in the light. "I'm glad this is almost over. I still can't believe Mitchell Sullivan is involved in all this. I didn't see that one coming."

Gunner leaned back against the sofa and ran his weathered hands along the smooth leather. "Nice home you got here. Must make you right proud."

Richard shrugged. "It's been a hell of a strain. Feels good to finally admit that truth. I'm tired of keeping up pretenses. Time for me to get serious about straightening up my problem and getting my family back to normal."

"That will be a relief to Kimber," Harper muttered.

"I ain't never had much, but I've seen more of this country than most men," Gunner said quietly. "It's been a grand ride, but I'm ready to settle." He grinned. "About time for someone my age, eh?"

The two men clinked their beers.

"Sorry to interrupt the bro-fest, but let's get to work." From his inside coat pocket, Liam withdrew a large, white cotton strip of cloth and a small box of makeup. "Lucky for us, it's Halloween season. Every store is carrying rows of monster makeup. Figured we can use this to draw a black eye. The cloth is for a makeshift sling. Might consider slightly limping on one leg when you meet Sullivan, although we don't want to overdo it with the acting."

Richard dubiously eyed the makeup kit. "I'll wear dark sunglasses so he can't see my eyes too closely. Maybe just a purple smudge peeking through the bottom rim."

"Perfect. I've got a small mike for you to wear under your shirt. Damn shame we can't do video, but it's too risky."

"Sullivan doesn't usually say much. Matter of fact, he doesn't even open the envelope in front of me."

"Then you say something short, like *here's my payment from last weekend's game*. See if you can draw him into a conversation. Maybe take off your sunglasses for a second and remark that you've learned never to be late again."

"Gotcha."

"Text me as soon as you get back in your car." Liam turned to Gunner. "And you text me as soon as the enforcer answers your message about meeting him for the money. Arrange for the payment to take place at camp, if you can. Hiding out in one of the tents will be easier for me than if he tries to draw you out to some remote area in the woods."

"Got it, boss."

"I've already reserved a bed for you at the YMCA and lined up a job interview at city hall. They need a good maintenance worker."

Gunner cleared his throat. "I won't let you down, boss."

"I know. Again, I'm offering you my spare bedroom tonight. Just to be safe."

"Take it, Gunner," Harper urged.

"Nah, I'll be fine with the other fellas. We look out for each other. Ain't nobody sneaking up on me."

"If you're sure." Liam didn't like it, but he couldn't force the man into accepting his protection, either.

"I wouldn't mind y'all driving me back to camp, though," Gunner admitted. "These old legs of mine are mighty tired from all that walking tonight."

Richard offered Gunner his hand. "Thanks for helping out. And thanks, Harper, for all you've done, too.

I'm fortunate y'all took the job. Otherwise, I'd have gotten my ass kicked tonight in front of my wife and kids."

"We all got what we wanted, including Liam." Gunner tipped up the beer can and finished it off. "Guess I should be heading on back."

Richard hustled to the kitchen. "Let me pack a to-go box for you." From the fridge, he pulled out sandwich meat and cheese, adding it to a bag where he tossed in chips, bread and canned goods. "Take the beer with you, too," he urged.

"Don't mind if I do," Gunner said with a grin. "We'll all have a grand time tonight at camp."

HARPER OPENED THE door of her house, and she and Liam were greeted with the children's shrieks.

Kimber rushed to the foyer. "How did everything go? Is Richard okay?"

"He's fine. Everything pretty much went according to plan," she assured her.

"*Pretty much?* What's that mean?"

"Like I said, Richard's fine." No point mentioning the enforcer had seen her enter the farmhouse. It would only needlessly worry her friend. Besides, there was nothing to be done about it now. Liam gave her a quick nod; they were in accord on this.

"Guess I'll be on my way," he said, edging toward the door.

Harper regarded him with suspicion. What was his hurry?

Kimber unexpectedly threw her arms around Liam's neck. "Thanks for everything," she said gruffly. "If anyone can help Richard and me, it's you."

"No problem."

"Back in a minute," Harper told Kimber, following

Liam out the door. "You don't have to run off. Why don't you stay for supper?" she asked.

"Got a couple things I need to check up on."

She pursed her lips. "You're going to keep an eye on Gunner tonight, aren't you? I'll go with you. We can take turns sleeping on your stakeout."

"You should stay with Kimber. She needs a friend tonight."

"She's a grown woman. I'm coming with you."

Liam cocked his head at the front window where Kimber's face was pressed against the glass, blue eyes huge with worry. The girls had joined her, their faces taut. "Grown or not, deserving or not, she needs you. So do her kids."

Harper sighed and threw up her hands. "If you're sure. I'll be glad when this is all over tomorrow. Whoever's behind this crime ring has to be the one responsible for shooting and chasing us."

"Exactly." Evidently mindful of their audience, Liam only gave her a reassuring hug before heading to his vehicle.

Back inside, Kimber had flopped into a chair and dropped her head in her hands. If Harper was tired, then Kimber was a total wreck. Judging from her swollen, red eyes, Kimber had been crying for hours.

"Girls, why don't you go upstairs a few minutes while I talk to your mom?"

Kimber straightened and pasted on a weary smile for them. "Go on and take a bath and get in your pajamas. I'll help you in a few minutes."

The girls left, albeit reluctantly.

"Richard hasn't contacted me," Kimber said, her voice rough. "We could go back tonight, but if he wanted us, he'd have called by now."

"He's probably scared to—or ashamed. Y'all didn't part on the best of terms. And he does want you to be absolutely safe here."

"But he should call me. I'm not the one who got us into this mess."

"This mess isn't one hundred percent his fault, is it?" she asked gently. "Surely, you two can work it out."

"I'll admit I've spent way too much money over the years, but the majority of this *is* Richard's fault. I thought when he finally agreed to counseling that we'd turned the corner, only to discover that he's lied to me yet again."

"It's your marriage. You know best." Who was she to offer advice or to judge?

Kimber nodded and blinked back tears. "I don't deserve your kindness. I'm truly sorry. It was horrible of me to try and scare you off with those noises."

"For the last time, apology accepted."

"Can you really forgive me?"

"Yes." And it was true. The trust had been broken and she'd probably never feel quite the same about her old friend, but Harper was willing to let bygones be bygones.

The doorbell rang, and Kimber's hand flew to her chest in alarm. It was as though she expected any second for someone to burst through the door and harm either her or her kids.

"Relax, I'll get the door. It's probably the pizza I ordered." Harper opened the door and stared in surprise. "Richard?"

A chair scraped in the kitchen, and a set of squeals erupted in the den. "Daddy! Daddy!" the girls cried as they ran to the door. They threw themselves against him as Kimber watched with widened eyes.

Richard stepped through the door and faced Kimber. "Are you ready to come home?"

Kimber looked ready to put up a fight, but instead, she ran to her husband and hugged him, the girls at their side.

Harper felt her own eyes moisten. This family was going to be okay, she just knew it. Silently, she retreated from the foyer to give them privacy.

Minutes later, a sheepish but much happier Kimber and Richard entered the kitchen, arms around each other's waists.

"I'm taking my girls home," Richard said, a grateful gleam in his eyes. "Thank you for letting them stay with you. We owe you."

"Glad to do it. You're welcome to stay for dinner. I ordered two large pizzas."

Richard pulled out a twenty-dollar bill and pressed it into her palm. "Thanks, but we want to get home. You understand."

Eagerly, the girls bounded to their rooms to pack their things. In record time, the family left, and she was alone once more. But at least now she could join Liam at his stakeout.

She headed up the stairs to change into dry jeans and socks, but stopped midway, blinking in surprise at the metallic glint on one of the steps. Slowly, she bent down and picked it up.

Another jack.

She turned it over in her hand, tamping down a frisson of fear. *Must have missed it earlier*, she reasoned. Yet both she and Liam had examined the staircase more than once to see if they could find the two missing jacks. *Stop. Just stop.* They'd simply overlooked the tiny object.

Harper pocketed the jack, quickly changed clothes in her room and headed back into the night to find Liam.

At the railroad camp, his car headlights were on bright,

illuminating the dark in all directions. What kind of quiet stakeout was this? Something was very wrong here.

Harper parked next to him, jumped out of her car and ran. "What's happened? Are you—"

Liam approached, his arms raised. "Don't come any closer. You don't want to see."

His warning came too late. She peered around him and spotted Gunner, facedown on the ground, blood seeping through his shirt.

Chapter Fifteen

Once again, Harper found herself back in the chilly, sterile atmosphere of the Tidewater Community Hospital. Inside the generic visitor waiting room with its plastic cushioned chairs, stale coffee and dog-eared magazines, she and Liam were the lone occupants. Did anyone even remember they were here awaiting news from the surgeon?

She pushed open the door and stared up and down the empty hallways. After the frenzy of the emergency room, the surgical waiting area had the silence of a morgue. Where was that doctor? What was taking so long?

Liam pushed past her and paced the halls, glaring every ten seconds at the closed doors leading to the operating room. She leaned in the doorway watching him as images of Gunner's battered, bloody body replayed in her mind like a series of snapshots—Gunner sprawled facedown in the dirt, his cotton T-shirt shredded with slash marks, his fingers clawing into the ground, the smashed cell phone by his side. Liam had bagged a few gum wrappers for the forensics team, which arrived at the camp in short order.

Worse was what *wasn't* at the scene—not a single man remained. Apparently, they'd each packed up their meager belongings and hopped a train car out of town.

All that remained of the camp was a pile of burned wood and empty food containers.

How could they leave their friend like this? Unless they'd been terrified and believed Gunner already dead. It had been a near thing. It was a wonder, given his age, that he'd survived such a brutal attack.

If Liam hadn't checked on Gunner, the man would have had no chance of recovery. But Harper could tell from Liam's haunted eyes that he blamed himself. She went to him and slid an arm around his waist. "Gunner's getting the best care possible," she said softly. "He's a tough ole guy. My money's on him to make it."

"This is all my fault. I never should have left him alone." Liam's voice was raspy, and he ran a hand through his cropped hair.

"Don't do this to yourself. You tried to get him to stay. He didn't want to."

"The enforcer realized Gunner was an informant playing a dangerous game. And I'm the one who put Gunner in that position."

"You were trying to get to the bottom of the corruption here in Baysville. Self-recrimination accomplishes nothing."

He let out a frustrated sigh. "You're right. This attack only makes me more determined to bring in the state police ASAP and get answers. First thing in the morning, I'm confronting Bryce."

"Bryce?" A ripple of surprise shot through Harper. She released her arm from Liam's back and stepped in front of him. "Confront Bryce about what?"

"He can't be blind to what's going on in his own town. I'm ready to lay my cards on the table and see what he's got to say about everything."

"I hope you're wrong." Bryce had a cocky attitude, but

she remembered the sweet boy Presley once tutored, and now she knew her sister had had a relationship with him.

"Actually, so do I. But if he's in on it, I'll try to break him down."

"Or Mitchell Sullivan," she reminded him. "Still can't get over that one."

"We owe that bit of the puzzle to Richard Collins. And at least now we know why the homeless men were killed. Their deaths are directly tied to the gambling and prostitution rings."

Harper stared at the closed doors down the hallway. "I want the name of the man who stabbed Gunner."

"Cowardly bastard, attacking an old man from behind. It perfectly fits the pattern of the other homeless deaths with those stab wounds in the back torso."

Her skin crawled to think of it.

"Of course, this investigation will be much easier *if* Gunner lives and *if* he can describe the attacker."

The operating room doors swung open, and a man in surgical scrubs strode forward. "You're the cops awaiting news on my patient?"

Harper didn't bother to correct his assumption they were both cops. She wanted to be with Liam when he got the news on Gunner's condition. She tried to assess the doctor's demeanor for a clue, but he merely looked professional and courteous.

"Did Gunner make it through surgery?" Liam asked.

The doctor nodded reassuringly. "With flying colors. His right lung was nicked, but we cleaned out the fluid buildup and inserted a tube to drain any residue. Also performed a blood transfusion to replace the lost blood, and then a mass of stitches to close the stab wounds. Despite his age, he's in stable condition and the prognosis of recovery is excellent, provided he doesn't develop pneumonia."

The heaviness in her chest lifted, and she let out a deep breath. "When can we see him?"

"He's being wheeled into recovery now. Normally, we don't allow visitors until later. Y'all need to ask him about the attacker?"

"Yes. Police business."

The doctor motioned for them to follow him. "This way."

They strode through two sets of double doors, down a corridor and then into a room filled with white gowns, hairnets, masks and slippers.

"He should be rousing from the anesthesia any moment. Ask your questions and then leave. My patient needs his rest."

The doctor led them to a room of curtained cubicles and pushed open one of the curtains. "In here."

Gunner looked as frail as Harper had ever seen him. His eyes were shut and his face was as pale as the white cotton bedsheets. An IV was attached to one arm, and he was hooked up to several monitors. They watched the rise and fall of his chest, loath to wake him from much-needed rest.

"Gunner?" Liam whispered. If Gunner didn't rouse easily, Liam would wait until he woke and was placed in a regular room. These killings had taken place over a decade. What difference did a couple more hours make?

Liam cleared his throat. "You doing okay, buddy?"

Gunner frowned, and his forehead creased in wrinkles. "Wh-what?"

"It's me. Liam. Harper's here, too." He stepped next to the bed and rested a hand on Gunner's thin forearm.

"You gave us quite a scare. But the doctor says you're going to be fine."

Gunner gazed blankly at them and then at the IV needle in his arm. Harper laid a hand over his trembling fingers, offering quiet reassurance as Liam questioned him.

"You were hurt last night, and now you're in the hospital. Do you remember what happened?"

Awareness dawned in his wide, frightened eyes. "So much pain," he murmured hoarsely.

"I'm sorry. But I need to know. Did you see who did this to you?"

Gunner licked his lips. "Just for a sec. Don't know him."

She and Liam exchanged a quick glance over Gunner's prone body. So the attacker wasn't the enforcer who had originally contracted Gunner to go after Richard.

Gunner struggled to rise and then sank farther into the bed. "The other fellas? Are they…?"

"They're fine," Liam reassured him. "You were the only one attacked. Tell me what you remember."

"We'd all finished supper. It was dark. A text came, saying, 'Got your money. Meet me behind your tent.'" Gunner stopped and drew a couple of deep breaths.

"You're doing good. Just a few more questions. What happened when you met him?"

"Someone grabbed me from behind. And then…pain."

"Did he say anything?"

"No."

"Any idea how tall he was, or did he have a tattoo… anything?"

"Beefy guy. Not fat. And not young, either. Gray in his hair."

The description wasn't much help. It could be almost any man over the age of forty. "Okay, then. Rest up and

I'll check back in with you later. When you're better, maybe you can give us more details and look through some mug shots."

She gave his hand a gentle squeeze, and they walked away from the bed. Harper was about to close the curtain when Gunner spoke again.

"Don't you do it."

Liam's forehead creased. "Meaning?"

"This isn't your fault."

Liam inhaled sharply. "You'll never again spend another night out in the cold and in danger. I promise you that."

THE DRIVE HOME was silent and tense. He pulled into her driveway, and she turned to him, wanting to offer comfort. "The worst is over. He's going to be okay, Liam."

"Yeah. No thanks to me." He gave a mirthless laugh, the heaviness of recrimination obvious.

"Don't. You can't protect everyone all the time. It's not your fault."

"Exactly what he said. Which only makes me feel worse."

"Come on inside and let's talk."

"No. You go on to bed. I'm dead tired."

"Then come in and sleep with me." The words slipped out of her mouth before she had a chance to think through the implications. And by *sleep* she meant *make love*. But it felt *right*. She longed to run her hands through his hair and kiss away the sadness. She wanted to become one with him, to experience him in every sense.

She loved Liam.

The knowledge burst onto her consciousness, full-blown and irrefutable. She wouldn't tell him the words tonight—she wanted her declaration unhampered with the tragedy of the stabbing. But she could show him love with her touch…with her body.

"Please say you'll come," she urged again.

His hesitation stretched on, but at last he got out, slamming the truck door shut. As they walked to the porch, she could see the exhaustion pouring from his lackluster eyes, unsmiling face and slow gait.

Harper sensed a certain guard from him, as if he were deliberately erecting a barrier. She'd never fallen for a cop before. Not even close. Liam seemed unable to divorce his feelings from his job tonight. Which was completely understandable. His compassion was one of the reasons she loved him. If she wanted to be a part of his life—and she did—then she needed to accept this was part and parcel of Liam. But how best to help him?

In the foyer, she leaned against him, resting her head on his broad chest. "Gunner's lucky to have you in his corner."

"Lucky?" He snorted and took a step back. "That's not the word I'd use."

"Want to talk about it?"

"There's nothing else to say. Probably best I go on home. I don't want you dragged further into this."

He was pushing her away. "I wish you'd stay," she said quietly.

"Why? I wouldn't be good company tonight."

"No problem. You don't have to be. I only want to be with you."

For the first time this evening, Liam's face softened, and he reached for her, pulling her back against his chest. His arms wrapped around her, and he stroked her back in long, firm caresses that left her craving more. Her skin tingled at the warm strength of his body through the thin cotton fabric of her shirt.

This.

This was where she was meant to be—in his arms. She cradled the sides of his face in her palms, feeling the abrasive scruff along his jaw. So masculine, so sexy. His mouth found hers, and the world faded to black as their lips and tongues danced. Heat bubbled in her veins, and she couldn't get close enough. She untucked his uniform shirt and ran her hands up his bare back. Muscles rippled beneath her fingertips, and his breath became jagged. Growing bolder, Harper moved her hands over his chest and then lowered them to trace his sculpted abs.

Liam stilled and pulled back a few inches, nailing her with the intensity of his smoky gray eyes. "Are you sure about this?" he asked, his voice ragged and deep.

Harper knew exactly what he was asking—and what she was offering.

In answer, she rose and held out her hand. "I've never been more sure of anything in my life."

Chapter Sixteen

Liam quietly entered Bryce's office, where his boss was engrossed in reading a file that lay on his desk. With a flick of his wrist, Liam forcefully shut the door. Bryce looked up, startled.

"What's the meaning of this, Andrews?" he asked with a scowl. "I'm busy."

"I think you'll want to hear this."

"Make it quick. I'm buried in paperwork."

"Maybe you should spend more time in the field and less time in the office if you really want to do your job effectively."

Bryce slammed the file closed. "This is *my* office, and *I'm* the chief. You'd do well to remember that. But now that you're here, answer this. What in the hell were you thinking arresting Mitchell Sullivan?"

"He collects money generated from a huge, illegal gambling ring that's been operating right under your nose for years."

"Mitchell?" Bryce scoffed. "I find it hard to believe that a man of his stature, a pharmacist, no less, would get involved in some penny-ante poker games."

"Make no mistake. This is no small-time ring. It generates thousands of dollars of income. It's even expanded into a profitable side business involving prostitution."

Bryce crossed his arms and leaned back in his chair.

"But I don't have to tell you all this, do I? You know what's going on."

"Why should I believe anything you say? You've been lying to me since the day you came in this office for a job interview. Should have trusted my instincts not to hire you."

His secret was out. Liam lifted his chin. "You call it lying, I call it doing my job."

Bryce's face flushed with anger, and he stood, glaring. "Why did you come to Baysville in the first place?"

He countered with a question of his own. "How did you find out I was working undercover?"

"Dad has lots of connections after decades working as an arson investigator. He'd worked with law enforcement agencies on a number of cases. One of his old buddies in Richmond ratted you out."

Liam made a mental note to bring Carlton Fairfax in later for questioning. "How long have you known?"

"Almost from the beginning."

No wonder his boss seemed to have taken an instant dislike to him. And no surprise Bryce was always trying to usurp his authority. His turf had been threatened.

"Why haven't you confronted me with that info before now?" Liam asked curiously.

"What's that old saying—keep your friends close but your enemies closer?"

"I'm not your enemy. We should both want the same thing. A town free of organized crime."

"Of course, that's what I want, too." Bryce sat back down. "Damn it, Andrews, why do you think I took this job?"

"Ego? You wanted to prove to your dad that you could run this place like he used to run the fire department?"

It'd been clear to him from the start that Bryce appeared to have an odd relationship with his father. The old man was always around, offering advice. It was as though he regretted ever retiring and wanted to continue running what he could behind the scenes.

A tiny muscle worked in Bryce's jaw, and the pencil in his hand snapped in two. The sound detonated like a firecracker. A stunned silence followed.

"Looks like I hit a nerve," Liam remarked drily.

"What's all this crap about organized crime? I assumed you were sent because you state guys found it suspicious we hadn't solved the homeless murder cases."

"It's what caught our eye at first," he admitted. Liam debated whether to say more, but he decided a friendly talk with Fairfax might elicit more info. The full heat of his division would be bearing down on Baysville by this evening or early morning at the latest. And he wanted to be the first to interview the chief, tap him out and observe his reaction to the pressure. "The murders are our top priority. But now I'm convinced the murders and gambling and prostitution are all related."

The angry flush on Bryce's face melted, replaced by a sheet of pasty white.

"You don't like my theory?" Liam pressed.

"I don't see any possible connection between the two crimes."

"Whoever the ringleader is, he's been hiring the homeless over the years to enforce people to pay their debts."

Light dawned in his boss's eyes. "And you think he later killed the men he'd hired to ensure their silence."

"In his eyes, they're an expendable commodity. Use them for a bit, then when they've seen too much or start asking questions, it's time to kill. After all, they're the perfect victims. Nobody reports them missing or brings public pressure to solve the case. Sometimes the victims aren't even identified."

"That's a lot of theorizing on your part. Where's the evidence?"

"Why should I show my entire hand to you?" The irony of using a poker analogy wasn't lost on Liam, but he plowed on. "Start talking. Prove to me why I should trust you."

"I'm not going to defend myself from your outrageous insinuations."

"Outrageous? Explain your reasoning."

"The murders have been spaced out over the years. And all the victims are transients. You know as well as I do that these people have a high rate of drug and alcohol abuse and mental illness problems. Those issues lead to violence. They're constantly vulnerable to becoming crime victims."

He thought of his uncle Teddy. "Doesn't mean their lives matter any less."

"I'm not saying that."

"Really? Because it's our observation that this department hasn't been aggressive in their investigations. I came to find out why."

"Not true. I've done all I can to solve the murders."

"Have you?"

Bryce slammed a fist on his desk. "How dare you. You feds think we have unlimited personnel to chase down clues? I do the best I can with the Baysville budget."

"Not good enough."

"Are you accusing me of incompetence—or something even worse?" Bryce pulled a stick of gum out of his pocket, popped a wad in his mouth and began chewing furiously.

Liam's gaze affixed on the crimson and white stripes

of the discarded wrapper, and then his eyes slowly traveled up to meet Bryce's dark eyes.

"What?" Bryce asked, bewildered.

Liam grabbed the wrapper and studied it more closely, then held it to his nose. The scent of cloves was pungent. Yes, this was it. A perfect match.

"I found wrappers just like this near Gunner's body," he said softly.

"So?"

"So I collected them as evidence, and it's been sent to the forensics lab in Richmond."

"You won't find my prints on them. Anyone could have dropped those wrappers at any time. Not like I'm the only one who buys this particular gum."

"It's a bit unusual. An old-fashioned brand. I haven't seen them in the stores much since I was a kid. And you always seem to be nearby when there's trouble."

Bryce's expression set into defensive stubbornness. "I'm not a murderer."

"But you know who he is, don't you, Bryce?"

His mouth worked the gum as he chose his words. "I've had suspicions over the years. Nothing I can prove."

"It's a cop, isn't it? Come clean. You protect a dirty cop and you'll only go down with him." His gut clenched as he recalled finding Gunner near dead, blood seeping out and darkening the back of his shirt. Liam couldn't even imagine the pain and suffering resulting from the multiple stab wounds. He'd vowed to protect Gunner and the other homeless men from sick predators. It was the least he could do after failing so abysmally last night. "I promise I'll make you pay if you could have prevented these attacks and did nothing," he threatened.

"I'm not defending a dirty cop. I interviewed Mitchell Sullivan extensively yesterday, and he denied all accusations. Apparently, he owns a home-remodeling company on the side and Richard Collins was paying him cash for an overdue bill."

"Did you ask to look at his accounting books?"

"Of course. He said he'd have his attorney provide that."

"He's lying. We'll crack him when the full force of the agency bears down on him."

"Good."

Liam eyed Bryce curiously. "I thought Richard Collins was your friend. You believe Sullivan over Collins?"

Bryce shifted his gaze to the window and steepled his fingers. Liam waited for his answer, sensing that the man was wrestling with a hard decision.

"Sometimes," he finally said, his voice heavy, "it's hard to know who to believe. Who to trust."

Liam sensed an opening. Bryce was struggling with something, and if Liam played his cards right, he'd find out what it was and how it connected to the activities he was investigating.

"We started on the wrong foot with each other, Bryce. What do you say we work together to bring down these criminals? Just tell me what's troubling you. I promise to listen and not make any judgments until all the facts are in. You'll find I'm a fair man."

Bryce nodded, but continued to face the window, as if expecting a miraculous solution to his dilemma.

"You know something, don't you?" he prodded.

"It's all suspicions. Nothing concrete."

"Listen. Wouldn't you rather talk to me than the suits who will be descending later from Richmond? Gunner will be shown photos of every cop on this force. If he recognizes one of them as his attacker, all hell is going to break loose in your department. At a minimum, you'll be fired and lucky to find any kind of security job in the future."

"To hell with that. My problem's a lot stickier than a damn job."

"Spill it."

Bryce scrubbed his face and then nodded slowly. He swallowed and looked down, and for a moment, Liam wondered if the man was about to cry. His eyes glistened as he spoke. "If there really is a hotbed of illegal activity connected to the homeless murders, then you're looking in the wrong place."

"I know your knee-jerk reaction is to protect your fellow—"

"The culprit isn't on the force."

"Then—"

"You need to be looking at an ex-firefighter."

Ex-? His mind spun as though he were on a high-speed carnival ride. His thoughts slowed and oddly settled on the image of one man. "You're not saying—"

"My father."

Carlton Fairfax.

Was Bryce low enough to deflect suspicion on his own father just to throw the heat off himself? Even as he pondered the question, Liam instinctively felt Bryce spoke the truth.

Bryce abruptly stood and paced the small room. "I hope to God I'm wrong."

Liam switched tactics and spoke in a reasonable, sympathetic manner. "Lay out your suspicions and we'll figure it out together."

"It started when I was in high school. Senior year, to be exact. Life was good back then. Uncomplicated. I was dating Julie, now my wife, and had received a scholarship offer to play football at Alabama. The only blip on the screen was my poor grades in math. But with his usual determination, Dad arranged to solve that problem. My future was set."

Bryce ran a hand through his hair and stood by the window, evidently contemplating his next words. "Then everything changed. I met Presley."

At the mention of Harper's sister, a knot of concern balled in his gut. "Your math tutor, I remember. Go on."

"Presley was…how do I describe her? She was unlike Julie or any other girl I ever dated. Genius-level smart. Very shy, but in a charming kind of way." A sad smile ghosted across his face. "Of course, I was determined to break down that studious wall of reserve."

"And so, you did." Liam paused before continuing, as he realized the implications of what he was learning. "You're the mystery father Harper's been trying to find."

Bryce returned to his seat. "It was a shock when she came to me with the news. Damn, I was so stupid. And careless."

Liam studied him objectively, sensitive to every nuance in Bryce's body language and voice. "Did the news anger you? So angry that you murdered Presley?"

"No. Never." He vehemently shook his head. "I would never have hurt Presley. She was adamant that she wanted to have the baby. At first, I tried to talk her out of it. I told my dad what had happened, and he exploded. Said giving up my scholarship was sacrificing my future. He had this grand delusion I could make it as a pro quarterback. Truth is, I never even enjoyed football all that much. A pro career was his dream, not mine.

"Anyway, we met that night—the night she died. After I'd had a day to absorb the news, I came over to talk with her and make plans."

"Where did you meet her? What did you tell Presley that night?"

"It was bitter cold, so we met at her house." A sheepish look flashed in his eyes. "Her mom was a little hard of hearing, which helped us from being discovered. Usually, she'd sneak out and meet me around the block, where I'd be waiting in my car. But this time, as arranged, Presley left the back door unlocked for me. When I came, she was there waiting, and we quietly slipped down to the basement. We were two scared kids, sitting on the rough, unfinished stairs, whispering in the semidarkness about what we were going to do. She hadn't even told her mom yet, because she was afraid of disappointing her."

Bryce's face was haggard, steeped in that long-ago memory. "But at least, for that one night, I did the right thing. I offered to forgo college and start working and paying child support as best I could."

Not that it mattered, but Liam was curious. "And how did Presley respond?"

"She was happy. Grateful. Promised that we'd figure it all out." He let out a long sigh. "At least I have that memory."

"And when you left—she was alive?"

"Yes."

"What do you think happened?"

"Can't say I'm one hundred percent sure. Or maybe I've pushed the truth way down deep inside. I wanted to believe that it was just an accident. She fell, hit her head and lost consciousness. The food she'd been heating on the stove caught fire. People die from freak accidents every day. Even sixteen-year-old pregnant girls."

"When did you realize it was no accident?" Liam asked softly.

"The very next day, when we heard the news of her

death, Dad actually smiled. *Smiled!* It chilled me, you know? I couldn't help remembering his rant when I'd confessed about the pregnancy less than twenty hours earlier. He'd claimed Presley was deliberately ruining my life. That I should talk her into getting an abortion. When I said I wouldn't do that, he'd grown livid and stalked away. I figured he'd cool down and over time he'd accept the situation."

He'd seen and heard plenty of chilling crimes, but this murder motive was pretty horrific. "You believe your own father killed Presley and his unborn grandchild? All for your football scholarship?"

"It's what that scholarship represented to him—a way to fame and fortune." A bitter laugh escaped Bryce. "Imagine his disappointment when I went to college and ended up sitting on the bench for two years. I finally quit and came home."

"Did he ever admit killing Presley?"

"Not directly. And I was too afraid to ask him straight up. Even if he'd confessed, what would I have done with that knowledge? I was young and he was a respected firefighter—captain of the department, no less. The man responsible for investigating possible arson. The one reporters interviewed and who publicly swore it was an accident. Who'd have believed me?" He paused, overcome with emotion. "And you know what? Part of me wanted to think it couldn't be true, that he couldn't have done it. He was my father. And to imagine him doing that…"

Liam could feel for the difficult position Bryce had found himself in. Tough for anyone, let alone someone so young. Carlton sounded like a bully, a man who controlled his family by intimidation. But it didn't necessarily mean he was a murderer. Perhaps he only wanted, in some twisted logic, for his son to believe he had the power to rule every aspect of his life. He had to ask.

"What do you mean by *not directly*? Did your father hint that he'd done this?"

"For years, it was this ugly, unspoken thing between us. I hoped—I tried—to believe my suspicions were ungrounded. But over the years, I became slowly aware that this gambling and prostitution ring existed. Even had a couple men tell me that Dad ran it. I finally confronted him."

Bryce stopped his tale and briefly closed his eyes. Liam leaned forward, eager to hear the rest. "What did he say?"

Bryce opened his eyes—twin pools of helplessness that fixed on Liam. "He laughed. Can you believe it? I threatened him with arrest, and that's when it all crashed down around me. He said that if I did, he'd ruin me. Dad turned on me, his own son. The former police chief, his best friend, had shown him Presley's autopsy report. Dad secretly made a copy of it and threatened to release the report revealing that Presley was pregnant at the time of her death. He'd claim that I long ago confessed to murdering her in a fit of rage. That he—a loving father—had protected me from my crime. But that now he'd had a change of heart and could no longer live with his guilty conscience. He wanted to come clean and expose my murderous crime of passion."

What a piece of work. Liam let out a low whistle. And here he'd imagined father and son were unusually close, when actually the lunches together and Carlton's presence around the office were nothing more than a form of intimidation.

"What you've told me is still not a confession of murder, though. But we can arrest your father on the gambling charges and try to wrangle a murder confession—or several murder confessions, in fact. As I said, I believe the homeless men were killed to cover up the organized crime."

Bryce covered his face with his hands and groaned. "Dad's out of control."

As sympathetic as Liam felt for his former boss, there was work to be done. And if Bryce wanted to right the many wrongs he'd allowed to occur in the town he'd sworn to protect, then it was time to act.

"You have to make a choice, Bryce. Today. Right now. We're closing in. Are you going to help us or are you going to keep being intimidated by your father?"

Bryce sat up straight and gave a curt nod. "Where do we start?"

"Before we confront your dad, let's line up all the evidence against him. First, we'll go together to interview Gunner in the hospital and take along photos of every cop on this force, along with your dad's photo. Hopefully, he can identify his attacker. Then we'll try and force Sullivan to admit guilt and name names when faced with evidence."

Officer Combs popped his head in the door. "Hey, boss. Your dad's here for lunch."

"Tell him I'm tied up today."

Combs nodded and left.

Bryce set his shoulders back. "I'm ready. Let's do this."

Chapter Seventeen

The hot spray of water, combined with the rose-scented body wash, felt rejuvenating. Or maybe it was merely the glowing aftermath of last night's lovemaking with Liam. Today, life seemed full of possibilities. Harper could resurrect her dad's dreams of turning this old place into a B&B and hire a manager to oversee the operation. She could even sell her firm in Atlanta and reopen a new interior design firm right here in Baysville. There might not be the same pool of potential clients as Atlanta, but living expenses were cheaper here than in the big city. She could get by quite nicely with a smaller number of clientele.

Doubts suddenly assailed her. How would Liam react to all this? He might not be another commitment-phobe like Doug, but he might view her plans as being too much, too soon. But the truth was, she didn't want to live in limbo indefinitely.

And what happened once Liam wrapped up his investigation in Baysville? Nothing tied him to this town. Richmond was his base of operations. Could she handle moving from town to town while he worked various investigations? Worse, could she live knowing that every day held the possibility he might get shot? What kind of life was she contemplating?

She turned off the water, wringing her hair dry. She'd handle this one day at a time. Keep exploring her options. Have a talk with Liam.

That decided, she dressed quickly and then turned on her computer and investigated everything involved in opening a new business.

Ding. A new email notification. Her eyes scanned the list and noticed a new email that had no subject line. Probably junk the spam filter missed. She clicked on it. It was again sent from loser@life, but this time it contained no message. *Who sends blank emails?* Had to be a computer glitch of some kind. Yet her stomach cartwheeled as she remembered the earlier email warning her to get out of the house. Dismissively, she turned away from the computer and resolved to push the unsettling nonmessage aside.

She arose, stretched and faced the large four-poster bed with the rumpled bedsheets. Her thighs tightened as she remembered the things she and Liam had done there last night. He'd been a passionate, attentive lover, and it had been every bit as good as she'd imagined. Better, actually.

The best ever, in fact.

With a satisfied grin, she flung back the comforter and straightened the sheets. She ran a hand down the smooth cotton. Her fingers hit a small, sharp object between the fitted and flat sheets. An earring, perhaps? Harper turned down the top sheet and stared, bewildered at the lone jack.

And that makes ten. The last missing jack.

It hadn't been there last night. Surely one of them would have noticed if it had. No one else had been in the house today. Liam had left early for work, and she'd fixed breakfast, done a little housecleaning, then hit the shower.

And yet…there it was.

A harmless trinket from a child's game.

Harper rubbed the chill bumps on her arm, trying to convince herself it meant nothing. She backed away from the bed. Should she call Liam? And tell him what…she'd found a jack that was out of place? Even she smelled the whiff of crazy on that one. And she'd been taunted for years by schoolchildren calling her nuts…not going there again.

She wasn't ever going to permanently live in this house. B&B or not. Irrational or not. One decision down, many more to go.

Harper shoved into her sneakers getting ready to head downstairs, wanting to be near an exit door…just in case. She berated her unease, even while taking measures to protect herself.

Ding.

Not again. She opened the second message from loser@life.

He'll be coming for YOU next.

Her breath hitched, and her heart pummeled against her ribs. Next? The implication was clear—someone had been after Presley.

Harper turned off the computer and went downstairs. Everything in the kitchen was as she'd left it earlier. Purse on the table, car keys lying beside it. The familiarity of everything in its proper place comforted her, but not enough to want to spend the day alone in the house. She'd escape to the friendly confines of the public library for more research on opening a new business.

The phone rang, and she jumped. An unknown number. She answered it.

"Have you talked to Andrews yet?" Allen didn't even bother giving his name before launching into his rude demand.

"Good morning to you, too. And yes, I talked to him."

"Is he going to help me?"

"That's his call, not mine."

"I promise I've changed."

What a loser. "Leave me alone, Allen. I'm busy."

"No need to be rude," he complained with a whine. "I'll let you get back to work or whatever you were doing."

Harper cut him off and began to stuff the phone back in her pocket when she heard it—a sliding, grinding noise from upstairs that pierced the silent house. This couldn't be happening. Her entire house had been swept by the police to remove any bugs.

A thump landed somewhere above her head. A high-pitched wail rang out that was drowned by the roar of blood pounding in her ears. Running footsteps followed, and her eyes involuntarily slid to the stairs.

A pair of white stick legs appeared and—God help her, she didn't want to see more—but her traitorous gaze continued its upward trajectory, feet rooted to the floor. A thin creature stood dressed in dirty rags that hung loosely on a frame that could have been a child's or a man's or… something else altogether.

And then she faced him.

It.

The thing of her nightmares.

The thing that had hovered over Presley's broken body.

It possessed large black eyes set in an emaciated face with sunken cheekbones. Dirt smudged its white cheeks, and the hair was thin, partly balding and hung in greasy shoulder-length clumps, the ends as ragged as if shorn by a pair of child's scissors.

The smell hit her senses next. Putrid. *That explains the mysterious odors*, she thought hysterically. It was coming for her. Just like it had for her sister.

"Get out! He's coming!" it yelled.

What did that mean? Was he talking about himself in third person? She didn't aim to find out. Her body caught up with her mind's urgent scream of *danger*, and Harper raced to the foyer on shaky legs.

A pounding erupted from behind the front door. A knock that reverberated in every cell of her brain.

"Don't open that door!" it—he—yelled. The thing—the man—was closer now, at least halfway down the stairs.

Like hell she wasn't opening the door. Harper snatched it open, gulping air. She blinked at the person standing before here. "Captain Fairfax?" He was retired, but everyone still addressed him by his old title.

She couldn't have asked for a more welcome sight, unless it had been Liam—rather, that's what her mind tried to insist. But her fear only grew.

Be logical. This was the man who'd patiently investigated the fire. The first on the scene that night to save her and Mom all those years ago.

Trouble was, Harper had never cared for him. Not then, not now. Especially not coming so close on the heels of the warning still ringing in her ears.

"Who else is here?" Fairfax asked in his booming voice. "Thought I heard a scream."

She glanced behind her, but the man had disappeared. It was the past happening all over again. Except this time, it was early morning instead of late night. Which somehow made it all the more terrifying.

Yet, a calm, still voice inside her warned, *don't let this man in the house.* So what if he found her mentally unstable for an irrational refusal to invite him in?

"If you'll excuse me, I was on my way out," she lied, making a move to cross the threshold.

Fairfax laid a beefy arm across the space between them, a barricade. His gaze shifted past her shoulder, to the kitchen table where her purse and keys sat in plain view.

"Leaving without your things?" he asked drily.

"Going for a walk," she countered, trying not to show she was flustered.

"We need to talk first."

"Okay, let's sit on the porch." She glanced at the driveway and frowned. "Where's your car?"

"Down the street," he answered evasively. "I had lunch in the neighborhood and thought I'd drop in."

He said it like this was a normal occurrence, as though they were friends who frequently visited.

They were not.

"Where did you eat? The Crab Shack? I love their shrimp tacos." She had this insane idea that if she kept him talking long enough at the door, someone would eventually stroll by and she could call out to them.

"Have you ever had their shrimp steamed in Old Bay seasoning?" she babbled on. "It's the best."

"Not here to discuss food." His mouth set into a determined line, and the yellow flecks in his brown eyes glowed in a feral manner. It made her think of hungry wolves closing in on their prey.

Don't let him sniff out your fear. Harper raised her chin and aimed for an attitude of cool indignation. "Mr. Fairfax," she said in a voice as cold and crisp as celery. "I told you I'm on my way out. Now step aside."

Gauntlet thrown.

He didn't even attempt a show of civility. "No. Get inside."

Abruptly, she ducked and tried to slip under his arm. He gave a mirthless chuckle, lowering his hand and forcing her back inside the house. Frantically, she searched the deserted street. Where was Mrs. Henley when she actually wanted to see her?

"What do you think you're doing?" Harper glared, faking a bravado she did not feel and praying that none of her fear showed through the righteous anger.

"I'm not leaving here until we've had a little talk."

Futile. She wasn't going to get past his tall, stocky frame blocking the exit. Perhaps even worse than that alarming fact was the knowledge that somewhere either behind her or off to the side—the creature lay in wait. *Be smart and focus. One enemy at a time. There must be a way out.*

And just like that, the answer arrived in a flash. Harper pivoted, racing to the back door. Her shins slammed against the kitchen table as she fled, but she barely registered the pain. There was only the roaring in her ears, the sharp, labored breath sawing in and out of her chest, and the overriding, screaming dictate to run. The command flooded her body with adrenaline.

Go, go, go.

If the creature was nearby, she didn't see it. Eyes trained straight ahead, Harper concentrated on the back door near the basement. Next to the door was a large window with a view of the backyard. A black truck was parked close to the screened-in porch. Fairfax's truck? Had he been the one stalking them all along? The sight filled her with more dread. No good reason for him to hide his vehicle from public view. None at all. She tried to banish an image of Carlton Fairfax dragging her into the truck, never to be seen or heard from again.

Or was she being ridiculous? He'd always been an arrogant, powerful kind of man. Perhaps today was only more of the same. Yet she dared not turn her head to see if he was closing the distance between them.

Halfway through the kitchen. Halfway to freedom. Her eyes locked on the prize, the cool brass knob of the back door.

Fairfax's longer, stronger arms caught up to her. He firmly laid hands on her shoulders, forcing her to turn around.

"Mite jumpy, aren't you?" he asked sardonically. "Always were a flighty little girl. Seeing things no one else can see. Hearing noises no one else hears." He gave a wolfish grin. "Oh yes, your mother told me. We talked regularly. She was quite concerned about you for the longest time. Said you trembled at every little creak and groan of this old house as it settled."

Only because she'd learned to keep her mouth shut. That way her mother wouldn't worry so much as she dealt with her grief. That way Harper could try and convince herself that all was well.

She bit her lip to stop the involuntary trembling. "Why do you want to talk to me?" She kept her voice calm and reasonable in order to appease the alarming tension that swirled around them.

"You and your boyfriend have been causing me lots of grief."

"I have no idea what you're talking about," she answered truthfully.

"Going around town, poking your nose in that old case."

"Which case?" she asked, genuinely puzzled. "The homeless murders?"

He waved a hand dismissively. "Nobody cares about those bums. World's better off without 'em."

And this guy used to be captain of the fire department? He had the sensitivity of a gnat. But she was hardly in a position to deliver an ethics lecture. "Then what case are you referring to?" she asked.

"Presley's death."

Her heart skipped a beat. "Why does that bother you?"

And did she really want to know the reason? Suddenly, she wasn't so sure. Not when Fairfax was standing so close, anger roiling off his massive body in waves.

"You don't believe her death was an accident," he stated. "You never did."

They stared at one another, and she felt herself unwilling to look away, mesmerized by the sparkling yellow flecks in his eyes.

"I have no grounds to prove otherwise," she said at last, eyeing him with what she hoped was a reassuring, steady expression.

Fairfax studied her for several moments and then shook his head. "Heard that you've stuck around Baysville this time for answers. You're determined to find out the truth."

With a casual violence that caught her off guard, he clamped a heavy hand on her elbow and pulled her.

"Hey, what are you doing?" she protested, struggling to escape his grasp. "Stop it."

He didn't even bother glancing her way as he strolled a few steps to the window and pulled the curtains closed.

The sunlight blocked, she trembled in the semidarkness. He faced her, his hot breath washing over her face. It smelled like a musky, holiday spice she couldn't quite name. Her own breath was rapid and shallow—loud in the lull that lay thickly between them. Somewhere in the darkness, the unknown shadow dweller also breathed—silent, but watching. Always watching.

"And now we talk," Fairfax insisted. His fingers dug deeper into her elbow, hard and bruising.

Cloves, she suddenly realized. That was the spice she couldn't name. As if that mattered a whit. Perspiration dampened under her arms and her mind raced in a fever of foreboding. "Why are you doing this?" she whispered.

LIAM WAS RELIEVED to note that Gunner looked much stronger today. He sat up in the hospital bed, chowing down on roast beef and mashed potatoes. At Liam and Bryce's entrance, he swiped a napkin across his mouth and then grinned.

"They sure are feeding me mighty fine food here," he said heartily. "Three hot squares a day. And anytime I want more tea or juice they bring it right to me. Can't beat that service."

"Never known anyone to rave about hospital food," Liam remarked drily.

"And this bed's so comfortable. They've already changed the sheets, and I only been here one night."

He and Bryce shared a brief, amused glance. Liam nodded in Bryce's direction. "You've met Chief Fairfax before, haven't you?"

"Yes, sir." The happiness in his eyes dimmed a bit. Liam didn't blame him. Bryce had always acted condescending to the men at camp.

"Sorry to hear of your attack," Bryce said, extending a hand. "I'm here to make a report. We'll do everything we can to find the culprit."

A bemused Gunner shook Bryce's extended hand. "Thanks for coming out, Chief."

Bryce opened a file stuffed with papers. "Officer Andrews has filled me in on everything that's happened, including the arrangement you made to be an informant. Based on that, we've compiled mug shots of men we suspect may have been your attacker. Can you look through them and see if you recognize anyone?"

"Glad to." Gunner placed the file in his lap and riffled through the papers, brow furrowed as he concentrated on each photo.

Liam practically held his breath. Were their suspicions about Carlton Fairfax unfounded? What if he'd hired someone else to kill Gunner?

Gunner frowned and shook his head until he came to near the end of the stack. He pointed a long, skinny finger on the page. "That's him."

Liam directed his gaze downward and nodded in satisfaction at Carlton Fairfax's unsmiling mug.

Bryce wasn't as satisfied. He frowned at Gunner. "You're sure? Not a sliver of doubt in your mind? It was nighttime, after all, and your visibility was limited."

"That's him," Gunner said emphatically. "No doubt at all. Neck thick as a linebacker and dark eyes with them weird light flecks in 'em."

"Very well, then." Bryce's face was as grim and resigned as Liam had ever witnessed. "I'll send Officer Denton to come take your formal statement."

"Hey, you know the guy?" Gunner asked.

Bryce collected the file and stuffed it under his arm. "Meet you in the hallway," he mumbled to Liam.

"What's wrong with him?" Gunner asked, gesturing at Bryce's retreating back.

Liam shrugged and changed the subject. "Doctors say anything about releasing you yet?"

"Later this afternoon." Gunner looked crestfallen. "Wish they'd let me stay a few more nights. I like it here."

Which showed how abysmal Gunner's homeless status had become in his old age.

"Don't worry. You can crash at my place for a week or so. Until you're healthy again."

"I don't want to put you to no trouble."

He'd put Gunner in mortal danger, almost gotten him killed, and the guy was worried about inconveniencing him by temporarily staying in a spare bedroom. "No trouble," he answered gruffly. "I've got to run. Check on you later."

In the hallway, Bryce waited, arms folded against his chest, his expression stern. "Let's do this. We have enough to make an arrest."

"You don't have to be part of it," Liam said. "I can get another officer as backup."

"No. I want to." A muscle worked on the side of his clenched jaw. "I have to do this."

Liam nodded. He could understand Bryce's need to be the one to confront his father. "Where would we find your dad this time of day? Can you call him and make a pretense for a late lunch, a rain check on bailing earlier?"

"Don't even need to do that. I can tell you exactly where he is at this very moment." Bryce pulled a cell phone from his back pocket and his fingers moved across the screen.

"You've got a GPS tracker on his phone?" Liam asked in surprise.

"No. He forgets to carry his cell phone half the time. I put a tracker on his vehicle a couple weeks ago. After the last murder." At Liam's raised brows, he explained. "I've had my suspicions about Dad for a long time. I'd hoped this might come in useful one day."

"Ever make any connections between him and the homeless murders?"

"Nothing definite."

They began walking down the hall, and Bryce tucked the phone away.

"Where we headed?"

"Seventeen thirty-eight King Street."

Liam stopped dead in his tracks. "That's Harper's address."

"Strange. What could he possibly want with her?"

"I'm about to find out. Let's move it." Liam jogged to the stairwell, his heart thrashing in his chest—wild as an animal trapped in a cage.

Chapter Eighteen

"Why am I doing this?" Carlton asked, mimicking her words. "I overheard Bryce and Liam at the station this morning. Like I said, you and your boyfriend have caused me nothing but grief."

As if she cared about his grief. Yet she had to reason with him, appeal to his logic—however faulty. "If you hurt me, Liam will see that you pay. Think this through."

He laughed. The glee in his eyes frightened her more than the anger. *He's off. Demented.* And people thought *she* was off her rocker? No, *this* was crazy. The bone-chilling grip of the real thing was undeniable. Fairfax's glittering eyes were a portal to an abyss of madness. Against dilated pupils, the yellow iris flecks whirled like pinwheels.

"What did you hear them say?" Maybe they had figured out Fairfax was a menace. Maybe Liam was on his way now. She clung to that hope.

"I'll be the one asking the questions here." He continued dragging her, and she stumbled beside him as he strode to the den.

"What have you told Andrews about your sister's death?" he demanded, pulling the curtains closed. The house darkened another fraction.

"J-just what everyone already knows."

"That ridiculous story about a monster in the house?" Fairfax marched to the front door and locked it.

The metallic click reverberated through her like a death knell.

His lips curled in rebuke. "Your story was another lie feeding the legend about Baysville's resident shadow dweller."

With her firmly in tow, he entered the kitchen, flicking the curtain closed on the lone window above the sink. Speaking of which... She peered desperately into the dark shadows. Where had *it* gone? Hysterical giggles at the back of her throat threatened to burst, like uncorked champagne bubbles rising to the surface. Was her shadow dweller a vision of death—a grim reaper who'd collected Presley's soul and had now reappeared to claim her as well?

Still—she feared the undeniably real Carlton Fairfax more. The merciless grip on her arm, the frigid eyes and the determined ritual of curtain closing to bar the outside world. It all pierced her with the promise of pain. And the possibility of death.

He reversed direction and headed to the back of the house again. Panic spiked more adrenaline through her body. "Where are you taking me?"

He ignored the question. "What else does Andrews suspect about me?" he continued in his hard, flat voice. One she was sure he'd wielded effectively against hundreds of criminals over the years. "I'm going to get the truth."

"Nothing! Liam knows nothing, same as me. It—it was all an accident."

"That's BS."

He yanked her to move faster, and her hip slammed into the edge of the tea cart. Grandmother Claudia's antique cups crashed to the ground. Porcelain shards scattered like snowflakes on the walnut flooring and crunched beneath her feet as she was relentlessly paraded through her own house. Desperately, she flailed her free arm, searching for a heavy object. Her fingers feathered against a glass candleholder, and she strained against Fairfax's pull forward. Two inches. That's all she needed. But her fingers tap-danced on empty air. The chance to grasp a weapon vanished.

Surprisingly, Fairfax moved past the back door. She'd been certain he meant to force her into his truck. Instead, he threw open the door to the basement.

The dark and relatively soundproof basement.

"No!" She dug her heels in, throwing the weight of her body toward the ground.

Pain exploded on her right cheek, stealing her breath, as he slapped her, hard. Hot needles of pain burned like a swarm of yellow jacket stings on the tender flesh. If she survived this day, Harper was sure her face would forever bear the imprint of his palm.

"You'll tell me everything Andrews knows about me," he continued. "Right now."

"And then what?" She kicked at his shins, and the man barely even flinched. "You'll kill me like you did Presley? Is that what happened?" If she was about to die, she could at least die knowing the truth about that night.

Fairfax stood at the doorway, gazing around her house with a thoughtful expression on his face. "It all started here. With your sister."

"What started?" Her throat threatened to close on choked sobs. "What did you do to her?"

"The killings," he answered, his voice as calm as though they were discussing how to solve a math problem. "Presley was the first." He chuckled as though he'd let her in on a private joke. "Turns out, I had a hankering all along for murder. A bloodlust I'd never suspected."

"What did you do to Presley?" she whispered.

He faced her with narrowed eyes. "You really don't know? You didn't see me that night?"

"No."

He gave a nonchalant shrug. "A quick kill punch to the back of her head where the skull base meets neck. Then I placed your sister in the kitchen and started a fire. Either her body would burn, or her lungs would fill with smoke. Death by fire or smoke inhalation, depending on when my fire department arrived."

Harper absorbed the full horror of his words. She imagined Presley's terror as Fairfax raised his hand, poised to deliver a fatal blow. Harper could only hope she'd been truly dead and had never regained consciousness to find smoke and flames licking the air, an inferno from which there was no escape.

And it had all happened as she and Mom had slept a floor above. Nausea rumbled in her belly.

"It was easy," he continued in the same singsong intonation. "Took her totally by surprise. No one heard a thing."

Except she had heard something—only she could never be sure exactly what it was. She'd only known that something horrible had taken place. Mom's partial hearing loss had prevented her from waking.

Harper didn't want to hear any more details. More words that would forever haunt her if she managed to survive her own encounter with evil. Yet Fairfax's confession relentlessly continued.

"Afterward, once I'd checked her pulse to make sure she hadn't survived the blow, I picked Presley up and carried her to the kitchen. Made it look like she'd slipped and fallen on the floor while heating up a bowl of soup. Easy enough to concoct a firebomb with chlorine and brake fluid in a plastic bottle, then set that in a pan on the stove. Untraceable." He laughed. "As captain, I was the arson investigator. I made damn sure there wasn't even a whisper that the fire might have been deliberately set. After all, why would anybody question my report?"

Bastard. Fury crashed over her in waves. For what he'd done to Presley, for what he'd almost done to her and her mom.

"You left Mom and me there to die," she accused.

"I had no beef against y'all and figured you'd wake up and escape before the house went up in flames. But if not, too bad. Funny." He chuckled again. "All these years, I kept waiting for you to remember something. A buried memory."

"No," she denied again. "Not you. I saw something else."

"The monster. Right. Maybe I'm the monster."

"No. He was thin, short. He looked nothing like you."

"Obviously, your mind has distorted my image. Could that be the truth?"

"No," she answered curtly. She wouldn't be drawn into his psychological games. His need to twist and manipulate her reality. She saw what she saw.

"But I was the only one there that night. Besides, Bryce, of course."

"Bryce?" Her belly took a nosedive. "Is he part of this?" If so, she feared her chance of escape had been reduced to zero.

"No. Boy's got a soft streak. Told me he wanted to forgo his football scholarship and stay here with Presley and her baby." His face darkened. "I couldn't let him do that."

Harper twisted and craned her neck, searching for a pale face in the darkness as Fairfax continued his poisonous confession. Where was the shadow dweller? *Help me*, she mouthed into the darkness.

For someone claiming he wanted her to talk, Fairfax was the one carrying the conversation. His words poured out in an angry braggadocio. "I took care of everything for Bryce. Protected him from a nobody girl who'd tie him down forever. He had a scholarship to the University of Alabama. Do you know what that means? Do you realize what kind of opportunity that was? A chance to make something of himself. I wasn't about to let your sister ruin his chances."

"You killed Presley and your own grandchild over nothing? You're the real monster here." Worse than anything her mind could have conjured.

"After that incident, I took everything to another level with my side business."

Harper reeled at his dismissive attitude. Her sister's life, her family's pain, meant nothing to him. Instead, he acted as though Presley's murder was merely a gateway for more business opportunities.

"Somebody didn't pony up on his gambling debt? Some hooker kept too much of her john's fee? I'd hire one of those bums by the railroad tracks to force them to do the right thing."

"Murder for hire?" she whispered.

"Nah, why let them have the fun part? Let them take the risk of enforcing my rules against some local who might recognize me. I prefer to run everything in total secrecy. But if my hired hands demand more money or threaten to blackmail me, why then—I kill them. You know what I discovered? Nobody cared. No victims' family members breathing down my neck to find a killer.

Hell, nobody missed the nobodies. I did the world a favor. When one of them bums got too big for their britches and demanded more money, I did what I had to do. Ain't nobody going to take what's rightfully mine. And you know what? I liked it. No, I loved it. That's right. I loved meting out my own brand of justice. To feel my knife slice through their scumbag, filthy skin. I have no regrets."

"You can't get away with this forever. If I die, Liam will hunt down my murderer like a dog."

"Dead dogs don't hunt." Fairfax laughed at his own black humor. "I'll kill you, and then next time, instead of hiring someone to take a potshot at Andrews, I'll shoot him down myself."

So that's who'd shot at Liam. No doubt he'd also been the one chasing them the night Liam was released from the hospital.

"No one will believe two women died in this same house from freak accidents," she pointed out, appealing to his brain rather than his nonexistent heart.

"They won't be able to prove otherwise. Besides, if I'm going down, you're going down with me."

He ran a callused finger from her chin to her gut.

"Too bad I can't cut you open, feel your warm blood in my hands, watch it ooze out of your body. Funny thing, I have to stab those homeless men in the back, so they don't see my face. Just in case. One day I want to run my knife down a woman. Watch her eyes as the life drains from her body. Maybe today's my lucky day."

Oh God, she had to distract him from this path. His breathing had gone huskier, and excitement crackled in his eyes. Would he lose control if he dwelled on this fantasy? Her mind scrabbled for a distraction.

"Wait! You were seen coming here today."

The excitement in his eyes melted. "You're lying."

"No. I was warned you were coming."

"Yeah, by who? Your make-believe shadow dweller?"

"He's here." Harper turned her face away. This was her one chance. He was out there, she was sure of it. She was not crazy. Whoever he was, he wasn't a killer. Fairfax was the murderer, not him.

"Help me," she screamed. "Please!"

"Shut up."

Fairfax lifted her in his arms as though she were as weightless as a rag doll, as though her kicking and flailing fell harmlessly against an armor of steel.

A flash of white materialized in the dark shadows, followed by a pop of brilliance as the lights switched on. The shadow dweller appeared, a cutlery knife clutched in one dirty hand.

"Drop her, Fairfax."

"What the hell?" he asked, bewildered.

His arms loosened, and she fell to the floor, scrabbling crab-like away from Fairfax and toward the other man.

Fairfax growled and lunged at her would-be savior. A sickening thud of flesh and bones hit the floor. He was astride the smaller man in a trice.

Outside, a siren sounded. Even though faint, she took heart that help was on the way.

She had a choice. Make a run for the door—or help the man who'd tried to save her. Damn it. That really wasn't a choice at all.

Harper ran past both the sprawling figures and returned to the dining room for that glass candlestick she'd missed earlier. The glass felt smooth and hard in her fist as she returned to the wrestling men. The smaller guy was pinned, and Carlton had seized the knife from him. He raised it, poised for a death blow.

"No!"

Fairfax paused, glancing up as if he'd just remembered her presence. It bought her a moment. With all her strength, Harper swung the candlestick, and the blow landed on his left temple. Blood erupted and arced over her and the floor. Fairfax dropped the knife, covered the wound with both his hands and then curled into a fetal position.

The shadow dweller snatched the knife and rose.

They faced one another in the darkness as outside the sirens drew nearer. He, knife at his side, and she, grasping the bloodied candlestick holder. Behind them in the shadows, Carlton groaned.

"Thank you," she whispered. "For saving me."

"You saved me," he countered.

"We saved each other."

The siren's blare had reached near-deafening level. Blue lights strobed into the den through the curtain cracks. Any moment, the cops would burst through. This was her moment.

"You're real. I did see you the night Presley died. You were there."

"I tried to help her. But it was too late. So, I ran away and hid. Like I always do."

"Where did you hide when—"

Pounding rained down on the front door. "Harper? Are you there? Open the door, honey."

Liam. The adrenaline that had fueled her energy—for what seemed to be hours but couldn't have been more then fifteen minutes—crashed and burned, leaving her exhausted. Her legs were concrete pillars, and it took a mammoth effort to walk the twelve feet to the door and unlock it. "I'm coming," she called through the barricade.

Sunlight and fresh air touched her face before Liam pulled her in for a quick, tight hug. "You okay? Where's Fairfax?"

Liam let go and entered the den. His hand reached for his sidearm. "Who are you?" he demanded of the shadow dweller.

"Ralph." The man's voice broke, and his skinny frame trembled so violently she was afraid he'd drop into a dead faint.

"It's okay," she rushed in. "He helped me. Fairfax is on the floor by the dining room window. I—I hit him." Belatedly, she stared down at the candlestick holder she still grasped.

Bryce entered, gun drawn. "I'll watch this guy," he told Liam. "Find my...find Carlton."

She set the candlestick holder on an end table and eyed Bryce as he stood there, gun aimed on Ralph.

Presley's lover. The father of the unborn baby that never had a chance at life. "Your dad confessed," she told him. "Did you know he killed Presley?"

Bryce didn't look at her, but the gun in his hands shook. "I suspected," he admitted.

From behind them, Liam's voice rang out. "Call an ambulance while I cuff him and read him his rights."

Oh, God. How badly had she hurt him?

"Bitch tried to kill me," she overheard Fairfax grumble.

"Too bad she didn't." Liam's voice boomed through the house as he read Fairfax his rights.

And then pandemonium.

More cops arrived and stormed through the door. She sat down on the sofa and indicated for Ralph to sit beside her. An unmistakable odor clung to him, but she was too tired and grateful to care. A stretcher was pushed through the door and Carlton was strapped onto it. Bryce loomed over his father, his face stricken. "Why did you have to kill her?"

Carlton didn't even pretend to not understand. He reached out a hand. "I did it for you, son."

Bryce ignored his father's outstretched hand and took a step back, signaling for the EMT workers to wheel him away.

"I did it for you," Carlton again insisted as he was pushed out the door.

Liam knelt in front of her, taking her hands in his. "Did he hurt you?"

"No."

He eyed her skeptically. "The side of your face is swollen. He hit you."

The outrage in his voice touched her. "It's okay." She squeezed his hands reassuringly. "If you need to go make reports, I understand."

"No way. That can wait." He cocked his head to the side, indicating the unlikely hero seated beside her. "How did this guy come to be here?"

Bryce shut the front door and returned. "Got two officers escorting my dad to the hospital. If you'd like, I can take this person down to the station and question him," he offered. "While you stay with Harper and get her statement."

"I want to hear more from him first," Liam insisted.

Actually, so did she.

Bryce positioned himself at the door and waited.

"My name's Ralph Poundstone." He gave them a wobbly smile, exposing a set of brown, crooked teeth. "Although people around here better know me as the shadow dweller. This has been my home off and on for a couple decades." He shot her an apologetic nod.

Her head reeled, her mind not fully wrapping around his bombshell news. "You've been living…here? In this house?"

"I'll show you." Ralph arose, and she and Liam followed him upstairs and then down the hallway past her bedroom. At the last guest bedroom on the right, Ralph unerringly headed to the closet and then pointed up for them to look.

A tiny crawl space in the ceiling was open, the small panel that normally covered it pushed aside.

"I never even knew this was here," she said wonderingly.

"Leads to the attic," Ralph offered helpfully. "Take a look for yourself."

He pulled a small bench in the closet directly under the opening and crawled through.

"You don't have to go up there," Liam said. "Why don't you wait for me downstairs with Bryce?"

"And miss this?" She gaped at him and shook her head. "I want to know everything. I *need* to see what's been happening right under my own nose. It will help me come to terms with my past."

Liam went in first, then reached a hand down and helped her as she wiggled through the narrow opening.

Her eyes watered at the smell as she scanned the tiny four-feet-by-six-feet enclosure that Ralph claimed as home. It was a walled-off portion of the attic. An old sleeping bag lay on the rough wood planking, surrounded by empty candy wrappers and litter. She recognized the mason jars of her mom's canned produce and preserves, and a pile of her father's old clothes. A few of her old books from middle school lay spread open on the floor.

"Why?" she asked him, shaking her head in bewilderment. "Why here?"

"It beats staying in the cold and the rain. Come spring and summer, I'd take my leave and ride the rails. Once the cold hit, I'd come back home."

He called her home his own? She shuddered and rubbed her arms. "We never saw you."

"I'd wait until you were all out of the house and then I'd slip back in. Easy to pop the lock on that back door. You should really get that fixed."

Hysterical laughter welled in her chest. The missing food, the unexplained noises, the smell, the sixth sense that screamed she wasn't alone in the house. And of course, that night he'd hovered over Presley. She should be furious, angry at the violation. While all that was true, it was also true that a weight had floated off her shoulders. She wasn't crazy.

"Why us? Why our house?" she asked.

"I was coming into town one day and happened to see your family getting in a car and going out. I was tired, cold and hungry. It occurred to me to check the doors and windows. Lucky for me, the back door was easy to pick. I came in and ate. Everything was all warm and cozy-like. So, I thinks to myself, *why not stay?* I looked around and found this hidey-hole. Hadn't planned on staying long but discovered I kinda liked it."

"Trespassing and theft." Liam quirked a brow at her. "We'll go on and take him into custody."

But she needed to know more. "Were you in the kitchen that night?"

"Presley." His hollowed-out eyes sank in deeper. "She was a good girl. She fed me several times over the years. Even brought me a blanket once."

Harper's looked at him in horrified disbelief. "She knew about you?"

"No. Not that I lived in your house. We met a few nights when I'd gone out for a bit of fresh air. She saw me shivering and brought me food and drink. I slept in your utility shed some that winter." He gestured at the tiny space. "Sometimes I felt closed in and needed a break. Anyway, that winter, I'd hear her sneak out at night. I saw who she was meeting, too. And then that night her boyfriend snuck in, I went downstairs to check on her. Heard them whispering in the basement, making plans. Then when her boyfriend left, that other man snuck in. The one that tried to kill you today."

"Carlton Fairfax. Go on."

"I seen him hit her in the back of the head and she was out cold. He carried her to the kitchen, all limp in his arms. Already dead, I think. He set her body on the floor and started fiddling around by the stove. He suddenly hightailed it out of the house, and then came the explosion. I didn't know what he was doing," Ralph assured her quickly. "It all happened so fast. When I saw the flames, I went straight to her. But it was too late. She was already gone."

None of them spoke, and in the silence, Harper sent up a little prayer to her sister. *We found him, sis. The man who murdered you. I'll make sure he's punished.*

"So that explains what you saw that night," Liam said. "Being a firefighter, Fairfax knew how to make a small, untraceable explosive. Figured there had to be a logical explanation."

"It was you who planted the jacks on the stairs and in my bed," she said in a flash of understanding. "And it was you who sent me the messages to get out of the house. Not Kimber."

"I picked up a thing or two when riding the rails. Even got me an email account. So I used it to reach out to you. I tried to warn you. To scare you off. I was afraid he'd come back one day and hurt you, too. But you wouldn't listen."

"You'll have to find another place to live now," Liam said. "You can't stay here anymore."

She completely agreed, even while pitying Ralph. "But where will he go?"

"For now, he'll go with Bryce and make a statement. We'll keep him a few days in jail on trespassing charges until we can find a shelter with an opening."

Ralph nodded, and tears ran down his dirty cheeks. "Can I bring something with me?"

"Depends on what it is."

Ralph picked up a tattered copy of *Charlotte's Web* and held it up for her permission.

"Of course, take it," she urged.

Her emotions were all over the place as she and Liam watched Bryce take Ralph into custody.

"That odor. Think your shadow dweller has bathed any the past year? Going to be a long ride for Bryce."

She laughed, the relief from escaping her ordeal draining away. "I should have offered him use of my shower and a pair of Dad's old pants and shirt."

"Nah, Bryce deserves it after all the hard times he's given me these last few months. Once Ralph gets to the detention center, they'll make sure he's thoroughly washed before issuing him a uniform."

"I still can't get over that he's been living with us all these years and we didn't even know it." She shivered and rubbed her arms. "So creepy. Even though he's turned out to be harmless."

Liam's face grew serious. "You've been through the wringer today. Sure you're okay?"

"Yes," she answered, surprised at the truth. "I feel relieved now that I know what happened to Presley and that her killer's been discovered."

She buried her head against Liam's chest. "Fairfax knocked her out and then started the fire. Can you imagine anything so horrible? And he had no remorse. None."

Warm fingers caressed her scalp, and she closed her eyes, concentrating on nothing but the comforting feel of his touch. Liam kissed her forehead, and she raised her eyes, finding love and concern written in his darkened eyes.

"When I knew Carlton was at your house…" His voice grew gruff, and he swallowed hard. "I've never been so scared in my life."

And this was a man who'd been shot at and faced danger every day. "I'm okay," she murmured, bestowing feather kisses along his jaw. This time, she was the one offering him comfort.

"I don't want another day to go by without telling you something I should have said almost from the very start. I love you, Harper."

She couldn't imagine a better ending to this strange, stressful day. His declaration of love helped counter Carlton's murderous revelations. Much as she'd always be saddened by Presley's death, it was time she moved forward with her own life. "Liam," she whispered, wrapping her arms around his neck, "I love you, too."

Epilogue

Harper followed Kimber around her old home, marveling at the changes she'd made in the last six months. A fresh coat of paint, combined with new flooring and light fixtures, gave the old structure a fresh boost.

"It's never looked better," she told Kimber.

"Thanks to your decorating skills. I didn't have a clue about paint colors and all that other stuff you picked out for us."

"Glad to help. Besides, it's good exposure for my new design firm."

"How's business?"

"Surprisingly good," she was happy to report. "Thanks to all your contacts."

"Good. Told you so." Kimber bounded up the stairs as she spoke over her shoulder. "Everything's on schedule for the tourist season starting next month. We're booked solid for weeks. And wait until you see what Richard and I have done with the attic."

Her old friend was beaming, like she hadn't in years. Harper obligingly entered the attic and blinked.

Drywall replaced the old brick and rough planks, and the same walnut flooring from the hallway extended here. The window had been replaced and enlarged. Sunlight poured through the room. Built-in shelves filled with books lined one wall, and a love seat and wing-back chairs were arranged in a casual sitting area.

"It's a reading room for our guests," Kimber said proudly. "A place they can privately relax in the evenings if they choose."

Curious, she stepped over to the far side where the plywood wall had been removed. Ralph's old, cramped hidey-hole was no longer. To think that for years, he'd made it his own winter home was still hard to wrap her mind around.

"Everything okay?" Kimber asked anxiously.

"Yes. Just remembering Ralph," she admitted.

Kimber shrugged dramatically. "What a creep."

"No. More a tragic figure," she gently admonished. "But he's better off where he lives now."

Ralph had been diagnosed with developmental and mental health disabilities and was eligible to reside in a halfway house, where he seemed to flourish.

"And, in the end, he was a help to you," Kimber admitted. "And to Liam's family."

The mystery of Liam's uncle Teddy had been solved. Ralph and he had been camp mates years ago at the tracks. Teddy had died of natural causes—probably pneumonia, from Ralph's description of the symptoms—and was buried in Baysville's pauper cemetery with an unmarked nameplate. Liam's mother had since erected a tombstone for her long-lost brother.

Loud footfalls ascended the stairs.

"Mommy! Someone's at the door for Miss Harper."

Surprised, Harper glanced out the window to see Liam striding up the front porch. "Wonder what he's doing here in the middle of the day?" she asked.

Kimber shrugged but looked a bit too smug. As if she was in on some private joke. "He's the new deputy police chief—reckon he can come and go as he pleases." Before Harper could question her further, Courtney, Anise and Layla appeared, chattering away in that delightful style of young girls.

Harper marched downstairs with Kimber and her girls. Her hand trailed along the familiar mahogany railing.

On the eighth step from the bottom, where Presley supposedly fell and died, she remembered her old mantra—*blessings, sis*. But it didn't fill her with sadness anymore. Like her, the old house was moving on. It felt right that it was inhabited by a family again. Hopefully, a family that would fill it with years of happy memories.

Goodbye, house, she added to her silent mantra.

At the doorway, Liam was bent on one knee, laughing at something Courtney said. Her heart flooded with joy. He'd be a wonderful father one day. Not that they'd even discussed the possibility of raising children. Yet. But they'd lived at his place since Kimber moved here. Their relationship was strong. Steady.

"What brings you here?" she asked curiously.

"Thought we could go out for a nice ride before dinner."

Funny, long drives weren't something they'd ever done before. He and Kimber exchanged a significant look. Fine, she'd find out soon enough what they were up to. So, she played along as she said goodbye to Kimber and her girls.

"Bryce know you're playing hooky?" she asked after they were underway.

"He insisted on it. Claims he can't have his top deputy working longer hours than him. Makes him look bad."

Liam smiled as he fiddled with the radio. He and Bryce had developed a close friendship after all the scandal and illegal activities they'd worked together to shut down.

And it was a gorgeous April morning, after all. Local

shops had opened along the downtown strip. When they passed the large stone church at the edge of town, Harper pointed at the marquee.

"Church social this weekend to welcome the new minister," she read aloud. "That's good news."

Liam nodded his head in agreement, and they were silent a moment, thinking of Allen's victims.

Allen Spencer had been found guilty on three counts of sexual abuse and was in prison.

"How's Gunner liking the new job there at the church?" she asked.

"Loves it. Takes pride in keeping the place spotless. The congregation claims it's never been so well kept. They shower him with attention and casseroles."

The bustle of town faded, and she relaxed, enjoying the view, not paying the slightest attention to where they were going. Until Kimber's old farmhouse came into view. To her astonishment, Liam turned off the county road and headed up their driveway. She was even more surprised when he pulled out a set of house keys from his pocket.

"Let's go inside and take a look."

Even with all the furniture gone, the house's charm remained. Harper strode into the kitchen and looked around. "I know Kimber and Richard are happy to be rid of the place, but I couldn't bear to sell it if it were mine."

Liam's arm wrapped around her waist from behind. "What do you say we buy it, then?"

"What?" She laughed and turned around to face him. "You're joking, right?"

"Perfectly serious. I know how much you love this place."

"But…" Her voice trailed off as she thought of all the reasons it wouldn't be a good idea.

Liam bent on one knee and took her hands in his. Seemed today was full of surprises.

"Marry me, Harper."

All her objections flew out the window. Together, they could work out the details. "Is that a question or a demand?" she teased.

Liam winked and tugged her down beside him on the kitchen floor. "Whatever you want it to be."

Much, much later, Liam surprised her yet again when he pulled out a bottle of champagne and a cake from the fridge.

"You were mighty sure of my answer, weren't you?" she said with a laugh.

This time, instead of laughing, he pulled her body up against his own in a tight embrace. "I'd never take you for granted like that. Now are you going to marry me or what?"

"You just try to slip away," she whispered, practically bursting with happiness. "And the answer is a big ole *hell yeah.*"

* * * * *

COLTON 911: DEADLY TEXAS REUNION

BETH CORNELISON

To Paul—my best friend for
more than thirty-four years!

Prologue

FBI Special Agent Nolan Colton hated suits almost as much as he hated today's unexpected summons to his boss's office. As he waited to be called back, he tugged at the collar of his dress shirt and readjusted the tie that threatened to strangle him. His knee bounced while he waited. Patience had never been his forte. What the hell could have happened to warrant this urgent confab with the special agent in charge? Nothing good.

Nolan reached in his coat pocket for an antacid and chewed it. His gut had been torn up with dread all night. His boss's tone of voice when he'd called last night instructing Nolan to report to this meeting had been grave and terse.

When the SAC's administrative assistant finally called him to the inner office, he took a deep breath, tugged his shirtsleeves to straighten them and strode into his boss's domain with his head high and his back ramrod straight.

The first thing Nolan noticed when he entered Special Agent in Charge Dean Humboldt's office was that they weren't alone. Deputy Assistant Director Jim Greenley sat in one of the chairs opposite Humboldt, and a man Nolan didn't know but who seemed vaguely familiar occupied the seat to the left of Humboldt's desk. The second thing Nolan noticed was he wasn't invited to take a seat.

He assumed a rigid stance, feet slightly apart, shoulders back, hands clasped behind him. "Good morning, sirs."

"Special Agent Colton," the deputy assistant director said by way of greeting, adding a quick dip of his chin.

The SAC's administrative assistant left, closing the door behind her, and Nolan experienced a brief moment of claustrophobia. His tie seemed to tighten like a noose.

"Thank you for coming this morning, Special Agent Colton," Humboldt said.

"I didn't get the impression when you called me last night that I had a choice."

Humboldt cleared his throat. "No. A rather serious matter has been brought to my attention, and we need to address it."

"I've never known the Bureau to handle anything that wasn't serious." He twitched a grin, but his attempt at humor fell flat. Humboldt scowled, and Greenley exchanged a look with the third man, who had yet to be introduced. "Sorry. What matter is that, sir?"

Humboldt opened a manila file folder and slid a large black-and-white photograph across the desk. "This."

Nolan stepped forward to look at the picture, and what he saw there shot adrenaline to his marrow. A shot of himself. In an erotic and compromising position with a fellow special agent.

Well, hell. He'd thought the ill-advised, one-time tryst with his partner had been discreet, something he could bury. They'd been alone in her hotel room. So where had the picture come from? The obvious answer rattled him. Angered him.

"Um." Nolan blinked. "Where did you get this?"

"We're asking the questions today, Special Agent Colton," DAD Greenley said.

"You recognize the woman in the photo, Special Agent?"

He jerked a nod. "Special Agent Charlotte O'Toole. We worked a case together last year in Portland." He drew a slow breath, deciding honesty was his best policy. "Obviously, things got out of control one night. It was a mistake, but it was just a one-time thing."

Humboldt divided a glance between the other two men. Greenley arched one graying eyebrow.

When Humboldt slid another picture toward him with much the same content, Nolan gritted his back teeth.

"What is it you say happened that night, Special Agent Colton?" Humboldt asked. His boss's continued formal use of Nolan's official title rather than his first name unsettled Nolan.

He frowned and tilted his head in confusion. "I'd think that was pretty clear. Are you asking for scurrilous details? Because, I have to say, sir, I find it crass of a man to kiss and tell."

Humboldt folded his hands on his desk. "Generally, I do, too. But considering the allegations Special Agent O'Toole has made against you, I think you'd be wise to share your side of the events of that night."

A chill raced down Nolan's spine. "Allegations?" He could barely choke the word out. His pulse thundered in his ears as he looked from one grim face to another. "Wh-what is she alleging?"

"She claims you assaulted her."

Nolan's blood froze, and he had the very real, very scary sense of his career, his reputation, slipping away like a wild mustang jerking the reins from his hands. He struggled for a breath. "What?"

"Special Agent O'Toole came forward last week with claims that you made advances toward her over a period of several days while you two were on assignment. She claims she consistently rebuffed your advances and reminded you such behavior was both unprofessional and unwelcome by her."

Disbelief clogged Nolan's throat. He made sputtering noises, but shock rendered him mute.

"Believing she would need evidence of your behavior to substantiate her claim, she hid a camera to capture further incidents as proof."

More like she wanted to frame me. Nolan's hands fisted. He'd been set up. But *why*?

Humboldt tapped the file folder. "There are more if you'd like to see them, but they are much alike and tell the same story."

Nolan glanced at the incriminating picture again, noting this time that the shot showed him bowing Charlotte back, as if the aggressor, while her hands were against his chest as if pushing him away. Her head was turned as if avoiding his kiss instead of providing access to her slim neck and bared shoulder.

Fighting for composure, Nolan said gruffly, "I'd like to see the other pictures, just the same."

His boss handed him the file.

Beside Humboldt's desk, the third man huffed irritably, but Nolan ignored him as he thumbed through the rest of the snapshots. Every one of the images gave the impression that Nolan had been an assailant and Charlotte his unwilling victim. Which was far from the truth. Missing from the file were dozens of other moments in which Charlotte had seduced him, pressured him, ravaged him. He saw now that she'd made a point of staging plenty of poses providing evidence to the contrary. But still he wondered, *why?*

He and Charlotte had worked well together. He'd liked her—obviously—and thought they had a good professional and personal relationship. So what had made her turn on him? No. Not turn on him. That indicated a change of heart. For her to plant the camera, pose the pictures and pursue him with the fervor that she had—because she had, in fact, been the instigator, pushing him to violate his professional ethics for the one-night stand—this whole situation had to have been premeditated. Charlotte had used him. Betrayed him.

"That bitch," Nolan muttered under his breath.

The third man puffed up and growled, "I'll thank you not to speak that way about *my wife*."

Freshly stunned, Nolan jerked his gaze to the older man. "Your wife?"

"You didn't know?" Greenley asked.

Nolan snorted, no longer caring about comportment or respect for his superiors. "Obviously not."

He was being railroaded with false charges, and he'd defend himself with everything he had.

Greenley turned up a palm. "Special Agent O'Toole married the senator five years ago."

"Six years ago," the third man corrected.

Nolan gave his head a small shake as if he'd heard wrong. "I'm sorry…the *senator*?"

Humboldt nodded toward the man in question. "Yes. US Senator George Dell of Nebraska."

Holy crap. He'd slept with the wife of a US senator? And Charlotte had said nothing about a husband—certainly not a husband with so much power.

The bad vibe he'd had even before entering Humboldt's office had cranked up by a factor of ten. A hundred.

Nolan's entire body tensed. Fire flashed through his veins. He thought his heart might pound right through his chest. A kaleidoscope of emotions battled for dominance as his brain numbly processed the accusation and ramifications. He had to lock his knees to keep his shaking legs under him. "Th-this is all, uh…a big misunderstanding."

"You're denying her claims?" Humboldt asked.

He jerked a stunned gaze to his boss. Humboldt had worked with him long enough to know Nolan's character better than that. How could his boss even *think* he was capable of such a heinous thing?

He threw the folder of photos back on Humboldt's desk. "Hell yes, I deny it! I'm not a sexual assailant!"

The senator shoved to his feet, his hands balled. "So you're calling my wife a liar?"

Nolan reeled in the curt reply on his tongue at the

last possible moment. He needed to be careful what he said, how he said it. He didn't want his accusers to have any more rope to hang him with. As it was, defending himself from charges of sexual assault would be tricky at best.

He struggled for a calm tone as he faced the senator, but a throbbing pulse pounded at his temples. "All I can tell you is that I didn't know Charlotte was married, and what happened between us was *not* assault. I know you don't want to hear it, but it was one hundred percent consensual."

Nolan stood his ground as the senator took two aggressive steps toward him, the man's teeth gritted and bared, his face florid. "You son of a—"

Greenley caught the senator's arm. "Sir, please. Have a seat."

Turning back to Humboldt, Nolan scrubbed a hand down his face. "Sir, you *know* me. You know these charges are preposterous. I would never...could *never*..."

"My personal opinion doesn't matter." Humboldt's expression was stern but apologetic. "A matter of this magnitude requires an internal investigation."

An investigation. Somehow knowing the incident would be explored gave Nolan a seed of hope. Surely the investigation would uncover the truth. He'd be exonerated and his name cleared, his reputation—

"Until the investigation is complete, you're hereby suspended without pay—"

"What!" he shouted, gut punched.

"Effective immediately." Humboldt stuck his hand out. "I need your badge and your service weapon."

Nolan gaped at his boss. This *couldn't* be happening. His career was *everything* to him. This smear to his character and reputation, even if found innocent, would follow him forever.

He cut a glance to Greenley, praying for reprieve, but met a stony countenance.

"I swear I didn't... I'd never..." He shook his head, and his chest contracted so hard he couldn't catch his breath.

Humboldt's hand was still extended to him, but Nolan refused to let the senator, whose smug grin gnawed at Nolan, see him surrender his weapon.

"This is bullshit!" Nolan turned on his heel and marched out of the office.

He'd made it as far as the elevator when Humboldt caught up to him. "Nolan, wait!"

Whirling around, he jabbed a finger toward his boss—ex-boss?—and growled, "You *know* I didn't do what she's accusing me of. I would *never* take advantage of a woman that way! Hell, man, you trusted me to drive your daughter to her apartment after the barbecue back in July!"

"I have no choice," Humboldt said, holding out his hand, palm up, again. "Damn it, Nolan. My hands are tied. It's your word against hers, and she has incriminating photographs."

Seething, Nolan unfastened his holster and slapped his service weapon into his boss's hand. "Yeah, well-selected photos. But where are the ones of the times in between the posed shots? She was all over me, Dean. It was her idea, and she took the lead, no matter what the pictures say."

"Your badge and ID."

Nolan groaned his frustration as he fished in his pocket for his credentials. "We've had this discussion before—how much we both abhor the sort of man who harasses and demeans women. God, it makes me *sick* to be lumped in the same category with scum like that!" He smacked his FBI shield and ID wallet into Humboldt's hand. "I have no idea what's behind all this. But, please, Dean, don't let them railroad me. This has to be political, or... I don't know. But it's a load of crap. I swear!"

To his credit, Humboldt looked grief stricken as he shook his head. "Go home, Nolan. Use the time to...go fishing or see old friends."

He scoffed. "Fishing? That's all you have for me?"

His boss lifted a shoulder. "I'm sorry."

Nolan jabbed the elevator button before deciding to take the stairs. He had adrenaline to burn off. Stalking away, he fisted his hands at his sides. The injustice clawed at him. After so many years working to get where he was within the Bureau, it had been snatched away in a heartbeat. And the best his boss had was "Go fishing or see old friends"?

As he slammed through the stairwell door and descended the steps two at a time, an image came to him, fixed itself in his head. And he knew where he'd go until this nightmare was resolved.

Whisperwood.

Chapter One

Whisperwood, Texas

"It's been a nightmare. My daughter, my precious girl, was murdered, and I need you to find out who did it."

Summer Davies held the haunted gaze of the man seated across from her, and her first thought after his pronouncement was, *The poor man. How he must be suffering!* Her second thought was *Finally, a real case!*

Since opening Davies Investigations LLC in Whisperwood, Texas, Summer had scrounged for work, taking more lost dog cases than she wanted to admit. All too often, when a potential client walked into her small, spare office, they assumed she was the secretary and gave her reluctant consideration when they learned she was the owner and sole private investigator.

Even Atticus and his son, Ian, who currently sat across from her, had exchanged hesitant looks when she'd informed them she would be the one handling any investigative work done by her office. But, used to the sexism, she'd smiled and asked for the details of the job. And Atticus dropped his bomb. A murder case.

Summer divided a concerned glance between the

two men. "You're sure she was murdered? She's not just missing?"

Ian sat taller in the wooden ladder-back chair, which was all she could currently afford for her clients, and snapped, "Of course we're sure. Her body was found in the Lone Star Pharma parking lot. What rock have you been living under?"

Summer let the snide comment pass as she narrowed her gaze on her visitors. "Wait. Lone Star Pharma? Are you Patrice Eccleston's family?"

The discovery of the young woman's body during repairs to the Lone Star Pharma parking lot had been a hot topic of gossip and speculation in town. Solving the much-discussed murder case would prove her mettle to the town and give her fledgling PI office the boost it needed.

And give Patrice's family the peace of mind and closure they were seeking, she mentally amended with a self-conscious pang.

Atticus blinked and dabbed at his eye, clearly fighting tears. "Yes. Patrice is my daughter." A pained look crossed his face, and he amended, "*Was* my daughter. I..." He heaved a shuddering sigh full of pain, and Summer's heart twisted. The grief etched in his face was heartbreaking.

"*Is,*" Summer said, leaning toward Atticus and flattening a hand on her desk as she reached toward him. "Patrice will always be your daughter. No matter what. I'm sorry for your loss, sir. I would love to be able to help bring in the person responsible for her murder."

Atticus met her gaze, hope lighting his eyes. "Thank

you. It rips me apart knowing that the cretin who did this to her is still out there. She deserves justice!"

Summer nodded. "She absolutely does."

While she was considering how to proceed and mulling the ramifications of taking the case, her dark gray feline companion hopped up on her desk and flopped on the paperwork she'd been reviewing earlier.

Ian's face reflected surprise then affront at the cat's appearance, as if Summer having her pet in the office with her was the height of unprofessionalism.

"Not now, Yossi." Summer lifted her cat to the floor and brushed stray fur from her desk. Continuing as if nothing had happened she asked, "Isn't the police investigation still open? While I'm happy to take your case, I don't want to step on any toes at the police department."

"Yeah," Ian said, "the police say they are looking into it, but we're not getting many answers outta them."

"Chief Thompson is a good man. I like him, and I know he's doin' what he can. But...we want answers. Right now, we just aren't getting anything with the cops." Atticus used his sleeve to wipe his face. "We figure, maybe people who know something are scared to talk to the cops. Maybe you could learn something Chief Thompson hasn't."

"Fresh eyes on the case and all that." Ian waved a hand toward her. "Maybe you'll see something they missed?"

Summer leaned back in her squeaky desk chair and nibbled a fingernail. It wouldn't do to get on the police chief's bad side. She couldn't appear to be second-guessing Chief Thompson's efforts in the case. She glanced out her office window, which had a view of downtown Whisperwood, and watched the pedestrians and pigeons ambling along the small-town street. Embarrassing the chief of police wasn't her worst consideration. If it looked like she was trying to interfere in his investigation, hinder his collection of evidence or—

And just like that her brain short-circuited. Her train of thought derailed, and her full attention snagged on a man in jeans and a snug T-shirt striding down the sidewalk at a brisk clip. His latte-brown hair, broad shoulders and loose-limbed stride tickled the back of her neck, stirring long-ago memories.

"Come on, Tadpole. Show these guys you're not scared!"

Surging forward, she grabbed the cord to the blinds and yanked them higher for a clearer view of the street. Yossi took this as an invitation to jump onto the wide windowsill, and her cat settled down to bird-watch. She squinted, trying to get a glimpse of the man's face, but his back was to her.

"Ms. Davies? Is there a problem?"

The man on the street placed a paper cup from JoJo's Java on the roof of his car, opened the driver's door, retrieved the coffee cup, climbed in and drove away. She continued to stare out the window at the empty parking spot for several heartbeats after the man's vehicle disappeared down the street.

"You're moving?" he asked. "Where?"

Twelve-year-old Summer frowned, shrugged. "Wherever the Army sends us."

He licked his lips and blinked hard, his eyes sad. "Will I ever see you again?"

No. As it turned out, she hadn't seen her best childhood friend since that goodbye seventeen years ago. They'd written to each other for a while, but—

A loud thumping drew her out of her musing. She gave her head a small shake and turned to find Ian Eccleston slapping his hand on her desktop. "Hell-oooo? Ms. Davies, are you listening?"

Atticus tipped his head. "My dear, are you all right? You look as if you've seen a ghost."

I may have. Summer raked her hair back from her face. Gathering her thoughts after what—or rather *whom*—she'd just seen was a bit like chasing down a spilled bag of marbles as they rolled in every direction.

"I'm sorry. I thought I saw…someone from my past. Someone important…"

But he hadn't been back to Whisperwood in years, to her knowledge. Why would he be here now?

"Can you help us with this case or not, Ms. Davies?" Ian asked. "I have to say, based on what I've seen so far of your operation…" He cast a disdainful look around her Spartan accommodations, allowing his disapproving glare to stop on Yossi, who crouched on the windowsill. "I'm not feeling especially confident in your ability to handle a matter as important as my sister's murder."

"I'm sorry you feel that way. I promise you, if I take your case, I will leave no stone unturned in searching for the truth. I provide the highest quality service to every client."

"*If* you take the case?" Atticus frowned and cast a side glance to his son before pinning her with his rheumy eyes. "You're not sure?"

"I want to take your case. I want to help you. But

considering the circumstances, I think it would be wise for me to do a little preliminary groundwork before I make any promises."

Ian rolled his eyes and grumbled to his father, "See, Dad. What did I tell you?"

"Hush, Ian. It may be a long shot, but Ms. Davies is our last best hope."

Last best hope? She wasn't sure if she should feel honored or insulted by the characterization. But being the grieving father's last hope for peace and justice was the red flag waved in front of her. A challenge. A mission. More than anything, she wanted to prove to these men, prove to the town, prove to herself that she hadn't made a mistake moving to Whisperwood three months ago. She was a good investigator—no, a *great* investigator—and she was determined to do what the naysayers and skeptics around her said she couldn't. She'd prove them wrong.

She cleared her throat and squared her shoulders. "Here's what I can do," Summer said, pulling out a blank notepad and clicking open her favorite pen. "I can take down your information, have you give me some background and insights into Patrice's life, and then I'll do a preliminary evaluation. If it looks like I can contribute something to the case that the police haven't covered, and that my efforts won't hinder or interfere with Chief Thompson's investigation, then we'll proceed. Deal?"

"What do you want to know?"

"What I like to call the big Hs—her hobbies, hangouts, habits and homies."

Atticus raised an eyebrow and sent her a puzzled look. "Homies?"

"Uh, you know, her friends. But homies starts with *H*, so…" She cleared her throat. "So what do you think?"

"I think I'll do whatever it takes to put my daughter's murderer behind bars."

NOLAN STUDIED THE storefronts along Main Street and reminisced about the summers he'd spent here in Whisperwood when he was younger. His cousins' ranch, a thousand-acre spread near Austin, had been the perfect place for a restless boy to spend his summers learning to rope calves, find the best fishing holes and ride his assigned horse, Joker, alongside his cowboy cousins. Sometime between first grade and graduating from high school, he'd fallen in love with the small-town charm of Whisperwood, as well. In the years since his last summer at the Colton Ranch, he'd missed the hot days wrangling cattle, the sticky nights chasing lightning bugs—and a special girl who'd made his early years at the ranch especially memorable. Summer.

With hair the color of beach sand, a laugh as bubbly as the sodas they'd sip under the cottonwoods and a smile as bright as the sun, Summer had been every bit as warm and wonderful as the season she was named for. As unlikely as the match had seemed, his cousins' neighbor had quickly become his best friend at the ranch. But then, she was no girly-girl like his sister, Emma, who preferred American Girl dolls and air-conditioning over the boys' rough-and-tumble antics in the great outdoors. Tomboy Summer had easily kept up with him and his cousins as they climbed, raced, dug, swam, wrestled, fished, mucked and sweated away the hottest days in the Texas Hill Country.

And then Summer and her family had moved.

Nolan sighed, remembering the June day when he was thirteen, and he'd learned his best friend was leaving town. He'd arrived at the Colton Ranch, raring to saddle up and go get Summer for a long horseback ride in his cousins' pastures.

"Dude, she's moving to North Carolina this weekend," his cousin Forrest had said. "Didn't she write you?"

Now Nolan rubbed his chest, feeling a hollowness behind his breastbone that paled compared to the sucker punch his younger self had experienced learning of his loss. He'd still had fun with his cousins in subsequent years, but the days lacked the nebulous goldenness and luster he'd known when he'd had Summer at his side.

Bending his neck to glance at the storefront signs out the passenger side of his car, he spotted a couple more new businesses mixed with the old familiar ones. He spotted the Whisperwood General Store, where he, Donovan and Forrest had filched a box of condoms—and felt so guilty about it they'd returned the same day to put them back. Down the block was the Bluebell Diner, where the chocolate chip pancakes were better than anything his mother or Aunt Josephine could make. His stomach rumbled appreciatively, even though he'd enjoyed a hearty breakfast at the ranch two hours ago. At the corner was a new business, Kain's Auto Shop, where the bay doors were open and someone in gray coveralls bent over the engine of a dusty pickup truck.

At one of the few traffic lights in the sleepy town, he sipped his coffee and decided the addition of JoJo's Java to the downtown storefronts was a definite boon. He didn't consider himself a coffee snob, but the rich house brew was excellent and hit the spot on this cool autumn morning. At his hip, his cell phone buzzed an incoming call.

"Special Agent Colton," he said out of habit, then frowned, wondering if he would still be a special agent when the trumped-up investigation was completed.

"How very official of you, Nolan," said a female voice at the other end of the line. "I wish I had a fancier title to throw back besides your cousin-in-law Bellamy."

He smiled, picturing his cousin Donovan's beautiful wife. "No fancier title needed. The fact that you put up with Donovan is credential enough in my book. What can I do for you?"

"If you have a little time today, could you come by my office and help me with something?" Bellamy, an accountant for Lone Star Pharma, asked.

"What kind of something?" Nolan switched to hands-free mode on his phone so he could drive.

"The ladies in the office organized a surprise baby shower for me this morning, and I have a lovely collection of gifts I need help getting home," Bellamy, who was eight months pregnant, said then rushed to add, "I know you're on vacation..."

He swallowed a scoff and a tinge of bitterness toward his employer when she referred to his unpaid leave as a vacation, but then, all he'd told his family was that he was taking some time off.

"…and I wouldn't ask normally, except Donovan is tied up working a case and Dallas—"

"No problem."

"—and Avery have their hands full with the twins, and Forrest—"

"Bellamy, stop. I'm happy to help," he said, even as he turned on Alamo Street to head toward the sprawling complex of the town's largest employer. He was, in fact, relieved to have something useful to do. He'd helped Hays muck stalls this morning and promised to drive Josephine to a doctor's appointment tomorrow, but he was woefully short on things to fill his free time. He needed something to occupy his hands, his mind for the foreseeable future or he'd go nuts stewing over the false charges being investigated back in Chicago.

"Are you sure? I hate to impose, but I'm not supposed to carry anything heavy and—"

He chuckled hearing the apology in her voice. "No imposition. Really. I wasn't doing anything except cruising around town, walking down memory lane. I'm on my way now."

"Thank you, Nolan! You're a lifesaver!"

"Helping you tote baby gifts hardly compares to saving a life, but you are most welcome."

He arrived at the Lone Star Pharma offices within minutes and parked in the visitor's spot closest to the door Bellamy specified. He climbed out of his car, coffee in hand, and scanned the complex, which was far larger than he'd remembered as a teenager. He'd heard the company was doing well and expanding, and the new buildings on the Lone Star campus testified to that fact.

At one end of the parking lot, he spotted an area marked off with yellow tape, and curiosity bit him. Crime scene tape or general cautionary tape? At dinner last night, his cousins had talked about all the damage done by Hurricane Brooke, the storm that had blown through the area a couple of months back. But hadn't they also mentioned a woman's body had recently been discovered buried under the parking lot? The back of his neck tingled, and he headed toward the yellow tape as if drawn there by some alien tractor beam.

His curiosity spiked all the more when he noticed a woman poking around the marked-off area. The woman, petite, with dark blond hair and curves, was crouched at the edge of the crime scene with a notepad, scribbling notes and taking pictures with her phone. A reporter maybe? But wasn't the story a few weeks old? Kind of late for the newspaper to be writing up the gruesome discovery. Whoever she was, her blue jeans fit her shapely tush in a way that made Nolan look twice...before mentally castigating himself for even noticing. He'd been suspended from the Bureau because he'd let a beautiful woman convince him to follow his baser instincts instead of his professional ethics. But never again.

He crossed the parking lot without saying anything, his athletic shoes silent on the asphalt. The woman was so absorbed in her work that she didn't seem to notice his approach. Not good, he thought to himself. What if his intent was to kidnap her or rob her? She really needed to be more aware of her surroundings.

He stopped a few feet behind her and observed for a few seconds before, without turning from her crouch, she said, "Just so you know, I'm packing a .38, and I'm trained to use it."

Nolan grinned and muttered, "Welcome to Texas."

"Is there something you want?" she said, still photographing the upturned earth and shallow trench where, presumably, the body had recently been found.

Nolan took a sip of his coffee, then said, "How about your name, and the reason you're nosing around?"

The blonde angled her head toward him. Blinked. Gasped. And sprang from her crouch, leaping toward him in one fluid motion. Squealing, she jumped against him, crushing his coffee cup and wrapping herself around him in a bear hug. "Omigod! Omigod! Omigod! Nolan!"

He had no choice but to catch the woman, or they'd both have tumbled to the pavement. Her legs hooked around him, and he put his hands beneath the shapely bottom he'd been admiring earlier to support her as she squeezed him and giggled.

And his heart stilled. He knew that effervescent laugh. "Summer?"

Nolan leaned back, trying to catch a glimpse of the woman's face. As she raised her head from his shoulder, she bumped his chin, making him bite his tongue. But, sure enough, the spitfire hugging him for all he was worth was Summer. His Summer.

"Yep!" she said, her full-wattage smile beaming at him. Her face had lost its baby fat, but not the elfin shape of her nose and full lips, her rounded cheekbones and wide almond-shaped eyes, the same color as the dark roast coffee now soaking his shirt.

He took a moment to catch his breath, then wheezed, "Holy cow! How the heck are you?"

When she finally put her feet on the ground and stepped back, she kept her grip on his arms, as if she were afraid he'd disappear if she let go. "I'm good. Excellent, in fact, now that you're here! Oh my god, Nolan, I'm so happy to see you!"

He chuckled and nodded to his spilled coffee. "Clearly."

She glanced down at the brown stain on his white T-shirt and cringed. "Oops. Sorry!"

"Forget it. The shirt will wash." He nodded toward the police tape. "What were you up to over there?"

"Oh, that?" She bent to retrieve the notebook she'd dropped when she'd hugged him. "Gathering info for a new case."

"A case? You're a cop?"

She wrinkled her nose in the captivating way he remembered and shook her head. "Not a cop. A private investigator."

Nolan raised his eyebrows and chuckled his surprise. "You're a PI?"

Her smile dimmed, and she narrowed a glare on him. "Why is that funny to you?"

"It's just—"

"A woman can be a PI same as any man!" She straightened her back, making the most of her five-foot-nothing stature as she squared off with him.

He raised both palms toward her. "Whoa! No offense intended. I just never would have pictured you becoming a PI is all."

Her hackles eased, and she gave him a lopsided grin. "Oh, yeah? And what did you see me becoming?"

He lifted a shoulder. "I don't know. Maybe joining the Army like your dad? Or working on the Colton Ranch wrangling cows alongside Jonah and Dallas?"

She twisted her mouth as if thinking. "Not the Army. Too transient. I had my fill of moving all over the place with my dad." Then focusing her attention on him again, she rushed forward for another hug. "I can't believe it's you! You're really here! It's been way too long."

He hugged her back, more awkwardly aware of the feminine curves snuggled against him. *It's Summer, for God's sake! You're not allowed to notice her figure!*

Leaning back to peer up at him, she asked, "What about you? What brings you here?"

He hitched a thumb toward the office buildings. "I'm meeting Bellamy. Donovan's wife?"

She nodded. "I've met her. She's great."

"Apparently her coworkers threw a baby shower today, and she needs help lugging some big items out to her car."

Her smile twitched playfully. "That's very kind of you to help her out, but... I meant what are you doing in Whisperwood?" Her expression changed instantly to excited hopefulness. "Did you move back here? Oh, Nolan! Say you did!"

He scratched his chin as he flashed a moue of regret. "Afraid not, Tadpole."

"Tadpole." She sighed happily. "It's been a while since anyone called me that." She cocked her head to the side. "So what did bring you to town after all these years?"

Whether she intended the scolding tone or not, he heard a mild reprimand in her question that chewed guiltily at his gut—followed immediately by the acid bite of anger and apprehension left by his suspension. "I'm taking some time off to…rest. Get some perspective on some things."

Rather than satisfy Summer, his vague answer seemed to intrigue her. Her gaze intensified, her mouth compressed and her brow wrinkled in consternation. "What the hell does that mean? Get some perspective?"

"It's a job-related issue."

She bit her bottom lip. "Were you fired?"

He rolled his shoulders, cleared his throat. "No." *Might as well have been.*

Her gaze narrowed further, and he recognized a deep insight in her espresso-brown stare. Summer had always been able to read him well when they were kids.

He drew his shoulders back and glanced away from her knowing gaze. This suspension was a crock, a humiliation. How would he ever be taken seriously by his fellow agents again?

"Nolan?"

He aimed a thumb over his shoulder. "Look, um… Bellamy is waiting for me, so I need to run. But it was great to see you, Summer." He smiled, meaning it. "I'd love to get together for coffee and a catch-up." He motioned to the front of his shirt with his empty cup. "You do owe me a cup."

Summer tucked her golden-blond hair behind her ear, nodding. "That I do, hoss." She patted her pockets, then frowned. "Dang, I left my business cards at the office."

Flipping a page in her notepad, she scribbled a phone number and ripped the sheet out. "Call me. I want to hear what you've been up to, what sort of perspective you need in this mysterious career of yours."

Folding the sheet, he tucked it in his back pocket. "Count on it."

He leaned in to give her cheek a peck, catching the tantalizing floral scent of her shampoo as he did. At the last second, he thought better of the platonic show of affection. Once bitten, twice shy and all that crap. He angled his face away so that they merely brushed cheeks. He took a long step back and rubbed his free hand on the leg of his jeans. Damn it, was this what he'd come to? Second-guessing every friendly gesture around a woman, afraid of his actions being misconstrued?

He continued walking backward, somehow reluctant to let Summer out of his sight. For so many years, she'd been the yin to his yang. Her energy and sunny disposition able to lift him from even the darkest mood. In light of his current circumstances, he could use a strong dose of Summer's friendship and positivity in his life. Running into her today felt like more than good luck. He didn't believe in fate or karma, but seeing Summer gave him a familiar sense of well-being and comfort, like the innocence of their younger days.

He lifted a hand, waving as he reluctantly turned to walk away. If he had the chance to reconnect with Summer while he was on leave, maybe his suspension wouldn't totally suck. He grinned to himself as he strode across the parking lot. See, Summer was already rubbing off on him. He'd found a silver lining in the disaster that was his life.

SO SHE'D BEEN right about seeing Nolan from her office window. A giddy revelry danced inside Summer, leaving her breathless and beaming. After several years of radio silence from her childhood friend, seeing him again was a bonus she hadn't expected when she'd moved back to Whisperwood. She pressed a hand over her scampering heartbeat and prayed he'd use her phone number to set up a date. Well, not a *date* date. That wasn't the kind of relationship they had. But she wanted a long sit-down, catch-up, revive-their-friendship meeting, coffee or not. Because, damn it, she'd *missed* Nolan.

When she'd asked her best girlfriend, Avery Logan— who was now engaged to Nolan's cousin Dallas—what the Coltons had heard from Nolan, she'd been told he hadn't been in touch with his cousins, either. His life for the past several years had been a mystery to her and his cousins. Why? What had led him to lose touch with the family and friends he'd once been so close to?

Summer watched Nolan walk away and couldn't help admiring his broad shoulders and lean hips, the confident swagger in his stride, and the shimmer of golden autumn sun on his light brown hair. She raised a hand to her face, still feeling the light scrape of his five o'clock scruff on her cheek. In that moment, she'd been sure he was going to kiss her, and when he hadn't, disappointment plucked at her. Not because she expected a kiss—they were just friends, after all—but because she'd detected a reticence on his part. He'd held back. Withdrawn.

As kids they'd had such an easy rapport. Even the last time she'd Skyped with him as a teenager, before her family had moved to Colorado and she'd lost touch with him, the comfortable camaraderie had been second nature. So what had changed?

Well, other than the fact that Nolan was no longer a rangy teenager with acne, but a tall, good-looking man with a sexy amount of beard stubble.

"Whew," she whispered on an exhale, mentally amending, a *very* good-looking man. Who'd developed muscles to match his height. Muscles she'd itched to run her hands over and explore after their hug.

Good grief! She gave her head a firm shake. Was she seriously ogling Nolan Colton?

Get that out of your system now, Davies. You want to make things awkward with your old friend? Just let him catch you eyeing him like he's the last slice of Aunt Mimi's chocolate cake.

Great. Now she wanted Nolan *and* cake. Huffing her pique with herself, she tracked Nolan's progress until he disappeared inside the Lone Star Pharma building. Nolan Colton. Here in Whisperwood. Wonders never ceased.

As she turned back to the taped-off area where Patrice Eccleston's body had been discovered, she sobered. She couldn't let Nolan's return distract her from the job at hand. She'd been charged with learning all she could about the monster who'd killed Patrice and why the attractive twenty-year-old had been targeted. If she'd been targeted. Had Patrice's death been planned, or was it a random act of violence?

As picturesque and homey as it appeared, Whisperwood was no stranger to murder and violent crime. In recent months, the man whom authorities had dubbed the Mummy Killer had been found. The murderer, Horace Corgan, had been on his deathbed and confessed to the crimes when presented with evidence of his guilt. Police had assumed Patrice was another of Corgan's victims, but the dying man, who had nothing to lose for speaking the truth, had vehemently denied killing Patrice.

In fact, the circumstances and evidence surrounding her murder and burial made her case an outlier. Unsolved. A raw wound for her family...which was what had brought Atticus and Ian to her office in search of answers, justice and peace of mind. Summer stared at the upturned dirt in the narrow ditch at the edge of the sprawling parking lot, and her heart ached. Poor Patrice. If construction workers hadn't been repairing the buckled pavement left by recent storms, the slain woman might never have been found. Obviously what her killer had hoped for when he— or she—had chosen the location of Patrice's shallow grave.

"Patrice," Summer whispered to the wind, "I promise to do everything in my power to find out who did this to you. If there is justice in this world, I *will* bring your killer in."

With her vow carrying to the heavens on the autumn breeze, Summer packed up her notes and headed back to town to begin fulfilling her promise.

Chapter Two

Summer's mind whirled as she planned her next step in her investigation. Who should she talk to first? How should she proceed so that she didn't burn bridges with the police department? What *need for perspective* had brought Nolan back to Whisperwood after all these years?

She shook her head. Letting Nolan distract her was no way to keep her word to Patrice or solve her first real case. She tucked her notepad under her arm as she fished the keys to her Volkswagen Beetle out of her purse and unlocked her car.

The clank of a metal door opening and the sound of voices drew her attention to the front entrance of Lone Star Pharma. Bellamy Colton, her belly swollen with eight months of pregnancy, held the door as Nolan struggled out the door with a pile of large boxes, stacked so high Summer wasn't sure how he could see where he was walking. Bellamy led him to a car parked in the employee lot and popped the trunk.

Discarding her purse and notepad on her passenger seat, Summer headed toward them to see if she could lend a hand.

"Need any help?" she called, and Bellamy flashed her a broad grin of greeting.

"Thanks, Summer, but I think Nolan's got it."

Summer rushed forward as the top item slid from its perch. She caught the tumbling package and grabbed the next box from the teetering stack, as well. "Are you sure about that?"

Nolan shot her an embarrassed grin. "Thanks. That was close."

Summer read the label on the pillow-like gift zipped in clear plastic packaging. "Boppy?"

Bellamy's face glowed. "I know! I'm so excited. I hear they're a must, and I hadn't gotten one before now."

Summer exchanged a curious look with Nolan as he loaded the gifts into Bellamy's trunk, and she mouthed, *What's a Boppy?*

He shrugged. "Don't look at me. I'm just the pack mule."

Bellamy swatted at his arm. "Oh, hush. It's not as bad as that. One more trip to get the swing, and we'll be done."

Summer added the packages she'd caught to the nooks in Bellamy's car and faced Nolan as he closed the trunk. "I was just finishing up my business here and thought I could buy you that cup of coffee I owe you now."

"Now?" He dusted grime from the car off his hands and arched one eyebrow.

"I didn't want to give you the chance to slip out of town and disappear before I could grill you about your mysterious absence from our lives."

He scoffed and gaped at her. "I disappeared? You're one to talk, Ms. No Social Media Presence."

She cocked her head, blinking. "Huh? I have social media accounts. What are you—"

Bellamy cleared her throat. "Um, I hate to interrupt this lovers' quarrel, but—"

Both Summer and Nolan jerked their heads toward Bellamy, chiming together, "We're not—!" and "What! No!"

Bellamy's grin reflected her skepticism. "Whatever... but my feet are killing me. If you don't mind grabbing that swing, Nolan? My lunch break is almost over, and I need to prop my feet up."

"Right." Nolan aimed a finger at Bellamy. "Lead the way. I'm right behind you." Then pointing at Summer, he added, "Yes. Now's good. But let's make it lunch at the Bluebell Diner. This pack mule is getting hungry."

Summer's mood lifted, and butterfly wings flapped in her chest. "Deal."

As he followed the waddling Bellamy back inside, Nolan motioned to the place Summer was standing. "Stay there. I'll be right back."

With a smirk, she saluted him. "Aye, aye, captain. I'll be right here."

Nolan returned five minutes later, lugging a large cardboard box. Summer eyed the box then the back seat of Bellamy's car. "Um, captain? I don't think there's room in the hold for that cargo."

"Not in that ship," he said, nodding to Bellamy's sedan. "I told her I'd put it in my car. This way. I'll drive to lunch."

Summer pursed her lips, and memories of days spent

rambling and relaxing on the Colton Ranch came back
to her. Specifically how bossy Nolan could be. Apparently, that hadn't changed. But she had. She was her
own boss now, and she'd learned the hard way not to
give any man control of her life.

Nolan started across the pavement, and when she
didn't follow, he glanced back. "Coming?"

"Yeah." She fell in step next to him and dug her
keys out of her pocket. "But I'll drive my own car to
lunch. That way we don't have to double back here to
pick it up."

He stopped at a dark blue Jeep Cherokee, where he
opened the tailgate and slid the baby swing box in the
back. "Suit yourself. If you beat me there, go ahead
and get us a table."

She chuckled lightly. "Bossy as ever, I see."

He frowned. "Bossy? I only said—" He growled
under his breath. "Whatever. Can I walk you to your
car?"

"Thanks, but I'm just there." She pointed three
spaces over to her yellow VW Beetle. "Meet ya in five."

Nolan gave her a wink and a nod that stirred a fresh
wave of giddy bubbles in her veins. She trotted to her
car, energized and more optimistic than she'd been in
months. But as she backed her Beetle out of her parking spot, a niggling warning tickled her brain. As kids,
she'd blown off Nolan's autocratic dictates or complied
happily enough. He was a year older, a boy, and usually had good ideas that she accepted at face value.
Good enough reasons for a nine- or ten-year-old kid to
be a follower. No big deal. But eight years later, going
along, appeasement and blind acceptance with Robby

had gotten her tangled in a dangerous and detrimental relationship that she still had nightmares about.

A cloud of doubt drifted in to cast her good mood in shadow. Summer squeezed the steering wheel and pulled onto the state road leading toward downtown Whisperwood. Nolan might be handsome as the devil and someone who'd graced her childhood with adventure and laughter, but she needed to proceed with caution. Clearly he was still a take-charge kind of guy. She couldn't let her golden memories of Nolan, her fondness for their old friendship color this new iteration of their relationship. She needed to stand firm and set the parameters, or she could too easily repeat mistakes she had yet to live down.

WHEN SHE ARRIVED at the Bluebell Diner, a popular place for locals to eat their fill of home-style Southern cooking and Tex-Mex favorites, Nolan was already ensconced in a booth at the back of the restaurant near the door to the kitchen. He sat with his back to the wall, watching the door, and lifted his chin in acknowledgment as she entered the bustling diner.

She greeted the older couple that ran the mercantile across the street from her office and Madeline Klein, for whom she'd handled a case last month, as she wended her way through the tables toward Nolan. The first thing she noticed as she reached their table was that he'd changed T-shirts. He'd replaced the coffee-soiled one with a simple heather-gray one that read FBI over the breast.

He stood as she approached, waiting for her to sit before resuming his seat. *He still has cowboy manners,* she thought, smiling, flattered, while another part of her brain chafed. Did his old-fashioned manners translate to old-fashioned opinions about women?

Shoving aside the itchy question, she slid into the booth and nodded toward his chest. "Where'd you get an FBI shirt?"

He shrugged one shoulder. "My gym bag was in the back seat."

She snorted. "I mean, how'd you come to own it?" She raised the ice water already at her spot for a sip.

He waved his fingers in casual dismissal. "Standard issue in the Bureau."

Summer choked on the water and set it down, sputtering, "Wait, wh-what?"

He handed her a napkin as she coughed. "Standard issue. They may have given it to me for a Bureau event. I don't remember for sure."

She clutched the paper napkin in her hand and gaped at him. "You're in the FBI?"

He scowled and grumbled, "A little louder, huh? I don't think they heard out on the street."

Nolan cut a glance to the table next to them, where a middle-aged woman with two small children sat. The woman gave him a curious glance, and Nolan flashed an awkward smile and smoothed nonexistent wrinkles from the blue gingham tablecloth.

"Yes," he said in a hushed tone as he handed her a plastic-protected menu from the stack behind the napkin holder. "I am."

Summer flopped back against the booth and stared at him, her mouth gaping. "Get. Out. Of. Town! Nolan!"

He shifted on his bench, and his hand fisted on the

table. "Well, technically I still am, but…" He exhaled heavily and sent her a dark look. "The real reason I'm in town is I've been put on administrative leave."

Their waitress arrived, placing napkin-wrapped cutlery at each of their places. "Y'all had a chance to look at the menu?"

Nolan picked up a menu. "Sorry, no. We need another minute."

"Take your time, but the pumpkin spice cake is going fast. If you want any, you better order it now."

"Hmm, that does sound good. Save us two slices," Nolan said, giving the woman a lopsided grin.

Pumpkin spice cake did sound great, but Nolan's high-handedness in ordering for her irked her. "Two slices? You are hungry, aren't you, G-man?"

He peered over the top of his menu. "You don't want cake? You used to love dessert."

"What kid doesn't? What I want is to order for myself." She softened the scolding with a playful scowl. Leaning forward, she flattened her hands on the tabletop. "Now tell me about this FBI thing. How did that happen? When? What department are you in? Jeez, the *FB freaking I*?"

He cleared his throat, dropped his gaze to the menu again and said, "I was training for the Fort Worth Police Department when I saw an article that said the FBI was recruiting. So I applied, got accepted and have been in the Bureau for the last six years."

A look of consternation crossed his face, and she recalled his comment about administrative leave. "And you're here in Whisperwood rather than on the job because…"

He poked the inside of his cheek with his tongue, tapped the menu on the table, then met her eyes. "I'm being investigated for sexual assault against a fellow agent."

As casually as if he'd just told her the sky was blue, he put his menu back behind the napkin holder. "I think I'll have the chili with jalapeño cornbread. What looks good to you?"

Summer's heart rose to her throat, and she squeaked, "What!"

"Chili and cornbread. I've missed Texas-style chili up in Chi-town."

She reached for his arm and squeezed. His muscles in his forearm were rock hard, and despite the serious topic of their conversation, her belly twitched in recognition of the skin-to-skin contact. "Don't pretend you didn't just drop a bomb. Explain that—" she stopped, giving the woman with the young kids a side glance and lowering her volume to a whisper "—sexual assault comment."

He firmed his mouth and withdrew his arm from her grip. "I'll fill you in on the specifics later, somewhere less public. Leave it at this—I didn't do what Charlotte's contending."

"Charlotte, huh?" She folded her arms over her chest and furrowed her brow. "I used to like that name. Not so much now."

"Why don't you tell me how you got started as a PI? And how long have you been back in Whisperwood? I tried to track you down in recent years and got nowhere. Where've you been?" He sipped his water, and his expression indicated he was closing the door on discussing his life.

"I've been a lot of places in the last seventeen or so years. You remember my dad reupped with the Army?"

He nodded.

"So we moved every couple of years. I started college in Georgia before…circumstances led me to change my major and transfer to Colorado State. Then after graduating with a degree in marketing, I decided I liked being my own boss. I'd gained a little experience and interest in private investigating thanks to those, uh, circumstances I mentioned…" She raised an eyebrow letting him know she'd be leaving that story untold for the moment.

"Mm-hmm, now who's being mysterious and coy?" he asked.

"Not coy. Just saving the details for our private heart-to-heart when you tell all."

The waitress returned and took their order. When they had semiprivacy again, she said, "I'd say the fact you couldn't find me on social media indicates you aren't a very good G-man, but, in truth, I tried to make myself hard to find."

Nolan's brow dipped. "Why would you do that?"

"A troublesome ex. That, and I've gone by different names over the years. The thing about moving to new schools every couple years is, you can reinvent yourself, be Victoria instead of Summer. Then I tried out Vee and by college I was going by Vicki. After Robby started hounding me, I switched to Tori."

"What was wrong with Summer?" His gaze narrowed,

and his hazel eyes darkened. "I liked Summer. Not just the name, but the girl I knew. Why reinvent yourself?"

She lifted a shoulder. "Boredom. Youthful experimenting. Because I could. New place, new name. It was a game."

The noise that issued from his throat said he was skeptical. "And now you're back in Whisperwood. Why?"

"That one's easy. I love it here. Of all the places we moved over the years, all the zip codes where I lived since I was a kid, nowhere ever felt like home the way Whisperwood did. Maybe it was nostalgia, maybe it was because we lived here longer than anywhere else, but Whisperwood has always represented home and roots. It's where I wanted to settle down and raise my family." She spread her hands. "So a few months ago, I made it happen. I packed up my cat and headed down here. I found office space on Main Street and opened my own PI biz."

"And got hired for a case that involves the crime scene at Lone Star Pharma." His arched eyebrow asked for her to supply details.

"My first big case here. I helped with criminal cases at my old firm, but since I opened my own business, I've mostly been following cheating husbands, looking for lost relatives and finding missing dogs."

He pulled an amused face. "Dogs?"

She chuckled. "Yeah. A little girl came in a couple weeks ago asking for help finding her dog. She had two dollars. I had a little time." She shrugged. "We found the dog a couple doors down from her house twenty minutes later. I didn't charge her. But word got around at the elementary school, and I've been hired twice more since then. Found both dogs at the same house as the first. It seems Mrs. Nesbit's poodle was in heat, and every male dog in the neighborhood was visiting Fluffy. Case closed."

He laughed, and the rich sound sent a quiver to her core.

Their food arrived, and she tucked in, more to occupy her restless hands and distract her mind from the odd hum that had vibrated in her veins since sitting down with Nolan fifteen minutes earlier than from hunger.

"And the case you have now? It's the real thing?"

"I'll say. A twenty-year-old woman was strangled and buried in the parking lot where you saw me earlier. Her family isn't happy with the way the police are handling the case, the slow trickle of information from the Whisperwood PD, so they've hired me to find the person responsible for killing her."

With his gaze fixed on her, Nolan set his cornbread down so hard, it broke in half. "You're investigating a murder? An open case with the local PD?"

She wiped condensation from her water glass with her thumb. Did she detect a note of disbelief or judgment in his tone? She prayed not. She'd come to expect a bit of sexism from the population as a whole, but she wanted to believe Nolan was above it. She bobbed a nod. "I am."

He said nothing as he popped another bite of cornbread in his mouth and chewed, watching her. She held his stare, wondering what was going on behind his mercurial hazel eyes. Where moments ago they'd been the gray-green color of a Texas river, now flecks of gold sparked in their depths, a sure sign his mind was churning. Once he'd swallowed the bite of cornbread, he said, "You're talking about Patrice Eccleston?"

"Yeah. You heard about her?"

"My family was discussing the case last night at dinner." He paused briefly before adding, "I'm staying on my cousins' ranch. Same room I used all those summers as a kid."

She smiled. "I'm guessing Josephine hasn't changed a thing in that room since the last time you stayed there."

"You'd be right." He stirred his chili, blew on a spoonful and said, "I want in."

She paused with a French fry halfway to her mouth. "Pardon?"

"Your murder investigation. I'm sitting on my butt out at the ranch doing nothing except mucking stalls in the morning and watching *Jeopardy!* in the afternoons with Josephine. I'm an FBI special agent, Summer. I can help you, and I want in."

Chapter Three

Summer dropped her French fry in a puddle of ketchup and frowned at him. "Who said I need help? I can handle the case by myself."

He raised a palm. "I'm sure you can, but I have time on my hands and investigative experience. Why not use me?"

Why not, indeed? She wiped her fingers on her napkin and considered his offer. "I can't pay you. I'm barely making my office rent each month as it is."

"I didn't ask you to. I'm volunteering." He crumbled a bit of his cornbread into his chili and stirred it up. "Come on, Summer. Think how great it would be for us to team up. Bullfrog and Tadpole, together again."

She sputtered a laugh. "Oh my goodness! We haven't used those nicknames in years!"

Teaming up with him, spending time with him would be great, if...

If he didn't prove a distraction. And *if* he didn't try to take over the investigation and push her aside. And *if* he could satisfy her questions about these sexual assault charges against him.

Dear God, *sexual assault*? He claimed he was innocent, and at face value, she believed him, but…it had been seventeen years since they'd spent any significant, quality time together. He could have changed. Knowing that the Nolan she'd known could be gone made her chest hurt.

But she wouldn't get the measure of him without spending time with him. A tingle of anticipation spun through her at the idea of having a legitimate reason to spend time with her old best friend. "I have conditions."

His head angled in surprise. "Name them."

"It's my case, so I'm in charge. Remember that."

"So noted."

"No calling me Tadpole in front of the client or anyone we're interviewing for the case."

"Of course. That wouldn't be professional. Understood. What else?"

She tore off a piece of her sandwich and nibbled it as she thought. "I…guess that's all. The first one is the main thing." She aimed a finger at him. "Don't be bossy."

He blinked. "Who me? I'm not—"

"You are, Mr. Two Pieces of Cake!" she said, laughing. "And you always have been!"

"Oh, see, now the cake thing…that's wasn't being bossy," he said, his expression the image of innocence. "That was foresight, thoughtfulness and practicality."

She tipped her head back as she laughed.

"I have conditions, too." His serious tone caught her off guard and quelled her chuckles.

"You do?"

He set his spoon in his empty chili bowl and pushed

the dirty dish aside. "If we work together, we keep our relationship completely platonic and professional."

She snorted. "Naturally. That kinda goes without saying."

So why did the term "platonic" cause the odd stab of disappointment? Summer could understand his caution since apparently someone was accusing him of untoward advances, but why had he felt it necessary to spell that out with *her*?

Okay, she had admired his fitness and the way his face had developed more chiseled and manly lines. Had he seen something in her face that he'd taken the wrong way? How embarrassing! Just in case, she added another eye roll and dismissive sniff. "No problem there."

"Good." He gave a satisfied nod. "Then we're in agreement? We'll work together on your murder case?"

"Uh...yeah." She blinked, letting the arrangement sink in. She would be teaming up with *Nolan*. Who was an *FBI agent*. To solve a *murder*. Holy crap! She released her breath, and an excited smile stole onto her face. "Okay. Let's do this!"

The cake Nolan had ordered earlier arrived, and she slid the biggest piece in front of her and dug in. It was divine.

THIRTY MINUTES LATER, Summer unlocked her office and led Nolan inside. A dark gray cat met them at the door.

Nolan paused, staring at the feline. "Summer, there's a cat in here."

"Uh-huh. That's Yossi." She slung her jacket across the back of her desk chair and squatted to pat the feline. "Say hello. He's very friendly."

Nolan held his fingers out for the cat to sniff, and Yossi rubbed his head on the offered hand instead. Giving the cat's cheek a little scratch, Nolan stepped deeper into the small office and surveyed the spare decor. The walls were bare, and her furnishings consisted of one wooden bookcase that was overloaded with books and stacks of magazines, two ladder-backed chairs facing a dented metal and faux-wood desk, a lamp and a metal file cabinet. In the corner was what he assumed was the cat's litter box.

Nolan rubbed his chin as he took a seat in one of the chairs. "Love what you've done with the place. If I move back to town permanently, you'll have to give me the name of your decorator."

Summer gave him a withering glance. "It's Sally *Bite Me*."

He chuckled and propped an ankle on his opposite knee as he watched her opening file folders and paging through the notebook he'd seen her scribbling in at the crime scene. "So where are you in your investigation? Lay it out for me."

She clicked open her pen and leaned back in her chair. "All right. So the victim is twenty-year-old Patrice Eccleston. Her family hired me first thing this morning, because they weren't getting answers from the cops."

"Not uncommon. The police often can't share details of an open investigation. What if it turns out a family member was responsible for the murder?"

She arched one blond eyebrow. "Preaching to the choir, Nolan."

He held up a hand. "Of course. Sorry."

"The autopsy shows she was strangled. Her hands

were bound by the time she was buried. No sign of sexual assault. Thank God. Broken fingernails indicate she struggled, but they found no traces of skin cells."

"Whoever strangled her was covered up, then? Long sleeves, gloves…and she didn't get his face, so maybe a mask. Or she was attacked from behind?"

She nodded and consulted her notes again. "She was last seen leaving Bailey's Bar and Grill the night she disappeared. She was alone at the time, according to surveillance camera footage." She tapped her pen against the notepad and looked up at Nolan. "I had her father and brother give me a list of her friends and hobbies, favorite hangouts and so forth—" She paused when Yossi jumped into Nolan's lap, curled up and lay down. She covered a smile with her hand. "I hope you like cats. Yossi is not much for personal boundaries."

He slanted a look at her gray feline, then rolled his eyes. "Yeah, it's fine." He scratched Yossi's cheek and nodded to her. "You were saying?"

"Right." She pulled out the forms that the Ecclestons had filled out and slid them across her desk to him. "Here's what they've given me so far. I went out to the crime scene this morning, as you know, to see if anything unusual or telling jumped out at me."

"And did anything?"

She twisted her mouth. "No."

Nolan leaned forward to take the papers from her desk, and Yossi dug his claws in to hold on as his lap bed shifted. Leaning back, Nolan began scanning the information and asked, "Who found the body?"

"Construction workers dug her up while renovating the parking lot. The storm that blew through here this summer caused a good bit of flooding, and the parking lot buckled and part of it washed out. It had to be completely redone. Originally they thought Patrice was another victim of a guy named Corgan, a serial killer who confessed on his deathbed to murdering several other women in the area. But Patrice wasn't mummified, and Corgan denied killing her, so…"

"So her killer is still out there. Thus the family's hiring you."

"Exactly."

He returned the pages of notes to her desk. "I think I mentioned that my cousins were talking a bit about the case at dinner. They've been pretty deeply involved with solving the Mummy Killer case and some other goings-on around town lately. I'll talk to them this afternoon and see what insights they might have that would help us. Things the police may not have shared with the family yet."

Summer perked up. "That'd be great! I'd planned to start interviewing some of Patrice's friends today. Want to divide the list?"

Nolan stroked Yossi's fur and shook his head. "Let's go together. Two sets of ears are better than one. I might pick up on something you miss—" her frown returned, and he added quickly, "—or vice versa."

Summer was certainly touchy about anyone denigrating her work or her abilities. What was that about? She'd always been such a confident and carefree kid when they'd hung out together those summers twenty years ago. Granted, a lot could happen, a lot could change in that many years. Not the least of which were her physical changes. The spindly-legged, flat-chested tomboy was gone, replaced by a beautiful, curvy woman with bedroom eyes that could seduce you in a heartbeat. Also the same were her expressive face and tendency to use big gestures as she talked. Summer had always been animated, full of life, with a magnetic personality. As a kid she'd played counterpoint to his quieter nature and penchant for observing rather than diving in and damning the torpedoes. Apparently that synergy still existed, still dovetailed with something in his soul, because he felt an old familiar warmth and tenderness toward her expanding in his chest.

He'd spelled out the need for the two of them to keep their working relationship platonic as much as a warning and reminder for himself as a guide for her. He'd sat across from her in the diner and been swamped with all kinds of nonplatonic urges. He'd had to remind himself about every five minutes that it was *Summer* sitting there looking like forbidden fruit. Every teasing twitch of her bow-shaped lips and disapproving wrinkle of her pixie-like nose spiked his pulse. Her thick golden hair and bedroom brown eyes had— Damn it! He was waxing poetic about her again. He pinched his nose and battled away the tug of lust.

"…her first. Sound good?" Summer was saying when he refocused his attention.

He cleared his throat, digging his fingers into her cat's fur and nodding stupidly. "Um, sure."

What had he just agreed to?

Chapter Four

"Maybe we should take your car," Summer said, suppressing a giggle as she watched Nolan fold his long legs and linebacker shoulders into the front passenger seat of her Beetle.

"No, I'm in now. Let's go."

Even before you considered his remarkable size, Nolan had a way of filling up a space with the magnitude of his presence. He commanded a room with his confidence and good looks, and now, in the tiny confines of her car, he seemed to suck all the oxygen out of the air. Or maybe that was just her reaction to his nearness. She'd been feeling a bit winded and dizzy ever since she'd hugged him at the Lone Star Pharma parking lot this morning. *Jumped him* was more like it. But dang it, she'd been happy to see him. She was impulsive that way. Was her overly enthusiastic greeting the reason he'd felt the need to put out his platonic-only condition for working together? Probably.

Okay, so she needed to try to check her impulses around Nolan. He may have grown up to be a walking dream, but theirs had always been simply a friendship.

Clearly he wanted no more than that, which was why he had been quick to put the kibosh on anything more.

He buckled his seat belt and slanted a wry glance at her. "Stop laughing, or I'll think this was a setup."

"I'm not laughing," she said, her lighthearted tone belying her assertion. "I Googled the directions on my phone." She handed him her cell. "Will you navigate?"

He swiped to open the proper screen and aimed a thumb down Main Street. "Sure. Head east toward Caldwell Street."

"Remember, I only moved back here a couple months ago. I'm still relearning street names and landmarks."

"Roger that."

A few minutes later, they arrived at the apartment complex where their first interviewee lived. Their knock on the door of 4-B was answered by a petite young woman with frizzy auburn hair and freckles. Her gaze locked on Nolan, the twinkle of interest in her eyes clearly saying she'd noticed how handsome the man on her doorstep was.

"Amanda Cole?" Summer asked, drawing the young woman's attention away from Nolan.

"Yes?" Amanda's expression modulated, as if disappointed to realize her hunky visitor had a female companion.

"I'm Summer Davies, a local private investigator, and this is my associate, Nolan Colton." They each offered their hand for Amanda to shake. "Do you have a few minutes to talk with us, please?"

Her green eyes darkened with doubt. "About what?"

"Patrice Eccleston. We understand you were roommates?"

"Well, yeah." Grief washed over Amanda's expressive countenance. Interviewing her would be all the easier, since her thoughts and emotions were written on her face.

"May we come in?" Nolan asked, and Amanda swallowed hard before nodding and opening the door farther to allow them inside.

The apartment was decorated in a style Summer would call Early College. Mismatched, inexpensive furniture mixed with older, worn pieces that screamed "castoffs from a parent's house," and the detritus of pizza dinners, studying and gossip magazines littered the living room. The scent of burned microwave popcorn hung in the air.

Nolan eyed a bright pink folding butterfly chair skeptically before seating himself on the garage sale–reject couch. Amanda perched on a red director's chair and chewed her bottom lip. Knowing she couldn't maintain an erect, businesslike posture in the butterfly chair, Summer joined Nolan on the sofa. A broken spring poked her butt, so she shifted closer to Nolan to find a more comfortable spot.

"What do you want to know about Patrice?" their hostess asked, a quiver of nerves in her voice.

"Basic information. Anything that might give us a picture of her life in the weeks before she was killed."

"Amanda? Who was—?" A second young woman with a long, lean frame, a mocha complexion and black hair pulled up in a ponytail sauntered in from the back of the apartment and stopped short when she spotted the strangers on the couch. "Oh. Hi."

Nolan stood and offered his hand as Amanda said,

"Maria, these folks are private investigators wanting to talk about Patrice. This is my roommate, Maria."

Summer smiled at Maria, who wore running shoes, yoga shorts and a T-shirt, then flipped to the front of her notepad asking, "Would you be Maria Hernandez, by any chance?"

Maria sent her roommate a worried frown before returning her gaze to Summer. "How did you know?"

"We got your name from Patrice's brother. You are actually on our list of people we wanted to interview. Ian and his father have hired me to look into Patrice's death."

"You?" Her tone echoed the dubious look she wore. "Why?"

"I'm a private investigator."

"What about him?" Maria asked, waving a hand toward Nolan.

"He's helping me with the case."

Maria shifted her weight uneasily. "We already told the police all we know."

Summer nodded. "That's good. I'm sure your information will be helpful to them. But we are working independently from the police department and want to explore…other options that the police might not."

"Do you have a minute?" Nolan motioned toward the empty butterfly chair.

Maria looked irritated. "I was just leaving for a run."

Nolan flashed a beatific grin that sent Summer's pulse scampering. "We promise not to keep you long."

Maria sighed and dragged a wooden chair in from the breakfast nook. "Before we start, can I see some ID?"

Summer dug out her wallet to show the girls her PI

license. When Maria's expectant gaze swung toward Nolan, he dragged a hand down his face. "I can show you my driver's license if you want, but my badge is in Illinois at the moment."

"Badge?" Amanda asked. "You're a cop?"

He hesitated before offering, "FBI. But I'm not here in an official capacity. Just backup for Summer."

Amanda and Maria exchanged wide-eyed looks.

"Anyway," Summer said brightly, "as Patrice's friends, we figured you two could tell us where she liked to hang out, if she had a boyfriend or a recent *ex*-boyfriend, her social media habits…that sort of thing. Let's start with the boyfriend question."

The both shook their heads, and Amanda added, "She had a lot of male friends, but none that were 'boy-friends.'" She drew air quotes with her fingers.

Summer glanced at the list Patrice's family had given her. No male names were among those provided. "Can you give us names of her male friends? How did she know these guys?"

"Classes, mainly. She was going to the vocational school in Hargrove to become a mechanic."

Nolan's chin jerked up. "A mechanic? Like to fix cars?"

Maria gave him a *well, duh* look. "What? Like a woman can't be a mechanic?"

Summer angled her body toward Nolan, narrowing a wry gaze on him. "Yes, Nolan. Is there a reason why a woman can't be a mechanic or whatever else she wants to be?"

He raised his palms. "Whoa. Easy, ladies. Just surprised me. It's not a common career path for a female.

But I have no beef with a woman being whatever she wants to be."

Summer flashed a satisfied grin. "Good. Now that we have that settled—" she faced Amanda "—those names?"

"I only know first names. She met most of the guys in class and only referred to them as Barry, Charlie, Tyler and so forth," Amanda said.

"Same when we all met up at Happy Hooligans for a drink," Maria added. "She only introduced the guys with first names. It was just a casual thing and…" She shrugged.

Summer clicked her pen and started writing, "So Barry, Charlie and Tyler. All students of the automotive repair program at the vocational college?"

Amanda nodded.

Nolan waved a hand toward the roommates. "Are you two students there, as well?"

Maria snorted. "Like I have the money for tuition. I wait tables during the early-morning shift at the Bluebell Diner and clean offices at Lone Star Pharma at night."

Summer scribbled that information down, then looked to Amanda. "And you?"

Maria gave a wry laugh. "Mandy's got a rich daddy who pays her rent."

Amanda scowled at her friend. "He's not rich. He's just helping me out until I graduate." Then to Summer, "I commute to UT in Austin two days a week. I'm in the early childhood education program. I want to teach kindergarten."

"How did you two meet Patrice?" Nolan asked.

"High school. We all went to Whisperwood High together," Amanda said. "I was in a lot of classes with Patrice. We hit it off, even though we were…kinda opposites."

Summer tipped her head. "Opposites how?"

Amanda flipped over a hand and gave a small shrug. "I don't do sports, and she and Maria were on the basketball team together. Then there was her whole love of cars and fixing engines. I totally don't get that. But she was super sweet and had a good sense of humor. We bonded because we'd both lost our moms."

Summer was making notes again when Nolan asked, "Did Patrice have any enemies? An ex-boyfriend who was bothering her? A rival she'd upset? Anything like that?"

Maria shook her head. "No. Like Mandy said, Patrice was really nice to everyone. Everyone liked her."

"So she hadn't mentioned any angry responses to posts on Facebook or arguments in class? Maybe one of the guys harassing her?"

Maria and Amanda both shook their heads.

"Patrice was a private person. She didn't share a lot with us about her private life, but I think she'd have mentioned something like that, and she didn't." Amanda divided a look between them. "She wasn't on Facebook. She had a Snapchat account and Instagram."

"Twitter, too, but she said she never checked it," Maria added. "We told all this to the cops already."

Summer smiled patiently. "I understand, but we may go a different path on this investigation than the police. So your cooperation is appreciated."

"No ex-boyfriend," Amanda said. "The guys from

her classes considered her a buddy, which is what she preferred, I think. Early on, I think she had a thing for Barry, but he seemed oblivious to her feelings for him."

"What about her family, her father and brother? What kind of relationship did she have with them?" Nolan asked, and Summer cut a startled look to him.

Summer tried to school her face. While she was in the middle of an interview, it wouldn't do to give away any of her personal feelings about the case, anything that could slant the interviewee's answers. But dang it, what was Nolan doing? Patrice's family was her client! Why would they hire her if they were involved in her death?

Summer bit back her discontent and fought to hide her irritation with Nolan as Amanda and Maria exchanged a look.

"Like I said, her mom died while we were in high school," Amanda said. "It's one of the reasons she and I became friends. When I heard about it, I found her in the lunchroom one day and told her I knew how she felt and if she wanted to talk ever, I was available."

Nolan nodded and offered a half smile. "That was kind of you. But what about her father? Her brother? Did she talk about them?"

"Some. Nothing major." Maria shifted her weight restlessly. "She'd eat Sunday lunch with them and watch the Cowboys game after church, and she'd check on her dad at some point during the week to cook for him, so he didn't live off fast food."

"Did you ever pick up on any resentment in the family relationships?" Nolan persisted.

Summer eased a hand to his thigh and pinched him.

Hard. Nolan grimaced, so slightly she'd have missed it if she weren't looking for a reaction to her silent message.

Maria hesitated, clearly having seen the brief interplay between her interrogators, then said, "Normal family stuff. Nothing big. She said after her mom died that her dad became super strict and overprotective."

Amanda added, "Also, more recently her dad had been pestering her to get a job to help with bills, which bugged her, because in his next breath he'd be nagging her about making good grades and spending more time studying."

"Did she get a job?" Summer asked. No one had mentioned to her a place of employment for Patrice.

"She applied at a couple places to appease her dad," Amanda said. "But no. She wasn't working when—" Her freckled face crumpled, and she didn't finish the thought.

"Did she say where she'd applied?" Summer asked. "Maybe someone saw Patrice as a threat to their own job?"

"I think she filled out an application at the Pizza Barn. We joked about the employee discount being a great benefit for us." Amanda flashed a sad smile. "She had a couple other interviews, but she wouldn't say much about them. Only that she didn't get the jobs."

"You could ask her dad about the interviews." Maria cast a telling look to the clock. "He drove her to most of them."

Summer and Nolan stayed about ten more minutes, gathering more specific information about Patrice's habits and hobbies (jogging with Maria, word puzzles and needlepoint, which her mother had taught her years ago), favorite hangouts (Bailey's Bar and Grill with her friends from class and JoJo's Java every Friday before class with Amanda) and other friends (Gail Schuster, another high school pal who was next on Summer's list).

When they returned to Summer's car, Nolan gave her a querying look. "There a reason you chose to abuse my leg while we were in there?"

She rolled her eyes and groaned. "You were hijacking the interview, asking questions about things that didn't contribute to the investigation."

He frowned. "I'm sorry, but what questions did you think were irrelevant?"

"The whole thing about her family. Did you miss where I told you they are the ones who hired me?"

"So?"

"So why would they hire me if they were involved in her death?"

He scratched his temple, his brow furrowed. "Um, you do know that when a woman is killed, the most likely candidates are always the people closest to her, right? The husband or boyfriend. A parent…"

She started the engine and shook her head. "I'm aware of that statistic, but in this case, the family doesn't make sense. I looked in her father's eyes and saw genuine grief."

"Sure it wasn't guilt?"

"Nolan!" She slapped a hand on the steering wheel. "This is my case! I told you I didn't want you trying to take over."

When she reached for the gearshift to back out of the parking space, he covered her hand with his to stop her, then turned the key to shut off the engine.

"Uh! What are you doing?" She gaped at him, trying to ignore the thrill that chased up her arm when he'd touched her hand.

"I don't want you driving while distracted. And I want to clear things up before we go any further with this case."

"Clear what things up?" Her heart struck a hard staccato beat when she faced him. His mercurial eyes bored into her, and his scruff-dusted jaw flexed as he clenched his teeth.

"Do you want me helping you with this case or don't you?"

"I do," she said with confidence, adding, "but only if you remember my terms. This is *my* case. Don't try to commandeer it from me."

His eyes clung to hers, but he said nothing for several uncomfortable seconds. Finally, his gaze softened, and he said, "Your case. I get that. Why is that such a sticking point for you? You seem hypersensitive about it. What's going on? The Summer I used to know wasn't this uptight."

She tucked her hair behind her ear and tried not to let memories of rampant sexism from her past elevate her blood pressure. Nolan had asked a fair question, and he deserved the truth. "The Summer you knew was included as an equal in all the stuff you guys used to do. You didn't defer to me or cut me out of anything muddy or rough-and-tumble because I was a girl. But this Summer—" she pointed to herself "—never got the lead on cases at her last investigative agency, despite the fact I had every bit as much or more training than the men in the agency. This Summer—" she tapped her chest "—was treated like a glorified errand girl, who always got sent for coffee or asked to do the copying and collating and transcribing notes for the men. I got leering looks at my chest and pedantic speeches and mansplaining out the wazoo."

His expression darkened at the mention of being sexually objectified by her colleagues.

"I finally had enough and quit."

"Good," he said, nodding his head in approval.

"I came here to start my own business and be the boss. But even here I get funny looks when I tell people I'm the owner of Davies Investigations LLC. I've lost business when people change their mind about hiring me when they learn a woman would be handling their case." She huffed angrily. "So, yeah, I'm a little sensitive to being pushed aside and treated with sexism, because it has been happening for years. And it drives me nuts!" Summer raised her hands, her fingers curled like claws as she growled her frustration.

Nolan again sat quietly, his gaze on her, steady and a bit unnerving with its penetrating power. Something deep in her core stirred in response to his hazel stare.

Finally he spoke, his voice calm and deep and lulling. "First of all, this Nolan—" he flattened a hand against his chest "—is the same Nolan you knew. I didn't discriminate against you when we were kids, and I will not now. I see ability and character in you. Not man versus woman."

Reluctantly, she said, "Okay."

His reply should have made her feel better, but the marrow-deep awareness he awoke in her deflated instead, leaving a hollow ache. She wanted to be treated as an equal, but would it be so terrible if he saw her as a woman? Did she really want to be just his pal? The feminine side of her said no, while a more practical part of her brain reminded her of his platonic-only rule.

"Second, I hate that you were subjected to that kind of discrimination and objectification. I'd love to set those men straight on a thing or two." His hand flexed as he scowled, leaving no secret *how* he'd set her sexist colleagues straight.

"And finally, the questions about Patrice's family were valid and necessary. I wasn't trying to take over. I was asking important questions, if only to legitimately eliminate them as suspects. It's not impossible that they hired you to throw the investigation off their tracks." He angled his head and wrapped his fingers around her wrist. "I think if you'll look past your sense of being overshadowed, you'll know I'm right."

The tingles were back. In spades. Her attention zeroed in on his warm hand, the sensation rushing through her blood, the hint of dizziness that swamped her.

"Summer?"

She jerked her gaze back to him, mentally replaying his last words. "Yeah. You're right. I'm sorry I overreacted." She exhaled a cleansing breath. "I'll try not to be so testy from here on out."

He lifted the corner of his mouth and gave her a wink. Before he withdrew his hand, he gave her shoulder a quick squeeze.

When she turned the key again to restart the engine, her hand was trembling. With a tight grip on the steering wheel to hide the tremors, she backed from the parking spot and headed out to the side street, praying Nolan hadn't noticed her show of nerves. Her crazy attraction to Nolan was her issue to manage. He'd been clear that he wanted their friendship to continue on the same course it had begun. Strictly buddies. Asexual pals.

And because she valued his friendship, his insights and his expertise on this case, she would find a way to rein in this new fascination with his *GQ* physique, thrilling touch and drool-worthy mug.

As she drove, Nolan opened her notebook and read over her notes. "I suggest we follow up with Patrice's dad on the job interviews and find these guys from her vocational classes."

Summer nodded. "I agree. I also want to look up her social media profiles and see if anything stands out."

He flipped the notebook closed and angled his body toward her. "Speaking of social media, tell me more about the troublesome ex you were trying to avoid when you made your profiles so hard to find. Robby?"

She cut a surprised glance to him. "Yes, Robby. Did I tell you that?"

"At lunch, yes. And I'm good with names. Comes in handy during investigations."

"I bet." She returned her gaze to the road and shrugged Robby off, even though just his name still caused an acid bite in her gut. "We dated briefly, but I knew pretty quickly he wasn't for me. So I broke up with him, and he didn't like it. Wouldn't take no for an answer."

"When was this? How long ago?"

"Mmm, end of my freshman year of college, so... nearly ten years?"

"When was the last time you heard from him? Is he still a problem?"

She sent Nolan a smile. His evident protectiveness spread a gooey, sweet feeling and a sense of safety through her. "Are you planning to beat him up for me, G-man?"

He flipped up a palm. "If needed."

"Well, thanks for the thought, but after a couple months and my threat to call the police on him, he took the hint." She twisted her mouth as she reflected on Robby's tactics of intimidation and stalking. "Thank God."

Had Patrice's murder been the result of a relationship gone bad? An ex-boyfriend who wouldn't take no for an answer? Her roommates hadn't known of anyone Patrice had been dating, but could a past boyfriend have been stalking her?

"Hey, make a note for us to ask Patrice's father about past boyfriends. Maybe Patrice wasn't as lucky to get rid of a bad penny as I was."

"Good thinking," he said with a nod...but didn't write it down.

"Uh, Nolan? Aren't you going to make that note for me?" She pointed to her pad.

He tapped his temple. "It's all right here. As your partner in this investigation, you share the benefit of my excellent memory and attention to detail."

She snorted. "And your modesty?"

He shot her a wry look. "And I get the benefit of your dry wit."

She laughed. "Yep."

He reached over to squeeze her shoulder. "It's one

of the things I love most about you, Tadpole. Don't ever change."

She knew he didn't mean love in *that way*, but hearing him say the word in reference to her caused a funny tickle in her belly. The weight and warmth of his hand sent sparks through her bloodstream, and her lips trembled as she sent him a smile of acknowledgment.

Don't ever change, he'd said. But did her reactions to the sexy adult version of her old friend mean something had already changed for her? Falling for Nolan, who was only in town while on suspension from the FBI, was a setup for heartache. She'd do well to remember that.

Chapter Five

When they returned to Summer's office, Nolan looked over her notes from the meetings with Patrice's family when they'd hired Summer and with Patrice's room-mates. He had to admit, her notes were meticulous, and the questions and insights she'd scribbled in the margins were on point and reflected a keen, analytical mind.

Summer continued to surprise him. Not that he hadn't known she was smart. Even as a kid he could tell that. And she'd always been able to make him laugh when they were younger, too. She'd been the ebullient, animated, energetic person she was today, full of sweeping hand gestures and expressive facial reactions. Larger than life. Was that the term they used?

So, in a lot of ways she was everything he remembered, but…holy cow! Every time he looked at her, he was stunned all over again by the sexy woman she'd become. Keeping his vow to maintain a friendly distance was proving harder than he'd anticipated. Her determination to make a go of her business filled him with pride. The stories of her teen years, a drifting soul looking for an identity, broke his heart. And that Robby punk who'd harassed her? Nolan wanted five minutes alone with the guy to teach him not to mess with his Summer.

Nolan frowned and mentally backed up. Not *his* Summer. Just Summer. He couldn't start thinking of her as *his* without repercussions he didn't want to deal with. He would be leaving again for Chicago in a few days, and the last thing he wanted was to give Summer the wrong idea about his intentions, potentially hurting her when he left town.

"Don't you think so, Nolan? Ahem! Nolan?"

Yanked from his musings, he jerked his gaze up to hers. "Sorry, what?"

"I was just saying the follow-up conversation with Patrice's father and brother can wait a bit. Tracking down the guys from her class should be our next move. Where were you just then?"

He waved off her question with a vague hand motion. "I can't get the conversation I had with my cousins last night out of my head." A lie, but a useful dodge of her question. No way he'd tell her he was obsessing over *her.*

"About the Mummy Killer?"

"Um…yeah."

"I thought the cops decided Patrice wasn't one of his victims."

"They did, but my cousins have been up to their Stetsons in all kinds of crazy, dangerous stuff in recent months. It may not be related, but it'd also be negligent of us not to at least consider there could be a link."

Summer nodded. "Okay. We can look into it."

Nolan spun the desk chair to look out the front window. He gnawed on the cap of his pen as he stared at the old buildings that lined the street and housed the small businesses that made Whisperwood so unique and special. Corporate America hadn't crept into town yet—much—to spoil the homey, personalized nature of the shops and services on Main Street. One could still buy fresh eggs, locally grown vegetables or a box of crackers from Whisperwood General Store, enjoy a custom-brewed cup of coffee at JoJo's Java or find the right tool for the job at B&P Hardware. *Small town...*

"I don't believe in coincidences," Nolan said, thinking aloud, "and this town is too small for those other crimes not to be related to Patrice's death somehow." He turned back to find Summer cuddling her cat as she paced. "I can feel it."

She nodded. "I trust your instincts. So let's head out to the ranch now and talk to them."

He twisted his mouth and cocked his head. "Not the best time to catch everyone at home."

She lifted a shoulder. "So when then? I'm flexible."

"Well, they're having a barbecue tomorrow night at the ranch as sort of a welcome thing for me. Everyone is supposed to be there. Why don't you come?"

She wrinkled her nose. "I can't crash a family event."

"You won't be crashing. Come as my date."

SUMMER'S PULSE SKIPPED. "Your date?"

He pulled a face. "Not a *date* date. My guest. Friend. Whatever. Don't get hung up on semantics, Tadpole."

She was sure he'd used the old nickname to put things in perspective and remind her how he viewed her. The shrimpy tagalong girl. His buddy. The tomboy who struggled to keep up with the guys.

"All right, *Bullfrog*," she said, emphasizing his moniker to say *message received.* "I'll come. It'll be a good excuse to catch up with Avery and see the twins again. I haven't seen the darlings since they were born."

He chuckled dryly. "They were only born a couple of weeks ago. I doubt you've missed much."

"Not true. Avery says they change a little every day."

"Hmm."

She felt the weight of his stare and shot him a glance. "What? I'm not allowed to want to keep up with my best friend's twins?"

"Best friend?"

"Well, yeah. In recent years." She set Yossi on the floor and brushed cat hair off her shirt. When she glanced at Nolan, his gaze was locked on her chest where she'd been tidying her shirt. Did his pupils seem larger or was it just the dim light in her office? She shook off the notion that he was ogling her and explained, "I knew her in elementary school, and after my family moved away, we were pen pals. We reconnected in the last few months. She's one of the reasons I moved here. She reminded me how great Whisperwood was for settling down and starting a family."

His chin jerked up, and he blinked. "You're starting a family?"

"Well, not yet, but someday. I hope." She pulled the guest chair closer and sat in it. Folding her arms on the desk, she pinned him with an inquisitive stare. "How about you? Ever think about settling down with a wife, two-point-four kids and a dog?"

One light brown eyebrow twitched up. "Not recently. The job's kept me on the road more than not, and that's not conducive to starting a happy home." He sighed heavily and stared at the desk, his brow creasing. "Although that could be changing soon, if this bogus investigation goes sideways."

Acid bit her gut, seeing the pain in his face. "Hey, we're not in public anymore. Can you tell me what the hell you were accused of and what really happened?"

He was silent for a moment, the muscles in his jaw working and his thumb tapping restlessly on her notebook. "Yeah, okay."

She reached across the desk and squeezed his restless hands in a show of support.

He seemed not to notice, and his gaze looked distant as he started, "Last year I worked a case in Portland with a female special agent."

"Charlotte," she said, remembering the name he'd mentioned at lunch.

His eyes flicked briefly to hers. "Yeah, Charlotte. She's an attractive woman. Tall, toned, in great physical condition for the job. So, yeah, I noticed her in *that* way."

Summer, who was barely five feet when she stretched her back and lifted her chin at the doctor's office and who hadn't been hitting the gym quite as routinely as usual, suppressed another spike of distaste for Charlotte.

"She made it clear, in obvious ways, that she was interested in me, as well. Touches, lingering looks, suggestive comments. So suggestive, in fact, that I started to get uncomfortable. There are rules, both written and unwritten, about getting involved with another agent. I did *not* want to cross that line and put our careers in jeopardy. I told her that. Repeatedly. To which she replied, 'I won't tell if you don't.'"

Summer growled under her breath, indignant on Nolan's behalf. The woman did sound like trouble.

"I stuck by my stance and thought the issue was closed. She backed off some for a couple days, then..." He glanced at her and scratched his chin. "One night she wanted to talk about the case and asked me to come to her room. We did have some matters related to the case to discuss, so I went. Turns out she had a hidden camera in her room and knew just where to stand to be full frame in the shot. She came on to me again. I told her no. Again. She continued kissing me and rubbing up against me, promising me no one would ever find out."

Summer squeezed Nolan's wrists harder, as if she were an anchor. As if she could keep him from sinking in the tidal wave she knew was coming in his story. Her stomach soured, and she tasted bile in the back of her throat.

Nolan pried a sweaty hand free and scrubbed it on the leg of his jeans. He muttered a curse under his breath. "I was so stupid. I knew better. Should have stuck to my guns, but damn it, she was attractive, and she got me all worked up... I caved. I threw caution to the wind, and we ended up in bed."

"Oh," Summer said quietly, disappointment pinging her. Despite indicators to the contrary, she'd been hoping he would say he'd nobly resisted.

"Fast-forward to last week, when I was called into my superior's office. I learned she was alleging *I* came on to *her*, that I forced unwanted advances on her and she had photographic evidence to prove it."

"She set you up!" Summer said hotly.

"Oh, it gets better," he said with a scoff.

She clenched her teeth, itching to pop Special Agent Charlotte in the kisser.

He explained how the pictures she'd presented featured images designed to make him appear the aggressor and her the unwilling victim. How he learned that day in his boss's office that Charlotte was *married* to a *US senator*. Ergo suspension, internal investigation, time on his hands to come down to his cousins' Texas ranch while the future of his career was decided.

"Oh, Nolan…" she said, groaning. "What a mess! Damn, I'm sorry. That's…she's…ugh!"

Summer fisted her hands, imagining Charlotte's neck there. "How dare she! What reason could she have for doing something like this? Accusing someone of rape is…super serious!"

Nolan's expression shifted. "That's another thing that seems…off."

She blinked. "What?"

As he raised his chin to meet her gaze, his eyes narrowed. His mouth pinched. His expression darkened with a deeper concern. "The term *rape* has never been used. I looked at the paperwork of the formal charges, and rape is not what she is alleging."

She blinked, processing this tidbit.

"*Sexual assault* is the term being used, and the specifics she lays out of groping, kissing and crude language do not include the sex act per se. Yet she knows full well we…" He paused, as if looking for a polite term, then with a sigh, said, "Slept together. So why stop at calling it groping, when, *technically*, she could charge rape? I'm sure she has the pictures of us in bed. Then again, the pictures of *that act* would show her taking the lead, fully capable of getting up and walking away at any time she wanted. I did *not* force her. Ever."

"I don't know. But…not being charged with rape is a good thing, right?"

He raised both palms toward her, and his face reflected tremendous relief. "Oh, don't get me wrong. I'm grateful that isn't on her list. It's just curious to me *why* it isn't."

Summer gnawed her bottom lip as she meditated on the disturbing story Nolan laid out. "Maybe it's as simple as the fact that she couldn't *prove* rape." She made finger quotes for emphasis. "No bruises, no incriminating posed pictures…"

"Hmph," he grunted as he pulled out his phone and dialed a preprogrammed number. "Hi, Stu, it's Nolan Colton." He turned to her and mouthed, *My lawyer.*

I'll be in the back, she mouthed back as she aimed a thumb to the kitchenette attached to her office.

Nolan nodded, then said into his phone, "I've been thinking…why didn't Charlotte allege rape? Why not go for the whole shebang instead of limiting her accusations to—"

Summer closed the door to the kitchenette, leaving Nolan to talk with his lawyer in private. She shivered despite the bright October sun that streamed through the window and warmed the room. Nolan was in serious hot water. Cases like his were notoriously he said versus she said. But Charlotte had planted a camera. That spoke to premeditation. Or…could her lawyer spin it that she felt threatened, and the camera was a safeguard? But

Nolan said she invited him to her room. Why do that if she felt threatened? But again, the invite to her room was a he said/she said issue, too.

Summer opened her mini fridge and took out a bottle of water. Yossi had followed her into the kitchenette and rubbed against her shins as he meowed for a snack. She squatted to pat his head and stroke his back. Typically Yossi helped calm her and center her after a troubling incident or when she was plagued with worry over a case. Though he rewarded her with a rumbling purr, today her cat couldn't quiet her spinning thoughts and the squeeze of anxiety in her gut.

Nolan finished his conversation with his lawyer and opened the connecting door to her office. He filled the doorway, an imposing presence, and her pulse hiked. For the briefest moment, she thought, *What if he did what Charlotte said?*

He held her gaze, and as if he read her thoughts, he said, "For the record, I know how my defense sounds. I know that a lot of women have legitimate cases of being assaulted and manhandled and intimidated. It makes me physically ill to think of anything like that happening to a woman I care about. My mom, my sister…" He paused, his hard gaze softening. "Or you."

Summer caught her breath.

He took a slow step closer, then another. "Men who take advantage of women that way are vile. There is no excuse for assaulting a woman. None. And I fully understand how, in light of recent movements on social media and in Hollywood, my defending myself sounds tone-deaf. But it's a two-way street, Summer. Women can take advantage of men, too."

The air she'd been holding stuttered from her. "I know that. And for the record, I believe you."

His face scrunched as if in pain, and he sucked in a sharp breath. "Thank you. That means—" when his voice cracked, he swiped a hand down his face and exhaled "—a lot to me."

Hard bands clamped around her heart, shooting pain to her core. She'd never seen Nolan so emotional before. She'd rarely seen *any* man look ready to crumble the way Nolan did in that moment.

Stepping around Yossi, who still wound around her ankles, she rushed to her childhood friend and wrapped him in a hug. "Oh, Nolan. You're gonna survive this. You'll prove your case and get your job back. Have faith."

He raised one wide palm to her back for a brief hug before pulling away. Clearing his throat, he pinched the bridge of his nose and gave his head a little shake. "I appreciate your support. Stuart thinks he can find enough holes in her story to give me a fighting chance. He's working every angle. Told me not to worry."

She chuckled without mirth. "Yeah, right."

He took a step back and waved a hand toward the office. "So...where were we on your case?"

Summer got Nolan a bottle of water, poured dry kibble in Yossi's bowl and returned to her desk. Nolan angled the wooden chair in front of her desk and took a seat. When Yossi snubbed her lunch offering and followed her back to the office, Nolan reached down to pat her spoiled cat.

Battling down the lingering emotion clogging her

throat, Summer tried to refocus her thoughts. She had a murder to solve.

"Well," she said and folded her arms on the file folders in front of her, "we'd need to find the guys Patrice befriended at the community college. We can start by calling the registrar and asking for a copy of her class schedule."

"Good idea."

"And if the Mummy Killer case or anything that's happened with your cousins is relevant to this case, I don't want to wait until tomorrow to talk to your cousins. If they have pertinent info about Patrice's case, then I'd like to hear what they have to say today. I figure we'll start with Dallas. With two newborns to care for, I doubt he and Avery will be at the barbecue."

"You're probably right. After everything that happened to Avery and Dallas last month, Forrest did say the new parents are sticking close to home for now." Yossi jumped in his lap and butted Nolan's chin with his head. Nolan grinned and obliged the feline with a scratch behind the ear. "Truth be told, I haven't seen Dallas since I got to town, and I have my own questions for my cousin."

"Then it's settled." She pulled out her phone and tapped at the screen. "I'll text Avery and see when might be the best time to come."

Nolan gave her nod and slow grin. "You're in charge."

While she waited for Avery to reply, she got up and added canned food, Yossi's favorite, to his bowl. He trotted over and began munching away. Summer stroked his back. "You watch the office while I'm gone, big boy. Okay?"

Her phone dinged, and she checked the reply from Avery.

You're welcome to come any time! It's not like I can go anywhere with two newborns who want to eat every two hours. LOL

She read the text to Nolan, adding, "What do you say? No time like the present."

Nolan stood and waved a hand toward the door. "After you, boss."

THEY ARRIVED AT Avery's house thirty minutes later after stopping at the Bluebell Diner to pick a casserole from the to-go freezer. When Dallas answered the door, Avery's black toy poodle danced around his feet yipping at their visitors. "Lulu, hush."

Summer handed him the pan. "Chicken supreme casserole. Avery told me the other day you were swimming in lasagna and were ready for something else."

Dallas gave her a wide grin. "Yes! Thank you. Come on in. Avery and the babies are in there." He hitched his head toward the living room.

"Ooh, let me at 'em! Auntie Summer's here!" Summer said as she headed into the next room.

Nolan shook Dallas's free hand. "Big D now stands for Daddy. Congrats, cuz."

The former Army sergeant's face lit like a happy jack-o'-lantern. "Best job I've ever had." He glanced toward the room where Summer had disappeared. "So you and Summer reconnected. That's great!" Lifting an eyebrow, he jabbed Nolan with his elbow. "So what's the story? You and she—?" He waggled his eyebrow suggestively.

Nolan scowled at his cousin. "Don't get any ideas. We're friends. Period. And we're looking into Patrice Eccleston's murder together, so any info you can share on that front is welcome."

Dallas's expression sobered. "Absolutely. Avery and I were investigating that before the twins came. Any help I can offer is yours." He paused, blinking tiredly. "I mean…so long as I can find someone to come stay with Avery. It's too soon to leave her alone with two babies."

Nolan nodded, reading more behind his cousin's reluctance to leave his fiancée than the newborns. Dallas had lost his first wife in a tragedy that had scarred him deeply, and from what Nolan had heard from the family, Avery's delivery of the twins had been touch and go for a while. "For now, information is what we need, thanks. I wouldn't think of tearing you away from diaper duty."

Dallas groaned. "An unending process. No sooner is one clean than the other has soiled his pants." He pointed to the casserole. "Let me put this away, send Lulu outside for a potty break, and I'll join you in the living room in a minute."

Nolan slapped his cousin on the back and turned to head into the front room. The sight that greeted him caught him off guard, and he pulled up short.

Summer, dewy-eyed and glowing with tender affection, held one of the babies and was cooing and nuzzling the newborn. His heart throbbed a couple slow, heavy beats, making his head feel light. He experienced an odd sort of déjà vu, which made no sense because he hadn't seen Summer in years. Yet she looked so natural holding the baby, so damn happy, that he had to take a minute and stare, to absorb the moment and process it.

Beautiful. His childhood friend was utterly beautiful and glowing. From the roots of his hair to his toenails, Nolan was filled with an urgency to find a way to make Summer that happy all the time. He yearned to have her look at him with that shiny-eyed joy and rapt attention. With a love that radiated from every pore.

"Hey, FBI guy, I got one here for you, too."

Avery's voice broke the spell that had mesmerized him, and he forced a smile of greeting to his face. What the hell had just come over him? Was he seriously having crazy flashes about Summer? Hadn't he just hours ago sworn to himself and stipulated to her that their relationship had to remain platonic? So where were these starry-eyed fairy-tale thoughts coming from? He exhaled and swiped a hand down his face, centering himself before entering the living room, where Avery and Summer were holding the two-week-old twins.

The new mother raised the bundle in her arms, offering for Nolan to hold her infant son. "I told Ezekiel his very important cousin Nolan was coming over, and he can't wait to meet you."

He waved her off. "I, uh…don't know anything about holding babies."

Avery chuckled. "Dallas was nervous at first, too. But it's really simple. You bend your arms to create a nest shape, then just snuggle him against your chest. Just remember to support his head for him."

"Go on, Bullfrog. He doesn't bite," Summer said, chuckling at him.

Avery sputtered a laugh. "Bullfrog?"

"That's the nickname I gave him when we were kids," Summer said with a sparkle of mischief in her gaze.

Nolan groaned, pleading with his eyes. "Don't…"

But she did.

"We were having this bonfire one night. I think it was the Fourth of July, and Nolan and his cousins had been drinking lots of soda at dinner." Summer's grin grew broader as she recounted the tale. "And boys being boys, they decided to have a burping contest."

Dallas returned from the kitchen at that moment. "Who burped? My boy?"

"No, you did, apparently. Along with your cousin here." Avery patted the couch beside her, inviting Dallas to sit next to her.

Nolan pulled a face. "Summer is determined to embarrass me in front of your fiancée."

Dallas smirked. "Please continue, Summer."

"Well… Nolan won the contest hands down when he let loose with a belch that was so loud and so deep I told him he sounded like a bullfrog."

"Oh, yeah. I remember that. Good times!" Dallas said, chuckling.

Avery laughed so hard that she woke the baby in her arms.

"And the name stuck." Summer settled back in her seat, clearly proud of herself.

"Seeing as she was my shadow that summer and half my size, I took to calling her Tadpole in return," Nolan said, finishing the story.

"Bullfrog and Tadpole, together again. Sounds like a children's book," Avery quipped.

Nolan studied Summer, her face lit with mirth and a wisp of dark blond hair curling in to tickle her full lips. Nothing about his male impulses at that moment was appropriate for a child's story. Before anything in his expression could give away the errant direction of his thoughts, he faced his several-times-removed cousin and cleared his throat. "The purpose of our visit is actually to get info from you about a case Summer's working on."

"Partly. The main purpose of our trip is to love on these sweet babies and see how my bestie is doing," Summer corrected.

An odd sensation poked him in the gut when she called Avery her *bestie*. *My God, Colton, you're a thirty-year-old man, not a jealous little boy. Why should you care whom she calls her best friend?* But that tiny suggestion that they weren't as close, didn't still have the tight relationship they'd once enjoyed did bother him. He'd tried to stay in touch with Summer over the years. He thought of her often, and when their letter writing dwindled and he'd lost track of her, he'd mourned the loss. Summer had always made him happy in ways no woman he'd dated nor any male friend had. That friendship, that sense of…what? Completion? Complement? Comfort? Whatever it was…had returned instantly when she'd hugged him so enthusiastically in the Lone Star Pharma parking lot.

"But while we are here," she said, narrowing a speculative look on the new parents, "we'd also like to hear anything you can tell us about Patrice Eccleston's murder." She scrunched her face in distaste. "Oh, man, how I hate to even bring up such a vile topic around these sweet, innocent ears." She raised the infant in her arms and pressed tiny kisses on the baby's tiny seashell ears.

Dallas and Avery exchanged a look—his concerned, hers stricken.

"What?" Nolan said, wagging a finger between them. "Why the look?"

"Your investigation just cuts close to the bone. We were interviewing a suspect a couple weeks ago with Forrest and Rae—Forrest's new fiancée," Dallas said, clarifying for his cousin as he took a seat next to Avery.

"Yeah, I'm staying at the ranch. I've met her."

Dallas nodded. "Right. Well, the suspect died quite suddenly and suspiciously while we were there for the interview."

"It was pretty horrifying," Avery said, her complexion piqued just from the memory.

"I can imagine!" Summer furrowed her brow and shot her friend a commiserating frown. Then tilting her head, she asked, "Are you referring to Horace Corgan? The man responsible for the Mummy Murders?"

Dallas nodded. "The same. Before he died, he confessed to killing the women who were found mummified, but he adamantly denied killing Patrice."

"According to what her father told me about the condition of her body when she was discovered, Patrice wasn't mummified like the others," Summer said. "So that rather supports the case that Patrice's killer was someone else, and Corgan was telling the truth."

Nolan made a mental note to finish reviewing Summer's notes from her first meeting with Atticus Eccleston when they got back to her office so he was up to speed on the key information about Patrice's remains.

"Seems that way," Avery said, shifting baby Zeke onto her shoulder when he started to fuss. "He went into rather disturbing detail about his appetite for *young beauties* and how he mummified them to, quote, 'preserve their beauty.'" Avery gave a shudder, her cheeks paling further.

Dallas slid a hand to Avery's knee and squeezed, and she responded with a shaky smile.

"For Corgan to have gone into such detail, to have confessed to his evil deeds and then flatly deny responsibility for Patrice's murder…" Summer chewed her bottom lip, a thought line creasing her forehead. "Did he give any indication he knew who *was* responsible?"

Dragging a hand along his unshaven jaw, Dallas nodded. "Maybe. When he was gasping, taking his last breaths, he said, 'Melody.' I've been wanting to investigate who or what he meant by that, but—" he stroked a crooked finger along Zeke's cheek and tugged up the corner of his mouth "—I've been a little preoccupied."

Summer grinned at Avery and Dallas. "I'd say so."

A niggling sensation stirred in Nolan's chest as he watched his cousin and Avery coo over Zeke. Dallas was so obviously over the moon in his new role as father. The pride and sheer bliss shone through the fatigue in his eyes. Nolan took a moment to consider what it would be like to be in Dallas's shoes. To suddenly discover he was a father. To settle down and start a family. To set aside his career, walk away from the danger of going undercover in homegrown terrorist cells, give up the constant travel and unknowns connected to his job in order to take care of a family.

His gaze moved to Summer, as if by their own volition. Which was crazy because, well…she was *Summer*. And he'd laid out very specific parameters for their collaboration.

After the debacle with Charlotte—

An icy feeling sank into his bones.

"You said Corgan died suddenly while you were there to interview him. How'd he die? What happened?" Summer's questions jerked Nolan from his disconcerting line of thought. He shook off the sidetrack in order to focus on the matter at hand. He would be no help to Summer if he allowed the mess with Charlotte to continue to distract him.

Avery drew a tremulous breath and rasped, "Corgan was murdered."

Chapter Six

"What!" Summer sat straighter, and her jaw slackened.

Dallas gripped his fiancée's arm gently, soothing her with the caress of his thumb. "Avery?"

Closing her eyes, Avery inhaled deeply. "I'm okay."

Turning back to Nolan and Summer, Dallas explained. "When we arrived at Horace Corgan's place, he was already in bad shape. He was in the late stages of lung cancer and had an oxygen tube in his nose. At one point, after he denied any responsibility for Patrice's death, Rae, Forrest, Avery and I stepped out of his room to confer. While we were out his oxygen tube was removed, and he started coughing badly. We rushed in to check on him. He was struggling to get air, coughing up blood, his color indicative that he was suffocating without the tube."

"Dear God! How awful!" Summer said, dividing a horrified glance between her friends. "Who could have done that? With you right there? I don't understand…"

"We tried to help him. He had a home health nurse attending him, but she wasn't able to save him. Later, when the cops arrived with the coroner, wanting to question us all, she was nowhere around. She was just…gone."

Nolan scowled. "Gone?" He fisted his hands. "As in escaped after sabotaging her patient?"

"Nolan? Why would his nurse—" Summer started.

"We suspect so, but we don't have proof. Like I said, the stress of seeing Horace suffocate was pretty distressing. We were all distracted, focusing on the clue Horace gave us, and didn't see the nurse leave."

"Clue?" Summer asked.

"Horace died before an ambulance could get there, but he gasped one word, *Melody*, before he succumbed. He was desperate to get it out, so we believe it has to be important," Dallas said.

"But important how?" Summer stood and placed baby Ariana Josephine in her bassinet. Shoving her sleeves up her arms, she faced Dallas. "Did you get the impression this Melody was another murder victim? A relative or old flame of Corgan's?"

"No clue. We had no context other than him gasping it out when he knew he was dying," Dallas said.

"So Melody might not be a person." Nolan rubbed the back of his neck, puzzling over the odd clue. "He could have been talking about a musical melody. Or a pet. Or a code for a safe or—"

"A computer password, street name, business…" Summer picked up. "It could mean anything."

"Exactly," Dallas said, discouragement heavy in his tone. "I hate to let this go hanging, but I'm not in a good position to dig further into what it means. I'd sure be grateful if you two would pick up the ball."

"Absolutely," Nolan said, but Summer's expression was skeptical. "What's wrong, Tadpole?"

"I…" She began pacing. "Do you think Melody is related to Patrice's murder? If Horace didn't kill her, are we muddying the water looking into what Melody means? I have a client—Patrice's father—paying me to find out who killed Patrice. That's where I need to concentrate my efforts."

"We really don't know more than what Dallas said." Avery passed Zeke to Dallas and scooped her daughter out of the bassinet. "I'm sure there was more to what Horace wanted to tell us, but *Melody* was all he got out."

Nolan rubbed his hands on the legs of his jeans. "Let's put a pin in Melody for now and come back to it later. Back up to the nurse. She would have been the only one in the room with Horace after you left the room, right?"

"As far as we know." Dallas held his son's pacifier in place until he began sucking it.

"It's *possible* someone was hiding while we talked to Horace or that she let someone in a back way unbeknownst to us. But we really weren't out of the room *that* long," Avery said.

"So his *nurse* killed him?" Incredulity filled Summer's tone. She pulled out her notebook and began taking notes. "Wow." She glanced up from her scribbling. "Any idea where this woman is now? I'd like to talk to her." She huffed. "And I'm guessing the police would like to talk to her." Tipping her head, Summer eyed Dallas. "Or have they already? What have the police done about Horace's murder?"

"Forrest would be in a better position to answer that,"

Dallas said. "I'm sure they *would* like to talk to the nurse, but I don't think they have. Last I heard no one has seen her since Horace died. If she did kill her patient, my guess is she didn't act on her own. Where's the motive?"

"Unless she's a pill pusher like some other nurses in town and thought Horace would rat her out," Avery said with a frown to Dallas. "You know the rumors that *you know who*—" her tone dripped venom "—is pushing illegal prescription pills through local nurses."

Dallas took a deep breath and gave Avery a sympathetic look. "And *you* know that those rumors haven't ever been proven, despite multiple raids on his shop. We gotta deal in facts, honey."

"You deal in facts. I know in my gut he's responsible for supplying the heroin that killed my brother."

Nolan divided a glance between his cousin and Avery. "Who are we discussing and why?"

Dallas scrubbed a hand down his face. "Avery's brother Zeke died of a drug overdose. She believes the gossip that Tom Kain, who owns an auto shop in town, is the local supplier. The rumors also pin him for bribing or blackmailing local nurses to sell opiates for him."

Avery scowled as Dallas continued, "Kain's garage has been searched multiple times, and the cops have never found anything to charge him with. If he is a drug dealer, he's really good at avoiding detection."

"They'll find something someday," Avery grumbled. "Or there is no justice in this world."

Summer twisted her mouth. "Okay, so whether or not this Kain person was behind it, couldn't the nurse in question be one of the ones dispensing illegal pills?

Maybe, like you said, Horace Corgan knew that about his nurse, maybe even benefited from her supply of painkillers, and she feared that he'd give her up while his tongue was loose. That could be her motive."

Dallas raised a hand. "Maybe. But I tell you, after hearing Horace describe how he'd targeted and killed those women, mummified them, even I wanted to kill him. She could have been outraged by what she'd overheard and decided to speed his dying process."

Avery gave her fiancé a raised-eyebrow glance.

He lifted a shoulder. "You see? Speculation is just that without proof."

Avery rolled her eyes and glanced away.

"Speculation on her motive aside," Nolan ventured warily, "I think we're safe to work on the assumption that the nurse is the lead suspect in Corgan's death."

"What's her name, by the way?" Summer asked, looking up from scribbling on her pad.

Avery screwed up her face. "Ugh. Baby brain and no sleep. Something with an *R*?"

Dallas pulled out his phone and tapped through a few screens. "Jane Oliver."

"Oh. Well, that ends in an *R*," Avery said, her lips twitching.

Summer wrote the name down. "What home health agency?"

"Whisperwood Home Health." Dallas stood when his son started mewling, patting his back gently and bouncing him lightly.

"So the assumption is," Nolan continued, "that Ms. Oliver was paid off, or blackmailed, or threatened in some way. Maybe she had ties to one of the murdered women."

Summer screwed up her mouth. "Like Dallas, I don't like assuming."

"Okay," Nolan said, "to be *sure* about what happened and why, we need to find Jane Oliver."

Summer pursed her lips as she got lost in thought, clicking her pen. "While it bothers me that this nurse disappeared, I keep coming back to the fact there's no link here to Patrice, and that's where I need to focus my efforts. If Corgan didn't kill Patrice, then her killer is likely still out there."

"Is there no link?" Nolan offered. "Do you really think it is a coincidence that a town the size of Whisperwood has had a crime wave of murders and disappearances without some tie? I'd like to be sure Jane Oliver isn't the latest murder victim."

Summer chewed her lips and finally bobbed a nod. "All right. We can stop by the home health agency when we leave here." She tapped her pen on the notebook.

"Thank you for helping out," Avery said. "It does my mind good to know someone is following up on all of this."

"Yeah, I was feeling a little guilty over leaving some of those issues unresolved, but we thought it best to step back from the case because of the twins," Dallas said. "Especially since we had the answers we wanted about the Mummy Killer and the Army buttons."

Summer's head shot up. "Whoa. Back up. Army buttons?"

Dallas blinked as if surprised they hadn't heard about the buttons he mentioned. "That's kinda how we got involved with the Mummy Killer case to start with. Forrest learned that some buttons were found where the mummified women were buried. The buttons turned out to be ASU, so he asked me to see what I could learn about Army vets in the area."

"I'm sorry... ASU?" Summer asked.

"Army standard uniform. ASU buttons haven't changed much in quite a while, so we were looking at a lot of years' worth of veterans."

"And the buttons led you to Horace Corgan? Horace was an Army vet?" Summer asked.

"Dishonorably discharged," Avery confirmed with a nod. Her expression brightened. "Wait! That's the connection!" She turned to Dallas for confirmation. "Wasn't one of the Army buttons found with Patrice's remains?"

The surprise on Summer's face reflected Nolan's own intrigue. "A button was found with Patrice?"

Summer huffed. "Woulda been nice if her father or brother had told me that. I got a copy of the police report, but that must have been part of the redacted info."

She bent her head over her notepad again, writing and drawing lines connecting bits of information.

Nolan studied her as she worked. A crease of concentration dented her brow, the sunlight from the front window cast gold streaks in her dark blond hair and she nibbled her bottom lip as she perused her notes, making him hungry to taste that plump lip himself. He couldn't deny his tomboy childhood friend had grown up to be a damn beautiful woman, a fact that would make his hands-off policy more difficult to adhere to. But adhere to it he would.

His renewed resolve caused a pinprick of disappointment in his chest. The voice of intuition, one he relied

on when solving cases and reading people in his undercover work with the FBI, whispered to him now. Was
his stubborn, well-meaning friends-only rule going to
cost him an opportunity he'd live to regret missing?

He shifted his gaze back to his cousin and found Dallas watching him with a knowing grin. Nolan's pulse
skipped. What had his face revealed? He shot Dallas a
scowl that asked, *What?*

Dallas's returned look said, *You can't fool me. I saw
how you were looking at Summer.*

Nolan gave his head a subtle shake.

His cousin's eyebrows lifted, and his expression mes-
saged, *You can't deny she is hot. Why wouldn't you
pursue something with her?* Or that's what Nolan inter-
preted, anyway. Close enough. Dallas was clearly asking about where things stood between him and Summer.
Nolan shook his head more definitively, his mouth firm.

Avery glanced up at that moment from dandling and
cooing over baby Ariana, and Nolan quickly schooled
his face.

He cleared his throat and backtracked mentally to
where the discussion had been. Melody. Buttons. A
murderous, disappearing nurse. "Sounds like we've
got our work cut out for us today. Anything else you
know of that might steer us in the right direction concerning Patrice's killer?"

Summer raised her gaze. "You said Forrest asked
for your help with the buttons. What's his connection
to the case?"

"Chief Thompson of the Whisperwood PD asked
Forrest to help out with the murder cases," Dallas said.
"Forrest used to be with the Austin PD and got a

special dispensation to work this case with the Whisperwood PD," Nolan added, expanding on his cousin's answer. "That's one of the reasons I want to go to the barbecue tomorrow night. He can fill us in on anything the police can share about the case."

Summer nodded. "Good." Then to Avery, "Any chance y'all will be at the barbecue?"

Avery laughed. "Listen to you *y'all*ing. You can take the girl outta Texas, but you can't take the Texas outta the girl!"

Summer's cheeks flushed, and her laugh filled Nolan with a sensation like carbonation bubbles tickling his belly. "True! I definitely got looks from classmates when I'd *y'all* in other states, but the Texas was well-rooted."

"I bet!" Avery said. "And, no, I doubt we'll make the barbecue, much as I hate to miss it. The twins are too little, and our pediatrician says there are already cases of flu reported in the area."

Summer gave an exaggerated pout. "Phooey. I understand why you can't, but you'll be missed."

Zeke released a high-pitched squeal of displeasure, arching his back and thrashing his thin legs. Nolan stood, taking the baby's unrest as their cue to leave. "We'll let you get back to the baby shtick. Zeke sounds like he's tired of us stealing your attention."

Avery sighed. "A touch of colic, but nothing we can't handle." She smiled tiredly at Dallas. "Right, honey?"

Dallas's answering smile demonstrated how completely smitten and happy Nolan's cousin was despite the lost sleep and barf stains on his shirt.

Summer gathered her purse and notebook and

crossed the room to give Avery and Dallas each a big
hug and kiss each of the babies on the forehead. "Call
if I can do anything for you."

Dallas headed for the door with Zeke squawking in
his arms, and Nolan stopped him with a raised hand.
"We can see ourselves out. You get that boy a bottle
before he busts a lung."

Once outside and tucked into Summer's tiny car,
Nolan had to swallow the impulse to direct Summer
to drive straight to the home health agency where Jane
Oliver was employed. Instead, he gave her a moment
to process all they'd learned, as her wrinkled brow and
meditative moue indicated she was. Finally she cranked
the engine, and he asked, "Well, boss, where to?"

"Where to, indeed." She rolled down her window to
allow fresh air to blow through the Beetle as she headed
back toward downtown. "As much as I want to find
out what happened to Nurse Jane, I'm not convinced
there's a link to our case. Finding Patrice's murderer
is my priority. I say we talk to the rest of her friends,
the guys in her classes, and follow up on our new questions for her family."

"All right." Nolan cast a side glance as he jerked a
nod. Summer's hair danced in the breeze from the window, the golden wisps fluttering and swirling around
her cheeks and teasing him with their floral scent,
stirred by the afternoon air. Being her partner on this
case, keeping a proper perspective on their relationship,
would be harder than he'd imagined. He wouldn't be
able to live with himself if he hurt Summer or betrayed
their valued friendship. If he couldn't rein in his grow-

ing attraction to Summer, his fascination with the intelligent beauty she'd become, he'd have to walk away from this case.

Chapter Seven

"There has to be a reason Patrice was singled out. Did she know the killer? Was it a matter of opportunity? She fit the profile of some sicko's perverted fantasy and was in the wrong place at the right time? Did she tick someone off?" Summer said, thinking aloud as she drove back to her office. "Could it have been a crime of passion? Maria and Amanda said she didn't have a boyfriend, but maybe one of the male friends she had wasn't happy with that status."

"Mm-hmm," Nolan hummed, clearly distracted. She angled a glance at him, trying not to notice how the October sun streaming through the windshield high-lighted the sexy two-day beard on his squared jaw. *Focus, Summer.*

She followed his gaze out the windshield to the businesses lining the street. Specifically, his attention seemed riveted on Kain's Auto Shop. She slowed and fixed her own attention on the nondescript cinder-block building with three garage bays and a small office that featured a large plate-glass window facing the street. A man in dirty overalls was bent over the engine of a pickup truck. Through the wide window, she thought she glimpsed someone behind the counter of the office, though she couldn't tell if it was, in fact, a live person or a life-size cardboard cutout advertisement like the one by the stack of tires at the second garage bay door.

She tapped her brakes, tempted to stop and satisfy her curiosity about the man, the business that Avery suspected so passionately of being connected to the drugs that killed her brother.

Nolan cut a sharp look her way. "Change in plans, Tadpole?"

She screwed her mouth into a frown and hit the accelerator. "One day. Not today. Too much else to do related to our case. But when I have more free time, I think I'll poke around at Kain's Auto Shop and see what's what."

Nolan's jaw hardened. "I'm not sure I like the sound of that. If this guy *is* involved in the drug trade, he won't take kindly to snooping."

She swatted at his chest. "Jeez, Nolan. Give me credit for having some discretion and common sense!" She straightened her shoulders. "What I meant to say was... I think I'm due for an oil change and tire rotation."

He snorted and rolled his eyes. "Just...be careful. Okay?"

"Always." She aimed a finger at JoJo's Java as it came into view down the block. "I'm ready for a caffeine fix. How about you?"

He nodded blithely. "I never met a cup of coffee I didn't like."

She grabbed a parking spot that a minivan vacated directly in front of the coffee shop, and as they entered, she inhaled the scent of fresh ground coffee, cinnamon and yeast deeply into her lungs and grinned. "Heaven, I tell you. This is what heaven smells like."

"What can I get you folks?" the woman at the register asked.

Behind the counter, Summer watched a barista taking a pan of hot cinnamon buns out of the oven. "One of those—" she pointed to the pan of pastries "—and a large house brew to go."

"Same." Nolan took out his wallet, adding, "My treat."

Summer nudged him. "Thanks, Bullfrog. I appreciate it. Especially since this month seems to be outlasting my bank account."

"You really took a gamble coming back here to hang out your shingle, didn't you?" He handed her a coffee as soon as the barista set it on the counter, then snagged the bag of cinnamon buns.

"Maybe. I don't mind pinching pennies until I get on my feet." She popped the lid on her coffee and added a generous amount of cream and sugar. "Yossi and I are living in the office, sleeping on a cot and cooking on a hot plate until I earn enough to start paying for a small house, and I haven't bought any new clothes in longer than I can remember." She stirred the coffee and replaced the lid. "But it's worth it to be back in Whisperwood. To be settled. To be putting down roots close to good friends and fond old memories." She sipped her drink and sighed. "Ah. That's good."

"So you're happy here?" he asked, drinking from his own black coffee.

"Yeah. Very." She smiled her thanks when he held the door for her, and they strolled out to her car together. "Only one thing would make me happier."

He arched an eyebrow. "Winning the lottery?"

"Well, there is that, but…no. I meant having you here. Permanently."

His dark eyebrows dipped, and his mouth firmed. "Sorry. I don't see that happening. Whisperwood is a great town to visit, but my job—" he huffed a sigh "—assuming I still have one, is in Chicago. My cases keep me on the road. I go where the need is. Besides, I've got a lot of years and hard work invested in the FBI. Too much to walk away from it without good reason."

"Oh." She schooled her face, trying to hide the disappointment that weighted her heart. And just what would qualify in Nolan's book as a good enough reason to leave the FBI and settle down somewhere? Why couldn't he work with the FBI from an office in Texas?

When they returned to her office, she handed Nolan her coffee to hold while she unlocked the back entry, but when she tried to push the door open, it resisted.

"Problem?" Nolan asked.

She grinned. "No problem. Just a cat." Putting her mouth near the open crack, she called. "I'm home, Yossi! Move it, buddy."

A soft meow greeted her, and a dark gray paw swatted through the crack.

Carefully she nudged the door open, and Yossi wound himself around her legs, purring loudly. She stooped to lift her feline companion into her arms, and he snuggled against her shoulder. "Good boy. Did you protect the office while I was out?"

Nolan set both of the coffees on her desk and took off his jacket. "So you're living here?" Her gaze followed his as he cast his eyes around the small office.

She knew it wasn't well furnished, knew most people would think her Spartan lifestyle was crazy. But in that moment, only Nolan's opinion mattered.

"I am," she said and gave him a quick tour of the kitchenette, half bathroom and a file room turned into a bedroom.

"Where do you shower?" he asked.

"The gym." She rubbed Yossi's head and saved her necklace when he decided to gnaw on it like a feline teething toy. "I get up at 5:00 a.m. to work out and shower. I wash my clothes at Spin and Bubbles laundromat and have already saved half of my goal for the down payment on a house."

His eyes grew. "That is dedication."

She strolled back to the office and set Yossi on her desk. "Well, having a real home is something I've wanted for years—ever since my dad started dragging us around the country like hobos. I told myself when I grew up I'd have roots—a roof and front porch with rocking chairs and a yard with a big flower bed and a kitchen that smelled like fresh-baked bread."

She lifted her coffee cup to drink and smiled to herself as she imagined the home she'd make.

"You can bake bread?" Nolan asked, taking the chair in front of her desk.

She snorted, almost choking on the swallow of coffee. "Heck no! But I can dream my kitchen will smell that way, can't I?"

"Touché." Nolan nodded his head toward her desk where her laptop sat. "Shall we start a bit of online research?"

"Good idea." Hustling around him to settle in her

battered chair, she woke her laptop, and the desktop screen glowed with a picture of Yossi. In her peripheral vision, she thought she saw Nolan give her side-eye. "Hey! I love my cat. Don't judge."

He chuckled and raised his hands. "Did I say anything?"

As she began navigating to a few social media sites and searched for Patrice's account, Nolan dragged a chair around from the front of the desk to sit beside her. The crisp scent of him, soap and coffee and something she could only call *Nolan*, wafted around her as he leaned closer to see the screen.

Trying to concentrate on the task at hand rather than the tantalizing aroma of her cohort, she pulled up Patrice's Instagram account and scrolled slowly through her pictures.

"Hmm."

She cut a glance to Nolan. "See something you think could be relevant?"

"Not yet, but I was thinking about the fact that her account was public. You wouldn't be able to see her pictures if it were set to private."

Summer frowned at the screen. "You're right. While that helps us dig, it seems careless of her. This day and age, a young woman really needs to be more cautious." She glanced at Nolan again. "By the way, when you go back to Chicago—" Just saying those words made her stomach cramp with regret. "I'll be sending you a friend request on Facebook. Look for it, okay?"

"I don't do Facebook."

"Oh. I thought you said you looked for me there."

"I created a dummy account long enough to look for

you then deleted it. In my line of work, I can't have personal accounts like that. Makes information about me and my family and friends vulnerable to the bad guys." He glanced at her. "Even with the tightest security settings. Can't risk it."

"Oh. Right. Of course." A knot in her gut, she went back to studying Patrice's photos. Most were of her and her roommates, inspirational sayings and vacation photos.

Nolan put a hand at the nape of her neck and massaged her muscles. "Summer."

"Hmm?" she hummed without looking at him, while trying to pretend his touch didn't have her insides sparking and crackling.

"No Facebook doesn't mean I can't keep in touch with you. You don't really think after finally reconnecting with you that I'm going to let you disappear from my life again, do you?" He lifted the corner of his mouth, and the sensation of a thousand feathers tickling her insides spread from her scalp to her toenails. Something warm and sweet filled his eyes, replacing the all-business veneer he'd worn as they interviewed people earlier. The tenderness in his gaze stole her breath, because she knew how easily she could fall in love with that look, with this man. If only...

Swallowing hard, she shut down that line of thought fast. Moving from one city to another with her military family for so many years had taught her the pain of letting yourself grow too attached to anyone when you had no one place to call home. And while she'd chosen Whisperwood to plant roots and build her life, Nolan was still a leaf in the wind.

His gaze shifted abruptly to the computer screen, and the affectionate glow in his gaze cooled to the serious professionalism that told her he was in full work mode again.

"Look." He tapped an image on the laptop screen that showed Patrice in class, taking apart an engine.

"Yeah?" Summer said. "We know she's a student of auto repair at the technical school. So…?"

"Look in the background. This guy is smiling at the camera, hamming it up and crowding in next to her, like he knows the picture is being taken. But this guy—" he pointed to a slightly blurry face at the edge of the shot "—is kinda glaring at the other guy."

"I repeat. So?"

"So…he wasn't happy with this first guy. Maybe jealous of him cuddling up to Patrice?"

Summer cut a skeptical frown toward Nolan. "Or he had a bad burrito for lunch. One picture of a guy caught in a scowl doesn't a killer make. Come on, FBI guy."

"I'm not saying he killed her. Just noting an interesting dynamic caught on camera." He reached past her to scroll farther down the page of photos. His arm brushed hers and reignited the frenzied feeling that skittered through her.

She squeezed the arms of her chair and took a calming breath before saying, "Do you suppose those are the guys her roommates mentioned? The guys from her class that she hung out with sometimes?"

"Makes sense that they are. These guys appear to be in her class, so…" Nolan met her eyes. "Let see if we can catch them on campus. We can check the class schedule at the college website and head out there tod—" He stopped. Twisted his lips in apology. Motioned to her. "If that's what you think is our next step."

She arched an eyebrow and chuckled darkly. "Clearly you think it's a good plan."

"But you're the boss."

She bobbed her head once in acknowledgment. "It's a good plan." Facing the computer again, she scrolled farther down the page in Patrice's pictures. A couple more pictures came up with the guys from her auto shop class, but nothing alarming stood out.

"Hmm, let's try this." Summer opened Facebook and searched Patrice's name.

"But her roommates said she didn't use Facebook."

When a list of results popped up with Patrice's name, Summer waved her hand at the screen. "Didn't use doesn't mean never created an account. Huh, she's been tagged in a few posts. Some since her death." She read a few of the posts aloud as she scrolled. "You'll be missed...never forgotten...love you always...gone too soon..."

"Back up. Who said 'love you always'?" Nolan asked.

"Uh, her brother." She cut a side glance at him.

"Oh." His expression reflected disappointment. "Okay."

"Thought she had a secret lover?" Summer asked in a singsong voice.

"Wouldn't be the first time I ran across it." His attention stayed riveted to the screen.

"You were thinking it was Mr. Scowl in the picture with her classmates."

"Just gathering facts. Too soon to draw conclusions, Summer."

His comment struck her as a rebuke. And it stung. She acknowledged that she wanted to impress him with her investigative skills. To have him school her pricked her pride. Sure, he had more experience with criminal cases, but she knew it was too soon in the fact-gathering process to assume anything. "Just teasing you, Bullfrog. Lighten up."

He wrapped his hand around hers and squeezed a silent peace offering, even as his gaze narrowed on the screen. "What's that?"

She didn't have to ask what he meant by *that*. The picture jumped off the screen with the chilling image it featured. She clicked the thumbnail to enlarge the photo in which a younger Patrice had been tagged by someone named Gail Schuster. Summer recognized the name as one Atticus Eccleston had given her as a high school friend of Patrice's. The caption read, Look what came up as a flashback on my feed today. Good times! I miss you guys! The photo was obviously from a past Halloween, and several of the teenagers in the picture were all dressed in gory costumes, yukking it up at a party. One boy posing next to Patrice had his hands around her neck, his teeth clenched in a snarl as if he were strangling her.

Nolan muttered a curse word.

"I know. It's creepy. They were just kids goofing around on Halloween, but…that's how she really died."

"Who is he?" Nolan asked.

She scrolled over the teenager's face, and a popup identified him as Henry Cunningham.

"Check his page. See if it says where he lives now."

She grunted. She wanted to defend Henry, saying

they were kids joking around on Halloween. Instead she mumbled, "No stone unturned," and navigated to Henry's account.

"He lives in... Morgantown, West Virginia, now. He's a student at WVU." She released a sigh of relief. "She died in April. Before summer break, after spring break. He'd have been in Morgantown."

"Likely. We can confirm that easily enough by calling to talk to his professors. See if anyone remembers him on campus that day." Nolan scrubbed a hand on his cheek. "But, yeah, he's low on our list of suspects. Let's see what else is on Patrice's account."

As the list of suspects and persons of interest grew, Summer's anxiety rose, as well. Initially, she'd been excited at the notion of having a real case to work, a chance to build a reputation for her fledgling PI company and earn more paying clients. But what happened if she never solved the case? This whole endeavor could backfire and leave her name sullied as incompetent. Gritting her teeth, she firmed her resolve to find Patrice's killer. But to solve the case, would she have to rid herself of the distraction that Nolan was proving to be?

Chapter Eight

The schedule for the students in the auto repair program showed the next classes meeting midafternoon the following day. After a couple of hours researching bits of information on the internet, from ASU buttons to confirming Patrice's old high school friend Henry Cunningham had been in West Virginia the day Patrice went missing, Nolan took Summer out for a pizza dinner.

While at the pizza parlor, they asked about Patrice's interview there for a job, and the manager confirmed she'd submitted an application, but they'd not been hiring. Nothing unseemly or unusual popped out to either Nolan or Summer in their conversation with the manager, so they settled in to enjoy the crisp crust, tangy tomato sauce and gooey cheese of their sausage-and-mushroom pizza.

Summer noticed how quickly they'd settled on their toppings. No haggling or disputes. As if they'd been of one mind. Bam. Mushroom and sausage. Done deal.

Okay, pizza toppings were insignificant in the big picture, but she saw it as more evidence that she and Nolan were simpatico. Connected. Peas and carrots, as Forrest Gump put it.

He brushed a chaste kiss on her cheek when he dropped her at her office after dinner and promised to meet her by nine the next morning, after he'd helped Hays with the ranching chores.

When he arrived the following day, he smelled of fresh-scrubbed man, the crisp scent of soap and his damp hair both evidence of his recent shower. Curling her fingers around the keys in her pocket, Summer steered her mind quickly away from any images that knowledge conjured. "Ready to head out? Our first stop today is Patrice's father."

"Lead on," Nolan said, patting Yossi goodbye and following her to her Beetle. He gave the tiny front seat a leery look. "Can we take my Cherokee? I chewed on my knees all day yesterday in this sardine can."

With a laugh, Summer tucked her keys away and waved a hand to his Jeep. "Of course."

They arrive in the Ecclestons' neighborhood moments later, and Summer ogled the houses, the quaint yards, the first signs of autumn color in the trees. Someday.

Seconds after their knock, Atticus Eccleston answered the door of his modest brick home on the shady street. When he spotted her and Nolan on his porch, his face brightened with a hopefulness she knew she'd have to dash, and her heart clenched.

"Ms. Davies, hello. Do you have news? Did you find my girl's killer?" he asked, opening the door and standing back to admit her and Nolan. Atticus gave Nolan a puzzled look before returning his wistful eyes to her.

Summer mustered a smile for the older man and shook her head. "No news yet. But we're gathering a lot of helpful information, so stay positive." She motioned to Nolan. "This is a friend of mine who is helping me work on the case." She introduced the men, and they shook hands. Summer followed Atticus into a living room that clearly had not seen a dust rag or vacuum in months.

"So what brings you by if you don't know who's responsible for killing my Patrice?" Her host moved stacks of magazines and unfolded laundry off the couch and motioned for her to sit.

"We wanted to ask more questions and update you on our progress. We thought you might be able to shed some light on a few bits of information we learned." Summer perched on the edge of the couch and took out her notebook. Nolan settled beside her, his eyes taking in the room and studying Atticus Eccleston with a casualness she knew belied the careful scrutiny and attention to detail he'd demonstrated earlier.

Atticus spread his hands. "Ask away."

Summer described the meeting the day before with Patrice's roommates, and Atticus nodded. "They're sweet girls. I'm glad they were helpful."

"Amanda mentioned that Patrice had, at your behest, applied for a couple of jobs. Do you know where or how those interviews went?"

"They went fine as best I know, although…she didn't get any of the jobs. But I don't think she minded getting turned down some of the places. Maria had soured her on the idea of waiting tables, serving the public. And she'd worried about the possibility of delivering pizzas to strangers' houses. Too dangerous."

He paused and laughed without humor, tears filling his eyes. "Ironic, huh?"

Summer gave him a sympathetic look. "Where else did she apply?"

Atticus shifted on his chair and fingered moisture from the corner of his eye. "I drove her to an interview at the auto shop on Main. She was more enthusiastic about working on cars, but that job didn't pan out, either. She never said why and didn't want to talk to me about it when we left, but she was pretty upset. She's pretty touchy…" he started, then frowned and started again. "She *was* pretty touchy about being a girl wanting to be a mechanic. I assumed that was why they didn't hire her, so I let it drop."

Summer could empathize with Patrice, and the feeling of being overlooked in a traditionally male field.

"Then she applied at the Whisperwood General Store," Atticus continued.

"On Alamo Street?" Nolan asked.

"Yeah, I think that's the address. But the store didn't need anyone at the time." Atticus shrugged in a what-are-ya-gonna-do? manner.

"Did she ever mention friends by the name of Barry, Charlie and Tyler?" Summer asked.

Atticus sat straighter. "No. Who are they?"

"Guys in her class," Nolan said. "She hung out with them from time to time, according to her roommates."

"Those names don't mean anything to you?" Summer asked.

Atticus's breathing grew harder and faster. His jaw clenched, and his hands fisted. "No. Do you suspect one of those…*boys* hurt my baby girl?"

"No." Summer raised her palms to calm the obviously agitated father. "We have no evidence they had anything to do with her death. Her roommates didn't know their last names, and we thought perhaps she'd mentioned—"

"No," Mr. Eccleston interrupted, shaking his head adamantly. "Patrice knew how I felt about her dating at such a young age."

Summer shot a glance to Nolan, wondering if he'd had the same reaction to the father's decree that twenty was too young to date. *Seriously? Overprotective much?* And yet all his overprotection hadn't saved Patrice from the hands of a murderer.

Atticus curled his lips. "I know what boys are after, and I promised her mother I wouldn't let anything happen to her. I—" he hiccuped a sob "—I would never have let her be alone with some grease monkey wannabe."

Sensing the male classmates were a dead end, Summer moved on. "Were you aware that the police found Army uniform buttons at the site where Patrice was buried?"

Atticus rubbed his eyes with the pads of his fingers and sighed heavily. "I'm sorry. This is all still so…hard to talk about."

"I understand," she said, giving him time to collect himself.

"I, uh…seem to recall they mentioned some button to me, but… I saw no connection between Patrice and Army buttons and I—"

The sound of a door opening stopped Atticus.

"Dad?" The door slammed shut. "Whose Jeep is—"

Ian appeared at the entry to the living room and pulled up short when he spotted Summer and Nolan. His eyes narrowed. "What's going on?" He hitched a thumb toward Nolan. "Who's this guy?"

Nolan rose from the sofa and extended his hand as he introduced himself. Ian shook hands warily as Nolan said, "I'm helping Summer look for the person who killed Patrice. Are you Ian?"

"Yeah. What's it to you?" Ian said gruffly, then to Atticus, "What the hell, Dad? We already talked to the cops and gave her all we knew about the case." He jerked his head toward Summer. "What more do they want?" He faced Summer, snarling, "Stop grilling my father and get your asses out there. My sister's killer isn't going to be found by harassing and upsetting my father!"

Nolan hadn't sat back down after introducing himself, and his posture grew defensive, his muscles tensing and his shoulders squaring. Summer popped up off the couch and eased in front of Nolan, surreptitiously putting a hand on his wrist in a silent signal asking him to stand down.

"We're not harassing him. And I'm sorry the questions are upsetting, but we have to have a complete picture of your sister's life and connections if we are going to do our job. When you aren't completely open with us and forthcoming about details you know, we can't do our job."

Ian snapped his head back as if slapped, and his expression soured further. "Excuse me? Just what are you accusing us of? Are you sniffing around here trying to pin this on us?"

"No one has said or implied that you—"

"The hell you haven't! I know how your kind work! Look at the family. The family is hiding something. What secrets can we dig up on the family?" Ian spat in a mocking tone. "Catch them in an inconsistency and drag their name and reputation through the mud!"

"That's not—"

Ian took a giant step toward Summer and yelled in her face, "You're pathetic! We did nothing wrong!"

The man's vitriol sent a shiver down Summer's spine, but she stood her ground.

In an instant, Nolan had shoved past her and stuck his nose in front of Ian's. "Easy there, pal. Wanna step back and cool down?"

"Ian!" Mr. Eccleston called as Summer warned Nolan with a low, "Don't."

"Get the hell out of here!" Ian shouted. "Either find my sister's killer or give my father his money back. But if I see you around here harassing us again, I'll call the cops!"

Atticus shoved out of his chair. "Ian Harold Eccleston, you are out of line! Sit down and be quiet or leave my house!"

Ian blinked at his father as if stunned to hear the sharp tone.

Atticus was shaking like an autumn leaf in the breeze, and his face was flushed. His expression crumpled when he met his son's glare, and his voice cracked as he said, "I will not have you disrespecting the people who are trying to help us catch Pattie's killer."

Ian's eyes were glacial as he stared at his father, and Summer felt that chill to her bones. She put starch in her spine, unwilling to let the men see anything but strength, competence and conviction. This was her first serious case as a solo investigator, and she had to show her clients they hadn't been wrong placing their trust in her abilities. Stretching to maximize her petite stature, she raised her hands, saying firmly, "Gentlemen, please! I understand this is an emotional and stressful time for you. But Patrice is not served by your bickering." Facing Ian, she added, "Our intention is not to harass your father, and I hate to cause further pain, but we need every crumb of information, no matter how trivial it may seem, to do our job. You never know what tiny tip may lead us to something that could crack the case wide-open."

Ian's hostile expression didn't change. Summer regarded him carefully. She knew everyone dealt with grief in their own way, but was Ian's bitterness and anger indicative of something more nefarious? She'd been quick to dismiss Patrice's family as suspects since they'd hired her, but had she been too hasty?

Summer divided a look between the men. Taking a slow breath for composure, she continued with her questions. "Did Patrice have a friend named Melody?"

"No," Ian growled.

"Not that I know of," his father said.

"Does that name mean anything to you?"

"No." Ian's countenance remained surly.

"Ms. Davies," Atticus said, drawing her gaze back to him, "if you don't mind, I… I'm not feeling well and would like to rest. I have your number and will call if I think of anything else I think could help you."

Beside her she felt Nolan stir, and she cast him a

quick, quelling glance. "Of course." She took her purse from the couch and shouldered the straps. "Thank you. We'll see ourselves out."

Nolan fell in step behind her, and she swore she could hear his teeth grinding and his mental gears turning. Ian, too, followed her to the door. She felt his minatory stare as prickles on the back of her neck as she crossed the yard to Nolan's Jeep.

"Wow," she said as soon as the Jeep doors closed. "Someone needs to talk to a counselor about his grief. That is some temper he has."

Nolan grunted as he started the engine. "Yeah," he said slowly, thoughtfully. "I think I'm going to take a closer look at Ian and see what shakes out." He glanced at her as if expecting a fight.

She flipped up a palm. "Probably not a bad idea."

"Where to?" Nolan asked as he cranked the engine. "The office?"

Summer twisted her mouth as she buckled her seat belt. "I guess. But on the way, let's stop at the home health agency where Jane Oliver worked and see what they can tell us about Horace Corgan's nurse. Maybe they have an idea where she might be."

"Roger that."

"Then after lunch we can go talk to Patrice's classmates. It bothers me that her father and roommates know so little about them, considering Patrice apparently hung out with them a good bit. If her father is as overprotective as he seems—I mean, really, not letting your twenty-year-old daughter date?—I wouldn't be surprised to find Patrice wasn't rebelling a bit behind her father's back." She watched the parade of houses pass

the passenger window as they left the quiet neighborhood. "Was she maybe sleeping with one of these guys?
Doing drugs? Using a fake ID to drink? What else was
she doing behind her father's back?"

A chiming tone sounded from Nolan's phone, and
he pulled to the curb to answer the call.

"Hey, Stu. What's up?" To her he mouthed, *My lawyer.*

Summer's gut tensed. She hated the accusations that
had been hurled at Nolan, forcing him to defend his
honor, fight for his career.

"Oh, really?" he said in response to whatever his
lawyer said, then dragged a hand over his face. "We
can prove that? It's not just an allegation?" He listened
for a moment. "Will they testify to that? It goes to state
of mind, right?"

Summer stared out the side window, trying not to
act like she was eavesdropping, even though she totally
was, to the point of straining to hear what the lawyer
was telling Nolan. She caught *divorce* and *revenge* and
something that sounded like *haunt* or maybe *taunt*?

"So you're thinking she had a change of heart, and
when he found the video, she had to devise a new story
to defend her actions?"

Now she did shoot a curious look to Nolan. He held
up a finger, saying, *Hold on. I'll explain in a second.*

"So when is your meeting with them?" Nolan closed
his eyes, listening. "Why not? Stay on them. Of course
it's relevant! It could explain everything!" He nodded.
"Right. Thanks for calling."

He disconnected the call and stared out the windshield for several excruciating seconds before he looked

at her. "So Stu says that Charlotte was planning to divorce the senator a couple of years ago because he had cheated on her. Stu found a couple of Charlotte's friends who are willing to testify to the fact that on a girls' weekend to Cape Cod, she'd said she wanted revenge. She was going to have an affair of her own. She had gone so far as to plan how to flaunt her infidelity."

"She told these friends her plan? Seems kinda careless. Especially for an FBI agent." She waved a hand, adding, "I mean, it's great for you that she did, but jeez!"

"I'm sure alcohol was involved, but yes. It was careless of her, no matter how much she trusted her friends."

"'Friends—'" she made air quotes "—who are now ready to break her confidence and sell her out. Again, great for your case, but odd that these women would turn on her."

Nolan just grunted as he started the car again.

She angled her body to face him more fully. "What else did these friends say?"

"That her plan was to get pictures of herself having an affair with a younger man to make the senator jealous."

Summer made a disgruntled noise in her throat.

"But..."

"There's always a *but*," Summer muttered.

"But...apparently her lawyer reminded her that, thanks to a prenup she'd signed, if she was caught in an affair, she would get nothing in a divorce. The senator comes from a great deal of inherited wealth, and his family wanted to be sure he protected that money. Once reminded of the terms of the prenup, she changed her mind about her revenge plan and was going to just grin and bear her husband's philandering."

"What changed to make her come after you?"

"Her friends claim the senator discovered the photos she made of us on her laptop. Charlotte had to come up with some explanation that would keep her husband from using the prenup to dump her and cut her out of all that money. So, of course, I became sacrificial lamb."

Summer said something unladylike, then, "So now what happens? You said these friends will give sworn testimonies?"

"Yeah. Stu's working on getting the women's statements on the record before they change their minds or their stories. He's also talking about counterlawsuits and suing her for defamation of character. But, really, all I wanna do is clear my name so I can get my job and my reputation back."

Summer wasn't sure she'd be quite so forgiving if someone lied so egregiously and harmfully about her. "Won't this information go a long way toward doing that? I mean, if you get the friends to back you up saying you were framed, wouldn't the FBI have to drop the case against you?"

"I wish it were that simple. Remember, the woman's husband is a US senator. He has power and pull. Stu said when he first approached my bosses with this new information, they refused to talk to him. The Bureau is only trusting the facts they turn up with their own investigation. They promise to talk to the women, but... who knows what they'll say when Charlotte, the senator and his band of lawyers are sitting in the room."

Summer groaned and leaned her head back against the seat. "Great."

He pulled back into the traffic lane, and she and Nolan made their way to the home health office where Jane Oliver was employed.

As expected, they were told that their interviewee was not available. Dallas had mentioned something about Jane Oliver disappearing after Corgan's death. The receptionist at Whisperwood Home Health confirmed that no one had spoken to or seen Jane Oliver since Horace Corgan's death.

"Do you have any idea where she might have gone? Does she have family in the area—or anywhere, for that matter?" Summer asked.

The receptionist shook her head. "None that she'd have anything to do with. She had an ex-husband, but she wouldn't see him if you paid her all the money in the world. That split was bitter, I tell you."

"No other family then? Parents, siblings, maybe some children?" Summer tapped her pen against her notepad, the lack of helpful information making her restless.

"Sorry, no. None that I'm aware of." The receptionist leaned to the side and waved to a nurse who was crossing the lobby. "Genny, come here, please. These folks are looking for Jane Oliver. Do you have any idea where she might be?"

The dark-haired woman wearing pale blue scrubs and a name tag that read Genevieve stepped over and eyed them warily. "Like I told the police when they were here a couple weeks ago, I haven't seen her. I don't know nothing about where she went."

"You haven't heard from her?" Nolan asked.

"No." Genny shifted the stack of files she held from one arm to the other, and her expression seemed nervous to Summer. Or maybe just impatient.

"Did she ever speak of a favorite vacation spot? Was there some place she liked to go to relax when the pressure was on?" Nolan asked.

Genny gave a snort of wry amusement. "Who has time for vacation? We're understaffed, and it's all hands on deck to cover all the patients. With Jane gone, things are even tighter. I haven't seen my kids in four days."

A wild thought came to Summer that prompted her to ask, "Do either of you know if Jane was a friend of Patrice Eccleston's?"

Nolan cut a surprised look at her, one eyebrow arched. The two women exchanged a blank look and shook their heads.

"I don't think so." The receptionist tipped her head in query. "Wasn't that the college girl they found buried in the Lone Star Pharma parking lot?"

Genny's mouth opened in surprise. "Do you think Jane had something to do with murdering that girl? That's insane!"

Summer raised a hand. "I didn't say that."

The receptionist narrowed her gaze. "Maybe you think there's a link between the murdered girl and Jane's disappearance. Is that what you're saying?"

Summer sent a side glance to Nolan, who was watching the women with a honed intensity. She shook her head. "I'm not. But I'm trying to find out who killed Patrice, and I can't ignore the fact that Jane has also apparently disappeared. If there is a link between the two women, it could help us find not only Patrice's killer but what happened to Ms. Oliver, as well."

"I never heard her mention anyone named Patrice. She said she knew Chief Thompson's sister, who was one of the Mummy Killer's victims, because they were neighbors growing up."

Summer made a note of the Oliver-Thompson connection, though she didn't see that it helped their case concerning Patrice.

A sense of defeat weighted Summer's chest, and she sent Nolan a frustrated looked before asking, "Can you tell us *anything* about Jane or her patient Horace Corgan that might help us figure out what happened to her or what went down the day she disappeared?"

Genny's anxious fidgeting returned, and her face creased with concern and reluctance. "Look… Jane is my friend. I don't want to get her in trouble. While I don't know where she is, she was bragging before she disappeared about expecting to get a 'big load of cash.' She wouldn't say from where or how, but she was counting on that money to pay off a bunch of loans and make a down payment on a new car."

Car. The word triggered a new thought for Summer. "Do you have any reason to believe she was involved with the illegal distribution of opiates in the area? We've heard from a few people that the owner of Kain's Auto Shop is the local dealer, and he's got help from nurses in selling prescription pain pills."

Genny straightened her spine. "I've heard that rumor, and it offends me. Nurses are healers. There's not a nurse I know that would push meds to addicts."

"Not even for a 'big load of cash' to pay off loans and make a down payment on a new car?" Nolan asked.

The receptionist gasped, and Genny divided a glare between Summer and Nolan. "I've said too much. I can't believe Jane would be involved with anything so nefarious, and I don't know where she is, so… I'm done here." She leveled her shoulders and drew her lips into a taut line. "I have work waiting."

Summer stared after Genny as she stalked away, wondering what they were to do with this information.

The receptionist broke Summer's line of thought, muttering, "She might not believe it of Jane, but I do."

Chapter Nine

Summer faced the receptionist, blinking her surprise. "You believe Jane could have taken a payoff for something illegal?"

The receptionist folded her arms over her chest and twisted her mouth. "Jane always struck me as the sort who'd cave to temptation and was willing to take short-cuts if it made her life easier. What's more, I think there's truth behind the rumors about nurses helping sell drugs. I know a couple folks who've suddenly been able to buy nice things, move to a better neighborhood or go on fancy trips to Italy and Paris. Things their salary had never afforded them before."

Nolan shoved his hands in his pockets and rocked back on his heels. "And the connection to Kain's Auto Shop? You know anything about that?"

"Nothing I can prove. But either Tom Kain is involved in something drug related or someone is real good at making it look like he is, spreading lots of suspicion around town. Way I see it, if it looks like a duck and quacks like a duck, it's not a kitten." She raised both hands and her eyebrows. "That's all I'm saying."

The phone on her desk rang, and the receptionist

answered the call, turning her back to them. Summer figured they'd gotten all they could from Genny and the receptionist, so she jerked her head toward the door, signaling as much to Nolan.

He followed her out to the parking lot, where he opened the passenger door of his truck for her. His kind gesture flowed through her like warm honeyed tea on a cold day. She wasn't surprised adult Nolan was thoughtful and chivalrous. Even as a kid, she'd known he had a good heart. But seeing all the ways the boy had become a man—beyond the obvious, *GQ*-worthy physical transformation—she loved discovering who Nolan had become, one hint at a time. She felt a bit like she was opening a delightful Christmas gift, finding another new shiny box inside each one she opened, until, at last, she reached the precious gem that was Nolan. Each hour she spent with him, every conversation, revealed a little more of who he'd become. She'd already seen his keen mind at work, his protectiveness of her and his kind heart when he helped Bellamy carry shower gifts. That his noble character had been called into question by his coworker's charges against him infuriated her.

He consulted the printout she'd made of the class times at the vocational college as he settled behind the steering wheel. "If we hurry, we can grab a bite of lunch and still get to the campus in time for class change to talk with the guys from Patrice's auto mechanic class."

Summer fastened her seat belt. "You read my mind."

"Bluebell Diner again?"

She slapped her hand on her leg, giving him a mock shocked grin. "Yes! Damn, that is downright spooky! Are you eavesdropping on my brain?"

He chuckled. "No, I just remember how much you love their Thursday lunch special of fried chicken."

She caught her breath and grabbed his arm. "And homemade mac and cheese. Oh. My. Gawd. The best ever!" Then with a shake of her head, she said, "Unfortunately, I can't eat like I could as a kid and still fit into my jeans. I have to reserve comfort foods for special occasions."

He dipped his head to look out the windshield at the sunshine. "Today seems pretty special to me." He cut a glance to her. "I will if you will."

Summer barked a laugh. "Oh, Nolan. How many times did you use that line on me as kids?"

He raised a finger. "The rope swing at the pond." Another finger. "Okra stew at your grandmother's."

"Ooh, bleck! That was nasty. Lighting firecrackers behind the barn," she added and pulled a guilty face.

He groaned at the memory. "We terrified the animals and got in so much trouble! That was Donovan's idea, though."

"You still led me into temptation with your 'I will if you will' line."

He flashed an unrepentant grin. "So comfort food for lunch?"

Her mouth watered as much from the chiseled cut of his cheeks and jaw as the thought of greasy, cheesy delights for lunch. "I'm in."

Nostalgia, as sweet and soft as a favorite blanket, wrapped around her. The most special part of her childhood memories of mischief and adventure had more to do with who'd been with her than what they'd done. Having Nolan back at her side did make today special.

She wished she could bottle this day and save it for the coming weeks. After Nolan returned to Chicago. After life returned to quiet, lonely evenings with only Yossi for company. Not that Yossi wasn't a great pal, but cuddling on her cot with her cat didn't compare to the sense of completion, the feeling of security and warmth and soul-deep joy she knew when she was with Nolan. Soul-deep…

Was Nolan her soul mate? The notion rattled her, and yet…damn, it made sense.

But he didn't want her *that way*. He'd insisted they keep things platonic. To protect the valuable bond of friendship? Probably. And that was smart. Losing his friendship would devastate her.

At the diner, Summer savored every bite of her fried chicken, macaroni and cheese, and homemade biscuits. She even added chocolate cobbler à la mode, vowing as they returned to his Jeep to add ten minutes to her elliptical workout in the morning.

"As if that'll be enough to counter the indulgences," she muttered, and Nolan wisely said nothing. Guilt poked her, and she revised the vow. "Okay, ten extra minutes every day this week. This month."

A dimple appeared in Nolan's cheek as he gave her a lopsided grin, and she sighed. "Aw, hell. You only live once, right?"

He fastened his seat belt and nodded. "Absolutely. Don't ruin the enjoyment the meal gave you with regrets, Tadpole."

"You're right, of course." She dug out her phone and looked up directions to the vocational college. "Head south down Main Street."

Once Nolan was on the highway headed toward their next interview, he shot a glance across the front seat to her. "So I've been thinking about what we learned this morning. That bit about Jane Oliver coming into a load of money. We need to be sure Forrest and Chief Thompson know about that."

"You're thinking Nurse Jane might have been paid to kill Horace Corgan?"

He lifted his palm from the steering wheel, gesturing agreement. "She had opportunity, and the promise of a big payout indicates motive. While it's not proof—"

"It quacks like a duck," she finished for him.

He tapped the tip of his nose.

"If she killed Corgan, do you think she could've killed Patrice, too? A nurse who moonlights as a gun for hire? Or an asphyxiator for hire, as the case may be?"

"Interesting theory. How does it match up with the autopsy report?"

She flipped through her notebook to the early pages, where she'd jotted her thoughts after reviewing the autopsy report. "The killer had a moderately large hand, based on the damage done to Patrice's throat during the strangulation. Can't rule out a large woman's hand, but more likely a man's based on the data."

"Manual strangulation takes some strength." He glanced at her. "Not that a woman couldn't do it, but again, more likely a man. Especially if the victim is struggling."

When his attention returned to the road, Summer continued staring at his profile. She mentally rejected the images of a young woman's last moments, preferring the view of the handsome man beside her. The manly changes weren't so many that she couldn't still see the boy she'd known, whose friendship she'd cherished. But she wanted to memorize the angular cut of his squared jaw, the dusting of short, dark whiskers on his chin for the day he left town again. She knew when the case against him was settled and his name was cleared— *please, please let his name be cleared!*—that he'd leave Whisperwood and go back to Chicago.

The slight bump on his otherwise straight nose hinted he'd broken it at some point since she'd last seen him. When? On the job, during FBI training, in a bar fight? Okay, the last one didn't fit Nolan. "Promise me something?"

He glanced at her, his lips twitching up. "What's that, Tadpole?"

"That you won't disappear from my life again when you go back to Chicago." He must have heard the same pained note in her voice that she did, because the humored grin faded.

"Of course not. I already promised I wouldn't." He reached for her hand and squeezed her fingers. "I missed you, Summer. More than you know. Finding you again is the one truly good thing that has come out of the mess Charlotte stirred up."

She squeezed his shoulder. "I believe, no matter how the case against you turns out, you will land on your feet. You'll be fine, and you'll move on to accomplish great things."

"From your lips to God's ears." He flipped on the turn signal and pulled into the drive of the vocational college.

"I mean it, Nolan. You're going to bounce back.

That's the Bullfrog I know and still see. Determined, astute, good to your core."

His mouth twitched in a brief smile. "Thanks," he said, his voice cracking. He cleared his throat and whipped the Cherokee into a parking space. "Way to get me choked up before I'm supposed to play the bad cop."

"You're the bad cop?" she asked, chuckling as she climbed out of the Jeep and followed him to the main class building.

"Have to be. No one would ever believe you in that role."

"Aw." She bumped him with her hip and began scanning the students that streamed out of classrooms into the wide hall.

When they reached the room where the automotive repair class was being offered, she picked a student at random and stopped him. "Hi. We're looking for some guys we believe might be in this class named Barry, Charlie and Tyler. Can you point them out to us?"

The rangy student looked up from his cell phone and turned. "Uh…" He scanned the crowded hall. "That's Barry over there with the blue hoodie. The short guy he's talking to is Charlie. Tyler's been missing class a lot lately. Don't think he was here today. Barry might know where he is. He's tight with Tyler."

"Thanks. Would you know their last names, by any chance?"

"Barry Grainger. Charlie's last name is…" He shook his head and shrugged. "Some Louisiana name that's hard to pronounce. The prof is always screwing it up."

They thanked the guy again and headed down the corridor to catch up with Barry and Charlie before they lost sight of them. When they got close enough, Summer tapped Charlie on the shoulder. "Excuse me. Is your name Charlie?"

The short dark-haired student glanced back, then stopped and turned to give Summer a slow look up and down. He arched a thick black eyebrow. "Who wants to know?"

Barry, who was taller, with a hefty build and dishwater-blond hair, stopped, too, when he realized his friend was no longer beside him. His expression puzzled, Barry wove back through the bustle of other students to join them.

Nolan and Summer introduced themselves and explained they needed information for a case they were researching.

"This about Patrice?" Barry asked, making his question sound more like a statement.

"It is. You have a minute to talk? We'll buy you a drink." Summer pointed toward the lobby where a small concessions stand sold coffee, sodas and snacks.

Barry and Charlie exchanged a look and shrugged.

"Not the kind of drink I usually get after class, but, sure," Barry said. "What the hell?"

After Nolan had purchased them each a cup of coffee, they took a seat on the vinyl couches in a corner conversation area.

Summer opened her notepad and wrote down Barry's name. "So you're Barry Grainger, right? And I'm sorry, I didn't catch your last name, Charlie."

"I didn't give it. It's Melançon." He pronounced the name May-LAHN-sah, his Cajun French accent thick in his voice. When Summer asked, he reluctantly spelled it for her. "We don't know nothin' about Patrice's death," he added, ignoring the coffee Nolan had set in front of him and rubbing his hands on the legs of his oil-stained jeans.

"You might be surprised," Summer said. "Sometimes little things that you see as trivial are the piece that investigators need to work out the puzzle."

"What do you want to know?" Barry asked, clutching his coffee between his hands as he cast a wary look to Nolan.

"How well did you know Patrice?" Nolan asked.

"Some." Charlie folded his arms over his chest, classic I'm-shutting-you-out body language. "Not real well. Just from class."

Barry shot his friend a dark look of disagreement.

Interesting.

"Patrice's roommates tell us that you two and Tyler would often go out after class with Patrice for drinks or dinner. Is that right?"

Charlie shifted on the couch and glared at Summer. "Yeah. So?"

"Look, Charlie, I'm not here to accuse you of anything. I just need to know what you know about the days before Patrice's death. Who she might have been involved with, what she might have done, where she might have gone."

Leaning forward, Barry said, "The thing is, we really only went out to blow off steam. We'd talk about classes and the professors and watch sports and have a good time. We really didn't get into any kind of deep conversations with her. It was all really surface stuff, you know?"

"Were any of you romantically involved with her?"

Charlie scoffed. "Is that your polite way of asking if any of us hit that?"

Beside her, Nolan bristled. His shoulders drew back, and his eyes narrowed on the dark-haired young man. "A little respect, please. That's no way to talk about a woman you claim to have been friends with. Would you want someone talking that way about your sister or mother?"

Summer cleared her throat and darted a glance to Nolan.

He returned a subtle nod. Message received. He clamped his lips together, as if physically holding back his words, and his body relaxed a degree.

"Okay—" Summer flipped up a hand in concession "—did any of you sleep with her?"

"No," Charlie intoned before finally picking up the coffee and taking a gulp.

"Me neither. But Tyler wanted to. Tried to. He hit on her plenty of times, but she turned him down cold."

Summer made a note of this and asked, "How did he react to being turned down?"

Barry and Charlie looked at each other as if sensing a trap and not wanting to get their friend in trouble. Finally Barry said, "He was pretty bummed."

"Bummed enough to hurt her?" Nolan asked.

"My eye!" Charlie said darkly. Seeing their curious looks, he said, *"No way."*

"Tyler didn't kill her," Barry said flatly.

"What makes you believe that?" Nolan asked.

"Because he wouldna!" As his temper flared, Charlie's Cajun accent deepened. "Tyler's a lotta dings, but ee's no murderer."

"Besides, he liked her. He *really* liked her. No way he'd hurt her," Barry added. "He might've been ticked about getting the brush-off, but he didn't kill her."

Summer wanted to say that a lot of abusive men claim to love the women they hurt, but she bit her tongue. She wouldn't bias the interview by inserting her personal commentary.

"Yeah," Charlie said, nodding his agreement. "When she disappeared, ee was *moitié fou*. Missin' class, *rougarouin'*, drinking. And when dey found her—" he shook his head, his expression grim "—it got worse."

Summer knew enough French to translate *moitié fou* as half-crazy, but had to ask, "Explain the ruga—whatever."

Charlie frowned impatiently. "*Rougarouin'* means—" he waved a hand "—making trouble."

Barry flashed a lopsided grin. "You should hear him when he gets drunk. Can't understand half of what this dang Cajun says."

Charlie poked his friend's shoulder with a play punch and gave Barry a wry look. *"Pshaw!"*

While the friends teased each other, Summer mulled the notion that Tyler had been romantically interested in Patrice and noticeably upset, his behavior changed for the worse after Patrice disappeared. Was Tyler's trouble-making just acting out his grief, or was there more to it?

Nolan cleared his throat and, as if reading her thoughts, asked, "In what way was he making trouble?"

Drawn back to the matter at hand, Patrice's classmates sobered. Nolan's brow had beetled, and his jaw clenched as he shifted his stare from one young man to the other.

Barry and Charlie exchanged a wary look, as if realizing their comments had cast suspicion on Tyler.

"Please," Summer said. "Your identity as our source will be kept in strictest confidence. Patrice was your friend. Don't you want her killer found?"

"Tyler is our friend, too. I won't help you hang him for something he didn't do," Barry said, setting his coffee down and leaning back on the couch as if to signal he was finished with the conversation.

"If he is, in fact, innocent, the facts, the evidence will bear that out." Summer touched Barry's knee, wanting to establish a physical connection to him to combat the emotional distance he was putting between them. A you-can-trust-me gesture. "We don't want to see the wrong person accused of killing Patrice any more than you do. We want the truth. Justice for Patrice. But we need all the facts to sort that out."

Charlie heaved a heavy sigh. "Ee was pickin' fights, mouthin' off…ee failed last semester 'cause he didna bother to show up for finals."

"And have you talked with him about what's going on in his head? Why he's acting out?"

Barry grunted. "It's pretty obvious why."

"Just the same, spell it out." Nolan arched one eyebrow. "Assumptions are bad practice for us."

The two were silent for a minute before Barry said, "Look. I'll tell you, but you gotta promise not to blow it outta proportion."

Summer's pulse spiked. That kind of preamble hinted they were finally getting down to the bare truth.

Charlie's head whipped toward his friend, his glare screaming a warning. "Dude!"

"Go ahead," Summer said, giving him a sympathetic look and specifically *not* making any promises about how she'd interpret the information Barry had.

Barry made a take-it-easy hand gesture to Charlie before he began. "The last night we saw Patrice, Tyler made a pass at her. We'd gone to Bailey's after class for drinks and to shoot a little pool."

Summer made note of the local bar with the intention of speaking to the employees about what they might have observed that night, then raised her gaze to Barry again as he continued, "Tyler said he kissed her in the back hall by the restrooms, and she got upset with him and walked out."

"She left the bar?" she asked for clarification. "Alone?" That would match up with what police reports said the security cameras showed.

"Normally when we go out after class, at least one of us would take Patrice home, make sure she got home all right." Barry stroked the side of his cup idly as he spoke. "You know, for safety."

"That was good of you," she said, smiling her encouragement.

"But that night you didn't?" Nolan asked, his tone nonaccusatory.

"No. She left early," Barry explained. "Took an Uber or something. Tyler said she was mad at him. She'd said she made it clear she didn't want to hook up with him, and he wouldn't let up. She wasn't at class the next day...or the next. She was officially declared missing by that weekend, then her body was found and..." He scrubbed both hands over his face. "So… Tyler blamed himself for what happened to her. If he hadn't kissed her, if he hadn't let her leave the bar by herself…maybe she wouldn't have disappeared."

"Did either of you actually *see* her leave the bar? Actually, physically, walk out the door, alive and well?" Nolan pressed.

Both of Patrice's friends frowned. They looked at each other and hesitated.

"I…" Charlie started, then shook his head. "I don't remember."

Barry shrugged. "Same here. Can't say for sure." Then clearly understanding the reason behind the question, he added, "But Tyler was with us the rest of the night. I drove him home, because he got wasted after she left. He was in love with her and kept saying that eventually she'd change her mind about him." He flipped up a hand. "That's all I know."

"What time was it when Patrice left the bar? Did any of you happen to notice? Pinning down the time when she was last seen is important."

Barry twisted his mouth and scratched his cheek as he thought. "Well, we got out of class about four thirty, grabbed a burger on the way to Bailey's, 'cause their food sucks." He hesitated, apparently still calculating. "I'd say we'd been there a couple hours having drinks."

"De Astros game had started ahready. 'Twas playing on de TV behind de bar. I was watching dat more than I was watchin' de door." Charlie added, "So… I'd say sometime after eight. It was early like dat. I remember thinkin' it was odd dat she split before de party got started good."

Summer made note of the timetable the guys laid out and specific details about the Astros game as a time marker.

"Man, you wanna find her killer?" Charlie said, leveling a hard stare on Nolan. "Go talk to her hard-ass father. He was crazy strict wid her. He's de reason she moved to her own apartment. She hated his rules."

Nolan straightened. "She ever tell you anything that made you suspect her father was abusive? See any evidence of bruises or scars?"

"Naw, but…dere's a first time for everyding, right?" Charlie said. "Just sayin', her father or brother is as likely de ones offed her as Tyler. Maybe he found out she was sneaking out to drink with us after class. Got mad." He shrugged and raised his hands. "Just sayin'."

Summer chewed the tip of her pen. "Okay. Fair enough. Anyone else Patrice mentioned that could have been trouble? Someone harassing her on social media? Another guy hitting on her at the bar? Someone she might have been dating on the down low?"

Charlie tongued his teeth and made a sucking noise as he thought. "No one I know of."

She glanced to Barry, and he shook his head. "Nope."

Summer pulled in a deep breath. "Okay. Well, thanks for your time."

Charlie stood and, taking the top off his coffee, downed it in a few gulps. After chucking the cup in a nearby trash can, he said, "Listen, I hope you guys find de bastard who killed Patrice and nail his ass to de wall. She was a good girl, funny, sweet and a great mechanic. She didn't deserve what dat guy did to her."

Summer nodded. "We'll do our best." She started to

close her notepad as Patrice's classmates stepped away. "Oh, wait! One last thing?"

"Yeah?"

"Tyler's last name?"

Again the two consulted each other with a slow glance. Charlie rolled his eyes, and Barry said, "Whit-more."

Summer bobbed a nod. "Thanks, guys."

Shoving their hands in their pockets, the two sauntered toward the lobby door.

"So we're agreed?" Summer watched Patrice's classmates leave the building. "We need to find Tyler and have a talk with him?"

"Damn straight." Nolan stood aside so she could precede him out of the conversation nook. "If he was the last person to have contact with her while she was alive, we absolutely need to question him."

As they headed back to his truck, he placed a hand low on her back to gently steer her through the swarm of students. The gentlemanly gesture was one she'd seen her father use to establish a link to her mother on many occasions. She'd always viewed it as practical, a way to keep them casually connected in a crowd. But the warmth and weight of Nolan's hand settled just above her fanny spread a wonderfully fuzzy feeling through her. His touch spoke of possession. Affection. Intimacy.

Her mouth dried even thinking the word *intimacy* in connection to Nolan. Her childhood friend, with whom she'd spent so many summer days full of innocent adventure and camaraderie, had become a virile man who radiated confidence and sex appeal.

Down, girl. As much as she wanted to pant at his feet,

maybe roll over and get a belly rub, he'd plainly stated his terms that they keep their relationship platonic. She would honor his request if it killed her. Because she understood his reasons—he'd been burned by his fling with Charlotte and had his hands full dealing with that fallout. Because she respected Nolan—he was an honorable man, a consummate professional and deserved her cooperation. And because she couldn't bear the notion of harming the friendship she cherished so much.

Even after they'd lost touch in recent years, her friendship with Nolan was an unvarnished bright spot in her life that she valued. Now that they'd reconnected, how could she do anything to cause a rift?

As they wove through the hive of bodies, they passed a couple in a serious lip-lock. Summer's steps faltered when she spotted them, and in her peripheral vision she saw Nolan turn to glance in that direction. The guy's hands were all over the woman, and her fingers wound passionately through his hair. The erotic display did little to quell the yearning that coursed through her own veins. She might have even moaned softly. Either way, Nolan snatched his hand from her back as if scalded, cleared his throat and pushed on through the milling students at a more determined pace. Summer had to jog to keep up with his long-legged stride.

By the time they reached his truck, she was winded from the brisk pace. She gulped air and said, "Hey, Bullfrog…where's the fire?"

He blinked as he faced her as if roused from deep thoughts. "Huh? Oh. Sorry." He flashed a small, lopsided grin. "I forget how short your legs are."

She play punched him in the arm, the way she used to as kids, and stuck her tongue out.

"Where to?" he asked, once they were in the front seat and buckling up.

She checked the time on her phone. "Isn't the barbecue at your family's ranch starting soon?"

He glanced at the Jeep clock and bobbed his chin. "To the ranch then?"

"To the ranch."

Chapter Ten

When they arrived at the Colton Ranch and knocked at the front door of the main house, the matriarch of the clan, Josephine Colton, answered the summons with a bright smile. "Nolan, hi! And could this beauty be Summer Davies? My goodness, it has been ages!"

Nolan pressed a kiss on Josephine's temple. Late-afternoon sunlight caught strands of gray in the older woman's blond hair and highlighted the perennial flush on her apple cheeks. Josephine stepped back and scrunched her face in an apologetic moue. "I'm afraid dinner isn't quite ready. We got a late start thanks to some issues with the herd. We'll eat in about an hour to ninety minutes."

"What sort of trouble with the herd?" Nolan asked.

"I said issues, not trouble. And it's nothing you need to worry yourself about, dear. Just the sort of ranching business that comes up every day. In the meantime, why don't you and Summer enjoy this beautiful fall weather and go for a ride?" Turning to Summer with a smile, Josephine said, "I bet it's been a long time since you sat a horse. Am I right, Summer?"

"Yes, you would be right. I think the last time I rode

a horse was with my family on a vacation in Colorado. I hope it's like riding a bicycle, and I'll remember what to do."

"If not," Josephine replied, a twinkle in her eyes, "I'm sure Nolan here will be happy to show you what you need to know."

"That I will," Nolan said with a nod. "What do you think? Wanna go for a ride?"

"It sounds like fun." Summer's expression, however, was skeptical. "But, um...didn't we come tonight to talk to the family about the case? Maybe we should find Forrest and talk to him about those buttons and the coroner's report first."

"Gracious, honey!" Josephine gave her a side hug. "Have you never heard the saying about all work and no play? Take a break and enjoy yourself for a little while. There'll be time to talk shop after dinner. We're planning a bonfire to let the neighbors' kids make s'mores."

"Just the kids?" Summer asked, a sparkle in her eye. "This girl loves a good s'more."

Josephine laughed. "The big kids are welcome to s'mores, too. Now scat!" She waved them toward the door, then pivoted to head back into the kitchen. "Go for a ride with your man and have fun."

Nolan opened his mouth to tell Josephine he and Summer weren't a couple in a romantic way, as her *your man* indicated. But the denial stuck in his throat. For one thing, contradicting her seemed rude. And for another, he kind of liked imagining himself as Summer's date. They might be keeping things platonic, but friends could be a couple for a relaxed family night, couldn't they?

Summer shrugged. "Fine. Talking shop can wait. Lead the way." She swept her arm toward the door.

Placing a hand at the small of her back, he steered her outside and across the ranch yard to the stables, where they found Hays and Jonah, the oldest of Josephine and Hays's sons, deep in conversation.

"Knock, knock," Nolan said as entered the main alley. "I heard we could rent a horse or two here for a little prebarbecue ride?"

"Nolan, my boy!" Hays said brightly, clapping him on the shoulder.

Jonah grinned broadly and shook Nolan's hand. "Hey, man. What's up?"

"Come in!" Hays said, then facing Summer, "And who is this lovely lady with you?"

"You remember Summer Davies and her family? Used to live across the lake? She hung out with us boys in the summers when we were kids."

"Little Tadpole Davies?" Jonah's laugh spoke of his delight. "Oh my God! How the hell are you?" Jonah stepped over to wrap her in a bear hug. Again, Nolan told himself he was not, definitely *not*, uneasy with the show of affection from one of his cousins. Even if Jonah continued to hold Summer's shoulders as he talked with her after the longer-than-necessary hug.

Chill, Nolan. Jonah is happily engaged to Maggie. He's not making a move on her. Nolan inhaled deeply, filling his nose with the scents of horse manure, hay and leather that were redolent in the air. Summer flashed one of her sunny smiles at Jonah and Hays, and the three exchanged pleasantries and caught up in generalities on the last two decades.

Finally Hays and Jonah helped them saddle Cody, Jonah's horse, and Ginger, Josephine's favorite mare, and Nolan and Summer set out, cantering across the ranch property toward their favorite swimming hole from days gone by. The late-afternoon sun cast the world in a golden glow, and a cool autumn breeze rustled the leaves of the cottonwoods and spindly black willow trees that lined the creek. The peace and beauty of this corner of the Colton Ranch, where so many of his best memories from those long-ago summers had been made, helped him relax. The murmur of water over the creek stones made it easy to forget the rest of the world, the stress of the FBI's investigation of Charlotte's accusations, the grim case he was working with Summer. A large dragonfly buzzed by, and Nolan tracked its path, darting from one plant to another, its gossamer wings catching the sunlight.

Summer reined Ginger in and sighed. "Wow. Nothing about this place has changed. The trees may be a bit bigger, but everything else is just the way I remember it." She swung her leg over the russet mare and dismounted. When she loosely wrapped her reins around the low branch of a tree, Nolan followed suit. He stroked Cody's neck as he stepped away, and the horse snorted contentedly.

Summer brushed aside weeds and scrub bush limbs as she made her way out to the edge of the stream and the large flat rock where, as kids, they'd sunned themselves after swimming on hot days. Swatting away a bee that buzzed in his face, Nolan ducked through the overgrowth and joined her. She sat cross-legged and surveyed the creek, the trees, the sky with an encompassing glance. With a gasp, she pointed across the stream and laughed. "Look, Nolan! Our failed tree house is still there!"

He turned to look where she pointed. Sure enough, a warped sheet of plywood was still wedged in the low V of a large oak's massive branches. Rotting pieces of two-by-four were nailed to the trunk to create a make-shift ladder.

"Well, I'll be." He chuckled and settled next to her, stretching his legs out in front of him and leaning back on his elbows. "Why didn't we finish that thing? Looks like we had a good start."

"As I recall, it started raining the last day we worked on it, and by the end of the week, the creek was swollen and flooding. We were warned not to go near it until it receded, and in the meantime, we got distracted playing with the Xbox Forrest got for his birthday."

"Oh, yeah. Then didn't someone have the idea to build a fort in the hayloft?" He glanced at her, one eyebrow cocked.

"Where we used the old hay pulley to make a rope swing," she added, completing the memory.

"That's right!"

She laughed, the sound tripping along his nerves in a most delicious way. His body hummed with contentment and a heady lethargy.

"Good times," she said. "Until Donovan broke his leg, and we were forbidden to play on it anymore."

Nolan scrunched his face. "Was it Donovan? I thought that was Forrest. Maybe my memory's blurred because of Forrest's more recent injury."

Summer cocked her head. "What injury is that? I didn't hear anything about it."

Nolan cut a side glance to her, and the dappled shade played over her face, deepening the frown that dented her brow. "He was shot in the line of duty. In the leg. You may notice he still has a limp. That's one of the reasons he moved back here. But Chief Thompson saw that he still had excellent investigative skills, bum leg or not, and he hired him to help with the Mummy Killer case."

"So *that's* why he left Austin? I thought he just wanted to be closer to family and get involved with the Cowboy Heroes."

Nolan arched an eyebrow. "Sorry? Now you've confused me. What or who are the Cowboy Heroes?"

"Really? I'm surprised your cousins didn't mention the organization to you. It's a search-and-rescue group that they got involved with when Hurricane Brooke hit this summer. Ranchers and EMTs trained in rescue techniques head out on horseback to reach areas vehicles can't go. They help in rescue operations when resources are stretched thin like they were in July. I think all of the Coltons are involved in some way. Some more than others. Avery told me about it. Dallas will be working with them full-time when his paternity leave is over."

"Horseback search and rescue," he said, as if testing the weight of the words on his tongue. "Interesting. I like it."

She sat up and turned to face him. "The group is looking at expanding into more parts of Texas and other states. I'm surprised no one mentioned it to you." Her expression grew speculative. "You'd be good at it. If…

well, if things don't work out the way you're hoping at the FBI, you should talk to them about helping out."

Search-and-rescue work? Intriguing. He mulled the notion until Summer lay back on the rock again and moved close to him. With a satisfied hum, she leaned her head against his shoulder. Without considering why, he reached for her hand and laced their fingers. The simple act seemed as natural and obvious to him as taking his next breath. Only when she tipped her head to smile at him and tightened her grip on his did he realize the implied intimacy. In the beat that followed, when his analytical brain might have kicked in and spoiled the moment, Summer sighed contentedly.

"This is nice, huh? Quiet and calm. Relaxing."

He shoved away the niggling concern about breaching the invisible wall he'd erected between them and inhaled a deep breath of autumn air. Fallen leaves and damp earth mingled with the floral scent that Summer wore. Intoxicating. He could definitely get used to spending stolen hours alone with Summer, especially if they escaped to tranquil places like this corner of the Coltons' ranch. He hummed his agreement and closed his eyes to listen to the babbling of the creek water.

"Where *do* you see yourself in ten years?" He heard, felt, more than saw Summer shift to her side to face him.

He was silent for a moment, not wanting to expend the mental energy to answer the question. She'd want more than the "I don't know" that was the simple truth. "Never really thought about it."

"Married?"

"Well, I guess. By then I should be."

"Kids?"

"Maybe. That's always been the vague plan." He paused, turning his face toward her. "My cousins all seem quite happy starting families, so that's got me thinking in more concrete terms. But I need a wife first, and…" He flipped up a palm and let the words trail off.

"Are you still with the FBI in ten years?" she asked, her eyes and her voice noticeably softer.

He snorted. "I guess that depends on how the Bureau's investigation into Charlotte's claims goes. I might not be working anywhere. 'Cept maybe the prison laundry room if criminal charges are brought." He flashed a wry grin and tried to laugh off the topic, even though the reminder twisted his gut into knots.

For her part, Summer leaned on an elbow and hovered over him, her expression fierce. The sun lit her gold hair from above, framing her face, so from his perspective she reminded him of a lioness defending her cubs.

"That will not happen. Not as long as I have breath in my body. I'll be your character witness, your alibi, whatever it takes. But I will not let them railroad you on charges so completely out of line with your true character that—" she sputtered. "That—"

The sunlight. The fire in her eyes. The passion in her voice. *Something* tipped the scales he'd been balancing.

Emotion surged in him, and he caught the back of her head with one hand as he levered the upper half of his body toward her. His eyes zeroed in on her pouting lips. He moved closer, his nose bumping hers and—

He balked. The image of standing in his boss's office defending himself from Charlotte's false charges roared through his mind, yanking him back from the brink.

He made a frustrated growling noise in his throat and flopped back on the rock. Clenching his jaw, he stared at the sky through the web of cottonwood branches.

Then Summer's face moved into view, a piercing truth shining in her eyes. "Nolan?"

He sighed and shifted his gaze away from hers. "I know. I almost… It was just…an impulse. Forget it happened. Okay?"

"Forget what? Nothing *did* happen."

"Right." He exhaled, but his nerves still felt jittery.

"Nolan," she said more determinedly and put her cool palm against his cheek, drawing his gaze back to her. Her cheek twitched in an impish grin, then she ducked her head and pressed her lips to his.

Chapter Eleven

Summer's pulse skyrocketed the instant her mouth captured Nolan's. The rush of sweet sensation that poured through her shocked her. She'd kissed her share of men before, but none had ever affected her the way this mind-blowing and impetuous kiss did. A crackling energy sizzled through her veins. Heat swamped her. Her intention had been just to press a flirty kiss on his lips then retreat. A taunt. An experiment, really, to explore an unknown. To test a theory.

Several stumbling heartbeats passed before she regained her senses and pulled away. She blinked Nolan into focus, prepared to flash a smile and tease him about his reluctance to be spontaneous, about him losing touch with the boy who used to take any dare. But the words died, unspoken, because the feverish look in his eyes shook her anew.

"Say yes," he said, his tone low and desperate. "Tell me you want me to kiss you back."

Say it? Did her kiss not speak for her? "Yes, Nolan. Yes."

Before she could crack a grin or form a wisecrack, he renewed the kiss, his lips parting to draw more deeply on hers. After that, Summer's mind shut down, and she operated on pure sensation, feelings. She let instinct and emotion take the lead. Her bones seemed to melt, leaving her mellow and pliant in his embrace. Coherent thought was replaced with the thrum of sheer bliss roaring in her ears.

Nolan's hand stroked down her body, tracing the dip of her waist and the curve of her hip. When his fingers reach her bottom, he squeezed gently, and fresh waves of heat and pleasure poured through her. She canted her hips forward, pressing closer to him, encouraging him. She wanted more. Craved his touch in her most intimate places. Needed to feel him in a deeper—

He broke the kiss with a gasp. She felt the shudder that raced through him as his lust-blurred eyes clashed with hers. When she tried to kiss him again, he caught her cheeks between his hands, stopping her.

"Why did you kiss me?" he asked, breathless, his hands still framing her face. "I thought we agreed to keep things platonic."

Her gut swooped. *What?*

"I…was curious." She gulped air, her gaze searching his before adding, "And the moment felt right, so I followed the impulse."

Lifting her eyebrows, she tossed his question back at him. "Why did *you* kiss *me*? I thought you wanted a strictly professional work relationship."

He released a slow breath, and the tension in his muscles relaxed. With his eyes sparkling playfully, his mouth twisted, and his gaze narrowed as if weighing his reply. "I do. But we aren't at work right now, are we? And you said yes."

"What if I'd said no?" she teased, and when a shadow crossed his face, she immediately regretted her thoughtless joke.

"Then I'd have backed away." His face contorted with pain. "I completely respect your right to say no."

Hoping to erase the darkness from his mood, she tweaked his chin and flashed a saucy grin. "Then it's a good thing I said yes, huh?"

She stretched forward to brush a kiss across his ear and whispered, "I dare you to do it again."

When he hesitated, as if rethinking the wisdom of following this path, she slid a hand to the back of his head and pulled him closer. She kissed him hard, leaving no question that she was all in.

Finally, he surrendered and sank into the embrace. Nolan wrapped his arms around her, anchoring her body close to him, and his hand traveled over the curve of her hip to her back. When his palm stopped over the clasp to her bra, he hesitated as if waiting, again, for permission.

Summer pulled back from their kiss long enough to catch her breath and repeat her consent. But as she opened her mouth, a disturbing noise reached her from the bank of the creek.

She froze, cocking her head to listen. The noise returned, louder, more urgent.

The horses were whinnying frantically, clearly agitated by something.

She braced a hand on Nolan's chest and turned her cheek when he moved in to continue the kiss. "Wait. Listen. Something's upset the horses."

He raised his head, casting a glance toward the area

where they'd tied the animals. Concern colored his face as he rolled to his feet. "You're right. C'mon."

He held a hand out to her to help her up. They hurried across the stepping stones, feet slipping and splashing in the cool water, as they rushed back to the bank.

Both horses pranced restlessly, tossing their heads, but Ginger was particularly agitated. As they approached, Ginger loosed a high-pitched squeal and bucked hard, jerking her reins free from the branch where Summer had tied her. Nolan ran forward, his hands raised, hoping to calm the frightened animal—and narrowly avoided getting kicked as Ginger reared again, tossing her mane and whinnying frantically.

"Nolan!"

Summer started toward him, and he waved her away. "No! Stay back!"

Ginger bucked again, then took off across the meadow, dragging her reins and a piece of branch she'd broken from the tree. Summer's heart sank as she watched the frightened mare bolt away.

Cody, too, yanked at his tether and danced sideways, his eyes wild.

Summer searched the ground, looking for a snake or some other reason why the animals had spooked. Until something flew in her face with an angry buzz. She feinted right, dodging and fanning at the hornet that hummed by her head. Then another followed, and she caught her breath. "Nolan, hornets! The horses must have disturbed a nest!"

He was already swatting the flying pests away from Cody and working quickly to unravel the knotted reins from the tree. "Get back. They're swarming!"

She hated to leave Nolan to rescue Cody alone, but it didn't take two people to untie a horse. Her heart thundered against her ribs as she stumbled away from the angry, circling hornets. Guilt stung her, realizing she should've scoped out the area better when she picked the tree to tie Ginger off. She cast a glance in the direction the russet mare had run. Gone. She was nowhere in sight now.

Nolan charged toward Summer, leading Cody. As they put even more distance between themselves and the disturbed nest of hornets, Summer fell in step beside Nolan. After they'd darted several hundred yards away from the tree and angry swarm, he stopped and bent at his waist to catch his breath. Summer, too, gasped for oxygen, but as she panted for air, she stroked Cody's withers and searched for evidence the horse had been stung.

"Easy, boy," she wheezed, her chest heaving as she gulped air.

Nolan straightened and began examining Cody's other side. "Did you see which way the mare ran?"

She nodded, then realizing that from his vantage point behind Cody, he hadn't seen, she said, "I did. But she's out of sight."

"We have to find her."

"Of course." Summer found a welt on Cody's neck and winced. "Poor boy. I'm sorry that old buzzer got you. It's my fault."

Nolan angled his head to see around Cody. "How is this your fault?"

"I chose that tree to tie the horses to, and I didn't see the nest in the ground."

"I tied off there, too, and didn't pay attention to whether there was a nest. I share the blame." He moved around the gelding, who still chuffed nervously. "Are you all right? Did you get stung?"

"I don't think so." She spotted the red welt on his neck then, and reach for him to examine the sting. "Oh, Nolan! Ouch. How many got you?"

"Just a couple, I think. I'll be fine." She watched him grit his teeth and pluck a stinger from a swollen spot on his arm.

She pointed out a spot or two on Cody where the insects had attacked the horse, and she gently stroked the gelding to ease its nerves.

Nolan frowned. "Let's get back to the house. I don't know what sort of first aid you give a horse for a sting, but I don't want to delay getting this guy attention for his."

"Agreed." Only then did her brain shift from the imminent threat of the hornets to the fact that her transportation back to the house had run off. "Um…"

Nolan continued murmuring softly to Cody, calming the horse. He glanced at her and quickly divined the reason for her hesitation. "We'll walk for a while, give Cody a few more minutes to settle a bit, then we can ride double. I think Cody can manage it. Right, boy?"

He stroked the horse's nose, and Cody's ears relaxed, a sign he was calming down.

"What about Ginger? We need to find her."

"We do," Nolan said, even as his gaze scanned the field. "Keep your eyes open for her as we go in. If we don't find her on the way, I'll head back out with a fresh horse and one of my cousins to find her."

They set a course for the stable, across the weedy meadow, and Summer's thoughts rewound to the moments just prior to the hornet attack on the horses. The kisses she'd been sharing with Nolan… His hands exploring her curves, sneaking under the hem of her shirt… The tantalizing warmth of his fingers against her sensitive skin—along her spine, at her nape, behind her ear.

Nolan seemed lost in thought as well, and she hated to ask where his thoughts might be. She could well imagine he was castigating himself for breaking his rule about keeping things platonic. When she reflected on what he'd told her about Charlotte and how she'd seduced him, pushed him to violate his ethics about working relationships, guilt bit her. She'd done the same thing, hadn't she?

"I'm sorry," she blurted in the taut silence.

He cut a side glance to her. "Stop kicking yourself. You didn't know there was a hornet's nest."

"I… I meant the kiss."

Now his gaze whipped back to her, and his stride faltered. "You're sorry it happened?"

She pulled her bottom lip between her teeth and ruminated on the question. "No." Drawing a slow breath, she met his penetrating stare. "I'm sorry I pushed. You set boundaries, and I ignored them." She huffed her frustration. "I'm no better than Charlotte."

"Whoa." He stopped walking and faced her. "Don't go there. This is entirely different."

She raised both hands from her sides, palms out. "Is it? I knew better, but I allowed my impulsiveness to override common sense."

He aimed a finger at her. "That. That right there is why this is wholly different. You acted on impulse. There was real emotion and genuine gut feelings motivating you."

She wrinkled her nose, not following. Impulsiveness and emotionality were anathema to the Nolan she knew.

"Charlotte set me up. It was a preplanned, devious trap. She used me to manipulate her husband, then when she changed her mind, I became the sacrificial lamb. She didn't care if I got hurt in the process." He pulled his shoulders back. "Did you set out to hurt me when we kissed?"

Her jaw literally dropped. "No! Never! Nolan—"

He jerked a nod. "I rest my case." The muscle in his jaw flinched as he gritted his teeth, and his eyes darkened. "Besides… I kissed you first. I'm the one who should apologize."

"Almost kissed me. I finished the job." She stepped closer, flattening a hand on his chest. "Are you sorry it happened?"

His gaze clung to hers, his pupils growing larger, and beneath her hand, she felt the rapid thumping of his heart. "No."

She smiled, then he spoiled the moment by adding, "I should be. And I know it can't happen again. So…let's promise not to talk about it anymore. Okay?"

Her heart plummeted to her toes. Her reaction to his request told her what she'd not dared to accept. She wanted more with her best friend than a quick exploratory kiss. She wanted to pursue a deeper relationship, a *physical* relationship, a *romantic* relationship with him.

A croaking sound escaped her throat, which he apparently took as assent.

Moving alongside Cody, he stroked the horse's withers and patted the empty saddle. "I think Cody's calmed down enough for us to ride now. Need a hand up?"

She swallowed her disappointment over Nolan's withdrawal and considered the climb into the saddle. Cody was at least a hand taller than Ginger. Not an easy step up for someone of her height.

Nolan, apparently reading her hesitation as a need for assistance, put his hands under her arms, his fingers splayed on her ribs. "On three. Ready? One, two, three."

Summer grabbed the saddle horn, poked her toe into the stirrup, and tried to swing her leg over Cody's back. But came up short. Her tight jeans just hadn't been designed with climbing or horseback riding in mind. Before she could change her mind, she felt Nolan's hand plant squarely in the center of her bottom. He pushed, and she was lifted high enough to settle in the saddle. Heat stung her cheeks. She couldn't decide if the prickle was embarrassment for needing so much help, or the natural response to having Nolan's hand grip her so intimately. Maybe some of each. She didn't have time to debate the subject long before Nolan swung onto Cody's back with her. She slid as far forward in the saddle as she could, but he was still pressed snugly against her—legs, lap and chest.

Summer squeezed the saddle horn and swallowed hard. The ride back to the ranch would be both excruciating and heavenly.

NOLAN WAS IN a special form of hell, where pleasure was his torment. Summer's tush was seated firmly against his lap, and no attempt at distraction was enough to keep his body from responding or his libido in check.

Summer couldn't be unaware of his arousal, yet she tried valiantly to keep the conversation on neutral topics. Her latest text from Avery about the twins. The questions she had for his cousins about the investigation into Patrice's death. Even stories of how she'd adopted Yossi, her cat.

"I'd gone through two rooms full of cats at the Humane Society and couldn't decide. I hadn't found the one that just…clicked, you know?"

He knew. He'd felt that *click* the moment his lips touched Summer's. Call it fate or kismet or soul mates, but the powerful *rightness* of kissing her had shaken him to the core. And scared the hell out of him. And like a coward, he'd retreated. He didn't know what to do with the intense feelings that had blindsided him. Because…it was *Summer. Summer!*

He responded, as he had throughout her monologue, with grunts and single-word answers. He was pretty sure if he said more, she'd hear in his voice the sexual tension that had a stranglehold on him.

"I was about to leave when someone pointed to the bottom row, a little out of the way. This gray kitten was sort of tapping on the window. When the shelter worker took that kitten out, the little guy leaped into my arms and settled right in like he belonged there. And just like that, I was decided. He was the one."

Again he grunted.

She sighed. "I'm boring you."

"No. You're not." *You're turning me on. I'm just trying to preserve my sanity.*

The faint rumble of engines drew his gaze toward the house. Two ATVs materialized in the distance, headed for them.

"Looks like the cavalry is coming," she said, and Nolan leaned to the side to peer past her.

When the vehicles reached them, Hays driving one and Jonah on the other, Nolan reined Cody to a halt.

The men cut the engines so they could talk without shouting over the roar of motors.

"Is everyone all right?" Hays asked. "We got worried when Ginger came back to the stable without her rider."

"Ginger's back at the stable?" Summer gave a relieved laugh. "Thank goodness. I was dreading having to tell you we lost her."

"Oh, yeah," Jonah said, grinning. "Ginger knows when and where dinner is being served, and she's not one to miss a meal."

Hays's expression stayed dark with concern. "How'd she get away from you? She didn't buck you, did she?"

Summer shook her head and explained about the unseen hornet's nest. "I'm afraid Cody has a few stings. Probably Ginger, too. That's why she freaked and ran away. I'm so sorry."

Jonah scoffed. "This is Texas. Snakes and hornets and scorpions and the like are part of the package. Just glad you're both safe." He aimed a finger toward Nolan. "A baking soda paste and some antihistamine should get you and Cody fixed up."

Hays squinted one eye as he appraised Cody. "The ole boy looks pretty tired. He's had a long day. Why don't you ride back to the party with one of us, Summer?"

While he understood the wisdom of sparing Cody the

extra weight, Nolan knew a moment of disappointment as Summer dismounted. *Crazy*...because he'd just been ruing the sweet torture of Summer's fanny against his groin and the scent of her hair as it teased his cheek.

Nolan followed the ATVs back to the stable and helped Jonah cool Cody down and tend the horse's stings. Ginger had been stung a few times as well, but the mare was contentedly munching fresh hay in her stall and barely noticed the ministrations of her keepers.

Hays and Summer left Nolan and Jonah to finish up in the stable and headed to the house to wash up before dinner.

Soon the scent of wood smoke reached Nolan, followed by the clang of a bell. Nolan grinned, hearing the low metallic ring. He remembered being called to supper as a kid by the ringing of an antique bell at the main house. "Josephine still uses that old dinner bell, huh?"

Jonah chuckled. "Occasionally." He paused and smacked his lips. "I'm a bit like one of Pavlov's dogs with that thing. My mouth waters when I hear it."

Laughing, Nolan slapped his cousin on the back. "Let's go eat then."

As they strolled back to the main house, Jonah nudged Nolan with his elbow. "So you and Summer, huh? Who'd have thought all those years ago that you'd end up together?"

Nolan cut a scowl to his cousin. "We're not a couple. Why would you say that? Can't a guy have a female friend without everyone assuming they're an item?"

Jonah smirked. "Wow. Did I poke a rattlesnake or what?"

"We're not a couple," Nolan repeated.

"Mm-hmm," Jonah hummed, but his tone said he was unconvinced.

"We're not. And I'd appreciate it if you wouldn't say anything like that around Summer."

"Mm-hmm."

Nolan stopped in his tracks and braced his arms akimbo as he faced Jonah with a frown. "Why do you think we're a couple? What...why—"

Jonah shook his head and laughed. "You can't even talk about her without getting flustered. You're a case, Nolan." He leaned closer and pitched his voice low. "I have eyes. I see the way you two act with each other. And that cozy ride together on Cody...?" He gave Nolan a knowing look. "What else happened out on the ride today?"

"Nothing." Nolan turned to stalk toward the house, then stopped again and faced Jonah. "We kissed, okay? That's all. But it shouldn't have happened. We're friends. Period. That's all we can be. It just complicates things that I let it get out of hand this afternoon." He jabbed his fingers through his hair. "I don't want to lose her friendship, and I'm afraid that if we get involved I could hurt her somehow without meaning to. It's not..." He huffed his aggravation. "I screwed up, Jonah, and I have to get things back on track. So don't..." He sighed. "Just be cool about it, okay?"

His cousin gave him a long steady gaze then nodded. "Sure, man. Whatever you say. But for the record, I think you two would be great together. Seems kinda like fate, ya know?"

Trouble was, Nolan did know. If his own life was in

better order, maybe he'd consider a different sort of relationship with Summer. But he couldn't drag Summer into the chaos his life was now. His career with the FBI was unknown. Hell, his entire *future* was unknown. If criminal charges were brought against him…

Acid bit his gut as he crossed the ranch yard. His lawyer had to find a way to clear him of the false allegations against him. Somehow.

When they reached the backyard behind the main house, a roaring bonfire blazed, surrounded by a semicircle of folding lawn chairs. He searched the cluster of milling family for Summer and found her seated in one of the lawn chairs next to Forrest's fiancée, Rae Lemmon. Summer was holding a baby and smiling at the child with heart-stopping affection in her eyes. Nolan's breath caught. Summer was destined to be a great mother. He couldn't imagine her life being complete without her own baby to cuddle and nurture.

Which made his own obscure future all the more bleak. Even if he wanted to defy common sense or practicality and explore the fiery attraction he felt for Summer, he couldn't give her the life she deserved. Once the charges against him were settled, he was either going back to the murky, unpredictable life of an undercover FBI agent or…he was going to jail.

Summer looked up then, as if she sensed his gaze, and her smile shifted to an exaggerated frown. She hitched her head, signaling him to come over.

"What's with the surly face, Bullfrog?" she asked as he approached.

"Was it surly? Sorry. Just…thinking."

"Well, whatever you were thinking about...stop. This is a party, and you're scaring the children."

He looked around and spread his hands. "What children?"

"Well, Connor here for starters." Summer held up the cherubic little boy.

"Have you met my son, Nolan?" Rae asked.

Nolan bent at the waist and took the baby's chubby hand in his. "Nice to meet you, Connor."

Connor pulled his hand away and started crying.

"What did I do?" he asked.

Rae took Connor from Summer and shook her head. "Nothing. He's shy, colicky *and* teething. He's been a bit of a grump all evening. Forrest is the only one who can calm him down some days."

"My ears are burning. What did I do?" Forrest asked, appearing beside Rae with a glass of iced tea for each of the women.

"Worked some kind of voodoo with the baby, apparently," Nolan said.

Once he'd passed the drinks to Rae and Summer, Forrest took Connor into his arms, and the baby immediately quieted.

"Amazing!" Summer cooed. "Forrest, you have the magic touch."

"Join us, Nolan," Rae said, pointing to the chair beside Summer. "Summer and I were just discussing the fact that she's been hired to find Patrice Eccleston's killer."

Forrest's head swiveled toward Rae. "Oh, really?" He took the chair on the opposite side of his fiancée, focusing his gaze on Summer. He stretched out his injured leg in front of him and furrowed his brow. "Hired by whom?"

"Patrice's family," Summer said. "And I have no intention of stepping on any toes at the police department. In fact, I'd like to work in conjunction with you, if possible. I'll share what I learn, and I hope you could steer me in the right direction."

Forrest faced Connor again and tipped his head. "What do you think, pal? Should we let them into the clubhouse?"

Connor cooed and giggled, producing a spit bubble that popped on his lip.

Nodding, Forrest said, "Right. I agree." Then to Summer, "How can I help?"

SUMMER WIPED CONDENSATION off her tea glass and searched for the best place to start questioning Forrest. "I just got the case, and we're still gathering information at this point. We've talked to her friends and roommates. Although I got a copy of the reports the police and coroner were able to share with the family, we still need to pin down specifics. Especially about the coroner's report."

"We?" Forrest asked.

She cut a glance to Nolan, then back to Forrest. "Nolan's sharing his FBI expertise to help me with the case."

Forrest and Rae exchanged a look. "I see."

She tried to dismiss the feeling that Rae and Forrest had just had an entire intimate conversation with that look. A conversation filled with conjecture about her and Nolan's partnership.

"So the coroner's report? Maybe we should start

there? When Atticus brought me the case, he said the coroner's report revealed Patrice had been manually strangled. Bruising on the neck and her crushed larynx established this. Suffocation was her official cause of death, but there were also signs she'd struggled with her attacker. Bruises on her arms and legs. Broken fingernails."

Forrest nodded. "That's right."

"Dallas and Avery mentioned something about Army buttons. What can you tell us about that?"

Forrest lifted a shoulder. "That's puzzling. On the surface it would indicate a link to the Mummy Killer, Horace Corgan. But on his deathbed, when he confessed his crimes, he vehemently denied responsibility for killing Patrice."

"Right. That's what Dallas told us." Nolan rubbed his jaw. "So are you working on the belief that Corgan had an accomplice? That Patrice was killed by a copycat killer? That the buttons were planted to throw the cops off the culprit's trail?"

"Any of those are possible," Forrest said, using a burp cloth to wipe drool from Connor's mouth, "and they all deserve consideration."

"Let me throw another bone into the pit for you to gnaw on." Rae cringed. "Oh, that sounded grisly, especially in light of the investigation. Sorry. I just mean I've been thinking recently about another fact worthy of exploring."

Summer shifted in her chair to face Rae. "What's that?"

The pretty brunette sighed and said, "One of the lawyers at my firm, Lukas, Jolley and Fitzsimmons—" she looked directly at Summer when she paused to name the firm "—had a brief affair with Patrice."

Adrenaline spiked in Summer's blood, and she sat straighter in her chair. "What? Are you sure?"

"Well, that's the rumor. And it comes from a reliable source at my office. She told me about it when I complained to her that Kenneth—that's the lawyer's name, Kenneth Dawson—was creeping me out with all the attention he was paying *me*. He made no secret of the fact he had a thing for me, despite my reminding him I knew he was married."

Summer noticed that Forrest had tensed, his jaw tightening and a darkly threatening look filling his eyes.

Rae continued, "He'd find ways to cop a feel, or I'd find him staring at me at meetings and he'd give me a smarmy wink. Once, he tried to corner me in the copy room to *chat*."

"Ugh," Summer said with a shudder of disgust. She cast a side glance to Nolan, knowing he had to be thinking about the accusations made against him.

"Anyway," Rae said, fanning a mosquito away from her face, "his affair with Patrice was pretty well-known around town, at least in some circles. Although I never saw them together myself, I heard people say that things between Kenneth and Patrice lasted two or three weeks. They were seen having dinner at that place right outside town…" Brow furrowed in question, she glanced to Forrest as if asking for help.

"La Cantina," he supplied.

"Right, La Cantina—great fajitas, by the way—and then they were seen riding in his car together about three days later."

"Wouldn't his wife have found out about the affair if he was so public about it?" Nolan asked.

"And Patrice's father?" Summer asked, a slow burn of irritation biting her stomach. "He swore she wasn't involved with anyone. Hadn't been involved with anyone…" She raked fingers through her hair, frustration gnawing her.

"I don't know if her father knew, but her brother did," Forrest said, the baby in his arms now close to asleep. "I understand that Ian confronted Kenneth in front of the law firm when Kenneth was leaving work. It got ugly, but Ian left before the cops were called."

Rae pulled a face and nodded. "Saw it. Ug. Ly."

Summer growled, then with drama said, "Oh, my kingdom for a client that would be forthcoming and honest when questioned."

Nolan chuckled and gave the base of her neck a quick, deep rub with his fingers. She savored the brief massage, not realizing how tense she'd become until he dug his thumb pad into her taut muscles.

Itching to take notes on what she was hearing, she glanced around her and scowled. "Shoot, I left my purse and notepad in the house." She shoved out of her chair and grabbed a napkin off the picnic table. Glancing to Nolan, Forrest and Rae, she asked, "Anyone have a pen?"

Nolan rose from his chair, gifting her with a charming half grin. "I'll get your notebook and purse. Hang on."

Forrest turned to follow him. "I'll go, too. I think this little guy has finally wound down."

"Thanks, honey," Rae said, beaming at Forrest and

handing him Connor's blanket and burp cloth to take inside with him. They shared a lingering look and blissful smile before Forrest headed into the house.

Summer allowed Rae to bask in her happiness bubble for a moment before returning the conversation to the grim topic of Patrice's murder. "So do you think this Kenneth fellow, the lawyer at your office, could have latent violent tendencies? Do you think he could have a connection to Patrice's death?"

Rae screwed her face into a frown. "He's a lowlife, cheating spouse, but violent tendencies? I don't know." She rose from her lawn chair and took a paper plate from the stack on the nearby picnic table. She loaded the plate with raw veggies, corn chips and two kinds of dip before she returned to her seat. "I told you about his fling with Patrice because I figured no one else had mentioned it, and I knew it *could* be relevant. An affair gone wrong *could* be motive for murder. Right?"

"Hmm. Right."

Rae held her plate out to Summer. "Try this taco dip. It's divine!"

Summer sampled the appetizer Rae offered and hummed her enjoyment. "Oh, that is yummy!" Then with her mouth full, "Have the police interviewed Kenneth?"

Rae nibbled a chip, nodding. "I would think so, considering his connection to Patrice. I told Forrest what I'd heard at the office about the affair the same day they found the body. But Kenneth is slick. His specialty is skirting all around the legal limits of the law and finding loopholes for his clients to slither through. I wouldn't put it past him to have found a way to avoid answering any real substantive questions related to Patrice's death." She popped another corn chip with dip in her mouth, adding, "It's embarrassing to say he's part of our firm, but his father-in-law is the Fitzsimmons in Lukas, Jolley and Fitzsimmons, so his job is pretty secure."

Summer helped herself to a strip of bell pepper and mused aloud, "Also gives him another reason to not want his affairs discovered. His father-in-law might not take kindly to learning about his extracurricular activities."

Rae aimed a carrot stick at Summer. "True that. If you're thinking of interviewing Kenneth, you'll have to wait. He's out of town on business until Monday." With a loud crunch, she bit the end off the carrot stick. "Now—" she glanced behind her as if checking to see that they wouldn't be overheard "—tell me about Nolan. Clearly you two have something going on."

Summer inhaled crumbs from the corn chip she'd just munched and coughed indelicately. "What?" she rasped.

Rae gave her a knowing look. "The touches, the subtle glances, the positive *reek* of pheromones surrounding you two."

Summer grabbed her tea and drank greedily before meeting Rae's gaze. "It's that obvious?"

"To someone who has recently fallen in love herself and watched other loved ones do likewise." Rae nodded toward the bonfire, where Jonah had his arm around a tall, beautiful blonde—his fiancée, Maggie, Summer presumed. "Yes. It is obvious."

Summer's face burned, and she pressed a hand to her cheek. "Oh."

Rae scowled. "You don't look happy. Was your relationship supposed to stay secret? 'Cause I have to say, Summer—" her mouth curved in a grin "—if it was, you need to learn better control of your facial expressions."

Summer stared at the condensation rolling down the side of her glass. "The thing is... Nolan is fighting it." When Rae lifted a skeptical eyebrow, Summer felt compelled to defend him. "He's going through a difficult issue professionally, and starting a romance at this point wouldn't be—" She fumbled then tried again. "He's just wary of mixing business and pleasure."

Pleasure had Summer flashing back to their kisses by the creek and the sweet pleasure of Nolan's body pressed against hers as they rode Cody back to the ranch. The warm sting in her cheeks flashed hotter, and her breath caught.

Rae didn't miss the telltale signs. "From the look of things, you disagree? Maybe you've already pushed the boundaries with him?"

Summer drank another gulp of cold tea and tried to calm her flustered heartbeat. "I... I want what's best for Nolan. I respect his wishes and the reason for his choice."

"But...?" Rae angled her head, obviously knowing Summer was holding back.

Summer sighed heavily. "Oh, Rae, I'm as surprised as anyone how my feelings for him have shifted. He's so sexy and so kind and so..." She huffed. "Good grief,

I spend most of my time around him wanting to rip his clothes off him and do him where he stands."

Rae laughed and reached for Summer's hand. Squeezing her friend's fingers, she said, "So do it! PDAs make it all the more exciting."

Shoulders drooping, Summer shook her head. "The more important thing is that I not do anything to ruin our friendship. We were best friends long before this crazy attraction to him tangled things up. I can't lose his trust or his friendship, Rae." A wave of panic and anxiety washed through her, remembering Nolan's withdrawal after the impromptu kisses. She swallowed hard. "And I may have already messed things up with him."

Chapter Twelve

Nolan measured his pace to Forrest's slower limp, and he rewound the conversation Summer had been having with his cousin moments earlier. "Before we got sidetracked to discussing this lawyer who works with Rae—"

A rumble of aggravation drifted to Nolan from his cousin. Nolan said nothing, but he could certainly understand Forrest's displeasure that such a man worked in the firm with Rae.

"—we were talking about the buttons found with the murdered women's bodies. Whether Horace Corgan denied killing Patrice or not, the buttons link her to the other women."

Forrest nodded. "And you're wondering if any other evidence was found that linked Patrice with the mummified women?"

Nolan flipped a hand. "Right."

He opened the door for Forrest, whose hands were occupied with the sleeping baby. As they entered, they encountered Donovan and his new wife, Bellamy, headed out to the bonfire, their arms laden with steaming bowls of baked beans, twice-baked potato casserole and a large platter of sliced beef brisket. Alex, Dono-van's black Labrador retriever, trailed behind them, av-idly sniffing the air.

Nolan stepped out of the way and held the door for his cousin.

"Hey, Nolan!" Donovan said brightly. "When did you arrive?"

Nolan stuck his hand out to shake Donovan's, then realizing his cousin's hands were occupied, he chuck-led and opted to scratch the dog's head instead. "A cou-ple hours ago. Summer and I rode out to the creek for a while."

He tried desperately to not let his thoughts stray to how they'd passed the time at the creek. Bad enough that Jonah had already guessed his true feelings for Summer.

Bellamy raised the dish she was carrying, revealing her pregnant belly. "Well, you two are headed the wrong direction. Soup's on. Get it while it's hot!"

Forrest nodded. "Be right back. Gotta put Connor to bed."

Nolan spotted Summer's purse on the family room couch and snagged it. He waited patiently in the front of the house for Forrest to return with a baby monitor with a video screen in his hand. "I bet even the FBI doesn't have the level of monitoring equipment Rae bought for Connor's room. This thing is so sensitive to noise, it will read your thoughts."

Nolan glanced at the camera, remembering another camera in another room that had caught him unaware, and his gut clenched.

"So I guess if you've talked to Atticus Eccleston

about what the police found at the burial spot, you know that Patrice's hands were bound?"

Nolan nodded. "Summer mentioned that, but she said Patrice wasn't mummified like the other women."

"Correct. Nor did she have a scarf in her mouth." Forrest hitched his head toward the door, and they headed back outside together. "My gut feeling is that somehow Patrice's killer found out about the buttons buried with the other women, acquired some—that'd be easy enough to do, since they were standard Army uniform buttons—and planted them at the scene when he buried Patrice."

Forrest slowed and faced Nolan before they reached the circle of chairs set up around the bonfire. The late evening sun cast harsh shadows on his cousin's face. Nolan noted the tiny creases bracketing Forrest's eyes and mouth, evidence of the stress he'd been under in recent months. Dallas had told Nolan on the night he arrived in Whisperwood that Forrest had been targeted by an assassin a couple months back in an attempt to scare him and Rae away from the investigation into the Mummy Killer. Death threats and assassination attempts were certainly enough to add a few stress lines to one's face.

Although the Mummy Killer had been found and the source of the attempts on Forrest's life captured, Nolan considered the fact that by investigating Patrice's death, Summer could be putting a target on her back. The thought chilled him to the marrow.

"Of course," Forrest was saying, "the fact that Patrice's killer put her in a parking lot that was being repaved tells me he was hoping no one would find her for years to come. The buttons could simply have been a way of hedging his bets if she was found. Something to muddy the evidence against him and mislead investigators."

Nolan nodded his agreement, then put a hand on Forrest's arm when he turned to go. "Forrest, be honest. Do you believe this case puts Summer in harm's way? Based on what the police have learned about Patrice's killer, do you think Summer's life is in jeopardy?"

Forrest's expression grew even more serious than it had been. "Come on, Nolan. You're FBI. You know criminal behavior. The perp has already killed once and has tried to cover his tracks. What do *you* think he'll do to keep his secret from being discovered?"

The chill in his bones crystallized, and acid filled his gut. "Damn. That's what I was afraid of."

"YOUR *FATHER* TRIED to kill Forrest?" Summer asked Rae, incredulous over what she was learning about events just two months prior when Forrest and Rae had gotten involved with the ongoing investigations in Whisperwood.

Rae bobbed her head, frowning. "Someone was apparently threatening my dad—and also me and Connor—in order to manipulate my dad. This someone apparently didn't like Forrest looking into the Mummy Killer and Patrice's death, and so, to protect his daughter and grandson, my dad tried to kill Forrest for this unknown person." Rae swallowed hard. "We believe whoever it was threatening my dad is also responsible for killing him."

Summer gaped at Rae. "Your father was killed because of the investigation into the Mummy Killer?"

"And Patrice's death." Rae's expression reflected grief and a weariness that Summer now understood wasn't entirely because of a fussy infant. "The first threats to us started arriving after Patrice's body was found."

Summer sank back in her lawn chair, her mind in turmoil as she tried to connect the dots of the case. "But, as I understand it, Horace Corgan admitted to killing the mummified women."

"Mm-hmm," Rae hummed and nodded.

"So couldn't he be the one behind your father's death? Even if he didn't kill your father personally, couldn't Horace have ordered the kill...and made the threats against you?"

"He said he wasn't. And the fact that Horace was killed while we were there talking to him leads us to believe he could have known who *was* behind it all and was silenced."

Summer bit her bottom lip in thought. "By his nurse? Jane Oliver?"

Rae pulled a face. "The nurse makes the most sense. She was the only other person there that we know of."

"We talked to Jane Oliver's coworkers earlier. They mentioned that Jane was bragging about coming into a load of money right before she disappeared."

Rae leaned toward Summer. "Yeah?"

"Our hunch, one we can't confirm yet, is that she was being paid off to be a pawn in some scheme, at least part of which includes being paid to kill Corgan or to let someone in Corgan's room to kill him."

Rae shrugged, then laid a hand on Summer's arm. "That does sound like the most obvious answer. Especially since we suspect Jane could have also been one of the nurses helping dispense illegal prescription pills."

"Avery mentioned rumors in town that some nurses were helping distribute illegal prescription pills. She tied everything back to the owner of the auto shop on Main. Um…" Summer snapped her fingers as she tried to come up with the name.

"Tom Kain."

"That's him." Summer aimed a finger at Rae.

"I can't tell you anything about the rumors regarding Kain, other than we've heard them. Forrest asked at the WPD about Kain. They'd love to catch him in the act if he is guilty, but so far nothing has turned up when they've raided the shop or his house based on credible tips."

"So he's as slick as your friend Kenneth."

"And Kain has a number of friends in high places who vouch for him being an upstanding community leader and benefactor." Rae shrugged. "So…"

Summer raised a finger to her mouth and chewed the nail as she processed the new information. "Patrice's killer could have had Corgan's nurse in his crosshairs, as well. We've been assuming she disappeared because she killed Corgan and used her payoff to skip town. But what if she ran because her life was in jeopardy? What if she thought Patrice's killer would come after her next?"

Rae scrunched her face as she considered that scenario. "Yep. Definitely possible."

Summer raked her hair back from her face. "So finding the nurse just got bumped up in priority on my to-do list. There are so many angles to this crazy case, and my gut says that, like some intricate spiderweb, it is all connected. The cast of characters Nolan and I need to interview keeps getting longer by the hour."

"Did I hear my name? What did I do?" Nolan asked, appearing behind her and handing over her purse.

"Thank goodness," Summer said, quickly digging a pen out of her purse. "I need to write all this down. We have a busy day tomorrow, Bullfrog. This case is growing by the minute."

Chapter Thirteen

The next morning, Summer woke to a gray cat begging for breakfast by hovering over her face and an insistent pounding on her office door. Smooching Yossi's head then nudging him aside, she raked her hair back from her face with her fingers and stumbled groggily to the door. She opened it a crack and peered through the opening. Early-morning sunlight glinted off Nolan's latte-brown hair and, ironically, lit his cloudy, frowning face with a warm glow.

"Jeez, Summer! You didn't even ask who it was before you opened the door. Are you nuts?"

She cracked a smile and opened the door wider to let him and the tray from JoJo's Java he held in. "And a cheery good morning to you, too."

"I could have been anyone. You have to be more careful." He held out the tray. "I brought coffee and sausage biscuits."

"One, this is Whisperwood, not Chicago. I'm not even sure why I bother locking my door at night." She closed said door and held her hands out for the food. "And two, those biscuits smell divine. I could kiss you."

His gaze flicked to her lips, and color filled his

cheeks as he passed the bag of breakfast to her. Her pulse spiked, realizing what she'd said. To hide her awkwardness, she led him to her kitchenette and turned her attention to the bag of biscuits and steaming coffee.

"The one with the X on top is fixed the way you like it."

"How do you know how I like it?" she asked, then yawned so hard her jaw cracked.

"I paid attention the other day."

Her already-pattering pulse skipped harder. She knew he had an eye for detail, but having him turn his skills of observation on her, that he'd taken note of her preferences, felt more than kind. The attention felt…intimate. Like something a lover would know about her.

Her hand trembled as she took a sip of her perfectly doctored coffee. "What time is it?"

"Seven thirty."

She sputtered and choked on the sip of joe. "Good grief, Nolan. It's Saturday. Sane people aren't even out of bed yet! Why are you here?"

"Early bird gets the worm, right?" He reached down to pat Yossi, who was rubbing against his legs and meowing for breakfast. "Besides, I couldn't sleep. Between this case and the matter back home, my brain wouldn't shut off."

She noted his reference to Chicago as *home*. And why wouldn't he? It was his home base. Still, the reminder that he wasn't in Whisperwood permanently, would be leaving…potentially within days, made her coffee sour in her stomach. Setting her cup on the small counter next to her hot plate, she grabbed a paper towel to wipe her mouth. "Who wants worms when you can have JoJo's biscuits?"

She reached in the paper sack and pulled out one of the hot breakfast sandwiches. Glancing at him, she added, "Thank you, by the way. This is nice."

His gaze was fixed on something at her chest level, and she glanced down, thinking she must have dribbled her coffee. "Wha—"

The question died on her lips when it dawned on her she'd answered the door in her pajamas—or what passed for pajamas for her. A thin T-shirt and short-short boxer-style bottoms. Without a bra on, her nipples were prominent, and his blatant notice of her dishabille only made them more erect. Heat rushed through her, chased by a tingling sensation that woke her up better than a double shot of espresso.

Nolan. You're getting hot and bothered over Nolan Colton. Good gravy, Summer! Get a grip!

"Um... I'll just go—" she aimed a thumb over her shoulder "—get dressed." She took a couple backward steps and almost tripped over the cat. "Um, would you mind feeding Yossi before he hurts himself begging? The cans of his food are in that cabinet." She pointed at the door below the counter, then fled the kitchenette.

In the bathroom, she studied herself in the tiny mirror. She'd intended to hit the gym and shower before doing anything else today. The desserts and dips at the barbecue, not to mention the indulgences at the Bluebell Diner, would start catching up with her if she weren't careful. But since Nolan was already there, she did the best with her ablutions as she could—spraying dry

shampoo in her hair and cleaning with scented body
soap and a washcloth at the sink.

Once she'd dressed, Summer and Nolan set out for
a full day of interviews and fact gathering. As Nolan
drove, she Googled Tyler's address then used her map
app to get driving directions to his apartment.

Their knock was answered by an unshaven, tousle-
haired young man, who squinted against the sunlight
as if he'd just woken up. "If you're selling somethin', I
don't want it."

"Tyler Whitmore?" Summer asked.

The bleary-eyed man scowled. "Who wants to
know?"

They introduced themselves, saying only that they
were helping Patrice's family learn all they could about
her death. Tyler didn't look like the sort who was keen
to spill his guts to anyone approaching law enforcement.

"So what do you want from me?"

Summer explained how, as the last person to see her
before she disappeared, he could have important information about what had happened to Patrice. When
he still seemed reluctant to speak to them, she added,
"Don't you want to help us catch the person responsible
for Patrice's murder?"

He raised his chin, and his expression darkened.
"Catch him? I'd like to strangle him the way he strangled Patrice." After another moment of scowling at
them, Tyler scrubbed both hands over his face and stood
back to allow them in.

As she passed him, entering the dimly lit apartment,
Summer got a strong whiff of unwashed body tinged

with the scent of alcohol. She took a seat on a futon across from the tattered recliner Tyler settled on.

The interview with Tyler went much the way it had with his friends at the vocational college. He confirmed having gone to Bailey's for drinks with the others after class the day Patrice disappeared and that Patrice had left the bar early, unescorted.

"I shoulda at least seen that she got home safe. We—the guys and me—usually followed her home. But she left so fast that night, without saying anything to us." He sighed, and a pained expression crumpled his face.

"Do you know what prompted her to leave early?" Nolan asked.

Tyler nodded, then hung his head. "I did." He admitted to having had feelings for Patrice, having been rejected by her when he tried to kiss her the night she disappeared. "It's my fault she's dead." He seemed on the verge of tears, and Summer cut a quick glance to Nolan to gauge his reaction to the young man's guilt and grief. "If I hadn't kissed her, if I'd followed her when she ran off, if I'd done *anything* different that night, she'd still be here."

Nolan moved to squat in front of Tyler, putting a hand on the young man's shoulder. "That kind of thinking is a dead end. Don't let yourself be sucked into that trap. Patrice's death is solely the fault of the person who killed her."

Tyler scrunched his eyes closed and pinched the bridge of his nose.

"Did you strangle Patrice, Tyler?"

Patrice's classmate jerked his head up, his eyes red and wild. "No! I loved her!"

"Then let go of this guilt trip you're on. The best thing you can do for Patrice now is honor her memory by living the best life you can. Would she want to see you shutting yourself up here and drinking yourself numb?"

Tyler shook his head.

"So go back to class. Finish your schooling. Cooperate with the police in finding her killer."

Summer's chest warmed as she watched Nolan console and advise the heartbroken, blame-ridden young man.

"Dedicate your life to being your best self. In her memory."

Tyler glanced up at Nolan and nodded slowly.

Nolan squeezed Tyler's shoulder and lifted a corner of his mouth. "And for God's sake, take a shower, man."

Summer curled her lips in and bit down hard to muffle the inappropriate giggle that rose inside her, then swallowed hard as a lump grew in her throat. Nolan's compassion for Tyler burrowed deep inside her, and she lost another piece of her soul to her childhood friend.

Tyler and Nolan talked in hushed tones for another minute or two before Nolan rose to his feet and signaled to Summer it was time to leave. She pulled out a business card and cleared a spot on the cluttered coffee table where she could leave it. "Please get in touch if you think of anything that might help us with our investigation."

Tyler glanced at the card, then met Summer's eyes and bobbed his head.

Back in the truck, Nolan sighed heavily. "He's not our man."

"Then the grieving, guilt-ridden, spurned love interest isn't an act to throw us off?" she asked, wanting confirmation of her own feelings.

He cast a glance to her, one eyebrow raised. "Didn't it look genuine...*smell* genuine to you?"

"Well, yeah. But the guilt could have been because he flew off the handle after being rejected and he strangled her in a jealous rage."

Nolan pursed his lips then shook his head. "Naw. My gut says he's not responsible for anything connected to her death."

She cocked her head. "Your gut? And how reliable is your gut? I thought you were a by-the-book kinda guy."

He reached for the ignition and started the engine. "Usually. But my gut's also very reliable." He put the truck in gear then added, "For what it's worth, in case you couldn't hear, Tyler just told me that the night he kissed her, Patrice admitted to being in a relationship with a married man."

Summer sat taller, her pulse accelerating. "Kenneth Dawson?"

Nolan flipped up his hand. "He didn't know a name, but... Dawson would be my guess."

Summer plowed a hand into her hair and expelled a long breath. "This case keeps getting more arms and legs all the time. I'm getting cross-eyed trying to keep it all straight."

"Whiteboard."

"Pardon?"

"This is the time in a case I'd start making a chart on a whiteboard and looking at the connections, asking what was missing. We need to fit some of these puzzle pieces together." He glanced at her. "Do you have a whiteboard?"

She wrinkled her nose. "No."

He flipped on his turn signal. "Then our next stop is the office supply store. We've got some charting to do."

YOSSI GREETED THEM at the door when they returned to her office, and Summer lifted her cat in her arms for a cuddle while Nolan hung the new whiteboard on an empty wall. Uncapping a marker, he wrote down the names of everyone they'd interviewed so far, including Patrice's roommates, her family and the guys from her class, plus Jane Oliver, Horace Corgan and anyone else of interest that had been mentioned in the interviews, putting a star by Kenneth Dawson's name. In another column, he wrote out facts they knew about Patrice in the months before her death. Classes she took at the vocational college, places she'd interviewed for work, the places she frequented, such as Bailey's Bar, and general information about her online social media accounts.

"We know Bailey's is the last place she was seen by Tyler." Nolan circled Bailey's on the board and drew a line to Tyler's name.

"We should go by Bailey's and ask about surveillance video from that night. Maybe they made an extra copy since they had to give one to the cops. It's been a long time, and I know places like that record over old video after a few days, but it can't hurt to ask. I want to study the other faces at the bar that night. Who could have followed Patrice when she left?"

Nolan jotted *Surveillance video?* over *Bailey's*.

Standing behind her desk, Summer bit her bottom lip

as she stared at the board. "When did Rae say Kenneth Dawson would be back in town? I really want to talk to him, especially in light of what Tyler told us about Patrice seeing a married man."

When she glanced at Nolan, he had an odd expression on his face. He seemed to be staring at her mouth. "Um, I don't... I don't recall. You...wrote it down, didn't you?"

"Right." Dismissing the strange look he'd given her, she bent over her notebook and flipped through the pages to find her notes regarding Dawson. "Here it is. He is scheduled to be back Monday. So that'd be the fourteenth."

Without straightening, she glanced up at Nolan, but his stare was fixed on something below her own gaze. Glancing down, she realized her bent-over position left her V-neck sweater gaping, and he had a clear view of her cleavage. Without thinking about who she was talking to, she spouted an automatic sarcastic response. "See something you like, pal?"

Nolan's gaze flew up to hers, and his face reddened with almost laughable guilt. He spun away from her and swiped a hand down his stricken face. She cracked a smile as she straightened until the depth of his distress dawned on her. He wasn't simply embarrassed at being caught gawking. Something had him truly upset. She could too easily guess what. And it all went back to Charlotte.

His friends-only, hands-off rule with her was based on his bad experience with Charlotte. He distrusted his own choices because of Charlotte. The barricade that kept her from pursuing the attraction she felt for Nolan was erected because of Charlotte.

A fury roiled inside her for all that the woman lying about Nolan was costing not only him, but herself, as well. What if she and Nolan were meant to be together, and the shadow Charlotte had cast over Nolan's life was the only thing keeping them apart?

Her fists balled, and her teeth clenched at the notion. Summer Davies was not the sort to stand by and let some scheming, manipulative bitch dictate what happiness she could have!

Her body trembling with pent-up rage, she stalked around her desk and yanked on Nolan's arm. Aiming a finger in his face, she asked, "Nolan Colton, do you have feelings for me?" Then, narrowing her eyes, she clarified bluntly, "Sexual feelings?"

He swallowed so hard, she saw his Adam's apple bob. "Summer, I'm sorry…"

She threw her hand up. "Stop with the apologizing and answer the damn question! Are you attracted to me that way or not?"

A muscle in his cheek twitched as he tightened his jaw. His eyes flashed hot as he stared back at her. "I'd have thought what happened at the creek yesterday had answered that."

The reminder of the steamy kisses they'd shared the day before sent a rush of heat through her. She trembled as a tingle of anticipation rolled through her. Summer squared her shoulders and canted toward him. "Okay then."

When she rose on her toes to kiss him, he put a hand on her arm and stepped back. "But that doesn't mean—"

She growled her frustration, cutting him off. "Screw the buts, Nolan! And screw Charlotte for making you so wary and reluctant to follow your heart! If you want something in life, you should go after it full throttle. Fight for what you want! No ifs, ands or buts." She stamped her foot as she jerked erect. Grabbing the front of his shirt, she pressed her body against his. "I want to kiss you, Nolan, and I'm prepared to fight your Charlotte-centric resistance to get what I want!" She rose on her toes and, getting in his face, she added in a low tone, "Because I'm betting it's what you want, too."

With that, she captured his lips and kissed him for all she was worth. He didn't fight her. In fact, he deepened the kiss, his hands framing her face as he swept his tongue over her lips. She opened to him, greeted him with a matching fervor.

When a tiny voice of caution whispered in her brain that Nolan would leave town again soon, that he was too dedicated to his career to be committed to her, she shut the voice down. The thrumming demand in her blood was too strong to give the what-ifs any consideration now.

She turned her thoughts, instead, to imagining Nolan stripped down to his birthday suit and twining his body in passion with hers. Summer's knees grew weak. If he hadn't wrapped an arm around her back, pulling her flush against him, she might have staggered.

When her lungs craved oxygen and she had no choice but to raise her head from their kiss, Summer gently pried loose of Nolan's embrace and stepped back, panting. Grinning.

His concerned expression was almost comical. Almost. Except she knew the source of his doubts and wanted to scream. Knew he was retreating into his head again, overthinking things.

"Summer, do you—"

Before he could finish the question, she swept her arm across her desk and sent all the papers, her mug, her stapler, her pen holder and her sticky-note dispenser onto the floor. She stared at her handiwork for a few seconds then laughed. "Oh my God! I've always wanted to do that! Always wanted a *reason* to do that." She turned to him, a wicked grin tugging the corner of her mouth. "And it felt so good."

He huffed his amusement and disbelief. "You really are something, you know that?"

"Yeah, yeah, FBI guy." She grabbed his shirt front and pulled him with her as she backed to the desk and scooted her bottom onto it. "Less talk and more kissing." She wrapped her legs around his waist and pulled him down with her as she lay back on the top of her desk. "Make love to me, Nolan."

His smile lit his face. "Can't be much clearer than that."

THE WARM BODY beside him on the narrow cot stirred, and Nolan roused from the lethargy that had overcome him after the most satisfying sex he'd ever experienced. Summer turned her head to peek up at him, and he brushed strands of her honey-toned hair from her face.

"Hey, you," she murmured drowsily.

"Hey, yourself. Did you know you snore?"

She twitched and frowned. "I do not!"

"Do, too." When she opened her mouth to protest, he kissed the tip of her nose. "And I think it is adorable."

"Look, it's allergy season in Texas right now, and—"

He chuckled. "It's always allergy season in Texas, Sum. I'd bet *Texas* is Spanish for 'allergies.'"

"Probably."

She wiggled to reposition herself, and the slide of her naked skin against his aroused him all over. "What time is it? I didn't mean to fall asleep."

He glanced around the small windowless space she used as a bedroom and spotted his pants discarded near the door. "My phone was in the pocket of my jeans last I saw it, and they are way over there." He pointed. "Getting to them would require leaving this toasty nest… and you—" he pressed a quick kiss to her lips "—so I'm not inclined to get it."

"Hmm." She gave him a mock serious look and nod. "And I think mine was on my desk before I cleared it for sex."

He chuckled, remembering her brash move. "That was classic."

"I think I broke my stapler."

He snuggled her closer and kissed the top of her head. "I'll get you a new one for Christmas."

"Christmas?" She leaned her head back and pulled a disgruntled face. "That's two months away! How am I supposed to keep papers together until then?"

"I don't know…paper clips, maybe?" His phone buzzed as he laughed at her teasing scowl. He considered ignoring the mobile, but his FBI training and his reluctance to miss an important message compelled him to crawl out from the warm blankets and retrieve his cell phone. He glanced at the caller ID. It was his lawyer. By the time he picked up, the call had gone to his voice mail. Like the cool air in the room on his sex-warmed skin, the reminder of his troubles back in Chicago doused him with a cold slap of reality.

What was he doing, making love to Summer? Why had he allowed himself to get more deeply involved with a woman who he knew invested her whole heart in everything and everyone she cared about?

A pit of regret balled in his stomach, and he grumbled a curse word.

Summer sat up on the narrow cot, clutching the sheet to her chest. "Nolan? What's wrong? Who was it?"

"My lawyer. I'll, uh…call him back from the bathroom." He glanced at his phone again before gathering his pants and socks from the floor. "Listen, it's three thirty. We should get going. Didn't you have more interviews on the docket today?"

She only stared at him, a knit in her brow. "What happened to staying in and…playing?" She lifted a corner of her mouth, although her eyes reflected wariness. "Didn't you have fun?" She hitched her head, indicating the bed.

He drew a slow breath, bent to pick up his shoes and glanced at a crack in her wall, unable to meet her sad eyes. "I did, but…"

"Nolan, don't—"

"Summer, we both know this was a mistake."

He heard her frustrated huff. "I know no such thing. It *meant* something to me!"

"And that is exactly why it was a mistake." He turned his back and started out of the room. He stopped long enough to whisper, "I'm sorry, Summer."

Chapter Fourteen

Summer had known Nolan might react like this, second-guessing their lovemaking, since he'd been so adamant earlier about keeping things platonic. But that didn't make his characterization of what had been so great, so special for her as a mistake hurt any less.

She'd also known, in the moments just after he'd left her bed, that he wanted to punch something. She'd watched him prowl her office like a caged tiger, his jaw tight and his fists clenched, and she hadn't needed their close connection to know he was strung as tight as a piano wire. Since she could stand to work out some tension and frustration, as well, she'd directed him to her gym. They'd both used the heavy bag equipment for a boxing-style workout, then grabbed showers before heading out for their next interviews.

Though Nolan appeared more relaxed after their workouts, Summer was bone tired and heartsore. But she refused to let her personal life interfere with her responsibility to her client.

"I want to talk to Tom Kain," she told Nolan as he tossed his gym bag in the back seat.

He slid behind the steering wheel and sent her a long, silent, grim stare.

"You can go with me or I can go alone," she said, guessing at the reason for his hesitation. "But I am going."

Nolan's expression shifted, reluctant resignation replacing the steely skepticism.

She flipped her hand over. "There are too many rumors about him for me to ignore the possibility of his connection to at least some part of this big puzzle."

He huffed. "Fine."

Falling quiet again, he drove out of the gym parking lot and headed back toward downtown.

She studied his profile, his damp hair, his stony jaw. "So is this how it's going to be now? You sullen and silent, withdrawn, giving terse answers to my questions and comments?"

He cut a glance to her, frowned, then rolled his shoulders as he sighed. "No. But…this is why…" He clenched his teeth and shook his head. "I need time to process. Us. This case." He flicked another quick look to her. "The call to my lawyer today."

"Did he have bad news?"

"No. Not exactly. He said Humboldt, my boss, called. They finished their investigation and interviews and will meet this weekend to review the information with internal affairs. I should have an answer soon about my future with the FBI."

Summer's gut kicked. "Oh. Wow. Um, that was fast. Do you think…did your lawyer think that was a good sign? That they wrapped it up so fast?"

Nolan shrugged. "He didn't say, and I didn't ask. It

is what it is. Is this the turn?" he said, pointing to the intersection ahead of them.

"Yeah. Left."

In the last couple blocks to the auto shop, no more was said about Nolan's future with the FBI, about their postsex relationship or about any of the things swirling in Summer's head and heart. Closing her eyes, Summer centered herself and mentally shifted into business mode. She needed to be on top of her game for this interview with the suspected drug dealer.

They arrived at Kain's garage just as a mechanic in oil-stained coveralls was closing the bay doors and moving inside a sign on a metal stand that read "Ask About Our Fall Tune-Up Special." Summer gave the man a convivial grin as she stepped out of Nolan's Cherokee, and the mechanic bobbed a nod of greeting.

"Sorry, ma'am," the coverall-clad man said, "but we just closed for the day. You'll have to come back tomorrow."

"We're not actually here for service. We'd like to speak to Tom Kain, if he's in." Summer estimated the mechanic to be in his late forties, based on his balding pate and threads of gray in his short-trimmed beard.

The man frowned and drew a rag from his pocket to wipe his hands. "He's in. What's your business with him?"

"We just have a few questions we'd like to ask him," Nolan said as he moved up behind her.

The other man's eyes narrowed on him. "You cops?"

"Why would you think that?"

"You've got that look about ya," the mechanic, whose name patch only said Walter, replied, eyeing Nolan.

"I do?" Summer asked, tipping her head. "I'm usually told I look like I'm still in high school. And a cheerleader at that." She snorted. "Which I wasn't. I played softball and was on the debate team." She flashed another friendly grin. "So would you tell Mr. Kain he has guests? We promise not to take too much of his time."

The mechanic continued to stare at them suspiciously for a moment before raising one shoulder and turning to stroll to the front desk of the auto shop. Summer and Nolan followed him inside.

"Wait here," Walter told them before he disappeared through a side door and down a short hallway. The scents of petroleum and mildew were heavy in the air, and Summer cast her gaze around at the cans of motor oil, filters, hoses and headlight bulbs that lined the shelf behind the counter. The wall to the work bays had a large picture window where old newspaper clippings, yellow and curled with age, had been taped. Another wall sported a calendar with a photo of some obviously pricey sports car Summer couldn't identify.

Hands in his jacket pockets, Nolan, too, was taking in the details of the business, and she wondered what he was noticing that she'd missed.

"Evening, folks. Walter said you were looking for me?" The amiable greeting brought her attention back to the door where Walter had left moments earlier. A man with light brown hair, a square jaw and startling blue eyes approached. Was *this* Tom Kain? Summer hadn't expected someone so...good-looking, so young, so clean-cut to be the owner of an auto shop. Her conscience pricked her for being guilty of stereotyping. Then she recalled Avery's belief that Tom Kain was dealing drugs from his shop and another stereotype was busted. Kain looked more like he should be selling life insurance or cleaning people's teeth than what she typically imagined drug dealers looked like.

"What can I do you for?" The hunky man in his thirties flashed a lopsided grin.

Summer extended her hand and introduced herself as a PI and Nolan simply as her associate. "If you have a minute, we have a couple of questions for you regarding a case we're working."

His smile dimmed with apology. "I *only* have a minute, I'm afraid." He glanced at the Pennzoil clock above the front door as if to reinforce his assertion. "I'm on my way out the door to a Whisperwood town council meeting."

"You're on the town council?" Nolan asked.

Kain shook his head. "Naw. I don't have the stomach for politics, but as a business owner, I feel it's my responsibility to stay abreast of what the council is doing."

"Right, well…we'll try not to keep you." Summer noted they weren't invited back to his office—another sign he was in a hurry to be rid of her and Nolan. "We're looking into the death of Patrice Eccleston, and we understand from her father that she interviewed for a position as a mechanic here a few months back. Do you recall that interview?"

Kain rubbed his chin and furrowed his brow. "Eccleston, you say? As I recall, we set up a meeting, and she came for the interview, but she left the office before we talked."

"She left?" Nolan narrowed his gaze on Kain. "Why?"

Kain shrugged, charming smile still in place. "I

couldn't tell you. I assumed she changed her mind about wanting the job. Or maybe she got tired of waiting on me. I was running behind that day, delayed at a lunch meeting with the mayor, and kept her waiting a good while, I fear."

"How late were you?" Summer asked.

Kain blew out a breath that made his lips buzz as he thought. "Half an hour or so. I'm not typically so remiss with appointments but, well, if you've ever met the mayor, you know his gift for gab. Seeing as I was lobbying for a better tax rate for small business owners, I didn't feel I could brush him off."

Nolan turned toward Walter, who was hovering in the doorway still. "Were you here with her while she was waiting?"

Walter appeared startled at being drawn into the conversation. He shifted his weight from one foot to another and folded his arms over his chest. "Uh, yes and no."

"Come again?" Nolan said.

"I, uh…" He glanced to Kain then back to Nolan. "I was here, but I didn't see her leave. I was doing some work from the creeper under a customer's car." Walter dropped his gaze to his shoes.

Summer glanced briefly to Nolan to gauge his reaction, but his face remained implacable. As she formed her next question, Kain cleared his throat and straightened a framed certificate on the shelf behind the counter, an obvious attempt to draw attention to it. She read the bold print about gratitude to Tom Kain for his continued financial support of the local library.

Kain caught Summer's eye, and, clearly feigning modesty, turned the certificate facedown. "I really should put this ole thing away, but I didn't want the good folks at the library to think I didn't appreciate the recognition of my financial support." He gave her a tight smile. "Then again, I don't want the Baptist church or the children's wing of the hospital to think I was looking for recognition of my contributions there, either."

Summer bit the inside of her cheek to keep from laughing aloud at his obvious attention grab. And deflection.

Kain looked at the clock again with a theatrical lift of his head. "I'm sorry. I really have to get going to the council meeting. Sorry I couldn't be of more help."

He made to leave, and Nolan stepped into his path. "One more thing. Does the name Melody mean anything to you?"

From the corner of her eye, Summer saw Walter's head jerk up, but Kain seemed unmoved. He twisted his mouth as if deep in thought. "No. I can't say as I know anyone by that name."

Walter's reaction to the name seemed to indicate he recognized it, but now his face was blank.

"You're sure? Does it mean anything to either of you in any other respect?" Summer included Walter in her question, sending her glance back and forth between the men.

The two men exchanged a brief glance, during which Summer read nothing telling. *Darn it!* She hoped Nolan had picked up on a subtlety she'd missed.

"If that's all." Kain sidestepped Nolan and took a jacket from a hook by the front door. "I really must go. Allow me to see you out."

Summer wanted to stay and speak to Walter without Kain hovering, but the friendliness in Kain's eyes had become hard determination. Summer reached in her purse and withdrew two business cards. Handing one to each man, she said, "Thank you for your time. If you think of anything that might help us with our investigation, please call. Day or night."

Each man took the card she offered them, and she followed Kain as he exited the business. He moved slowly for someone in such a hurry to get to a meeting, and she got the sense he was watching, waiting to make sure they left the premises before he would.

Nolan paused by the driver's door of his truck and leveled a steady gaze on Kain as the auto shop owner slid behind the wheel of a well-kept Mercedes-Benz S-Class sedan.

Finally, once they'd pulled out of the parking lot and headed back to her office, the Mercedes exited the driveway and turned the opposite direction toward town hall.

After a moment of mulling the brief meeting with Kain, Summer broke the silence.

"Look at me. I give money to charities," Summer said in a mocking low voice. *"I'm an important and benevolent businessman."*

Nolan chuckled. "Right."

Hearing Nolan respond with a laugh did wonders for her mood. At least some tiny piece of their rapport had survived. Maybe more, please?

"So...thoughts?" she asked, but before he could speak, her cell phone rang. The caller ID showed an unfamiliar number. "Hello?"

"Meet me on the south side of the auto shop. Kain

has security cameras that see everywhere except that side by the fence. Don't park anywhere near the property, neither."

Summer's pulse spiked. "Walter?"

"Yeah. Meet me there in five minutes." The line disconnected.

Nolan cast a querying look toward her. "What'd he say?"

"He wants to talk but gave explicit directions how not to be spotted by Kain's security cameras." She stashed her phone and told Nolan what Walter had said about staying out of the cameras' view. "I think we're finally about to catch a break in this case."

Chapter Fifteen

Before leaving his truck, Nolan took his personal hand-gun out of the glove box and loaded a sixteen-round magazine. After ensuring the safety was on, he stashed the gun in the holster at his hip and pulled his jacket over it to hide the weapon. Summer gave him a grave look, and he said, "We need to be careful. I want you to stay behind me until we're sure this isn't an ambush."

"An ambush?"

"If Avery is right about Kain being a drug dealer, he could have Walter on more than one payroll, if you get my drift."

"You think we've kicked a trip wire by talking to Kain." Summer's eyes reflected her concern as she nibbled her bottom lip.

"I think we'd be foolish to ignore the possibility." He reached to stroke her cheek but jerked his hand back. He'd never keep the reins on his desire if he didn't stop touching her, didn't stop thinking about how good it had felt to hold her and be inside her. He sighed and fisted his hand. "I won't let anyone hurt you, Summer. I promise." *Including me.*

Shouldering open his truck door, Nolan waited for

Summer to join him before cautiously approaching Kain's auto shop. He stopped every dozen yards or so, sidling up to the corner of buildings, vehicles or trees, anywhere they could stay hidden. The sun had just set, casting long pools of darkness on the streets, and he scanned his dimly lit surroundings for anything suspicious.

"There he is," Summer said, pointing to the orange glow of a cigarette tip in the shadows beside the garage. She set out across the street toward the dark meeting point, and Nolan hurried to catch her arm.

"Stay. Behind. Me," he grated through his teeth.

She faced him, her mouth in a taut frown. "This is my case, Nolan. Don't think that because you have the gun that makes you boss of me."

"It makes me your best chance to stay alive if we are attacked. Do you really think a suspected drug dealer is going to ignore the fact that private investigators came sniffing around his place today?"

Beneath his hand, he felt Summer shiver.

"All I'm saying is we need to be careful. You lead the conversation, but keep your eyes and ears open. And if I say run, or get down, or *do the damn hokey pokey*, do it. Immediately. Got it?"

She wet her lips and hesitated before nodding. He clenched his back teeth tighter, shoving the mental image of her tongue sweeping her plump lip from his brain. It was essential that he focus. He couldn't let thoughts of how he and Summer spent the afternoon distract him. Their lives could depend on it.

He eased in front of her, his hand ready on his weapon, as they crossed to the spot where the dark figure waited for them. As they approached, the glowing cigarette was dropped on the ground and crushed out.

"Hands out where I can see 'em," a male voice hissed, "or this is over before we start."

Summer held her hands out, but Nolan called back, "Likewise, pal."

When the man held up his hands, Nolan inched his up, as well. Not until they got right up next to the man could he make out the man's face and confirm it was the mechanic in the coveralls that had been party to their conversation with Tom Kain.

"Hello, Walter. Thank you for calling." Summer let her hands drop, and Walter visibly tensed.

"Hands back up, sweetheart. You wearin' a wire?"

"No. I—" She gasped as the mechanic stepped up to her in one long stride.

"Hey!" Nolan placed himself between them and grabbed the front of Walter's coveralls. "Easy, buddy."

The mechanic lifted his chin defiantly. "I'm patting you both down for wires or weapons, or I'm gone."

Summer put a hand on Nolan's arm. "Let him. We have nothing to hide." Then to Walter she added, "My associate has a gun—"

The other man stiffened.

"—but only for our protection. It will stay holstered so long as you give him no reason to draw it." Summer stepped out from behind Nolan, adding, "And fair is fair. You pat us down, Nolan here pats you down. Got it?"

The man's eyes darted from Summer to Nolan and back again before he jerked a nod. While the mutual pat downs were conducted, Nolan kept checking the street, the shadows, the corners of the building, prepared for attack. As Walter frisked Summer, Nolan gritted his teeth so hard his jaw hurt. He hated the idea of the mechanic's hands on her, touching the curves he'd caressed intimately earlier today.

Finally, searches satisfied, Walter stepped back and dragged a hand down his mouth. "Before I say anything, I gotta have your solemn word that Kain never hears I talked to you. If you do, I'll deny every bit of it and—"

"You have our word," Summer said. "Anything you tell us will be strictly confidential. I protect my sources one hundred percent. I promise."

Walter looked to Nolan.

"You have my word, too."

Walter nodded and rolled his shoulders. "You asked about Melody. Why?"

Summer straightened her shirt where it had been mussed during her pat down. "You know a Melody?"

"Answer my question. Where'd you hear the name?"

"You just had me swear not to reveal you as a source. My other sources deserve the same favor. Who is Melody?"

He rubbed his hands on his coveralls, shifted his weight and sighed. "She's not a who. She's a what."

"Excuse me? What do you mean?" Summer asked, pulling out her notepad.

Walter eyed the notebook uneasily. "Nothing in writing."

She held up a hand signaling surrender and put the notepad back in her purse. "How is Melody a what?"

"Melody is… Kain's Benz."

"His Benz," Summer repeated, then, "You mean a car? A Mercedes-Benz?"

Walter nodded. "Melody is his pride and joy. Fully loaded, highest-quality leather seats, not a scratch in her paint. He's obsessed with that car."

Nolan thought back to earlier in the evening when they'd played chicken with Kain to see who'd drive away from the auto shop first. That car had been a black Mercedes sedan. "Do you mean the one he was driving tonight?"

Walter's head twitched back, and he blinked. "He drove Melody tonight?" He gave a gruff chuckle. "That's rare. He typically keeps her under a protective canvas in the back of the shop. When he does drive her, he's showing off for people he wants to impress."

"Like the members of the town council?" Summer said.

"Well, yeah." The mechanic glanced around them nervously. "But he's already got most of them hood-winked, I thought."

Nolan checked their surroundings again, as well. Everything seemed quiet, empty...but he knew better than to assume anything.

"What do you mean by hoodwinked?" Summer asked.

"Deceived folks. Fooled people," Walter explained in a tone that said his meaning should be obvious.

"Fooled people how?" Nolan pressed.

"Look, I shouldn't be talking to you." Walter stepped backward and raised both hands. "If Hands-On Tom found out I said anything..." He released a restless sigh.

"We won't let anyone know you talked. Please,

Walter..." Summer spread her palms, and her tone beseeched him. "We're just trying to get justice for a young lady who was brutally murdered."

Walter's agitation grew, as evidenced by his ragged breathing and constant fidgeting. Finally he said, "I lied."

Summer glanced at Nolan then back to their informant. "When? What did you lie about?"

"I saw her—that gal that was killed—when she came in the shop for the interview."

"You saw Patrice Eccleston?" Nolan asked, wanting confirmation. "Did you speak to her?"

"I did. Briefly. When she first got to the shop. Told her Kain wasn't back yet. She was supposed to wait in the front, but..." He hunched his shoulders. "She came in the garage bay where I was working. I saw her feet. She was looking around at the equipment. I didn't see any harm. She was interviewing to work here, after all." He sniffed and wiped his nose as he glanced away, checking the shadows again.

"And?" Summer prompted.

"Kain had Melody parked in the garage that day. Uncovered. He'd been out somewhere in her earlier in the day and hadn't put her back in storage yet."

Nolan scratched his chin, wondering if it was as odd to Summer as it was to him hearing Walter refer to the car with feminine pronouns. The effect was...unsettling.

"Anyways, I was under that customer's car like I said, but from my angle I could still see the gal's feet, right?"

"Okay." Summer's gaze narrowed on the man.

"Well, I saw her walk over to Melody and peek in the windows. I mean, why wouldn't she? Melody is any car enthusiast's wet dream." He stopped abruptly and shot a guilty look to Summer. "Sorry, ma'am. What I mean is, the car's, uh…"

"I know what you mean." She motioned with her hand. "Please continue."

"Well, I don't really know what happened after that. I was concentrating on the repair I was doin', when I hear her sorta gasp. Scared-like. I turned my head and see her getting up from a squat by the front tire. She stumbles back a few steps then just takes off. Leaves the shop without staying for her interview."

"Did you follow her out or go look around the front tire area to see what might have upset her?" Summer asked.

Walter shook his head. "Didn't see it as a big deal, really. The shop's got spiders. Roaches. I figured the gal saw a bug she didn't like and got spooked."

Nolan cut a glance to Summer. He was growing irritated with the mechanic's reference to Patrice as "the gal" and the insinuation that because she was a female, she'd be frightened away from a job interview by the likes of an insect. How must Summer, who was especially sensitive to sexism and patronization, be feeling?

A muscle in her jaw ticked as if she were gritting her teeth, and her hand fluttered restlessly at her side. Her tone, though, was remarkably calm and encouraging when she asked, "How did Mr. Kain react when he learned she'd left?"

Walter shrugged. "He didn't, really. At least, not until

I said she'd been admiring Melody. Ole Hands-On Tom didn't like that a bit. He's real protective of her."

"So you've said." Summer raised a fingernail to her teeth and nibbled as her brow creased in thought. "You said Kain has security cameras everywhere. Could the cameras maybe have caught an angle that would show what she found?"

"No doubt." Walter rolled his shoulders. "Hands-On Tom reviews his security tapes every night. The man's nothing if not watchful over his property. Only reason there ain't no camera here is—" he motioned his hands to the empty yard and blank concrete-block wall of the shop "—nothing here to protect."

"Explain what you meant by Hands-On Tom and his reaction to—"

The mechanic muttered a curse word and turned ninety degrees, eyeing the dark night edgily. "I need to go. I've said too much as it is."

"Wait," Summer said, catching the sleeve of Walter's jacket. "Just one more qu—"

"No!" He pulled away, waving his hands. "I shouldn't have said anything. I—" He took a quick step closer to Summer and stuck his face in hers. "You gotta swear you won't let anyone know I talked to ya."

Nolan planted a hand on Walter's chest and shoved him back from Summer. "Back off, man."

Without missing a beat, Walter lifted pleading eyes to Nolan. "You gotta understand. I have a family. A mortgage. I need this job. If Kain even gets a whiff that I told you anything…" He shook his head. "I can't say if the rumors around town are true or not. But I know better than to cross him." As if realizing at that moment he *had* crossed his boss by meeting with them, Walter trembled visibly and backed away with quick stumbling steps. "Don't push Kain, friends. He's got a bad temper. You've been warned."

Chapter Sixteen

"I want a look at Kain's Mercedes," Summer said several minutes after they returned to Nolan's truck and sat in mutual silence digesting what they'd learned from the mechanic.

"Ditto." Nolan rocked his head from side to side, stretching his neck muscles. "Especially the tires."

"Yeah. But if Kain is as protective of Melody as Walter says, then how are we supposed to get close enough to poke around?" Summer angled her body to better study Nolan's profile in the dim glow of his dashboard lights. She'd tried to put the memory of their lovemaking out of her mind so she could focus on the case, but the scent of him surrounded her. She was attuned to his every breath, every tiny movement. And every whiff of the shampoo he'd used at the gym, every subtle rustle of his clothes and every brush of his hand renewed the thrum rooted in her core. Then his words would replay in her head like a bad dream she couldn't shake.

This was a mistake. I'm sorry, Summer.

And her heart would sink to her feet, a leaden weight dragging at her, crushing her, killing the hope she'd nurtured in recent days of building something lasting and true with Nolan. Something like Avery had found with Dallas. Or Rae had with Forrest. Or—

"We know he's driving the Mercedes tonight. That he's at the town council meeting." Nolan's voice dragged her back to the topic at hand—figuring out what Patrice had seen while snooping around Melody that sent her fleeing the auto shop.

"Yeah. Allegedly," she replied. She struggled to keep her mind on Kain and his beloved car when Nolan rubbed the stubble on his chin, creating a quiet, scratchy noise. The sound reminded her how it had felt to have his bristly beard lightly scraping her cheeks, her breasts, her thighs. She balled her hands in her lap and added, "He could be anywhere, in truth."

Nolan cranked the truck to life, and the engine gave a rumbling purr that sounded like the moans of satisfaction that had come from Nolan's throat when—

For the love of bacon, Summer! He said sleeping with you was a mistake! He doesn't want what you want, so just deal—and move on!

"Let's just see if he's really at the town council," Nolan said, cutting the wheel to turn down the street toward the municipal building.

As they cruised past the parking lot, the flow of people and cars from the area made it clear the council meeting had dismissed. But Summer pointed to the back corner of the lot, where the handsome auto shop owner was waving goodbye to another man and climbing into the black Mercedes sedan. "There he is."

"And there she is." Nolan tapped his fist on his steering wheel and drove away. "Melody." He cut a look to Summer and scoffed. "He named his car."

She crossed her arms over her chest. "So?"

"Don't you think that's kinda…" He stopped short and arched an eyebrow. "Wait. Did you name *your* car?"

She should have been offended by the humor and disbelief in his tone. Maybe she was. Hard to tell when her heart was still bruised by his characterization of their lovemaking that afternoon. "Not my current car, but… I named the first car I had in high school."

He curled his lips in, clearly trying to hide a grin. After a beat, he finally asked what she'd feared he would. "What did you name it?"

She drew a breath and pinned a hard look on him. "Nolan."

He met her gaze, as if merely responding to his name. Then he blinked, realization dawning in his eyes. "Wait. That's what you named the car? Nolan?"

"I missed you. It made me feel close to you. And the car was cantankerous and stubborn like you, so…" The last bit wasn't exactly true, but she felt the need to minimize the significance of her confession.

He stared forward through the windshield again. "I don't know what to make of that."

"Nothing. There's nothing to make of it." She flicked a hand at him in dismissal. "Could you take me back to my office?"

"Okay. Why don't I stop on the way and pick us up something for dinner. A pizza, maybe?"

"No. Thanks, but I'm tired. I might do some work on my notes or something then hit the hay early." In the bed that still held Nolan's scent and the dent of his head on her pillow. *Crud.* How would she ever sleep in that cot again without thinking of him?

SUMMER DODGED NOLAN the next day. She told him she wanted to go to church—alone. Wanted to catch up on some internet research for another case—alone. Overnight a cold front had moved in, along with a layer of clouds. Despite the gray gloom, she took a long jog through the more scenic parts of Whisperwood, past single-family dwellings where children played on manicured lawns. The kind of homes and children she'd always dreamed of having…someday.

Fighting off the negativity that dragged at her, she raised her chin and hurried her step. She *would* have a home and family. Maybe not soon. Maybe not with Nolan—her heart gave a painful throb with that admission—but someday. She finished her run at the gym to clean up before retracing her steps at a leisurely pace to get home again. Like her mood, the autumn leaves that had seemed vibrant and glowing in the sun earlier that week were more subdued in the drab of cloud cover. She spent the rest of the day with Yossi curled in her lap while she read, napped and caught up on episodes of *The Marvelous Mrs. Maisel.*

But having respected her wish for distance on Sunday, Nolan was at her office door with coffee and cinnamon bagels first thing Monday morning. She forced a cheery smile as she accepted the offering of caffeine and carbs. "Good morning."

Nolan set the bag from JoJo's Java on the counter, and she felt his gaze as she bit into the still-warm bagel.

"Are we okay?" he asked, leaning back on the counter and folding his arms over his chest as he eyed her.

She feigned nonchalance, lifting a shoulder and talking around a mouthful of bagel. "Sure. We're fine."

He continued to stare as if he saw through her act of indifference.

She took a big swig of hot coffee and set the cup aside. "We have a few things to follow up on today. Kenneth Dawson should be back in town, and we need to talk to Forrest and Chief Thompson about what Walter told us."

"Mm-hmm," Nolan hummed. "Why won't you look at me?"

She cut a quick glance to him as if to disprove his theory. "What?"

He sighed and pushed away from the counter. Opening his arms, he drew her into an embrace. "You know I never wanted to hurt you. I tried hard to avoid…*this*."

She faked a laugh. "I'm fine, Nolan."

He tightened his hold, and she put an arm around his waist, leaning into his chest and fighting back the sting of tears in her sinuses. She had to get a grip on her emotions or she'd never get through the day, working beside him and hiding the extent of her crushed ego.

"If you're sure…"

"Mm-hmm."

He kissed the top of her head then stepped back. "So, Dawson…check. And talk to Forrest about Melody. Definitely."

Thirty minutes later, they were at the law offices of Lukas, Jolley and Fitzsimmons, asking the receptionist to show them to Kenneth Dawson's door.

"I understand you're interested in speaking to Mr. Dawson," she said, "and he directed me to tell you he has no comment. He's quite busy today and asked not to be disturbed."

"I bet he did," Nolan said darkly. "Which office is his?"

"I'm sorry. I can't—"

Nolan braced his arms on the woman's desk and leaned across her desk until his nose was inches from hers. "We're not leaving until he talks to us, so just tell us where to find him and we'll get out of your hair."

The receptionist clamped her lips in a discouraging frown and shook her head. "He's my boss. Or one of them. And he can fire me if I don't—"

A door opened down the hall behind her, and a middle-aged man with thinning blond hair stepped out, bellowing, "Candace? Did I get a fax from the Gieger office in Dallas?"

The receptionist sat taller, her eyes drilling into Summer's. *That's him*, she mouthed before turning to face the lawyer.

"I'm sorry, Mr. Dawson. I haven't seen it come in yet."

Dawson grimaced. "Damn it! They promised it would be here first thing this morning." He smacked a hand against the wall and turned to retreat to his office again.

"Um, Mr. Dawson?" Candace called after him, "These folks need a moment of your time."

Dawson turned, lifting his gaze to Nolan and Summer. "Car accident? Divorce? Contested will?"

"Murder case," Summer replied.

Dawson raised a hand and waved them off. "I don't take criminal cases, but I'm sure someone else in the firm could—"

"We don't want to hire you. We need to question you." Summer circled the receptionist's desk and stuck out her hand. "Summer Davies, Davies Investigations. We understand you knew Patrice Eccleston."

The man's pale skin blanched even whiter. His mouth moved, but only choked sounds emerged. He sent an accusatory look to Candace before returning his attention to Summer.

Nolan joined her and added his own introduction and offered hand, which went ignored.

After a few awkward seconds of silence and blinking, Dawson said, "As I told Candace to relay, I…have no comment. Can't comment, really. Client-attorney privilege."

Summer cocked her head to the side. "Patrice was a client of yours? In what matter?"

"That's, uh… I can't…" Dawson cleared his throat and pulled his shoulders back, seemingly regaining his composure. "I'm very busy today. I really don't have time to—"

"We promise not to take but a moment or two of your time," Nolan said, brushing past the lawyer and boldly stalking toward the office Dawson had emerged from.

"Hey!" Dawson aimed a finger at Nolan. "Come back here. You can't just barge—"

But Nolan was already entering the door Dawson had left open. Summer hid a grin at Nolan's presumptuous move. Leaning close to Dawson, she whispered, "Don't worry, Kenneth. They're easy questions…assuming you don't have something to hide. And since we've already heard about your affair with Patrice, there's no point trying to cover it up."

The man's eyes widened, and he cut a quick, guilty look toward the receptionist, who was pretending not to be listening.

The muscles in his jaw flexed as he gritted his teeth. "Not here."

"Of course not." Summer waved a hand down the hall. "After you."

"I WASN'T LYING when I said Patrice was a client," Dawson said quietly, the minute he'd closed his office door.

Dawson didn't offer Summer or Nolan a chair, but Nolan sat in one of the leather chairs with brass nail head trim anyway. Nolan propped one ankle on his opposite knee and leaned back, assuming a casual pose. "Do tell."

Summer didn't like the insouciant attitude Nolan had assumed and tried to signal him discreetly with her eyes. He only lifted his fingers from the arm of the chair, as if to say, *It's okay. I know what I'm doing.*

Summer took the second chair and directed her full attention to Kenneth. "We have a friend of Patrice's on record saying she told him she was having an affair with a married man. Were you that man, Mr. Dawson?"

The lawyer dropped heavily into his desk chair and glanced past them, avoiding eye contact, as he stammered, "I...she didn't...my wife..."

"Will not hear anything about this from us," Summer assured him. "That's not our job."

"Although based on rumors we've heard around town and claims made by another woman we know, you should probably think about having a conversation with your wife," Nolan said. "Soon." He narrowed his eyes in a menacing way. "And then quit messing with other women. It's called harassment, and it's *not* okay." Nolan's glare darkened further. "Am I clear?"

Kenneth squeezed the burgundy leather arms of his desk chair and jerked a nod. After another beat or two of silence, he blurted, "Originally, Patrice came to me for advice. She wanted legal guidance on a matter, and... due to the nature of her problem, I met with her several times over the course of two or three days."

"What was the issue?" Summer's pulse accelerated as she flipped open her notebook and started recording the conversation. Patrice had consulted a lawyer? She had a tingling sense they were on to something that could explain Patrice's murder.

Dawson waved a finger at her. "What are you writing there?"

"Just notes on our interview with you, so I'm sure I remember things correctly."

He frowned. "I don't like you writing down everything I say."

Nolan pulled out his phone. "Would you prefer we record the conversation? We want to be accurate with our fact gathering."

Kenneth divided a look between them. "I told you. I can't reveal anything about her concerns because of attorney-client privilege."

Summer pursed her lips in frustration. She knew they were close, *so close* to solving the case. She had to find a way to get Kenneth to talk. "But couldn't you reveal the information if you knew doing so could prevent a violent crime?"

The lawyer blinked rapidly and angled his head. "Pardon?"

"Is it possible that what Patrice told you could be a clue as to who killed her?"

Dawson's expression said what he didn't. *Yes, it could.*

Nerves jumping, Summer cast a glance to Nolan.

"And if you could prevent someone else being hurt or killed by sharing with us what Patrice told you, don't you think you have a moral obligation to prevent another attack?"

Nolan leaned forward. "She's right. In Texas, you can waive client privilege to prevent another killing."

Kenneth closed his eyes and pressed his mouth in a distraught line.

"You need to help us put her killer behind bars." Summer scooted to the edge of her chair and flattened her hands on the man's desk. "Please, Mr. Dawson?"

Yeah, she was fishing for a loophole, a technicality, a nuance that would give Dawson the out he needed to talk to them. But the anxious look in his eyes told her that he was considering their arguments, that he *wanted* to talk.

Finally, Dawson's shoulders drooped, and he leaned closer. "If I talk, *I* could be the next one killed."

Summer and Nolan exchanged a tense look.

"My cousin Forrest Colton works for the Whisperwood PD," Nolan said. "I can see that you get protection—added patrols in your neighborhood."

Kenneth stared at his desk where his hands were

propped, his fingers laced and his thumbs fidgeting. "I want protection for my family, as well."

"Done."

Summer wasn't sure how Nolan could promise protection without consulting Chief Thompson or Forrest, but she didn't comment.

Dawson sighed and lowered his voice to almost a whisper. "All I'll say is this—she told me she saw something. Evidence of illegal activity. She wanted to know if she was required, by law, to report what she'd seen. She was afraid if she reported her find, she could be putting her life at risk. She was torn between reporting what she'd seen and protecting herself."

Summer blurted the obvious question. "What did she see?"

He raised a hand and shook his head. "That's all I'm saying."

"Mr. Dawson, can't you just—"

"No!" he returned, his tone firm. "She feared for her life, and I believe that, somehow, someone very dangerous discovered her secret, and she was killed to keep her from talking. I don't want to be next victim."

Nolan edged forward on his seat and raised a palm in appeal. "We could do a better job of protecting you if we knew who or what we were protecting you from."

Kenneth shot to his feet, adamantly shaking his head. "No. We're done here."

"But Mr. Dawson, if we could—"

He cut Summer off as he lifted the receiver of his desk phone. "Will you call security to see Miss Davies and Mr. Colton out, please?"

Nolan rose to his feet. "No need. We're going."

A panicked sense that they were inches away from resolution to the case and losing the only chance to close that gap swamped Summer. "But..."

Nolan took her arm and guided her toward the door. "Thank you for your time, Mr. Dawson. Please remember what I said about respecting women, huh?"

Dawson scowled and dropped back in his chair.

As Nolan hustled Summer out of the law firm, she replayed what the lawyer had said. Patrice had seen something. She'd been afraid to report her find. *Her find?* Did that mean she hadn't seen an action, such as a murder or a theft, but had found an incriminating object? A murder weapon? A body?

She squinted against the autumn sun as Nolan led her outside, his hand at her back. "Nolan, we left too easily. With a little more cajoling, he might have given us the last piece of the story."

He pursed his lips and shook his head. "No. He was done. I recognized the moment he shut down. That moment when a suspect realizes he's said too much and buttons up."

Summer stopped walking, shooting Nolan a sharp look. "You think he's a *suspect*?"

"No. He's a philandering jerk, but I don't make him for a killer." His brow dented in thought. "He's terrified of something. Of some*one*."

"Right. The person who killed Patrice," she supplied. "So..."

He twisted his mouth and drummed his fingers on

his thigh. "Let's head back to your office and lay out all the pieces. We're close. I can feel it."

He opened the passenger door of his Jeep for her, and she nodded. "I agree. It's whiteboard time."

Chapter Seventeen

Yossi was napping in a pool of sunshine on her desk when they returned to her office. Summer's gut tightened and her chest ached remembering what *she'd* done recently on that desk. With Nolan. Who wasn't staying in Whisperwood. Who didn't love her and had called their lovemaking a mistake.

She shoved aside the painful memory and drew a careful breath. If she was going to live and work out of this space for months to come, she'd have to get over the reminder of what would never be that her desk represented. Because she didn't have the funds to buy a new, unspoiled desk.

Calling to Yossi, she enticed him to vacate her workspace by opening a can of his favorite flavor of food and clinking a spoon against his bowl. "C'mon, Yossi boy. Dinner!"

Her feline hopped down and trotted quickly over to eat, purring his thanks. She longed to cradle her furry friend and curl up on her bed for a good sulk, but responsibility called. With a scratch on Yossi's cheek, she returned to the office, where Nolan had already set up the whiteboard and was jotting comments and Venn diagrams.

For a moment, she just stood in the door to the kitchenette and studied her longtime friend and partner on this case. Nolan's lean body and efficient movement as he wrote new facts on the board and folded his arms to study the flowcharts he'd created was a thing of beauty. Controlled power. Like a panther, patiently watching his prey.

Her lover. Once. One precious time that she'd have to cherish and hold quietly in her heart the rest of her life.

Closing her eyes, she sighed. *Stop it. Now is not the time.*

She and Nolan had important work to do. Dawson had given them little, but his one admission cast a fresh and meaningful light on the whole investigation. Was Nolan on the same wavelength she was? She would soon see.

Summer straightened her desk where Yossi had nudged files and her cracked stapler out of his way to nap. Reaching in her purse, she took out her notebook and flipped to the most recent pages. "All right, add Dawson's name and a line linking him to Patrice. Label it 'client-slash-affair.'"

Nolan stepped aside to show her he had already added these pieces to the board.

"Good. Then under the facts column, add the bit about Patrice seeing—" she consulted her notes to be completely accurate with how Dawson had worded his claim "—evidence of illegal activity."

"Right." Nolan faced the board as he made the note.

She drummed her fingers on the desktop, concentrating on the tantalizing tidbit and trying not to let the view of her partner's tush and broad shoulders distract her. "He didn't specifically mention Kain's garage, so what she saw could be anything from jaywalking to treason."

Nolan pursed his lips, his brow furrowing. "I think Occam's razor applies here." He capped the marker and turned toward her, his eyes intense. "The easiest and most obvious explanation is likely our answer."

She lifted a hand, inviting him to continue. "And which obvious answer do you see? There are lots of options, as I see it. We have a serial killer who confessed on his deathbed. A nurse, likely paid off to kill her patient, who has since disappeared. A college classmate with an unrequited love who was last to see Patrice alive. An overprotective father who didn't even know his daughter was friends with boys from her class, let alone that she was having an affair with a married man."

Nolan tapped the whiteboard pen against his palm. "All serious stuff. But none of those feel right as motive in this case. I'm talking about this." He used the pen to point to the name Melody.

"Tom Kain's car killed her?" she said with a wry grin, but a prickle at the base of her neck told her they were on the same track.

Nolan gave her a withering glance before turning back to the chart he'd drawn. "Think about it, Summer. Horace Corgan thought Melody was important enough that he gasped the name on his dying breath."

Summer flipped back in her notebook to the pages related to their interview with Tom Kain and later with Kain's mechanic. She tapped the page with her fingernail and read for a moment before looking up at Nolan.

"The mechanic at Kain's Auto Shop, Walter, said Patrice was snooping around Melody while waiting for her interview with Kain. He said she gasped, then quickly left the shop without ever talking to Kain."

Nolan twisted his mouth. "That's right. So could the something Kenneth Dawson said she was scared about having seen be the same something that frightened her away from the auto shop?"

Summer sat taller. "Certainly makes sense." Summer followed that train of thought to the next logical station. "And after Kain lied about not knowing who or what Melody was, Walter was anxious to tell us about the car. But not where Kain's security cameras could see us talking to him."

"Security cameras...that means..." Nolan turned back to the board, his face lighting with discovery.

"Kain likely saw Patrice snooping around Melody when he reviewed the security tapes. Walter told us Kain did that every night, and that was why he was so careful to meet us out of camera range."

Nolan rocked back on his heels and scratched his chin. "If the rumors about Kain being a drug dealer and distributor are true, he would definitely be interested in keeping a close eye on his shop."

"And if Patrice found something incriminating when she was snooping around Melody, and Kain knew it..." A chill sluiced through Summer. Nolan met her eyes, his expression echoing the conclusion she'd reached. "He could have killed her to keep her quiet about whatever she'd seen. A stash of drugs, perhaps? Or money?"

"It makes sense. But..." He frowned and began pacing.

Finished with his dinner, Yossi returned to the office and jumped up to finish his sunbath on her desk.

"Not now, Yos." Summer lifted her cat off the notebook where he'd sprawled. "We're about to crack this case. Go sleep on the bed. You can even get on my pillow. Special privilege today if you let me work."

Yossi blinked unhappily at her, and Summer tried to ignore the guilt trip from the feline as she flipped through the pages of her notes to find anything else that might support their working theory. "Could Horace Corgan have known about Kain? Not just damning evidence about Kain's drug business and whatever the link is with Melody, but even suspecting that Kain killed Patrice?" Summer's heart raced as she saw all the pieces begin to fall into place. "Kain could have paid Jane Oliver, the nurse, to kill Horace Corgan if he talked about Melody or gave up anything about his drug deals. That could be the *big haul* she bragged about coming into."

Nolan pulled out his phone and started dialing.

"Wait," she said, rising from her chair and crossing the room to him. "Who are you calling?"

"Forrest. It's past time we bring him and Chief Thompson in on what we've learned."

"Hang on." She grabbed his arm and pulled his phone away from his ear. "This is my case, remember? I'm not ready to hand it off to the police!"

"Summer, if we're right about Kain, we owe it to Patrice and her family to see him arrested as soon as possible. Besides, I promised Dawson I'd arrange protection for him until we're sure any threat to him has passed."

"I know you did, but—" Firming her resolve, she

raised her chin. "Let's do one last thing to confirm our suspicions first."

Nolan's brow dipped. "What's that?"

"I want to take a closer look at Melody for ourselves."

"How do you plan to do that?" Nolan braced his hands on his hips and arched one eyebrow. "Kain has cameras everywhere, remember? He'll be on to us within hours, assuming we can even get at the Benz. It's not like he leaves it parked in front of the shop."

"But Melody isn't always at the shop. He drives it to town council meetings, remember?"

"But the council just met a few nights ago. I doubt they'll meet again for at least a couple weeks. Are you really willing to wait that long to get a look at Melody?"

Summer folded her arms over her chest and prowled the confined space in her office. "Maybe we could arrange for there to be an emergency meeting called. I'm sure your family knows the mayor. You could ask Hays or one of your younger cousins to ask that a special meeting be set up for tonight."

"Under what guise?"

"Well, they could say it was about public safety, which wouldn't be too far from the truth if it means we catch a murderer who's currently walking the streets." She chewed her bottom lip as she paced. "Or a just-discovered financial error that's created a crisis in funding daily operations. Money matters always bring people to the table. Once the council is gathered and they waste some time taking roll and covering minutes from the last meeting, yada yada, they announce the error has been corrected or it was a false alarm and apologize, but the ruse buys us enough time to check out Kain's car."

"Without a warrant, searching his car is illegal," he reminded her.

She growled her frustration. "If you're worried about getting yourself in hot water with the FBI, then you don't have to come. I'll go alone, and I'll be... 'Oh, my! What a lovely car,' said the private citizen as she peeks in the windows and kicks the tires."

Nolan scowled. "Summer..."

"If we see anything questionable, we'll let Chief Thompson know, and the police can get the necessary warrants."

Nolan continued to glare at her, his disapproval plain.

Her shoulders dropped, and she spread her arms. "What else can I do? If we're right, and whatever Patrice saw is the key to this investigation, I have to get a look at that car!"

"And what if you see whatever Patrice saw, and it gets you killed, too?"

A shiver raced through her. Would she be poking a rattlesnake by snooping around Kain's prized car? Probably. But could she ignore the mounting evidence that Tom Kain was linked to Patrice's killing? She owed it to Patrice to get justice for her murder. She wanted closure for Atticus. Resolution for her first big case. She couldn't let fear of reprisals stop her. Reckless? Maybe. But making love to Nolan on her desk and again in her bed had been reckless, too, and she wouldn't trade that memory for the world, no matter how much his rejection stung.

Fisting her hands at her sides, she gave Nolan a stubborn stare. "I'm going to get a look at Kain's car, one way or another. Now are you going to help me or aren't you?"

Chapter Eighteen

Nolan couldn't begin to count the ways that what he was doing was wrong. How in the hell had he let Summer talk him into this? And how had she sweet-talked Hays and the mayor into calling this emergency meeting of the Whisperwood town council? Summer had some mad persuasion skills.

From the time as kids when he'd joined Summer in using the worn-out rope swing at Gilbert Pond—a poor choice that earned him a broken arm—to his most recent experience of making love to her in her office, he, too, had a long history of conceding to Summer against his better judgment. Because he wanted to make her happy. Because deep down, he admired her sense of adventure and devil-may-care attitude. Because she had a mulish streak a mile wide, and he had to go with her to protect her.

At least he'd stood his ground on alerting Forrest at the last minute to their plan—a plan Forrest was every bit as displeased with as Nolan. "Don't make me have to come up there and arrest you two for trespassing or B and E."

Nolan had explained Summer's determination and

added, "Just be on standby. We may need a search warrant by the end of the night." He'd hung up before Forrest could say more. He really kind of hoped Forrest and Chief Thompson arrived at the municipal parking lot in time to stop Summer. It might save her life.

Clenching his jaw to suppress the gnawing sense of impending doom, he tucked his personal handgun in the waist of his jeans and quietly closed the door of his Jeep. Flashlight in hand, he followed Summer across the city hall parking lot to examine Melody. The black Mercedes S-Class was parked in a dark corner of the small lot, at a selfish angle, such that Kain took up three valuable parking spaces, thus ensuring no one parked close to him and dinged his precious vehicle.

He grabbed the back of Summer's T-shirt, bringing her up short as she set off across the blacktop. "Easy, partner. Before we barge over there and start snooping, we need to case the area and make sure we aren't being watched."

Her eyes went up toward the halogen security lights, where a camera had been mounted. "Wrong angle. I don't think we'll be in the shot." She snorted derisively. "Probably why Kain parks there, huh?"

He agreed with a low grunt and scanned the area. "Security cameras are only one set of eyes. Kain could have his own." Nolan attempted to appear nonchalant as he lollygagged at the fender of his Jeep. He pulled out his phone and pretended to be texting while his gaze swept from shadowy landscaping bushes to the dark front seats of the other parked vehicles.

Summer hung back, but he could tell by the energy vibrating from her whole body that she was champing at the bit, eager to prove her theory come hell or high water.

"Remember, Tadpole, let the evidence lead you. Don't try to fit the evidence to match your assumption. If Kain's—"

His phone startled him, vibrating with an incoming phone call. Had he not already been holding his cell phone, he might have ignored the buzz. But the screen lit with his lawyer's name and number. Nolan only debated a couple of seconds before answering the call. Summer gave him a frustrated, impatient look when he tapped the screen and said, "Hi, Stu. This isn't a good time. Let me call you later."

He hung up without letting his lawyer respond. He didn't need a distraction now, not if he was going to keep Summer safe.

He caught the flash of curiosity and wariness that crossed her face. His own emotions, given their risky mission tonight, were already in tumult. Summer's questions would have to wait until he got his own answers. *Later.* After this fool's errand was over and they were back at her office.

He poked the phone into his back pocket, his head a bit muzzy.

"You're not going to talk to your lawyer?" Summer asked, her tone quiet.

"Not right now. One nightmare at a time, huh? For the moment, I want to concentrate on Kain and what we need to do tonight."

He saw a shiver chase through her, and she jerked a nod. "Right." She set out across the blacktop again.

"Come on. The mayor can only stall in this fake meeting for so long."

"Summer—"

But she didn't stop, didn't slow down until she was within a car's length of the black Benz. Pulling a mini flashlight from her jacket pocket, she switched it on and aimed the beam at the wheels of Kain's sedan. Checking over her shoulder, she hurried to the far side of the Mercedes, away from town hall, and crouched to examine the hubcaps.

His gut tightening, Nolan cast another uneasy glance around the front walk to city hall and the dim parking area. "Make this quick, Summer. Someone could come by any minute."

"Keep your pants on, Bullfrog. I'm not leaving until I find whatever Patrice saw." She angled the light under Melody's frame. "You look inside and under the hood. I want to come away with something incriminating."

He groaned. "That's what I was talking about earlier, Summer. Don't assume there's something here and make snap judgments. Don't forget, the police have searched Kain's properties multiple times and never found anything." He sidled up to the Mercedes and shined his flashlight in the front seat. The back seat. Along the dashboard.

"But Patrice found something. Something that got her killed. I just know she did. I feel—" Her gasp cut her off.

"Summer? What?"

"I got the hubcap loose. Help me with it."

"Jeez, Summer. You're going to get us thrown in jail." He imagined one of Kain's goons showing up, and his stomach pitched. "Or worse." But he crouched beside her and helped pry the ornate, custom hubcap from its clips with the flat blade of a screwdriver.

"A rather fancy hubcap. That's a lot of shiny chrome." Summer took the piece from him as it popped off.

"Custom order, I'd wager. Check it thoroughly to see just *how* customized it is." While Summer scrutinized the hubcap, Nolan lay on his back and scrunched as close to the Mercedes as he could, shining his flashlight into the wheel well.

Nothing immediately stood out as suspicious, and he was about to scoot out from under the frame when he realized part of the wheel well wall was cleaner than the rest. Or rather, the standard grime had been smudged and, upon more careful inspection, fingerprints were recognizable.

"Summer, hand me the screwdriver."

She did, and using the screwdriver so he wouldn't leave his own fingerprints, he tapped on the smudged area, pushed on it. The spot buckled, revealing edges to a false wall. Pulse racing, he wedged the screwdriver blade under the loose piece to pry it free. He shined his flashlight into the dark wheel well. Behind the removable hard plastic barrier was a small enclosed space.

And a zip-sealed plastic bag containing a white powdery substance.

Nolan's pulse spiked. "Summer, I think we just hit pay dirt."

"What did—" She started, then gasped, "Nolan!"

The alarm in her tone shot adrenaline through him, even as a male voice said, "Pay dirt, eh? Too bad it's the last thing you'll do."

Chapter Nineteen

Panic swelled in Summer's chest as she crab scrambled back from Tom Kain. Before she could do more than shout a warning to Nolan, Kain had jabbed a syringe needle through the leg of Nolan's jeans and injected him with…something. Nothing good, she imagined.

Nolan groaned and rolled out from under Melody, scrabbling at his waist before his eyes rolled back and his body went limp.

She fumbled for a weapon, but she didn't even have the screwdriver anymore since passing it to Nolan. The hubcap? It was heavy. Too heavy for her to swing effectively.

"Looks like I left that bogus council meeting just in time." Kain pocketed the syringe in his jacket and drew out a pistol. "I knew something was up the minute the mayor started reading that rambling proclamation. I know a filibuster tactic when I see one."

Ice filled Summer's veins. She sucked in a deep breath to scream for help, and Kain aimed the pistol at Nolan's heart. "You make a sound, he dies."

"Nolan?" Summer crawled to him, despite the

weapon that was trained on her again. She sent Kain a sharp glare. "What did you give him?"

Kain eyed Nolan with a smarmy grin. "A tranquilizer. Jane promised the stuff was fast acting. She didn't lie." He dug in his pants pocket now and pulled out a key fob. With a click, Melody's doors unlocked. "We need to hurry before anyone sees us."

Summer tensed. What did he mean by that? Her gaze cut to the front door of the city building. *Please, someone come out, someone drive into the lot, someone—*

He jerked open the back seat door, growling, "Get in. *Now.*"

His tone brooked no resistance…and yet she hesitated. She *wouldn't* leave Nolan. And she knew, without a doubt, if she got in Kain's car, she'd be dead within the hour.

When Kain set his weapon aside and grabbed Nolan's legs, dragging him roughly across the pavement to the back seat door, Summer saw her chance. She tucked her feet beneath her and sprang at Kain, her fingers curled, ready to claw him as he struggled with Nolan's deadweight. But Kain reacted instantly, dropping Nolan's legs and backhanding her chin with a powerful blow. Her head snapped back. The impact of the strike sent her reeling, and she stumbled and fell to the pavement with a tooth-rattling thump. As quick as she could, she shook off the stars filling her vision and mounted a fresh attack.

This time when she lunged at Kain, she managed to swipe her fingernails across his cheek, drawing blood.

"Bitch!" he snarled and grabbed her hair. A thousand pinpricks ravaged her scalp as he used her hair to drag her to Melody's open back door. Though she struggled, kicked and swung at him with closed fists, even her adrenaline-fueled muscles were no match for him. He lifted her like a doll and tossed her into the car. She tumbled in a heap, half on and half off the seat.

Twisting and clambering, she righted herself. She grabbed for the door handle on the opposite side to flee, but something hard cracked against the back of her head.

Her vision narrowed to a small dim circle...then went black.

Summer's head throbbed. She groped awkwardly to rub the ache. Found she was slumped in an uncomfortable position. More than her head hurt. Her side ached. Her jaw, too. And she tasted blood. Groggy. So groggy and...sore.

It didn't help matters that someone was leaning on her, crushing her. Or that she seemed to be bouncing roughly like she was on a carnival ride. Groaning, she cracked open her eyes. Tried to orient herself.

And immediately wished she hadn't.

She was in a car. Melody. Nolan was slumped, unconscious, on top of her. Her hands were bound with a plastic zip tie. And Tom Kain was behind the wheel, driving them God knows where. To kill them.

Before she could catch it, a whimper of fear squeaked from her throat. A small noise, but enough to alert Kain that she'd roused.

He met her gaze via the rearview mirror. He grunted. "Sorry about the bump on the head, but I only had the one syringe." He paused as if thinking. "I'd hoped you'd stay out until I finished you two off. It makes it so much simpler."

His attention returned to his driving, and he added blithely, "Oh well. It gives me the opportunity to cleanse my soul. Purge the wrongs I've done through confession." He raised his gaze to the mirror again, grinning smugly. "Can't go to a priest, after all. Too likely their conscience would lead them to break the confidentiality of the confessional and turn me in to the cops." He hummed a note of regret, then added, "But you know who never breaks a confidence?" His face morphed with a sadistic grin. "Dead people."

Bile rose from her gut, and she had to swallow hard to keep from vomiting. She shifted her arms and grabbed Nolan's sleeve. The handful of fabric wasn't much, but it was a link to him. She tugged the fabric and tried to jostle Nolan, praying that she could revive him before Kain carried out his plan to murder them. With a bit more struggling, she managed to lever up, such that Nolan's head was now in her lap. If she'd had a better position, she could have freed her hands. Breaking the zip tie was a matter of the right angle and a lot of force, neither of which she had at the moment.

"When I killed that girl who discovered Melody's secret stash—Patricia something, I think the newspaper said her name was…"

Anger roiled in Summer's veins. Not only had Kain murdered the innocent young student, he couldn't even be bothered to know her name.

Kain was saying, "I told her all about taking out Beau Lemmon."

Summer jerked her head up, startled. "Rae's father?"

Kain seemed surprised Summer had spoken. "You know her? Huh. That's a small town for you. Yeah, well, he'd done a job for me and started growing a conscience over it. I had to neutralize him before he talked."

Her heart galloped like a wild stallion. Rae's father... Patrice... The man was truly evil, and she was in no position to stop him, reveal his crimes.

"I guess I should claim Horace Corgan, as well, even though it was Jane that killed him. Pulling his oxygen cannula was a stupid way to kill him, since it was so obvious she'd been the only one with him at the time. But I didn't pay her for her smarts, just her access to Corgan." Kain turned his head to look in the back seat, directly at Summer. In the dim glow from Melody's dash lights, Kain's chiseled face struck her as frightening and monsterish. She couldn't believe she'd actually thought him handsome the day they interviewed him at his auto shop.

She saw no remorse in the harsh lines of his face and grim set of his mouth.

She angled her head to try to get a sense of where they were. Wherever he'd taken them, it was dark. Frighteningly dark. No streetlights or business marquees broke the endless black. The night sky was filled with thousands of stars.

The stars at night are big and bright, deep in the heart of Texas. The famous song lyrics she'd sung with the Colton family around summer bonfires popped in her head, and pain lanced her heart. What would she give to go back to those carefree childhood days? Her biggest trouble then had been the biting mosquitoes and a 9:00 p.m. curfew. And her relationship with Nolan had been straightforward and uncomplicated. They'd been best friends, plain and simple. No jobs calling them out of town. No intervening years full of burdensome events and vindictive people. No confusing complications from sex to muck things up. A mistake, Nolan had called it. Damn, that still stung.

A tear leaked from her eye, and with her hands bound as they were, she couldn't catch it before it dripped onto Nolan's cheek.

Nolan's brow flinched, and, eyelids fluttering, he glanced up at her. Her mouth opened as she sucked in a silent gasp. Quickly, Nolan shook his head, telling her without words not to let on that he was awake.

Glancing to the front seat to make sure Kain wasn't watching, she gave Nolan a tiny nod of understanding. The element of surprise might be their only weapon against Kain.

Knowing Nolan had revived gave her a thin layer of comfort against the chilling specter of Kain's plan to kill them. Also of small comfort was knowing she had proof now who had killed Patrice. She'd solved her first big case. Too bad it would also likely be her last case.

Stubbornness pricked her. *Damn it, if I'm going down, I'm going to get answers to* all *the questions this town has been asking.* She shoved down the niggle of fear and pinned a hard look on Kain's profile. "So the rumors about you being a drug supplier and dealer are true, I take it."

Against her, she could feel Nolan tense, and in the front seat, Kain seemed startled from deep thoughts. He raised his gaze to the rearview mirror again. "The drugs. Yes, they're very profitable."

"So how did you avoid detection for so many years? Your place, and surely Melody, was searched more than once, to no avail, I hear."

Kain smiled proudly. "You heard right. Lucky for me, the police must follow certain rules of law. A warrant, for example. And I have a well-placed snitch at the courthouse on my payroll who tips me off whenever a search warrant for any of my property is applied for. With the heads-up, I'm able to clear any evidence of my side business before the cops show up. A valuable asset, my informant."

"Then you *were* behind the drug supply that killed my friend Avery's brother."

Kain scowled and scoffed. "Perhaps. I'm just a businessman selling a product. I don't shoot the stuff into their veins."

Summer gritted her teeth, wishing she could smack the blithe sneer from his face. "And you've manipulated local nurses to help supply addicts with illegal prescription pills, too. Haven't you? Jane Oliver, for example."

Kain nodded. "Oh, Miss Jane did more for me than just peddle pills. She proved a key asset when Corgan took ill. I learned things about his killings that helped throw the cops off my trail when I buried Patricia."

"Patrice…" Summer corrected through clenched teeth.

"Wha—oh, right. Patrice. Pretty girl. Hated to waste her, but when she snooped and found Melody's secret, she had to be handled. So I acquired an Army button to mislead the cops—you know, just in case—and took advantage of the repairs to the Lone Star Pharma parking lot to hide my transgression."

The drug lord quieted long enough to consult the map on his phone. "Aw, hell. I missed my turn thanks to your yapping." He slowed the car and, using the shoulder of the isolated road, made a wide U-turn.

Summer squinted at the glowing phone screen, trying to get some idea where they were. She couldn't make out any details to orient herself. Other than one green line indicating the road they were on, the map was essentially blank. No landmarks, crossroads or town names. In other words, the boonies. Somewhere in the vast emptiness that Texas had plenty of. The hope of rescue she'd clung to took a nosedive.

A short distance down the dark road, Kain took a left turn onto a rutted lane crowded by scraggly cottonwoods and scrub brush. Branches scraped against the windows and sides of the Mercedes with a macabre screech.

Kain barked a curse. "The damn trees are scratching Melody's paint!" He turned and looked directly at Summer. "This is your fault. Yours and lover boy's there."

"Our fault? We didn't tell you to drive your precious car out here in the middle of nowhere."

"When you poked around Melody, you left me no choice. If you'd minded your own business and kept out of mine, Melody wouldn't be out here." He turned back to the front, grumbling, "I'll have to take her to Houston for a custom paint job, and that'll cost thousands."

"Oh…boo-hoo." Summer couldn't help the sarcastic retort, even knowing her snark would aggravate Kain more. He already planned to kill her. What did she have to lose? But she felt Nolan's fingers squeeze her wrist, and she took the signal as a warning not to push Kain.

Recalled to the urgency of her situation, she knew she might not get another chance to pump Kain for information. "Do you…" Her voice cracked, and she tried again, "Do you know where Jane Oliver is? Where she went after you paid her for killing Corgan?"

Kain nodded. "Oh, I know where she is. Same as where you'll be shortly. Out here under the trees. Or under the dirt and rock, really. Unless you'd like me to leave you for the animals to scavenge. Circle of life and all that?"

Summer's gut curdled. "You killed her, too?"

"She knew too much. Just like you do. And why pay her off when I could kill her off and save the fifty grand I'd promised her?"

She had to take several deep breaths and swallow a few times to keep from throwing up. "You're a monster. You know that, right?" Her tone was low and menacing, all of her fear and spleen poured into the words.

"Am I?" He screwed his face up as if considering it. "That sounds rather harsh. I have secrets. I've done things that most people call sins. But I believe those things will be weighed against the nice things I've done, and I'll be okay in the end."

"Nice things?" Summer couldn't believe what she was hearing.

The car bumped hard over a pothole, but once they hit smoother ground, Kain glanced back at her again. "I did tell you about my contributions to local charities and the town library when you stopped by my shop the other day, didn't I?"

"You think you can buy your way out of all the evil you've done?" She scoffed, aghast at his hubris.

"Not entirely. That's why I've spent all this time confessing to you. I tell you everything, clear my conscience, get forgiven and move on with my life."

Summer couldn't believe what she was hearing. "I don't think that's how it works. If you're looking for forgiveness from me, you won't get it. And God only forgives those who are truly repentant."

"Well, I guess we'll see one day. Huh?" He lifted a corner of his mouth in a grin that made her skin crawl. "You sooner than me, of course." He glanced to the left out his side window. "In fact, here we are now. The official middle of nowhere."

Though Summer wanted to ask what made this remote spot any more officially isolated than any other, her anxiety choked her.

Kain parked Melody and cut the engine.

Summer listened for clues to where they were—the sound of water would mean a river or stream, road noise might mean a highway was close by—but the pounding of her pulse in her ears made it hard to hear anything but the snick of the driver's door as Kain climbed out. The thunk as he closed the door.

In the two seconds it took Kain to move to the back door and yank it open, Nolan whispered, "Follow my lead."

Then the car door at Nolan's feet opened, and Kain peered in. "Welcome to your final resting spot."

Chapter Twenty

Nolan had been fighting the lingering effects of whatever drug Kain had shot him up with, trying to clear his mind and focus his limited energy. But when the car stopped and Kain opened the back door, a spike of adrenaline helped fuel his muscles. He swung his foot up, into the drug dealer's chin, sending him staggering back a step.

Behind him, Summer gave a startled yelp. Kain recovered his balance within seconds and bared his teeth as he gave an ominous growl.

Having used his element of surprise, he prayed he could, at the least, muster the strength to keep Summer safe. Nolan groped at his waist for his weapon.

"Looking for this?" Kain asked, pointing Nolan's gun at him.

Nolan's heart plummeted to his stomach. Without his weapon and with his muscles still weak from the sedative, he stood little chance of overpowering their kidnapper. While he didn't like the idea of dying tonight, he *hated* the thought of Summer being murdered because he couldn't protect her.

"Come on, man," Kain said, rubbing his sore jaw

with one hand while extending the gun with the other. "You didn't think I was stupid enough to knock you both out and load you in my car without also searching you for wires, cell phones and weapons, did you? Your phones were left crushed back in the parking lot, but I figured this might come in handy." He waggled the weapon and motioned it toward them. "Get out. Both of you."

Nolan set his teeth, glaring at his opponent as he calculated strategy, weighed options.

Summer's hands were bound with a zip tie, but she scooted her arms close enough to grab a handful of his sleeve.

"Hurry up!" Kain barked, motioning with the gun. "Out!"

Shaking his head, Nolan settled back against the seat. "Don't think so. I'm good here."

"Nolan?" Summer whispered, her voice rife with terror.

"Fine." Kain gripped the gun with both hands and aimed at Nolan's head. "I'll shoot you where you are."

Summer sucked in a sharp breath, and his heart squeezed, wishing he could do more to allay her fear.

"I don't think you will," he told the drug dealer, "'Cause I don't think you want my blood and gore all over Melody's nice seats and floors."

Kain blinked, and his mouth compressed in an angry line. His nostrils flared as he huffed a few heavy breaths. Then, cursing under his breath, he lowered the gun and stalked around to the opposite side of the Mercedes. Jerking open the other back door, he reached in and grabbed a handful of Summer's jacket.

She yelped and struggled as Kain dragged her toward him. "No! Stop!"

Panic surged in Nolan's gut, and he grabbed for her legs. His hold on her slowed Kain until he shifted his grip to Summer's arm. Though she flailed and fought, with her hands bound, her attempts to loosen his grasp did little. In seconds, Kain had dragged Summer from the Mercedes, and she bumped to the ground with an uncushioned flop. Her cry of pain twisted inside Nolan and sank sharp spikes into his soul. "Summer!"

When Kain jabbed the gun against Summer's skull, Nolan's blood froze.

"Get out of the car, or I'll waste your pretty little girlfriend here and now," Kain said through gritted teeth.

A sense of helplessness, even greater than the day he'd first learned of Charlotte's false charges and his suspension, filled Nolan and left a rock of despair in his gut. His heart raced as he scrambled to find a way to rescue Summer. He couldn't let anything happen to her. No matter what it cost him.

SUMMER TASTED BLOOD, and the metallic tang made her already churning stomach heave. She must have bitten her tongue as she tumbled from the car to the hard ground. With her hands bound in front of her, she hadn't even been able to catch herself and break the fall. But now that she was out of Melody's cramped back seat…

She squirmed and got her legs under her, but as she positioned herself to rise on her knees, Kain grabbed her hair, and the cold kiss of steel greeted her temple.

Her ears buzzed as their kidnapper threatened to kill her if Nolan didn't comply with his demands. Her pulse seemed to slow, stall. If Nolan got out of the car, she knew they would both be dead within minutes. But she also knew, in her heart, Nolan wouldn't do anything to put her in harm's way. Her gaze cut to the open car, where Nolan moved slowly to the end of the seat. A murderous expression darkened his eyes, his glare fixed on Kain. The dim glow spilling from Melody's roof light cast dramatic shadows on their macabre scene.

"You know that if you kill us, you're signing your own death warrant. My cousins will not let our deaths pass without hunting you down and seeing you put on death row."

"Your cousins?" Kain scoffed. "You mean those cowboys out at the Colton Ranch?" He shook his head. "They don't scare me. Old Hays might think he has clout in this town, but the real power is mine. It's money. Secrets. Controlling someone else's nasty addiction. That's the real power."

When Nolan stopped at the edge of the seat and eased his legs out of the car, Kain waved the weapon, motioning to the ground. "All the way. Facedown, hands out."

She had no more time. She couldn't wait for a better opportunity that might never come. Swallowing hard to gather her courage, Summer rose on her knees, screamed like a banshee and pulled both arms straight back toward her stomach. She kept her wrists stiff, and the tension on the zip tie caused the thin plastic strip to pop off.

Her scream startled Kain, and, for an instant, he acted disoriented, confused. With her hands freed and her feet under her, she lunged up. Her kidnapper still had a grip on her hair, so the surge jerked at her head and shot pain along her scalp. But she managed to land an elbow in his solar plexus. Knock his gun hand up with her shoulder. And create the distraction Nolan needed.

He rocketed toward Kain, shoulder first, plowing into him like a linebacker. No, more than an athlete. A trained killer.

Just as Nolan had been taught to use a weapon when he joined the FBI, he'd almost certainly learned lethal hand-to-hand combat techniques.

Kain released Summer's hair in order to defend himself from Nolan's blow, but the force of Nolan's tackle knocked Kain onto his back. Given the chance, would Nolan kill Kain?

Summer gathered her balance and spun to face the men. Kain kicked out at Nolan then scrambled to his feet while Nolan swayed. She cringed seeing Kain deliver a blow to Nolan's jaw with the butt of the gun. Nolan swung, too. A glancing blow to Kain's cheek.

Summer's attention narrowed to the lethal weapon Kain clung to. If she could get her hands on the weapon…

Even as that thought entered her mind, Kain angled the gun…and fired.

Chapter Twenty-One

The blast of the gun so near his ear sent waves of pain through Nolan's skull, and the anguished timbre of Summer's scream caused terror to flood his soul. Had she been hit?

Even the hint that she'd been hurt infuriated Nolan. He channeled that ire to fuel his drug-weakened muscles. The first gunshot had been fired randomly. Or so Nolan thought. Kain only had one hand on the weapon, and that arm was partially trapped under Nolan's knee.

Nolan's only advantage against Kain was his position, hovering over him, and he could lose that high ground at any moment. He had to strike hard, strike fast, before the drug dealer gained the needed aim to put a bullet in his heart.

Nolan balled his fist and smashed it into Kain's throat, right in the windpipe. The blow caused Kain to choke, gasp. Nolan closed one hand around Kain's neck, holding him down with his thumb pressing hard into Kain's Adam's apple. Predictably, Kain flailed and grabbed at the hand choking him. While Kain struggled to breathe, Nolan used his other hand to gouge at

Kain's eyes. This was a street fight. A no-holds-barred battle for the upper hand.

And Nolan could feel his energy, his strength draining. Whatever adrenaline had fired his limbs to action was now waning.

Still gripping the gun, Kain swung at Nolan's head. Hit Nolan in the temple with a strike that made his ears ring and his vision dim. As Nolan blinked, stunned, Kain bucked, pushing up with his legs and twisting his torso. He wrested Nolan's hand from his throat and scrambled to his hands and knees, gasping air.

A blurry movement flashed past Nolan, too quickly for him to react. Head throbbing, he jerked his gaze toward Kain. The blur had been Summer. Nolan's heart rose to his throat, and he rasped, "No!" as Summer tackled the drug dealer from behind. She wrapped her legs around his waist, one arm around his neck, and her free hand grabbed a fistful of the man's hair. Yanked.

Kain cried out, and Summer grunted. "Doesn't feel so good, does it, you bastard!"

"Summer!" Nolan called, fumbling to his knees.

When he couldn't shake Summer loose by twisting his body and shoving at her legs, Kain gave a small jump and flopped backward in a wrestling move. Summer's head struck the ground with a terrifying thump.

"Summer!" Nolan crawled toward them, alarm streaking through him.

Summer wasn't moving.

SHE COULDN'T BREATHE. Her lungs were paralyzed, unresponsive.

Pain lanced her skull. Buzzing filled her ears, as if

she were trapped in a beehive. Muted sounds wafted around her. Unfocused images moved before her. Fuzzy, as if seen underwater. A small pool of light from the Mercedes' interior gave the only illumination in the darkness that surrounded her. *Melody.*

Acid swamped her gut as her mind cleared and the horror of her situation returned. Though her brain shook off the brief fugue, her lungs still struggled to recover. Her fall had winded her, and she gasped, trying to re-store the lost oxygen.

"Summer?" Nolan appeared beside her, stroking her face, his expression stricken. "Can you hear me?"

She blinked and managed a small nod, a wheeze. Then a chilling voice pierced the night and sent fresh waves of revulsion to her core.

"I have to say, that lady's got spunk. Jane and Patrice both just cowered and sniveled, pleading for their lives."

Sucking in a thread of breath, Summer said, "I hate...being called spunky."

Kain laughed as he raised the gun. "You see? Feisty 'til the end."

Nolan moved in front of her, his arms spread. "You son of a bit—"

Three loud pops rang through the dark and echoed off the trees. Summer jerked. Scrunched her eyes shut waiting for the pain.

"Drop the weapon!" came a shout from behind them.

More gunfire. Ear-shattering blasts that reverberated through her. Terrified her.

Nolan shifted. Grabbed her. Rolled with her across the rocky ground.

"Police! Throw the weapon away and lie down!"

Dizzied by their rolling, she felt as if the earth was moving, seesawing beneath her as more shots went off. The rustling sound of feet rushing forward through weeds.

Above her, shielding her, Nolan groaned. Summer trembled from head to toe. Nausea gripped her. Hands shook her.

"Are you all right? Answer me!"

Nolan.

She lifted her eyes to his shadowed face. Gave a weak, twitchy nod.

When more shouts filled the night, she glanced toward the dark figures that appeared from each side. One ran like a crouched tiger, fast and agile, leading with a gun. The second had a more loping cadence to his step, a slower pace, but no less menacing as he barked directions and aimed his weapon. The two men descended on Kain, who lay spread-eagle on the dirt and grass.

Nolan released a shuddering breath. "It's over, sweetheart. The cavalry's here."

Her gaze moved to Nolan, relief filling her eyes with tears. "Thank God. Oh, Nolan, I—I'm sorry. You...you were right. I should never—"

"Shh," he said, pulling her into his arms for a hug.

When she squeezed him back, he grunted, and she levered back to study him. "What?"

She followed the direction of his eyes and spotted a dark stain spreading on his shirt.

"Nolan! You were shot?" She yanked at his clothing, trying to rip the shirt away from his wound. "Lie back. Don't move!"

He winced as she tried to push him back onto the ground. "I'm okay. It's just a graze."

But she had his shirt up, examining the neat hole in his side. "That's no graze. Omigod, omigod!" She pressed the heels of her hands to the bleeding gunshot wound. "Nolan was shot! He needs help!"

The two men who were securing Kain's hands behind his back looked over. One of the men muttered something to his companion then peeled away to limp over to Nolan. When he moved inside the circle of light from Melody's open door, Summer recognized Nolan's cousin.

"Show me," Forrest said as he knelt awkwardly beside her, holding his previously injured leg.

Nolan shrugged. "It's just a scratch. I'll be fine."

Forrest pulled out a small flashlight and shined it on Nolan's bleeding side. He ducked his head to examine the wound and scoffed. "You definitely need to go to the ER. That's a good bit more than a scratch, Nolan."

Summer sat back on her heels. "We don't have our phones to call an ambulance. Kain destroyed them when he grabbed us."

Forrest's mouth twisted. "Probably faster for us to drive you to the ER than wait for an ambulance to find this place in the dark." He clicked off the light and divided a scowling look between them. "How exactly was Kain able to kidnap *two* of you? And one a trained professional?"

Nolan's head rolled forward, his chin to his chest, his expression full of shame. "Can we talk about it later?"

Summer cringed, not willing to let Nolan bear any of the blame. "It's my fault. I insisted on examining Melody."

Forrest cocked his head to the side. "Melody?"

She waved a hand toward the Mercedes. "His car. He calls the Benz Melody. We had reason to believe there was proof of his illegal drug connection and, therefore, motive for him to kill Patrice Eccleston hidden somewhere in the wheel well or tires." She took a breath before adding, "And there was. We found a hidden compartment and a stash of what is likely meth."

Forrest arched an eyebrow and glanced at the Mercedes. "You don't say?"

"Forrest," Summer continued, feeling the need to defend Nolan, "Nolan was drugged. Kain had a syringe out and ready when he snuck up on us and—"

"It's no excuse." Nolan talked over her, shaking his head.

"He injected Nolan before we could—"

"Whoa, whoa, whoa…" Forrest stopped them both, raising his hands to quiet them. "We'll sort this out at the police station." Then, narrowing a concerned frown on Nolan, he said, "And after you've been checked out at the hospital." With a grunt of pain, he shoved to his feet and rubbed his bum leg. "Right now I'm going to help Dallas with Kain."

As Forrest started moving back across the clearing, Summer called, "Forrest."

He stopped and glanced back at her.

"Thank you." Emotion welled in her throat. "You saved our lives."

His expression darkened with something akin to fear or grief. "I believe you're right." He exhaled sharply and flashed a relieved grin. "And you're welcome."

ALTHOUGH THEY WERE initially taken to separate exam rooms at the ER, once Summer had a CT scan of her head and a minor concussion was confirmed, she went to wait with Nolan for his test results.

The majority of the Colton clan had descended on the ER waiting room soon after Forrest dropped Summer and Nolan off, then taken Kain to the police station for processing.

The ride back to town had sure been interesting, Summer ruminated—Kain handcuffed and sitting between Dallas and Nolan in the back seat of Forrest's cruiser while Forrest drove and Summer rode shotgun up front. Previously chatty, Kain had clammed up and sat with a dark scowl on his face the entire ride back into downtown Whisperwood. Melody had been left out in the woods, undisturbed, so that the forensics team could search the Mercedes and gather evidence in the morning.

"How did you find us out here?" Nolan had asked, dividing a look between his cousins.

Forrest had shifted his gaze to study Nolan in the rearview mirror. "A lot of luck and calling in some favors. After you called me this evening, I hopped on the phone to Dallas, since he lives closer to the city administrative building."

"I saw your Jeep in the parking lot but not a Mercedes, so I was instantly alert to something having gone awry," Dallas said, picking up the story. "An older lady that lives diagonally across the street from the city building was in her yard, and she flagged me down and said she'd heard a scream moments earlier and looked out in time to see a struggle then a Mercedes pull away headed south."

"Since the WPD has been trying to catch Kain red-handed for years, we already knew his cell phone provider and had them ping his cell phone. Once we had a general location and which direction he was headed, Dallas and I threw on the cruiser lights and sped out here with updates from the cell provider."

Summer tipped her head, her nose wrinkling. "But this far from town, the cell towers are farther apart and wouldn't give you a specific location. How did you know to come *here*?"

"A good point, Ms. Private Investigator," Forrest said. "We figured he might be driving to a specific place, so I had Dallas phone my contact in the county records department to run a search of Kain's land holdings out here, along with any other recent transactions for properties Kain might know about. The clerk remembered filing records last month on the sale of a tract out here for a hunting club. Kain wasn't listed as a member or investor per se, but there was a TKI Inc."

"TK... Tom Kain..." Summer said.

"Tom Kain Investments Inc.," Dallas confirmed.

"When we reached the turn to come in here, we heard the gunfire," Forrest said.

"I jumped out and ran like hell in the direction the shots came from." Dallas dabbed at a dribble of blood on his cheek. "Ran through some thorny vines, but it was worth it to take down the guy responsible for the drugs that killed Avery's brother."

Now, sitting in the ER with Nolan, Summer lifted a prayer of thanks that the Colton brothers had reached them in time.

Dallas had left his cell phone for Summer and Nolan to use until they could replace theirs. When the doctor officially discharged them from the ER, she stepped outside where cell phone use was allowed and called Atticus Eccleston. "We found him, sir. Nolan Colton and I found the man responsible for killing your daughter."

She heard a long shuddering sigh, then a broken, "Who?"

"Tom Kain."

"You…you mean the auto shop owner?"

"The same. He was involved in a lot more than fixing cars at his shop, and we believe that Patrice found evidence of that when she went to interview for a job at the garage. He saw her come across that evidence via his security tapes and murdered her to keep her quiet."

Another long silence followed. When he spoke again, Atticus's voice was taut with emotion. "I'll kill the son of a bitch."

"I understand the sentiment, sir, but it is likely the state of Texas will do that for you. He killed a number of other people, directly or via a second perpetrator, and the DA could seek the death penalty."

She didn't bother to tell Atticus that Kain was spilling his guts as part of a plea deal to avoid death row. Let the grieving father rest in the comfort of knowing his child's killer had been caught. The trial and sentencing were worries for another day. "I'll fill you in on the details later. It's been a long night, but I wanted you to know Patrice's killer has been arrested."

She heard a quiet sob, then a broken, "Thank you, Ms. Davies."

By the time Nolan and Summer were discharged from the hospital, Jonah had retrieved Nolan's Jeep from the municipal building parking lot. Maggie and Josephine had purchased a hot takeout meal from the Bluebell Diner for each member of the family, and Forrest had phoned to say Chief Thompson wouldn't be officially questioning Tom Kain until the man's lawyer could get in from Austin the next morning. Kain would spend the night in the town jail and be arraigned in the morning.

The adrenaline that had kept Summer going for the past few days, and especially the last several hours, dissipated once the danger had passed and she was certain Nolan hadn't sustained serious injuries in his fight with Kain. Exhaustion and body aches crashed on her with a one-two punch as they headed to her office home for a change of clothes before dinner with the Coltons.

While she cherished the thought of celebrating the wrap-up of a case that had dragged so many members of the Colton family into life-and-death situations and brought surprising happy endings to each of the brothers, Summer begged off.

"I think tonight I have a date with that takeout box of comfort food, a couple ibuprofen and an early bedtime," she told Jonah. "Tell Josephine and Maggie thank you for the dinner—" she patted the warm takeout box in her hands "—and give everyone my best."

Jonah cast a look to his cousin. "How about you? You coming with me or staying with your lady?"

"She's not—" Nolan began before pinching the bridge of his nose, clearly as fatigued as she was and choosing not to spend his energy debating the status of their relationship with his cousin. Instead, he deferred to her. "You want company or are you ready to get me outta your hair?"

What she wanted was to lose herself in slow, gentle

lovemaking with Nolan, but echoes of his characterization of their last "mistake" quelled that idea. Besides, he looked as tired and sore as she felt, and she knew the best course for both of them when they were this worn-out was a bit of downtime. Alone.

Tomorrow morning was soon enough to begin untangling the knots that had crept up in the ties that bound them. "Let's call it a night. I'll see you later."

With a brief nod, a squeeze to her shoulder and a sleepy half grin, Nolan left her alone with Yossi to sort out a way forward.

SUMMER'S FIRST THOUGHT upon waking the next morning was of Nolan. With Patrice's murder solved, they could now focus on their relationship. Assuming there was a relationship left to consider. Her foolish insistence on snooping around Melody had almost gotten Nolan killed. She'd forced his hand more than once, pushed him to do things he'd thought unwise. Her stubborn impulsiveness may have cost her Nolan's respect. His loyalty.

This was a mistake.

Had her seduction of him ruined the chance for them to be friends going forward? She fumbled for the replacement burner phone she and Nolan had bought after leaving the hospital and swiped her hair back from her face as she began punching in the digits of Nolan's new temporary phone. Then stopped.

This was a conversation they had to have face-to-face. After rousing Yossi from the end of the bed so that she could swing her feet out from the covers, Summer dressed quickly and set out for the Colton Ranch.

Josephine answered Summer's knock on the main ranch house door, smiling brightly when she saw Summer on the porch. "Hi, darlin'. Come in. What brings you out here this morning?"

Summer stepped into the cozy ranch house and inhaled the scent of something sweet and spiced with ginger in the oven. "I need to talk with Nolan, but it's not a conversation I wanted to have over the phone or by texts. Is he here? Maybe out in the pasture with Hays or the guys?"

Josephine's face fell. "Honey, didn't he tell you? He left last night."

Summer's heart clenched so hard she couldn't breathe. "Left?" she rasped. *Without saying goodbye.*

"Yes. He got a call from Chicago and lit outta here within minutes. Didn't even take his Jeep. Said he was going to catch a flight from Austin. Donovan drove him to the airport."

"Um," Summer stammered, wiping her hands on her jeans. "What happened? Why—"

"He said he was needed in person for an important meeting today. No time to delay or drive his car back."

The case with Charlotte? Likely. But couldn't he have called from the airport? Texted? Something!

"I see." Summer's voice cracked. "But his injury…"

Josephine rushed forward to wrap an arm around her shoulders. "I was worried about that, too. I made him promise to go slow and take his antibiotics on schedule." The older woman gave her a squeeze. "Don't fret, Summer dear. He'll be back. Has to come back to get his car, if nothing else." Mrs. Colton smiled at her. "Since you're here, why don't you join me in tasting the pumpkin bread I just took out of the oven? We better get it now. Once the men get back from the tending to the herd, that loaf will be gone in a blink."

"Thanks, but…no." The spicy aroma that had enticed her when she'd first come in now sat uncomfortably on her churning stomach. Nolan was gone. Without a word to her.

She'd known he'd leave Whisperwood to return to Chicago eventually, but she'd thought she'd at least get the chance to say goodbye. Was his silence an indicator of how much damage she'd done to their relationship? Her heart gave a painful throb, and it was all she could do not to crumple on the Coltons' floor and weep.

"Darlin', you're white as a ghost. Are you okay?" Josephine asked.

Summer couldn't talk. The tears she battled back clogged her throat with a hard knot. She forced a tight grin and nodded as she backed to the door.

"Well, do you want me to give Nolan a message when he comes back for his Jeep?"

Her fingernails bit her palms as she struggled for the composure she wanted to show Josephine. She shook her head and managed a weak, "No. Thanks."

If she melted down now, showed her heartbreak, she knew the entire Colton clan, including Nolan, would know of her devastation within the hour. And she refused to let Nolan know how deeply his silent departure had hurt her. That was on her. She'd fallen in love. Despite his warnings, despite red flags, despite the knowledge she could irreparably damage their friendship.

Raising a hand in a pathetic goodbye, she spun on her toe and hurried out to her Beetle.

Her vision blurred as she drove away from the main house, and she blinked hard, scolding herself for her situation. He'd given her ample warning that reviving their old friendship was all he was after. He'd tried to be gentlemanly on so many occasions, and she'd bulldozed past his platonic barriers. Because it was what *she* wanted. What she'd convinced herself was right for both of them.

Well, now you have what you deserve. Nothing. You pushed Nolan when you should have respected his wishes. How are you any better than Charlotte? She might not have thrown him under the bus professionally, but she'd ignored his wishes, put their friendship at risk, hadn't taken his wants at face value.

She felt like a heel. Worse. She was the bug beneath a boot heel. And she was crushed.

NOLAN SAT AT a conference table at the FBI's Chicago field office, staring at Charlotte. She wouldn't meet his eyes. If she had, she'd have seen the hurt, the disappointment, the anger that he didn't even try to mask in his expression. He continued glaring unapologetically at his accuser while Stu handled the details of the conversation for him. Nolan's supervisor and a representative from internal affairs were at the other end of the table, and Charlotte's husband was beside her, their personal lawyer in tow.

"You realize my client could sue for defamation of character? This whole ordeal has been damaging to Nolan's reputation and career."

"He has his job back, and my wife has recanted her accusations. We're going to pay the man's legal fees.

Isn't that enough?" Senator Dell asked, his face mottled with red splotches.

"Would it be enough for you, Senator? Special Agent O'Toole?" Stu asked.

Charlotte sighed, her guilty gaze still fixed on the table, and mumbled, "Probably not."

The senator shot a look of disgust at his wife. "Sh. You're not helping. Do you want them to bleed us dry?"

The Dells' lawyer put a hand on the senator's arm and gave his client a warning look.

"I won't," Nolan interjected. "I'm not interested in vengeance."

"There." The senator waved a hand toward Nolan. "He doesn't want monetary reparations. So let's just sign these papers and put a period on the end of this unfortunate episode so we can move on."

Beside him, Stu turned his chair. Nolan felt his lawyer's eyes studying him. "Are you sure, Nolan? You're satisfied with this agreement?"

Stu motioned to the papers on the table that spelled out Charlotte's withdrawal of her accusations, the return of his position and pay grade, and the agreement of the Dells to cover all of Nolan's expenses for his defense.

"I am. I only want one last thing." *Well, two, really.*

But neither Special Agent O'Toole nor the honorable senator from Nebraska could get him what he wanted most—to undo the things he'd done that hurt Summer.

"What's that?" Senator Dell asked, his tone suspicious.

He flattened his hands on the table. "I want to hear from Charlotte."

Charlotte squeezed her eyes closed, and her head remained down.

"She hasn't said anything to me since we began these proceedings," Nolan continued. When she still didn't respond, he said sharply, "Charlotte!"

Her chin jerked up, and her tearful, startled eyes found his.

"Don't you have anything to say?" he asked, incredulous. "Don't you care what you've done to me?"

She swallowed hard, and her throat convulsed. "I—"

The senator drummed his fingers impatiently. "Damn it, Charlotte. Give him what he wants, or so help me…"

"For the record," Nolan said, cutting a quick, hard look to the senator, "I'm not happy with you bullying her, either."

The senator's expression of shock and affront was almost comical. Almost. But Nolan couldn't find humor in any of what was happening. He shifted his gaze back to Charlotte. "Well?"

Her shoulders drooped, and her face crumpled with compunction. "I screwed up. I should never have drawn you into my personal problems."

He arched an eyebrow. When she fell silent, he tipped his head. "Two words, Charlotte. I still haven't heard two simple words."

She wet her lips. Swallowed again and whispered, "I'm sorry."

Nolan turned to Stu with a nod. "We're done."

Picking up a pen, Nolan scribbled his name at the bottom of the document on the table and rose from his chair. Relief should have felt sweeter. He should be overjoyed to have his job back, his name cleared and his life back on track.

But since leaving Whisperwood, nothing about his life had felt right. He missed Summer. He missed her smile and positive energy. He missed seeing her nose wrinkle in thought as she puzzled out the details of her case. Heck, he even missed Yossi.

How could he have ever wanted someone as morally warped, as selfish and cowardly as Charlotte? Having seen Summer in action this past week, her courage and optimism, her determination and grit, he found Charlotte all the more lacking.

Summer had taken on the challenge of starting her own business, had pursued what she wanted in life, not by destroying someone else but by hard work and sacrifice. And Summer had faced each setback with grace and humor, sharing her joy for life with everyone around her. Summer was…inspiring. She buoyed him when he needed hope to cling to. She was, quite simply, a treasure. And she deserved better than the mess he'd left in his wake.

He pulled out his phone as he marched to the elevator and opened a new text to her.

Summer—Charlotte recanted and I'm officially back on the job with the FBI. I thought you'd want to know.

I miss you. You're the best thing that ever happened to me and—

Nolan stopped. Sighed. Backspaced to erase the last lines. Hit Send. He wouldn't make the mistake of giving her false hope again. He had his job back, his career was once again on track and Summer had made it clear that traveling the country, having a husband that would leave her to go undercover for months at a time, was not the life she dreamed of.

A front porch with rocking chairs, a yard with a big flower bed and a kitchen that smelled like fresh-baked bread. That was her dream. As he stepped onto the elevator and rode it down to the main lobby, he had to admit her vision sounded pretty good to him, too.

He swiped a hand over his face. *What are you thinking, Colton? You just got your job back. A job you worked hard for. A job you love.*

When the doors parted, he strolled out of the elevator, across the lobby and out into the brisk October chill. When he'd left Texas, the temperature had been seventy degrees. Chicago was thirty-nine before adding the effect of a stiff wind. He huddled deeper into his coat and turned to look up at the glass-and-steel edifice of the FBI offices. The large windows reflected the gray sky and looked as cold as the air felt. The severe building held none of the charm that the old brick and river-stone buildings along Whisperwood's Main Street had. Another pang assailed his heart.

Whisperwood. Summer.

You're not thinking of leaving the FBI and going back to Texas, are you? Leaving undercover work for a second chance with Summer?

And yet the idea didn't seem so off-the-wall. Being near his cousins, working with Summer, *making love to Summer* all felt so *right* in hindsight.

Despite the windchill, a warmth flowed through him.

Was he ditching the FBI to start a new life with Summer? "Damn right, I am!"

Smiling to himself, he hurried to flag down a cab. He had plans to make.

WHAT FAINT HOPE Summer had of hearing from Nolan, working out the issues that had marred their last moments together, repairing the damage and moving forward with their relationship dimmed further with each passing hour she didn't get even a text of explanation. Not even delivering the details to Atticus and Ian Eccleston of Kain's arraignment, that Kain had confessed to killing Patrice and would remain in custody until trial, was enough to alleviate the weight of loss in her chest. She'd wanted Nolan at her side when she gave her clients the good news. He'd helped her, guided her, buoyed and supported her on her first big case. He should have been there to share the rewarding moment.

Instead, sitting alone on the Ecclestons' couch, she'd watched father and son embrace, crying tears of joy and relief—and renewed grief—when she told them what had transpired the night they'd been kidnapped and in the courtroom that morning.

Summer glanced at her phone when it beeped an incoming text. And her heart jolted. Nolan. Finally! As quickly as she could without appearing rude, Summer bade the Ecclestons goodbye and hurried to her car. Only once she was ensconced in the semiprivacy of her front seat did she read the text. It was short and to the point—Nolan was vindicated and had his job back. As happy as she was at his news, the terse message, the lack of any further explanations or greetings hurt. If she'd had any doubt before, the text answered her questions. Nolan was back in Chicago for good, and she needed to move on with her life.

SEVERAL DAYS LATER, Summer sat at her desk, scratching Yossi behind the ears as he lounged on the file she'd been trying to review, when she heard a knock at her door.

Hadn't she unlocked the office and flipped the sign to say Open that morning? Why was the person knocking? She glanced out the window to the sidewalk, and her breath caught. Nolan?

She hurried to answer the door, remembering Josephine had said he had to come back to retrieve his Jeep. Maybe he just wanted to say goodbye, find some closure.

She swallowed the lump that swelled in her throat and opened the door, offering him a friendly, but subdued, smile. "Well, well. Look what the cat dragged in. The conquering hero."

His mouth slid up in a lopsided grin. "Hi, Summer. You busy at the moment?"

She considered telling him she was. She wasn't sure she could stand a long, emotional goodbye. Instead she shrugged. "I guess Yossi can handle the file I was reading by himself. What's up?"

He rubbed a hand over his mouth and squared his shoulders. "I have something to show you."

She arched an eyebrow, and a bittersweet pang twisted inside her. "Oh?"

He hitched his head and reached for her elbow to lead

her to the street. To a large, shiny blue pickup truck. "I traded my Jeep for a pickup. What do you think?"

Summer knitted her brow, confused. "It's nice. And…big."

"All the better for hauling stuff." His face glowed with the expectancy and joy of a kid on Christmas morning.

After a moment's awkward silence, she asked, "Is this all you came to do? Show me the truck?"

"No, there's more." He pulled a folded section of newspaper from his back pocket. "I saw this listing for a house on Bonita Street. The price is right, and I thought you might be interested in looking at it. What do you say? Are you ready to move out of your office?"

She looked at the listing he pointed to and shook her head. "It's lovely, Nolan, but that area is too expensive for me. I need a smaller starter house that—"

"Hold that thought!" He seized her hand and led her closer to the new truck. "I also have an early Christmas present for you. Three, really."

"Nolan, I don't—"

He quieted her with a finger to her lips. "Just wait."

She stumbled along behind him as he ushered her to the cargo bed, where a tarp covered a large lump. "What in the world?"

He slid his mouth into a lopsided grin and whipped the tarpaulin off to reveal two finely crafted wooden rocking chairs. "For the front porch."

Her chest squeezed, and tears stung her eyes. "Nolan, they're beautiful!"

"I saw them at a roadside woodcraft shop as Dallas

drove me in from the airport at Austin, and I immediately thought of you."

She pressed a hand to her mouth and swallowed hard. She didn't want to cry, or she might not stop. And crying in front of Nolan was the last thing she wanted to do. He couldn't know how much she ached for missing him, wanting him, losing him. "Thank you. They're... perfect."

He smiled proudly. "Good. I thought you'd like them. Next, I got you these..." He opened the passenger door and handed her a plain brown paper bag.

When she peeked inside, she blinked, uncertain for a moment what she was seeing.

"Flower bulbs," he said, clarifying what she suspected. "The lady at the nursery said it's a mix of hyacinths, tulips, crocuses and daffodils. She said now's the time to plant them so they'll bloom next spring."

"But—" she glanced to the concrete sidewalk in front of her office "—where—?"

He pulled out the home listings again and tapped it. "The house on Bonita has a big flower bed all the way along the front porch."

Her heart lashed her ribs with a staccato tattoo as the meaning behind his gifts crystallized.

Rocking chairs on a front porch, a flower bed...

"And since I know you're not a baker..." He reached in the back seat again, then handed her another sack with a bakery insignia on the side. Three boxes were nestled inside and the top one read Country Wheat— Ready to Bake.

"The directions say you just thaw and let the dough

rise and bake for fifty minutes. I got sourdough white, whole wheat and cinnamon swirl."

Moisture dripped onto her cheeks. "So my kitchen will smell like fresh-baked bread," she squeaked through her tears.

"That was the dream, right? Your goal for the perfect home?" His bright smile dimmed when she continued sniffling softly. "Summer? What's wrong? I thought you'd love all this." He swept an arm toward the chairs on the back of his truck. "You said this was what you'd longed for since you were a kid."

She bobbed her head and wiped her nose. "I did say that. And I do love that you remembered. That you tried to—" Her voice broke, and she had to pause and take a deep, calming breath. "The thing is, Nolan, in the last couple of weeks I've discovered a flaw in my dream."

"A flaw?" He set the bag of frozen bread dough on the seat and faced her with a deep furrow in his brow. "What flaw?"

"I realized that the dream home I wanted wasn't about rocking chairs or flower beds."

His shoulders drooped, and he heaved a disappointed-sounding sigh. "Oh."

"It's not even about Whisperwood...or any one place, for that matter."

His mouth firmed in a line of frustration. "I don't get it. You said that you wanted roots and—"

"I know. But I realized that the home I really wanted, the real dream wasn't about where the house was or what went on the porch or in the yard. The home I wanted to build was about who lived in the house with me. Roots, family, love. That's what home is."

The shadows of disappointment lifted, and he nodded. "I see."

"My dream now is about…who." Her throat tried to close with knots of emotion, but she shoved the rising melancholy down. This was her chance to tell him what her heart had always known. Raising her chin, she rasped, "It's about…you."

Nolan fell back a step, and he sucked in a sharp breath. "Oh."

She dug her fingers into the front of his coat to keep him from backing any farther away. "I didn't tell you that to pressure you or make you feel guilty or awkward. I…maybe I shouldn't have even told you at all."

"Summer—"

"I mean, I know you have your own plans for the future. You have a job that you love, that you just got back after fighting for it, and you have to travel for the FBI, so—"

"I left the FBI."

She had to let his words replay in her head to be sure she'd heard him right. A low buzz started in her ears, and her pulse thumped harder as a hope she was afraid to acknowledge swelled in her chest. "But you told me once that you had worked too hard to get where you were with the FBI to walk away," she said, her confusion rife in her tone.

"As I recall, what I said was I wouldn't walk away *without good reason*. And you, my dear, are a damn good reason."

"Me?" She was afraid to move, afraid to breathe and break the spell. She tried to quell the surge of expectant excitement that coiled inside her, ready to spring.

Nolan rolled his eyes and mimicked her, like he used to when they were kids. *"Me?"*

His wide, warm palms framed her cold cheeks. "Yes, *you*, you goof. It's always been you, even when I was too dense to recognize the truth. I love you, Tadpole. And not just as my best friend, though you are that. You're the reason I bought the truck. It's more practical for ranch life. For Whisperwood. I want to make Whisperwood my home because you're here. I love you. Will you let me be the reason your house is a home? Will you marry me?"

Joy sprang inside her, and, with a squeal of happiness, she leaped into his arms. "Oh my God, yes! Yes, yes, a thousand times yes!"

Epilogue

One month later

"To Emily Virginia Colton!" Hays shouted as he raised his glass of champagne to the family members assembled in the ranch house living room—a tight fit now considering all the new members of the clan.

"Cheers!" they all chanted and clinked their glasses. From the couch where she sat cradling her newborn daughter, Bellamy smiled at Donovan beside her and kissed the baby's head.

Nolan cast his glance around at all of his cousins, their spouses and children—and, most important, at Summer beside him. Happiness, more intoxicating and bubbly than the champagne in his flute, swelled inside him. Family. Love. A bright future. He was rich in every way that mattered.

"To Maggie and Jonah finally setting a date!" Forrest called out, lifting his glass.

"Hear, hear!" Nolan said as everyone drank to the engaged couple.

Beside him, Summer raised her glass. "To Davies and Colton Investigations!"

"Soon to be Colton and Colton Investigations," Nolan amended, giving his fiancée a wink.

"To your new partnership," Dallas said, "and I don't just mean your PI gig."

"Yes! Cheers!" Avery said, raising her sparkling cider to toast.

His family cheered and drank to them, and Nolan pulled Summer close for a kiss.

"And to the twins' excellent two-month doctor checkup," Summer said, returning a toast to her best girlfriend.

Avery bobbed a nod of thanks, adding, "And to them both sleeping for five hours straight last night so Mama and Daddy could get some rest!"

"Funny, I don't remember us resting," Dallas said and waggled his eyebrow seductively.

"To Dallas gettin—" Jonah started before Maggie elbowed him in the ribs with a wide-eyed look.

The Coltons laughed and raised their glasses again.

"To Forrest's new *permanent* position with the Whisperwood PD!" Donovan said, and hearing his master's raised voice, Alex gave a happy bark.

The room reverberated with "Cheers!"

"Whew!" Rae said, swaying a bit before she took a seat on the couch beside the new parents. "I think I'm going to be sloshed before we finish toasting all the good news in the family!"

Amid the chuckles, Josephine said, "So be it! After the last few trying, trauma-filled months this family has had, we deserve a spate of good news to toast."

"To getting sloshed with good news!" Forrest shouted as he drained his champagne glass and refilled it. A rousing chorus of "Hear, hear!" and "I'll drink to that!" lifted around Nolan.

"To…" Jonah said, then hesitated. "Hell, there's got to be something else we can toast. I feel like we're just getting started."

Moving to the center of the room, Hays raised both his empty hand and his glass of bubbly. "To the Coltons. May our family's love, laughter and joy continue for years to come!"

All the flutes clinked in salute. "To the Coltons!"

* * * * *

COMING SOON!

We really hope you enjoyed reading this book. If you're looking for more romance, be sure to head to the shops when new books are available on

Thursday 17th October

LET'S TALK
Romance

For exclusive extracts, competitions
and special offers, find us online:

MILLS & BOON
Desire

Indulge in secrets and scandal, intense drama and plenty of sizzling hot action with powerful and passionate heroes who have it all: wealth, status, good looks… everything but the right woman.

Six Desire stories published every month, find them all at:

millsandboon.co.uk/Desire